SPEAKING DREAMS

SPEAKING DREAMS

BY SEVERNA PARK

Firebrand
Books

Book and cover design by Betsy Bayley
Typesetting by Bets Ltd.

Printed in the United States by McNaughton & Gunn

Library of Congress Cataloging-in-Publication Data

Park, Severna, 1958–
    Speaking dreams / by Severna Park.
        p.   cm.
    ISBN 1-56341-015-X — ISBN 1-56341-014-1 (pbk.)
    I. Title.
    PS3566.A6747S64   1992
    813'.54—dc20   92-5384
                                                                         CIP

Acknowledgments

For all their support, Cinder, Natalie and Shoshana; to my parents for their enthusiasm, even when they had no idea what I was doing; and for Phil, thanks for the computer.

The following people are intimately involved in this book—thanks from a reader and a listener: William Burroughs, Sam Delaney, Keri Hulme, DPM, P. Gabriel, O. Haza, HoF.

Many, many thanks to Nancy Bereano for her amazing patience.

Mostly for Vicki, my main muse.
I'll always be yours.

1

Because of the dream, she knew no one would come until much later. Costa crept into the low, dark shed, feeling along the dirt floor for the chains and then the clasp that held them. It opened at her touch. She'd known that as well.

She pulled the chain slowly, link by link, through the ankle cuffs of the line of sleeping slaves. It caught on one boy's foot, and he sat up groggily. The same as in the dream, he stared at her, then hesitantly reached down and untangled himself. She pulled again, and the chain snaked away.

It was all she needed to do. Costa bent through the low opening and hurried past the slavers' house into the night mist and tall grass. At the edge of the woods, she stopped and looked back. There were still no lights in the main building where Raffail lived, and only a vague passage of shadows as the slaves filed silently out of the shed and into the trees on the other side of the clearing.

Further ahead, her sister's black mare stood patiently, invisible except for the bit of white on her forehead. Costa slid onto her back, guiding her through the thinning trees and down the hill toward the village. Both moons were just beginning to edge over the ragged, distant mountains on the horizon. She looked back one last time, but there was no one behind her—and there wouldn't be. The same as the dream, she urged the mare into a trot. Everything was right. She would be back in bed before sunrise.

The day was hot well before noon. Costa straightened, smearing the sweat out of her eyes. One of her chores was weeding, and today she'd spent most of the morning in the gardens, digging out the tenacious, startlingly blue flowers that coiled around the more mundane vegetables. A little way down the hill, her aunt Nisai eyed her occasionally, mending clothes in the shade of the small house. The rest of the village spread along the edge of the lake further below, a collection of worn wooden houses, patched against the severe winter storms, solid enough, but dilapidated in a kind of spiritual way, as though the only thing that really held them together was the slavers' insistence that they *would* stand. A little like Nisai, thought Costa, bending back over the helpless flowers, yanking them out by the roots. Her aunt was thick and old with childbearing, having produced five boys and a girl for Raffail, pregnant again with her seventh child. Both of the older boys had been taken away several years ago by the slavers. No one had said anything. That was entirely normal. It was only a question of who would be next.

Emielle came out of the house with her bucket of dirty water and the scrubbing brushes. Except for her shorter hair, she and Costa could easily have been mistaken for twins. The resemblance would have been unusual for cousins anywhere else, but in this population of soft grey eyes and golden hair, the similarity was expected, required, and valued.

Emielle dumped the water at the bottom of the hill and sat down next to her mother, speaking with her hands. Nisai's deafness was a result of Emielle, if rumor was to be believed, a product of her punishment for bearing a daughter instead of another boy as Raffail had planned. As if it were something she could have controlled. Costa squinted in the bright sunlight, trying to see what they were saying, but they were too far away. She tossed her fistful of weeds over the fence and smoothed the rich, black dirt with a bare foot, waiting for her cousin to come up the hill.

"You're not doing a very good job," said Emielle. She pulled up another bright vine and added it to the armful she'd collected between the bottom of the short slope and where Costa was standing. She pushed the wad of wilting plants at her cousin, scowling. "Where were you last night?" she whispered. "I woke up and you were gone."

Costa shrugged uneasily. This was not something she'd expected. "I couldn't sleep."

Emielle glanced back at her mother as though the old woman could hear everything. "You're dreaming again," she said in a low, accusing voice. "What did you do this time?"

"Nothing." No one but Emielle knew about the dreams, and that was only because they'd been sharing a bed in the small house since they were children. Sometimes Emielle was part of what Costa saw. Months ago they'd gone together, letting Raffail's horses loose in the middle of the night, chasing them off into the plains that spread to the west of the village. It had taken the slavers almost a week to find them all, but that had been perceived as an accident, or carelessness on the part of one of Raffail's own slaves. This would be different.

"Don't lie to me," whispered her cousin fiercely. She seemed to have a lot more to say, but she stopped suddenly, frowning at something past Costa's shoulder.

A thin cloud of dust hung in the hot sky, roiling gently over the hills. The sound of horses was just audible, and someone was shouting.

Emielle pushed back her short hair nervously. "It's them," she said, and brushed at Costa's shirt. "You're dirty. He doesn't like that."

Costa straightened her clothes as the horses crested the hill, moving slowly along the trail that ran past the fenced edge of the gardens. Raffail rode in front, tall and unmistakable even though he wore the same white head-to-foot robes and blue eye stripe as the rest of the slavers.

The captured slaves straggled between him and two other riders. They were tied together by ropes running through their chain collars—a girl and three boys, dark-haired and foreign. Two of the boys were shirtless, grimy from the run. Costa could see their branded shoulders clearly, a combination of outworld numbers no one here on Jahar could read, and below that, the simple, almost hieroglyphic lines of the Eye, identifying them as slaves that had been taken by Raffail or some member of the Sector clan.

Emielle grabbed Costa's elbow, and they sank to the ground together, kneeling as the horses came closer. Raffail halted his horse in front of them, still on the other side of the fence.

"Emielle."

"Yes D'sha," replied the girl politely, just loud enough for him to hear.

"Tell your mother I'll be stopping in to see her this afternoon."
Costa heard her swallow. "Yes D'sha."

Raffail gave her an easy, reassuring smile. "I have a husband for
you," he said. "That's not such bad news, is it?"

"No D'sha."

Actually it was very good news. Emielle was only weeks away from
her eighteenth birthday, only a few months younger than Costa. None
of the four unlucky slaves standing in front of them were any younger
than eighteen, none older that twenty-two. Those were the years to be
careful—extremely careful—and as productive as possible.

"Costa," said Raffail, and she looked up cautiously. His outworld
accent was nowhere as thick as some, but he always pronounced her
name with a long *oh* instead of a short one.

"Yes D'sha?"

"Where's your sister?"

"Ari?" She forgot her manners and stared up at him. "Hunting
with my uncle, D'sha."

"And where is Tomas?"

Why was he asking her where Ari's husband was? "With the babies, D'sha?" she stammered. "I haven't seen him—"

Raffail cut her off, shaking his head in irritation. "We had some
trouble last night," he said, and glared at the nearest boy. "I'm still missing
two."

Emielle looked up quickly. "We can help you look, D'Raffail," she
said, sounding oversincere. "I'll get the horses."

"No," he said. "Jezr'el can find them."

He gathered the reins up and tapped the horse with his heels.
The procession moved slowly away, along the fence, out of sight.

Emielle practically jumped to her feet. "Are you out of your mind?"
she demanded in a hissing whisper. "You did *that?*"

Costa nodded, her mouth still dry. "I didn't think he'd catch them
this fast."

Emielle grabbed her by the shoulders and shook her. "What are
you trying to prove, anyway? What if one of those slaves recognized you?"

It had been too dark, Costa was pretty sure of that. What frightened her more was that Raffail had somehow gotten the idea that Ari
or Tomas were somehow responsible.

"You're going to get us all in trouble." Emielle turned around and stalked down the hill, past her mother, heading toward the lake.

Costa watched her go, knowing she was exactly right. If Raffail was unable to identify the true culprit, he would find a way to punish the entire village. Nobody with an ounce of good sense was willing to risk the consequences the slavers were perfectly capable of doling out.

But the visions were compelling, and what she was doing seemed so necessary. Still, it was better to lie awake in bed, wrestling with her better judgment, than to risk her sister being mistakenly involved. Costa smoothed back her long braid, then brushed off her knees and followed her cousin down to the water.

The lake wasn't much more than a large pond, brackish and brown with silt during most of the summer, frozen uselessly solid in the winter. A thin tributary fed into it from the far side where there were no buildings, only ancient, thirsty trees. They bunched together on the shore like old men, their roots knotting over half-sunken boulders, twisting into the cool water.

Emielle was sitting on one of the stones, toes in the lake, not watching as Costa came around the beach, walking with her feet in the other girl's prints.

Costa stepped into the shade at the edge of the water. "Are you angry?"

Emielle shook her head and slid over so there was room for two.

As children they had swung on branches from one end of this grove to the other without setting foot on the ground. Costa slipped through the tangle of roots and limbs easily and sat down next to her in the dappled shade.

"I'm worried about you," said Emielle softly, in more of her normal tone. "You're too old to be getting into trouble. It was different when we were too young for them to take us away."

"No one knows it was me," said Costa. "It was the middle of the night."

Emielle sighed. "I don't understand you sometimes. What did you think you were going to accomplish?"

She shrugged, staring across the water. "Maybe I just want to show them that they aren't wanted here."

"Don't you think they know that?" said Emielle sarcastically. "I suppose you think they should get back in their ships and leave us alone, too."

In fact, that was exactly what she thought but Emielle didn't wait for her to answer. She gestured vaguely at the tilled hillsides and fenced pastures. "How do you think the horses feel about being ridden? What about the vegetables? And what about the reshie? What would you do if they could suddenly object to being hunted?"

"It's not the same," muttered Costa. "You know it isn't. Besides, you weren't talking like this six months ago. Now you sound like your mother."

"My mother is still a free woman," replied Emielle. "Not like yours."

Jaleela had been taken away *in collar*, as people said, when Costa was four and Ari was six. Most of the time Costa couldn't remember much more than her name, but sometimes at night there was an indistinct memory of reddish blonde hair and strong arms. Maybe the memory was really Nisai in her younger days. Ari remembered more, Costa was certain of that, but her sister would never talk about it.

"They took her because she stopped having babies," said Costa. "She turned out to be sterile."

"Maybe," said Emielle. "Maybe there was more to it."

"What do you mean?"

Emielle leaned back on her elbows. "My mother talks about her sometimes, when you're not around."

That was unusual, especially for docile, obedient Nisai. People who were taken by the slavers were never seen again and rarely discussed. When names did come up, there was a tendency to refer to them as some kind of ghost, as though they were no longer really alive.

"What does she say?"

"She says you're a lot like her—not just looks. It's the way you act. She says you think too much."

Costa shrugged, trying to appear indifferent. The truth was, she would have given anything to know more about this woman that no one ever mentioned, even in a whisper. "Is that all?"

"No." Emielle gave her an odd half-smile. "She told me everyone was sure Jaleela would end up in collar because she was headstrong. But she was so beautiful, Raffail decided she'd be a better breeder than a slave."

"He was wrong, though," said Costa. "She only had two babies, and we're two years apart so she probably miscarried at least once."

"That's not what my mother thinks."

Costa frowned at her, mystified. "Well? What does she think?"

"Maybe she refused to do what she was told. Maybe he finally punished her by putting her in collar."

"Nisai said that?"

"No," admitted Emielle. "But I'm pretty sure that's her opinion."

"And you're saying she thinks that's what's going to happen to me?"

"We're only as good as our breeding," said Emielle softly. "I just think you need to be more careful if you want to stay free."

She meant it as friendly, sisterly advice, but it made Costa's skin prickle with anger. "I'm not the only one who takes chances." She gestured across the lake at the village. "People do what they can get away with. Ari takes chances sleeping with Ofre. They don't know about that."

"You don't think so?" asked Emielle, suddenly very serious. "Why do you think they married her off so young? Why do you think Raffail was just asking about her? Lucky for her she was a long way from here while you were stirring things up last night."

Costa let out a worried breath. "But why would they suspect her? She always behaves for them."

Emielle shook her head. "They may not know everything but they think they do. That's why they use the Eye as their mark. They're always watching."

"What about you?" Costa persisted. "You've done some pretty wild things yourself. Not just the horses." She closed her mouth and used her hands to say it. *That boy you slept with.*

"Stop it." Emielle narrowed her eyes and scanned the opposite shore. "I never got pregnant. I just wanted to know what it was like." She arched one eyebrow at her cousin. "And anyway, at least it was a *boy*, not a girl."

"All I ever did was *talk* about *that*," hissed Costa. "Not like *you*."

Emielle grinned and slid closer, pushing her right to the edge of the boulder. "You won't make any babies with those kinds of ideas," she whispered in her cousin's ear. "What would D'Raffail think?"

Costa looked away, ignoring her.

Emielle snickered. "You'd make a terrific slave. Young and beautiful, but she doesn't like men much. No wonder they haven't found you a husband yet."

"Stop it." Costa pulled away, stumbling in the shallow water and tangled roots. Emielle was laughing at her.

"What are you going to do when they bring you a man?"

"The same thing you did."

Emielle rolled on her back, grinning. "It wasn't so bad. You might even like it."

Costa stood knee-deep in the lake, hands on her hips, working herself up to a really devastating reply. Neither of them heard the horse coming until the Sector rider shot past the grove, the fifth slave tied across the front of his saddle.

Emielle crouched against the trunk of the nearest tree, out of sight. She caught Costa's hand and practically dragged her out of the water.

"Did you see who it was?"

Costa nodded quickly. "Jezr'el." She shaded her eyes against the early afternoon sun, watching the rising dust as the black horse thundered around the edge of the lake and stopped on the village beach. "We'd better go."

They came up behind the crowd gathering on the beach and crawled onto the neighbor's roof for a better view.

Raffail was already standing on the shore, his son Jezr'el on his right, and the five captured slaves kneeling in the sand on his left. Whatever Raffail had in mind to say to the crowd would be lost on them. The slaves spoke an outworld language that no one here understood except the Sector. Raffail made sure there was as little communication between the Jahari locals and his slaves as possible, and whatever the Jahari knew about outworld servitude was limited to what they could infer, or whatever half-truths they were told.

Two other slavers hovered at the edge of the crowd, counting heads, listening, but right now no one was saying much of anything. Reprisals were rare here. The last public punishment anyone could remember was for Nisai's passive act of giving birth to Emielle. Costa shivered in spite of the temperature. Such a tiny, unavoidable mistake could not compare to what she'd done last night. Did they know who was responsible already? She bit her lip hard and told herself again how impossible that was.

Raffail pushed the white cloak back from his shoulders, waiting for the signal from his lieutenants that everyone was there. In spite of the heat, there wasn't a drop of sweat on him, not that Costa could see. The only skin the Sector ever seemed to expose to the sun was their faces, and even their eyes were covered by the stripe of blue, like a mask.

Jezr'el took a step forward, glaring at the people who had been foolish enough to stand so close to him. Most fled back into the body of the crowd, and a few dropped reflexively to their knees. Where Raffail was a despot, Jezr'el had the potential to be a tyrant, and everyone knew it. His father was at least fair on most occasions, even merciful. Jezr'el had no such compulsions. He considered it a waste of his time. He was young and zealous, and that made him even more dangerous. When Raffail was away, often for months, leaving the young man in charge, people put on their most obeisant behavior and did their best to stay well out of his way.

Raffail held up his hand, and what mumbling there was stopped instantly.

"A few months ago," he said, quietly in the silence, "a number of our horses escaped. You may remember. The stable hands were punished for their carelessness. You may remember that as well." He took a step toward the line of slaves, and the nearest one shook visibly, laying her head on the ground at his feet. "Last night," Raffail continued, "there was another incident." He reached down, winding his fingers into the girl's hair, and jerked her head back sharply. "They know the consequences of their actions, but I believe someone here was involved." His eyes flickered around the crowd.

Costa flattened herself against the rough thatch, trying to look innocent and invisible at the same time.

Raffail let go of the girl and nodded at his son. Jezr'el stepped around him and yanked one of the boys to his feet, pinning his arms back, painfully high. He snapped out something in the boy's own language, and the slave surveyed the crowd, trembling. He took a good long time, searching every face, but he never looked up where Costa and Emielle were. Finally he swallowed hard and mumbled something.

Jezr'el's face tightened. He glanced at his father, but Raffail shook his head. "Later," he said. The word floated menacingly on the warm breeze, and Jezr'el let the boy drop back to the sand.

There was a ripple in the crowd at the far end of the road.

"Look," whispered Emielle, and Costa lifted her face cautiously out of her arms.

"I can't see."

"It's Triez," said Emielle, sounding shocked. "They're taking Triez."

She was a young woman, no more than twenty, very pretty. She'd had a number of fervent admirers when she was a teenager, and rumors had circulated wildly two years ago when Raffail announced he'd decided on a match for her. Her new husband had been brought from the south and was the object of a lot of jealous contempt from the local boys. Now he hovered in the doorway of their house while the two slavers led her down to the beach. As far as finding a radical element to make an example of, Triez was an odd choice. She was as faithful and obedient as anyone could be, dutifully producing two children and working on the third, at least until a few weeks ago.

"I can't believe this," whispered Emielle, almost to herself. "She's good enough for a whole brood! One miscarriage. . . ."

They were going to do it in public, too. That was even more unusual. Costa crouched against the rooftop, afraid to watch, wondering how much of this was a reprisal and how much had already been planned.

Triez was pale and worn out from the difficult pregnancy and didn't look like she had the strength to resist. She sank to the ground at Raffail's feet, her back to the crowd, her family and friends.

Raffail waited for the dismayed group to quiet down. "Who freed my slaves?" he demanded. "We all know Triez didn't do it. Who's going to be honest enough to keep her out of collar?"

There was no sound, no motion except for the wind in the trees.

Raffail nodded slowly. "I see," he said, and to Costa it seemed like he was looking straight at her. He took a step back as Jezr'el pulled Triez to her feet—too eagerly. Jezr'el reached into his cloak and took out the tiny hypodermic that fit against his palm. He laid his hand on Triez's throat and squeezed. Her face flushed as the Drug entered her body. It would heal whatever was wrong with her, and the dose was strong enough to last for almost twenty years. Mostly though, it would keep her young and lovely for a long, long time.

Costa covered her eyes as Jezr'el snapped the chain collar around the woman's neck. She heard the rip of fabric as he pulled the shirt off her shoulder—it would be the left one—and Triez's thin shriek as he pressed the brand against her arm. Then there was silence. Costa looked up, holding her breath. Maybe Triez was only the first to go this afternoon.

But Raffail was getting on his horse. He waited for Jezr'el to mount, with Triez in front of him.

"No more trouble," said Raffail sharply. "I can do much worse than this, as you know."

There was a hushed chorus of *Yes D'sha*. No one budged until they were all well out of sight.

"He looked at me," breathed Costa, finally.

"He looked at me too." Emielle laid her head against the thatch and closed her eyes. "Maybe he thinks we both did it."

Below, people were beginning to wander away, back to whatever they'd been doing, nervous now, tense.

Something slapped hard against the roof, and Costa jerked away from it in alarm. Nisai's wrinkled face appeared at the back of the house. She hit the roof again with the broom.

"This trouble is from idle hands," she snapped, too loudly, because she could hardly hear herself. She pointed an accusing finger at Costa. "Get back to your garden. And *you*," she waved the finger at Emielle, "why didn't you tell me he had a man for you?" She grabbed her daughter's arm and hurried her through the back yard to their own house. Costa watched them disappear inside and wandered slowly back into the gardens.

There was a place at the top of the hill, between the rows of heavy-headed grain, where she could sit, unseen, with a view of the village, the lake, and the rolling, lightly forested hills beyond. Blue flowers entwined at her feet, thick and brilliant, choking off the roots of the reddish grain. She pulled at the blossoms without much enthusiasm and ended up with a handful of petals, leaving the rest of the plant still intact and alive.

Costa stared out across the hot, shimmering valley, past the clumps of trees, already starting to turn from green to gold as the summer came to a gradual end. The sheer black peaks of the mountains quivered beyond them in the distant east. In more normal times, hunting would have started in a week or two, when the weather was cooler and the reshie were closer, following their migratory path from the plains to the foothills. The furthest kill had been less than a day away from the village in years past. Now the rules were suddenly different. At the beginning of this summer, to everyone's surprise, Jezr'el had announced that hunting would be done on the plains, not the foothills, and anyone found east of the lake would be dealt with. No one had the audacity to ask why. Instead, every able-bodied man, woman, and child had been out at least twice this season, riding nine or ten days in the sweltering heat, trying to stock enough meat for the winter when the new boundaries would put the reshie out of reach.

A number of conditions that people had thought of as stable and time-honored had changed recently, not just the hunting season. Jezr'el was being given more responsibility, and that in itself was frightening. Nobody openly criticized how the Sector ran things, but now it no longer felt safe to even have an opinion. At the beginning of the summer, one bright young woman had brought home a pair of yearling reshie with the idea of breeding them, like horses, eliminating the problem of hunting altogether. She had disappeared the following morning. The animals were found soon after with their throats cut. Not another word was said about the incident, and the hunt went on as planned.

Although this was certainly not the first time Costa had felt trapped here, something was different: things were changing too fast. Maybe Raffail's son was simply flexing his muscles, as some whispered, and it was only a matter of time until life was back to normal, but to Costa it was more than that. Now there were days when the very air seemed different, almost tainted.

She pushed herself to her feet, suddenly feeling her aunt's suspicious eye, even at this distance, and began pulling the weeds with a false kind of diligence. Last night everything had been so clear to her, so assuredly right. What the dream had shown her were specific details: where and when to go, the position of the chain, and where to place her fingers to open the lock. Now the results of what she'd done eddied around her tasting unmistakably of real disaster. What Costa had thought was a decision to do a correct, even moral thing was starting to feel more like an uncontrollable compulsion. She dug her fingers into the dirt and roots and pulled hard. She could promise Emielle not to act on what she saw, but she was beginning to think the only way to keep herself out of trouble was to somehow avoid the temptation altogether.

Costa glanced back down at the house and out again at the low hills. There had been plenty of times in the past when she'd been angry enough, or bored enough, to fantasize about wandering quietly off, never to be seen again. Fantasy was all that had ever been. Only the occasional outworld slave had any illusions about being able to outrun Jezr'el, and the example he set with them made the consequences for leaving without permission extremely clear. Still, the slaves were not native to this planet. They didn't know how to hunt or how to survive the winters here. They didn't know where to hide.

Costa turned back to the flowers and vegetables, afraid of what she was thinking, but more afraid not to consider it. Some strong undertow of events was swirling around her, drawing her out of familiar waters. Running was the wrong thing to do, but there no longer seemed to be a choice. If she accomplished nothing else, she could at least take the burden of Raffail's suspicion off of Ari. She knelt in the spread of flowers and began to work more methodically, digging them out, one by one.

By late afternoon she'd made enough progress to satisfy Nisai, should she be in a picky, investigatory mood. Costa straightened up, listening to the sound of approaching riders, and made her way over the fence to the crest of the hill.

The low sun caught in the cloud of dust, gilding it, cutting through in shafts to the riders and burdened horses below. It was cooler now, and Costa stood in the pleasant breeze, trying to catch a glimpse of Ari in the pack of hunters. Someone was waving at her—slow, tired sweeps of her arm. Costa waved back energetically and ran down the hill to meet her sister.

Almost half the village had gone this time. Emielle's younger brothers and father were leading their loaded mounts. They hardly noticed as Costa pushed past them to the back of the line.

Ari slid stiffly off the horse and gave her a tired, grimy smile. She was taller that most of the other Jahari women, with enough energy and optimism for a dozen people. Right now, though, she looked like she could sleep for a week.

"Is that all you got?" asked Costa, falling into step with the horse, running her hand over the glossy brown pelts of the limp carcasses. There were only three.

"This is my average," replied her sister. She pointed across to the plodding pack animals. "Fifteen in five days." She grinned. "Think you can beat that?"

"Depends how many you missed." Costa smiled back and took

the reins from her. She wanted to tell her everything, every detail of what had happened since last night, but she didn't dare. "How far did you have to go?"

"Three days. We did pretty well this time, but there's going to be another trip out tomorrow. You should go."

It was such a simple solution. Costa nodded too quickly, nervously. "Will you come too?"

Ofre, said Ari with her hands, and gave her a secretive grin. *It depends what he wants to do.*

Costa wound the reins through her fingers. Raffail's careful manipulations of Jahar's gene pool made Ari's unapproved trysts a dangerous game. Her assigned husband, Tomas, knew what she was doing, but as long as she continued to have children with him and not Ofre, he really had no reason to complain. In fact, on a number of occasions he'd actually gone out of his way to make sure the two of them could have a little privacy. This illicit romance had been going on for over two years, and so far Ari had managed to satisfy herself, the slavers, and apparently her lover as well without making any unfortunate mistakes. If Raffail ever found out what she was doing, Ofre would probably be sent far, far away. If it was Jezr'el who found out, the consequences would be much worse.

Costa looked up at her sister, trying to decide how much she could safely tell her. "I saw Raffail this morning," she started. "Emielle's going to be married."

Ari nodded approvingly. "That should keep her out of trouble." She put a friendly arm over her sister's shoulders. "You'll be next, I think. Did he say anything to you?"

"Sort of." She looked away quickly from Ari's questioning glance. "He wanted to know where you were."

Ari frowned. "Why?"

"There was some trouble last night. Some of their slaves got out. They think someone helped them run. One's still loose." She licked her dry lips, thinking she'd spoken much too fast.

Ari wasn't listening that carefully. "Did he ask about anyone else?"

She meant Ofre. Costa shook her head. "Only Tomas."

Her sister stopped, worried now. "Have you seen Ofre since this morning?"

"No." The slavers had probably been too busy with Triez and their runaways to bother with Ofre, even if they did suspect him of something. Costa opened her mouth to say so, but Ari was already running across the road, cutting up the hill to take the short way home through the gardens. She stopped halfway up the slope and Signed across the distance, *See you at the lake. Tonight.*

Costa nodded back, wanting to explain. Instead she ran a forefinger across one eyebrow. *Understand.*

Emielle was on the beach helping to unload the horses. She blinked in surprise when she saw Costa and the dusty gelding.

"Where's Ari?"

"She went home." Costa fumbled with the knotted ropes, easing the carcasses to the sand. Someone else would take them to be skinned and butchered. She caught her cousin by the arm as Emielle reached for the next horse. "Help me wash him off."

The other girl followed as Costa led the horse into the shallow water, away from the others.

"Mother's in a complete panic about the wedding," said Emielle conversationally. "We've got eleven days to get ready. She's convinced it's not enough time."

Costa threw the reins over the gelding's neck and smoothed wet hands against his sweaty black hide. Emielle was trying not to sound as excited as she felt, but this marriage was a precious gift. Her older brothers were already gone, and it was expected that the younger ones would be taken away when they were old enough. For Nisai's error to be worked into the breeding scheme was an incredible act of generosity.

"Who did you get?"

"I've never heard of him," said Emielle. Her mouth quirked into half a grin. "His name's Ephraim. What kind of name is that?"

Most likely another stranger from the south. Costa shrugged while her cousin chattered on about the dresses and flowers and the food.

"There's a lot of cooking," said Emielle. "You're good at that. Mother wants you to be in charge of it."

"I can't," said Costa. "I'm going hunting tomorrow."

Emielle frowned at her. "Someone else can go. I need you."

"I'm going," repeated Costa quietly. "I have to. I'm not coming back." It still sounded so wrong. Emielle was staring at her, speechless.

"How can you talk like that?" hissed her cousin. "Didn't you see how fast they caught those poor runaway bastards? And you know what's going to happen to them." She turned away, splashing water on the horse's legs, glancing around to see if anyone was close enough to overhear.

"I'll be further away," said Costa. "You could come too. We could be ten days from here before anyone knows we're gone."

"Not me," snapped Emielle. "Not a chance. They'll bring you back in collar. They'll beat you." Her voice was starting to shake, and she wouldn't look up. "You *are* out of your mind."

"They won't find me," whispered Costa. "I'll know if they're coming. I'll dream it before they get there."

Emielle stared at her, her eyes full of tears. "You're really going to do it."

Costa looked down at the water, almost convinced of it herself.

"You can only go west," whispered Emielle. "There's nothing out there. In two months you'll be freezing to death, or starving."

Costa shrugged. Her plan was to circle north and then head for the mountains. Off limits or not, if she could stay out of sight long enough, with the winter storms covering her tracks, the Sector might never be able to trace her. She didn't want to tell Emielle. If she wasn't coming, it was better that she didn't know. "I'll be alright."

"You won't," said Emielle. "You don't know what you're doing." She grabbed Costa's arm and squeezed hard enough to hurt her. "What's the matter with you? Why can't you just do what everyone else does? You don't have to fight. You can't fight. . . ." She let go, wiping her eyes. "I don't understand you anymore." Emielle turned away and stumbled to the beach, disappearing into the crowd of people and animals.

Costa spent the remainder of the afternoon helping with the butchering. She would catch occasional glimpses of her cousin on the other side of the beach, pretending to be cheerful, but Emielle never looked at her. The only tension in the village seemed to be between the two of them. Everywhere else there was a feeling of vast relief that the summer was nearly over, the crops were ready to be brought in, and that the last hunt of the new season would be leaving in the morning.

The two moons they called the Sisters came up together in the darkening evening sky. The lake silvered in the soft light, no longer a low, muddy pool, more of a mirror. Costa waded into it, rinsing off her face and hands. The smell of sizzling meat hung in the cool air as the fires were stoked down over open pits. On the shore behind her, clay jugs of bitter, fermented berry juice had already been brought out and were being passed from hand to hand.

Early stars glittered behind her reflection as she pulled her hair back, watching herself in the water. A single bright light, like a languid comet, drifted slowly overhead. Costa watched the Sector ship as it disappeared behind the thin clouds in the north.

Realistically, there was only one sure way of escaping this world, this limited way of living. Space travel was as abstract a notion for her as it was for everyone else here, but it was common knowledge that Jahar was not the only place where people were bred for the service and pleasure of others. Sometimes she tried to imagine what it was like where her mother and so many of her relatives had been taken, and sometimes she wondered how much worse it could actually be.

Costa turned back toward the shore, her stomach knotting. There was still one whole night for her to change her mind. Maybe she would stay home, stay awake, and stay as free as she was right now. Someone on the beach was calling her name. She waded back to join the rest of the village as they prepared to celebrate the early hunt.

Much later, after the dancing started, Emielle collapsed next to her, panting, more than a little tipsy. She pushed the damp tendrils of hair away from her face and leaned forgivingly on Costa's shoulder.

"Come and dance," she murmured. "Everyone's asking about you."

"I don't feel like it." Actually, she wasn't sure she could stand. Costa had discovered that the more she drank, the less worried she felt. At the moment, her optimism was so palpable, she could almost touch it.

Emielle picked up Costa's cup, tilted her head back, and swallowed what was left. Which was quite a lot. Costa tried not to snicker as Emielle choked on a mouthful, and bright red liquid dribbled down her neck, onto her shirt.

"You're a mess now," she said. "What's your future husband going to think?"

Emielle grabbed her hand and hauled her to her feet. "Come on."

Costa stumbled along behind her and found her hands gripped on either side by other people, twisting and spinning through the traditional steps. She did her best to keep up with them, and was actually quite impressed with herself when her feet hit the ground with everyone else's. Overhead, the stars swam around in the warm, warm night, swaying with the repetitive, staggered drumbeat and shrilling flutes. The only thing missing was Triez, who usually sang. Someone else was belting out the ancient lyrics about home and hearth and faithfulness, soddenly. Not as convincing as Triez.

The singer's voice wavered, high and unpracticed, as he finished the song, but the flutes and drums suddenly faltered in what was supposed to be an emotional crescendo. The singer stopped mid-lyric. The dancing slowly came to an unorganized halt.

Costa lurched against the girl next to her, dizzy with the alcohol, her head pounding so hard she felt like the ground itself was shaking. But it was. And the sound wasn't from inside her head. It was an approaching rider, someone coming very fast.

For a moment there was no other noise except the crackle of the fires and the breathlessness of people listening intently. Off in the darkness, the horse slowed to a trot, and Jezr'el's harsh voice snapped an order in the outworld language.

Firelight flickered over the sweating black horse as the young slaver rode onto the beach, scattering people too drunk or too foolish to get out of the way. The animal was flecked with foam, and Jezr'el's white robes were streaked with dirt. Something. . .someone was trailing behind, tied to a long rope. Jezr'el slowed the horse, and the last of the runaway slaves came into the circle of firelight.

Costa watched from the safety of the crowd as the boy swayed with exhaustion, ashen, even in the red glow of the fire. He had his hands wound into the rope that ran from his chain collar to the saddle to keep himself from being strangled if he fell while the horse was running. He looked like he'd been running all night. He was gasping for breath, quite literally dripping with sweat. Something was wrong with him, beyond being chased and captured and probably knocked around. He collapsed in the sand, trembling, and she finally recognized him. Everyone here knew who he was. The Sector called him something unpronounceable, so the Jahari had shortened the name to the first syllable: Fray.

Raffail had given him to his son when Jezr'el was about ten years old, unluckily for Fray. The young man's meanness had developed at an early age, and the slave had been the victim of tremendous abuse when his master was in the mood to hurt him. Still, for all the mistreatment, Fray was a remarkably good-natured sort of person. Even though he didn't speak a word of the local language, he was well-known in the village, and sometimes, when the slavers sent him on some errand, he would hand out candy and trinkets from faraway worlds. Of all the slaves the Sector had brought to Jahar, Fray seemed to be one of the most intelligent. It was obvious he'd gotten further than the others before being caught, and if he'd managed to escape, he probably could have survived. Costa closed her eyes, feeling incredibly sorry for him. She hadn't realized he was in the coffle she'd set free.

Jezr'el had dismounted by now and was pacing back and forth on the beach, his whip trailing in the sand. People were clustered just at the edge of the firelight, close enough to be counted, hopefully out of range of the young slaver's temper.

Jezr'el held up a hand for quiet, but no one was talking.

"My father is a lenient man," he said in his thick accent. "Wouldn't you agree?"

"Yes D'sha," whispered Costa, with the rest of the crowd.

"Yes D'sha," he mimicked, and scowled at them. "A crime has been committed by someone standing here. Unlike my father, I believe you all know who it is."

He was wrong, but that wasn't going to make a difference. Costa glanced around the dark beach, wondering where Raffail was and if he knew his son was about to put on his own show of discipline when the message had already been driven home that morning.

Jezr'el put his hand into the crowd like someone picking fruit off a tree and pulled out a woman, heavy with her pregnancy.

It was Nisai. "Who did it?" he snapped at her.

Deaf Nisai nodded her head frantically. "Yes D'sha," she whispered, terrified.

Raffail at least remembered who he'd crippled in the past. Jezr'el had no interest in things like that. He was frowning at the old woman, confused and irritated.

Costa pushed forward, not sure what she could possibly say or do, but her uncle stepped out first and fell to his knees on the sand.

"She has no hearing, D'sha," he whispered in the complete silence. "She can't understand you."

Jezr'el scowled. "No hearing?" he repeated. "Then ask her in Sign."

He probably could have done it himself, but the slavers never used the silent language, and there was some debate as to whether they even understood it. Jezr'el waited while Nisai watched her husband carefully, then stared at the slaver in alarm, shaking her head emphatically.

Costa shrank back in relief as Jezr'el turned away from her aunt, but it wasn't over yet. Jezr'el took a step backward, eyes narrow, scanning the crowd. Costa held her breath as he glanced past her, then froze as he looked back, nodding with sudden understanding.

"Ari," he said, very clearly. He caught her arm and pulled her into the light of the fire. "You're Jaleela's daughter."

Costa shook her head frantically, and the haze of alcohol vanished abruptly, leaving her frighteningly close to his hard, angry face and the smear of blue paint across his eyes. "I'm Costa," she whispered, absolutely dry-mouthed, but his fingers only dug harder into her shoulders.

"Where were you last night, Ari?" he snarled.

"C-C-C-Costa!" She tried to say it, but all that came out of her mouth were guilty, useless, inarticulate sounds that would do nothing but incriminate her. And her sister.

"D'Jezr'el," said someone behind Costa, and his grip loosened as he looked past her.

Ari dropped gracefully to her knees in the sand, the picture of self-possession and sobriety. "Excuse me, D'sha," she said, as though hesitant to point out his mistake. "I'm Ari."

He narrowed his eyes at her, then scowled at Costa, studying her face. "Costa," he said, in exactly the same tone, "where were you last night?"

Costa opened her mouth, but the voice that answered was her sister's.

"She was with me, D'sha. We came back from the hunt this morning."

Jezr'el let go, and Costa fell at his feet, limp with fright. Ari caught her hand, pulling her into the shelter of the crowd. Costa clung to her, trembling, as Jezr'el turned back to Fray.

The boy was curled up on his side now, shivering like a sick animal. Jezr'el stuck his toe under Fray's face. The boy managed to put his mouth against his master's boot, but couldn't move fast enough to dodge the kick.

Jezr'el pulled his foot back and raised the whip.

"Pay attention," he said to the villagers in a low, dangerous voice.

"These are your consequences as well."

Fray writhed and howled as he was beaten, and Jezr'el laid into him with a vengeance. The Sector never broke their routine when it came to runaways, but there was nothing systematic about what Jezr'el was doing. It was easy to see he enjoyed every minute of this. The fact that he had a captive audience made it that much better.

The woman standing next to Ari covered her mouth and looked away. She may have felt a certain sympathy for Fray, but it was probably her own relatives or her children she was thinking about. Costa put her face against her sister's arm, listening to the whistle and crack, and the boy's thin cries, trying not to think about her mother.

It was over sooner than anyone expected. Jezr'el stopped with his arm in the air, the bloody cord trailing against his clothes. Fray was spasming, convulsing at Jezr'el's feet, no longer even conscious, just flopping like a landed fish.

Costa had seen this happen to slaves before. When the Drug ran low, they simply died. Fray was old, as far as his years in collar went, but he'd had time left. Costa was fairly sure of that. Jezr'el had forced him over the brink. Without realizing it, by the look on his face. The young man lowered the whip in disgust as his slave gave a final, wrenching shudder and lay still.

Jezr'el glowered at the people watching him and pushed the corpse over with his heel. "You," he said to someone, "bury this."

2

Of course after that it seemed much easier to leave.

Costa shaded her eyes as the sun sank lower over the broad sweep of prairie, letting her gelding follow the others at his own pace. The rolling hills and valleys were well behind her now, and the village was completely out of sight.

Her winter clothes were packed in saddle bags, stuffed around her boots and a couple of small cooking pots she didn't think Nisai would miss right away. No one took very much on hunting trips, and she felt conspicuously loaded, but so far, if anyone had noticed, they weren't saying anything.

The bow lay unstrung across the front of the saddle, and she ran her fingers along the smooth, familiar wood. At least she had an excuse to be armed. Without being at all vain, she knew she was a very good shot.

Costa closed her eyes, letting her shoulders slump. The idea of trying to escape was making her absolutely ill. Ari was riding with the rest of the hunters up ahead, and every once in a while, Costa could hear a snatch of laughter or singing. Her sister's clear voice harmonized with the other women. The lyrics from the song last night drifted back faintly in the dry air.

The slavers' lessons about "right" and "wrong" had never been lost on Ari, but even so, she always seemed to be able to do whatever she wanted without overstepping Raffail's boundaries. Costa watched her sister laughing in the distance, as though nothing in the world could go wrong. She wrapped her hands in the gelding's reins, weaving her fingers through the worn leather, needing something new to concentrate on.

The song ended, and Ari circled her mare back, waiting for Costa to catch up.

"You're not very sociable this morning," she remarked.

Costa shrugged unhappily.

Ari raised an eyebrow and glanced at the overstuffed saddlebags. "Aren't you feeling well? You seemed to be drinking a lot last night."

Costa nodded, unable to look at her.

"Too bad about Fray," Ari went on. "I wonder how far he got before Jezr'el found him."

"He probably ran all night," said Costa.

"On foot," agreed her sister, "because ever since somebody let the horses out, Raffail's kept the corral locked." She rode for a while in silence, letting the accusation settle, like the yellow dust around them. "I just can't figure out why Jezr'el thought I was responsible."

Costa bit her lip—too hard. "He's just trying to scare us."

"He's certainly scaring *you.*" She leaned closer and lowered her voice. "How far do you think you're going to get?"

"I'm not going anywhere," Costa whispered.

"Is that so?" Ari hissed back. "If *I* can tell, don't you think *they* can?" She sat up straight again, eyeing the other riders, but they were well out of earshot. "Did you do it?" she asked softly.

Costa stared at the pommel of her saddle. "Yes."

Ari let a breath out between her teeth. "What else did you do?"

"The horses," said Costa. "Emielle and I let them go."

Ari rubbed her forehead. "But why?"

"Because. . . ." Because she was terribly afraid of the things she knew she would be forced to do as she got older. Because there was something fundamentally wrong with the only two options in her life. Costa stared at the ground, not wanting to say anything about the dreams. "I'm not sure anymore."

Ari frowned, sensing the lie. "Seems like a lot of trouble to go through if you're not sure why you're doing it."

Costa didn't say anything.

"Are you that unhappy here?" asked Ari. "Because doing that kind of thing is a sure way to leave. It might be a lot easier for you to just knock on Raffail's door and ask him to please put the collar on."

"That's not what I want," said Costa, irritated at her sarcasm.

"So what do you want?" Ari waited for an answer and then went on more sympathetically. "You want to be free," said Ari. "Isn't that right?"

It was as good an answer as any, and closer to the truth.

Ari sighed. "Trying to run away won't make you any freer than you are right now. You understand that, don't you?"

"They won't find me," said Costa.

"Yes they will," said Ari. "It's just a matter of time, and then they'd have their fun with you, like Jezr'el did with poor Fray. It isn't worth it." She put a hand on Costa's shoulder. "You may not be happy with the way things are here, but if you're not careful, you could end up with a lot worse. Have you thought about what it's like to be a slave for them?"

"Sometimes."

"I don't think you'd like it much," said Ari. "Although I suppose for some people it's no different than being here."

"What do you mean?"

"Triez, for example. She never gave them any trouble, no matter what they wanted her to do. Being a slave isn't really that big a change for her." Ari shrugged. "You and I aren't like that, and Raffail knows it. His biggest fear is that we'll start making plans, or start fighting back."

"You think that's wrong?" whispered Costa.

"It is if you want to stay alive," said Ari blandly. "You've seen what happens to runaways. What do you think they'd do to someone who had the nerve to pick up a rock? Or a knife?" She frowned at Costa's look of indecision and didn't say anything for a while. "What do you remember about Mother?" she asked at last.

Costa looked up in surprise. "Not very much."

"Do you remember Father?"

She'd never even heard him mentioned. "No."

"I'll tell you why," said Ari. "Mother kicked him out when you were two years old. I was sitting on the porch with you when she did it. She threw him right down the stairs, and he never came back."

"You were four," objected Costa. "How can you remember that?"

"I remember lots of things." She squinted into the distance. "Would you like to hear what happened the day they took her away?"

Costa frowned. "She threw out her husband?"

Ari shook her head. "Raffail let her alone for two years after that. They didn't touch her until I was six." She lowered her voice. "It was spring. Everyone was busy digging in the gardens, getting ready to plant. There were plenty of hoes and shovels, things like that. She took us both up to the top of the hill and picked up the first thing she saw—a rake, I think." She stopped and took a breath, hesitating. "She started waving it around, like a weapon. She was shouting as loud as she could, and everyone was staring."

"What did she say?"

"That's harder to remember," admitted Ari, "but it was something like not letting the greedy bastards at her daughters and that anyone with any decency would fight back."

Costa stared at her in astonishment. No wonder no one ever talked about Jaleela.

"Raffail was there so fast, I think he must have been listening. Maybe she already knew that. She took a couple of swings at him before his brothers showed up. They knocked her down." She shrugged. "You can figure out the rest."

"What was everyone else doing?"

"Standing around," said Ari bitterly. "Like stupid reshie." She shook her head. "She was very intelligent, but she made one mistake."

"What?" asked Costa.

"She loved us too much." Ari took Costa's hand and squeezed it. "She knew if she had a big family, like Nisai, all her children would be taken away the minute they turned eighteen. So she quit having babies, and then she provoked Raffail into taking her instead." She glanced meaningfully at her sister. "It's important not to love anything here, Costa. It just makes life that much harder."

"But you do," said Costa. "What about your babies?"

Ari shook her head. "Not even them. They're just replacements for the children Jaleela didn't have. Why should I torture myself?"

"You don't know that."

"Yes I do," said Ari. "All of mine—and all of yours."

Costa took a breath. "You don't love Ofre?"

"Not even him," said Ari. She laced the reins through her fingers.

"He's almost twenty-two, and they still haven't married him off. We're both pretty sure he'll be gone by spring." She smiled tightly. "Unless they've forgotten about him."

That was patently unlikely. Costa frowned at her own hands, struggling with this ridiculous, useless outrage, and with the most obvious of questions. "You don't love me either?" she asked finally, not looking up.

"You're the only reason I even know what it should feel like." Her grip tightened on Costa's hand. "You can't leave me," Ari said in a low, unsteady voice. "Come home with me after the hunt. You can stay in my house. I'll keep an eye on you, and we'll talk Raffail into bringing you a husband. The sooner you get pregnant, the better off you'll be."

It was the wrong solution, and Costa knew it. Still, she found herself nodding weakly in agreement.

There were three days of riding before anyone expected to see the reshie, and four days before anyone actually shot one.

It was a small female. Costa sat by the fire, working the arrow out of its ribs while someone else sharpened the knife to skin it.

"Not very big," said Ari.

The man who'd killed it shrugged. "We're lucky to find any still out here. The rest are probably across the river by now."

Costa ran her hand over the rough brown fur. Reshie were deer-like, not much bigger than a half-grown horse or a large pony. This one had a knob of badly healed bone on one leg. Maybe an injury from when it was a calf. It was rangy and looked underfed. She twisted the arrow again, and it snapped in her hands.

"Bad luck," said the man. He smiled as she gave him the pieces.

Actually, things seemed much better. She'd slept soundly and dreamlessly for the last three nights, and just the change of scenery had cheered her up. The trouble at home seemed much further away, unimportant, almost improbable. When she thought about it—and she tried hard not to—the dream of freeing the slaves began to blend with the event itself until she wasn't really sure what she'd done. It was such an incredible act of brazen disobedience, there were times she could almost convince herself the slaves had escaped some other way, that she'd had nothing to do with it.

On the fourth night all of that changed.

In dreams, her soul followed her, invisibly, just above her head.

Sometimes things moved slowly, like a pebble in honey. Sometimes colors were brighter than they should have been. In this one there was no sound at all, and she was flying.

Two reshie ran below, dodging one way and then the other, bounding over the low prairie scrub, running for their lives as two blonde riders on black horses closed in on them. Not far ahead, a river snaked along its wide, ancient bed, and from above, Costa could see where the outlying marsh began. The reshie were heading for the narrowest point in the river where it was shallow enough to cross. Beyond the water, the plains stretched to the horizon, empty and peaceful.

One rider bolted forward, suddenly passing the largest of the two animals, cutting it off to drive it back toward the slower horse. The reshie swung around, churning in the mud, and the horse tried to follow but lost its footing and went down. Costa watched from the sky as the girl flung herself off, rolling into a bank of grass, while the other charged after the escaping reshie.

Costa opened her eyes in the darkness.

The river was another one of the boundaries they were forbidden to cross. But it was never guarded.

She turned over carefully, not disturbing Ari who was curled up next to her, sound asleep. Costa laid her head back against the saddlebags and stared at the sky. Not even the Sector ship disturbed the glitter of sharp stars overhead. On the eastern horizon, the Sisters were beginning to rise. It was only a matter of hours until daylight. Costa closed her eyes again, filled with familiar confidence. There was no doubt at all in her mind that she could cross the river and follow it as far as she needed to. No one would follow her, and Raffail would not know anything until the hunting party returned. At the very least, she would have four full days to go in any direction at all, and by then she would be far, far away.

The first reshie they saw were nowhere near the river. There were three of them anyway, not two.

The heat was making her sister short-tempered, but the fact that Costa was so obviously thinking about something besides hunting exasperated her beyond the usual limits of her patience.

Watch where you're going, Signed Ari, as dry twigs snapped loudly under the gelding's hooves. *Stay over there—.* She pointed off to the right. *Try to keep your mind on what you're doing.*

Costa nodded, flustered and anxious. She guided the horse carefully through the patches of dry scrub. Something moved ahead in the shimmering mirage, and she halted the horse, glancing at Ari. Her sister Signed across the short space.

Three reshie. Go around the other side.

Costa pulled the gelding back, circling behind a clump of straggling trees, guiding the horse with her weight and heels while she strung the bow and set an arrow on the string. Reshie were nervous, flighty creatures, with remarkably good hearing. Strategies for hunting them were fairly straightforward, but getting close enough was a challenge. Voices, or sometimes even the sound of the wind, would send them racing away. Although horses were generally faster, a frightened reshie could usually get an unbeatable head start.

On the other side of the thicket, Ari was just visible, lying against the mare's neck, watching. She saw Costa and pointed.

The reshie were grazing not far ahead, oblivious, short tails twitching against insects. Two adults and a calf.

Which one? Signed Costa.

On your side, replied her sister. *The male. Ready?*

Costa made sure the arrow was tight against the string, gathered the reins in her other hand, and dug her heels into the gelding's side.

Her horse, Ari's mare, and the reshie all bolted forward at the same time.

Costa dropped the reins over the pommel of the saddle, crouching into the wind as the gelding raced through the tall grass. Ari was already ahead, and the reshie were attempting to scatter, the female and her calf cutting off to the left. That was fine. Costa leaned more to the right, watching the male as Ari closed in on him from the left, driving him toward Costa. She would press him from her side until he was running between them. Then the only thing that remained was to kill him quickly.

Ari swung the mare closer to the fleeing animal, her unstrung bow bouncing against her back. She was a fair shot, but not off the right side of a moving horse. Costa pulled her own bowstring tight, aiming over her left leg as the reshie was forced closer and closer to her.

He was a handsome buck, ears flat back and muscles straining. His neat cloven hooves moved faster than she could see, and sweat darkened his glossy coat. Costa leaned down a little, watching the movement of his right foreleg, matching the rhythm of his stride, aiming for the space between two ribs, right next to his heart. She let the arrow go as the leg moved forward, and it sank in deep, solid.

The creature stumbled and then dropped like a stone, immediately dead. Costa let the gelding run a little further, slowing down, circling back. Ari was already on the ground, a knife flashing in her hand as she bent over the carcass.

"Nice job," said Ari as Costa slid off the gelding. "For someone who's not awake."

Costa blinked at her. "What?"

Ari shook her head. "You haven't said two words to me this morning and you look like you didn't sleep at all. Are you feeling alright?"

"I'm fine." The truth was that she felt quite exhausted and was afraid anything she said would come out as some form of good-bye. "I guess I didn't sleep very well." She could smell the metallic stink of the marsh from where she was standing. The landscape was starting to look familiar too, long grasses giving way to low thorny brush, scorched from the last hot days of summer.

Costa straightened, squinting at the uneven slopes in the distance, trying to decide exactly how close the river was. Ari frowned at her and stood up, wiping off her hands.

She shaded her eyes. "What do you see?"

Two reshie, Costa Signed, almost against her will, and pointed at the indistinct black shapes. Only a person with extraordinary eyesight could have seen so clearly over that stretch of space, but Ari wasn't arguing.

She caught her mare by the reins and swung into the saddle. "Hurry up!" she hissed. "They're heading for the river!"

Costa closed her eyes for a moment, lightheaded in the bright, midday sun. The images of the dream came back vividly, even more tangible than the landscape around her, too compelling to be dispersed by her own fears or Ari's good sense.

She clambered onto the gelding as Ari rode ahead, peering back over her shoulder. Costa urged her horse forward, desperately trying to think of some other escape, dizzy from the height inside her head. She fitted an arrow against the bowstring and took a deep, deep breath. Ari's horse leaped abruptly forward, and the gelding bolted under her. Costa hung on helplessly, mired in events she had no idea how to control.

The two reshie seemed nothing less than astonished. They ran together instead of trying to split up until Ari began to bear down on the largest. He swerved and dodged, but the mare was much faster. Costa found herself paralleling her sister and the reshie, moving at an angle toward the river bank. The air was abruptly thick with insects, and the hard ground became a layer of crusted mud. The reshie slowed, just slightly, and then wheeled around, doubling back.

Costa reined the gelding around hard to follow, then felt him slipping. She managed to let the arrow go as the reshie charged past her, catching it in the shoulder. That was wrong. She hadn't shot him in the dream. The gelding churned under her, struggling for balance, kicking mud in all directions as she threw herself off into the coarse, high grass, and lay there, completely disoriented.

"Are you alright?" Ari slid off the mare and crouched next to her, breathing hard.

Costa stared up at her, and at the empty blue sky beyond. Two young blonde women on black horses was what she'd seen last night. One fell and one kept going. The only distinguishing mark that would have separated them was the star on the mare's forehead, and she hadn't paid any attention to that. She'd been thinking about the river and the safety beyond it. In the dream she'd never actually gotten that far.

Costa closed her eyes, oblivious to Ari shaking her, calling her name. Uncontrollable events pressed around her making it difficult to breathe, and for a moment she felt as though she was deep underwater, out of air. Ari's voice got fainter, and the essence of the vision throbbed inside her head, taunting and tantalizing, more vivid than ever.

Late summer storms were building in the western sky as the hunting party headed for home. The thickening humidity mixed with the dust in the hot, sticky air, and the animals lagged, even under the light loads.

Costa led the gelding on a long rein, glancing back at the enormous thunderheads piling on the horizon. Lightning flashed inside the clouds, and sheets of rain fell over the grasslands, now almost three days behind them.

Ari was walking next to her, lost in thought. In fact she hadn't been more than an arm's length away since the abortive reshie hunt. Thunder rolled overhead, and she looked up gloomily. "Bet it hits us at midnight." She grimaced at the thought of trying to sleep in the rain and squinted at the inviting, tree-covered hills, still hours away. "Should have left a day earlier."

In terms of the hunt, stopping early would not have made any difference. The take had been depressingly small, less than ten reshie between a dozen people, and nothing on the last day.

Costa wiped the sweat out of her eyes, gauging the distance to the hills again. At this rate, they would be home tomorrow, probably sometime in the early evening.

She stayed awake as late as she could that night, as thunder rumbled and lightning fluoresced through the dense clouds chasing across the sky. She huddled deeper into her cloak, wrapped against the chill of the approaching weather, staring into the dying fire. Ari snored softly next to her, exhausted. Costa was in no rush to get home. She'd spent the last three days and nights trying to imagine what Raffail would say when Ari demanded a husband for her. None of the scenarios were encouraging: the first thing Raffail did in each of them was ask why they were suddenly in such a hurry. The answers she could come up with did not seem especially convincing. They led to more questions, suspicions, and then frank accusations. When she had been able to sleep, her nightmares were frightening but not prescient. Those dreams seemed to wait until the events were practically upon her.

It was after midnight when she finally fell asleep, and in the dream, she was running as fast as she could. The moons raced along with her, one above the other, passing quickly behind occasional clouds as if they were afraid to lose sight of her. The fields were the familiar ones behind the village, and she could see herself below, moving effortlessly up the side of the hill. Even from high in the air, she could feel the rough bundle of unlit torches in her hand and the pouch of flint and tinder bouncing against her chest. Her soul in the sky swooped lower, close enough for her to make out her own features. The plan was suddenly so obvious it seemed stupid not to have come up with it before.

Raffail's house appeared through the short brake of trees. The windows were lit, and shadows moved inside against the steady light that didn't come from candles. Costa crouched at the edge of the woods while her soul hovered behind one shoulder. She laid the torches out and struck flint over the pile of tinder until it began to burn.

The dry thatch roof caught instantly with the first torch. Flames shot up in a column, engulfing half the building in seconds. Her reflection flashed in the near window, a threatening, omnipotent darkness, surrounded by fire. She lit the rest of the torches, throwing them one by one onto the burning roof. She heard shouting, then crashing, as the building began to collapse. Costa watched her body turn and run as low branches started to catch as well. One strange star hung near the ground in the frantic tree shadows, but there was no time to see what it really was.

She woke up, breathless, drenched by the breaking storm, understanding everything.

Alone, even in the dark and the rain, the ride back to the village was really quite short. Costa urged the gelding along the muddy path as fast as she dared. The storm had thinned to a drizzle now, and the clouds were breaking around patches of indigo sky. Moonrise could not be far off, and both moons had been up in the dream. There was plenty of time to set her fire and be back at the campsite by dawn. No one would ever know what she'd done.

It was clear that not even Raffail had any real idea who'd let the slaves out of the shed that night. His next and most likely step would be to wait for another round of trouble and then pin the blame on whoever seemed guiltiest. And if Ari continued to lie to protect her, it would be Ari who would be collared and taken away.

But what if there was no Raffail? What if there was no Jezr'el to replace him?

Murder. That was a word she wasn't used to. Enough consequences in two syllables for a dozen villages, a hundred sisters. In the dream, though, no one had escaped. The house had burned to the very ground. Hadn't it?

The weather broke as she reached the outermost fences. Costa turned the gelding off the main path, guiding him silently through the lush grass. It wouldn't take long to reach the slavers' house from here, even on foot. And she had been on foot in the dream.

Costa slid off the horse's back and tied him securely to a tree, out of sight. She looped the pouch of flint and tinder around her neck, made her way out of the shelter of trees, and began to run.

The two moons were just rising, gleaming like a pair of eyes. They didn't seem as worried as they'd been in the dream. Right now they were vengeful goddesses, guiding her through the tall grass, pulling her like she was on a cord, straight for the Sector house.

She crouched down at the edge of the woods, not even panting. The same as the dream, some outworld device cast shadows on the windows, shining with a warm yellow light.

Costa untied the torches. She was so close, even a fair throw would hit the roof with no trouble.

The tinder caught quickly, and she lit the first torch, aiming carefully despite the short distance, and tossed it into the thatch. Fire licked up immediately, but not as fast as she'd thought. She lit two more torches and straightened up to throw them further back on the roof. Flames flashed off the glass in the nearest window. She saw the reflection, but it wasn't hers.

Some other young woman stared back at her, filthy and starved, distorted by the leaping fire. The torchlight gleamed off the chain around her neck, and the image lowered its grey eyes.

Ari?

Inside the house someone was shouting, but the dead weight of her mistakes and assumptions held Costa where she was. The face in the window darkened abruptly as the roof began to collapse. It became unidentifiable, like someone peering from inside—strangely calm, with dark, slanting eyes.

Costa's heart clenched in her chest. She threw the torches, anywhere, and ran.

Behind her, the house was indeed burning, roaring with fire. She could hear Raffail's voice now. Tree shadows jumped around madly, and hot wind gusted through the branches as the building fell in on itself, completely engulfed.

At the far edge of the woods she looked back long enough to see the silhouette of the horse running in front of the fire, charging toward her. She pressed herself against the nearest tree, crouching down, waiting to be discovered.

The horse thundered past, riderless, reins flying. Costa put one hand over her mouth, holding back the sound. There was no mistaking the white spot on the forehead of her sister's mare.

3

Costa lay at the edge of the woods, unable to move, not even when the rain began pelting down again.

She hadn't killed anyone. That, at least, was certain. Ari had followed her and was now taking the blame for everything Costa had ever done to irritate the slavers. She realized numbly that she would never see her sister again.

By dawn the rain had stopped. Costa managed to get to her feet, almost nauseous with guilt. In the grim, cold hours before morning, it had become clear that her options had narrowed to one: she would get on her horse and head back toward the plains, putting as much distance as she could between herself and this last incredible error. Going home was impossible. There were more dreams coming, lying right behind her eyes. If she was far enough away, she might eventually learn to find the grain of truth in them, and hopefully, a way to stay one step ahead of the Sector.

Costa made her way slowly up the hill to where her horse was tied. Her bow and quiver hung dripping from the saddle, and she climbed wearily onto the soaked, unhappy gelding, slinging the weapons over her back.

Meeting the rest of the hunting party on the road would only raise questions she didn't have the strength to answer. Costa guided the tired horse along the crest of the hill, intending to cut through the woods, avoiding the main path altogether.

The village straggled along the misty lakeshore below, nothing but a ramshackle collection of sticks and stones and memories. A few people were already up. She could see the decorations for Emielle's wedding—garlands of autumn flowers hung on every door. Tables had been set up for the meal Nisai had probably spent the last four days preparing. At the near end of the village she could barely make out the front porch of the house that had belonged to Triez, gifts and furniture stacked to the ceiling for Emielle and her new husband.

Costa swallowed her tears and fury. She started to turn the gelding away, back into the woods, but there was something else moving on the shoreline.

Two black horses drifted weightlessly through the pink morning mist hanging over the lake. Three riders. Jezr'el and his father, and the tall blonde woman in front of Raffail, her hands cuffed tightly behind her back. She was still wearing her own clothes, not the uniform white of a slave.

Costa wrenched the gelding around and slammed her heels into his sides. Maybe there was still time to take responsibility for her own actions and save Ari from her pointless altruism.

She seemed unnoticed as she bolted down the hill, coming up just behind the gathering crowd. No one with any sense would be absent from something like this, and in moments, the entire village had gathered on the beach.

Costa slid off the gelding, pushing forward as far as she could as Jezr'el dismounted, holding his father's horse while Raffail pulled Ari down.

Someone banged open a door. Someone else hushed a baby. Raffail waited, counting heads until he was sure everyone was there.

"There was a fire last night," said Raffail in the total silence, his tone sharp, dangerous. He took a step forward and Costa caught a glimpse of Ari's husband, Tomas, as Raffail grabbed the front of the young man's shirt and pulled him roughly onto the beach. "Where were you last night?" demanded Raffail.

"Here, D'sha," stammered Tomas. "I w-was home."

Raffail let go of him and folded his arms as Tomas dropped to his knees, head bowed. "You're still young enough to sell," he remarked. "I want the truth."

"It is the truth, D'sha," whispered Ari. "He doesn't know anything about it. Nobody does." She raised her head a little. Costa could see the bruises on her face and the dry smears of blood on her shirt.

"Nobody?" Raffail nodded to his son. Jezr'el waded into the crowd and pulled Ofre out.

He was a beautiful young man, with long blond hair that fell constantly and endearingly into his eyes. He didn't struggle. Kneeling resignedly, as though he'd expected this all along, he laid his head in the sand at Raffail's feet and crossed his wrists behind his back, like the slaves did.

Raffail gave him a contemptuous look. "There's a lovely girl in the village south of here," he said. "She's just old enough now, and you can have her, but only if I get some facts. Who else is involved in this?"

Ofre wasn't expecting a reprieve. He lifted his head, not sure how to respond.

Costa's knees were trembling, about to give way. Tomas obviously knew nothing, but she had no idea how much Ari had confided in her lover. If she waited too long, these consequences would spread to everyone she'd ever touched, no matter how innocent.

"D'Raffail," said Ofre slowly, struggling with his answer. "I don't know who started the fire, but she didn't do it." He glanced up to see if he was making any impact. "I know her, D'sha," he insisted, "she would never do a thing like that."

Jezr'el kicked him hard for his opinions.

Ofre writhed in the sand, clutching his side, and Raffail scanned the crowd. "We know there's an accomplice." He pulled out the handful of unburned torches and tossed them on the ground. "There was someone around the back of the house."

Jezr'el stepped past him, toward Ari, with a hand inside his cloak. Instead of the needle, he pulled the whip out, slowly, inch by inch. Ari was watching him and opened her mouth, but no sound came out.

"This is no slave," said Jezr'el to the crowd. "She's still one of you. And she's only the first." He snaked the whip through the sand, furrowing it. Ari bent back down, shaking, her hair falling over her shoulders, and Costa felt her body step forward.

"No." It came out as air, not even a word, but it surprised her so much she couldn't even try to repeat it.

Raffail scowled at her. She knew she was supposed to kneel, but her knees were locked so she just stood there.

"I did it," whispered Costa, terrified of the things coming out of her mouth. "I let your slaves go. I let your horses go." She could see Emielle from the corner of her eye, tears streaming down her face, Nisai holding both her hands as tightly as she could.

Raffail gave Costa an odd smile. "Well, well," he said softly. "If it isn't little Jaleela, all over again." He pointed to the torches. "You admit to doing this?"

"Yes D'sha."

"And you've come here to kill me?" he asked. "With your bow and arrows?"

Costa stared dumbly down at the quiver and her unstrung bow. She'd forgotten all about them. She could have shot the slavers easily, the moment they'd set foot on the beach.

"It isn't true!" Ari shook her head furiously at Costa, struggling against the cuffs.

"I know," said Raffail mildly. "Real killers never miss such a perfect opportunity." He slapped her hard across the face, and she fell onto her knees. "Next time you lie to me, make your story a little more convincing."

Costa touched her burning cheek, not watching as Jezr'el pressed the Drug into her sister's veins, branded her, and snapped the chain around her neck.

When she had the courage to look up, Ari was slumped in the saddle, this time on Jezr'el's horse.

Raffail turned around, almost as an afterthought. "Costa."

She bowed her head to show she was listening.

"Tomas is your husband now," said Raffail. He eyed her horse standing patiently at the edge of the crowd. "I hope you aren't thinking about leaving us. You have a lot of work to do for me."

"Yes D'sha."

"One child every year," he said. "At least."

He didn't wait for her to answer. She shut her eyes, listening as the horses moved softly away over the sand. Tomas picked himself up and stood next to her for a hesitant moment, then turned around and went back to the house. After a while, everyone was gone.

At first Costa hardly noticed how alone she'd become. Tomas worked in the gardens with the others, taking both the children with him, leaving her to herself because that was what she wanted. But as time went on, she realized that the people who stopped by the house sympathized only with Tomas. Even Emielle and Nisai avoided her.

One night, after the babies were in bed, he put his hands on her shoulders, gently, but she pulled away. "I won't do it," she whispered.

Tomas let out an irritated sigh. "People are starting to ask questions about you. It's been weeks since they took Ari. It's time to get back to normal."

"I'm not going to get pregnant," said Costa. "That's all you have to say. It isn't you, it's me." She'd been spending her nights on the floor for the past few weeks. Tomas was not the type to force anyone to do anything, but she still had no intention of sleeping with him.

"It'll make things so much easier for you," her husband persisted. "You only have to do this one thing. After that, everything can be the same as it was."

It was exactly the wrong thing to say to her. "What's the matter with you?" shouted Costa. "Is it that easy for you to give up your wife and your children?" In the next room, one of the babies started to cry. Tomas took a step away from her, but she caught his arm. "He'll only be a slave when he grows up," she snapped. "Let him cry. He might as well get used to it. "

Tomas pulled his arm away. "What does it take to teach you?" he muttered, and went to comfort his son.

After that evening, he only spoke to her when he had to. Costa steeled herself to her isolation and spent most of her time as far from the village as she could get without arousing Raffail's suspicions. The Sector were always around these days, either observing from a distance, or patrolling the streets, waiting for the first winter storms that would make travelling impossible.

Costa watched from across the lake as Raffail guided his big horse through the village in the late afternoon sun. Golden leaves floated in the water, and there was still a little ice from the night before in the shadows between the stones. Raffail hadn't said anything to her since he'd taken Ari, but she could feel his eyes on her all the time now, like an itch in the middle of her back.

She huddled deeper in the cloak, wrapping her hands in the thick cloth, hoping he wasn't looking for her. Even in her bulky winter clothes, he would not be fooled into believing she was pregnant. One day his patience would run out. She doubted that she had the six months until spring when the weather would be clear enough to escape.

There were times when she simply wished he would come to the house and get it over with. Mostly though, the idea of submitting to him terrified her, and every day that he left her alone made her more nervous. Noises in the night sounded like Raffail walking across the front porch. When she could sleep, her dreams were vivid and incredibly realistic, but her unwelcome prescience had changed abruptly from visions of the improbable to mundane foresight. More and more often, just washing a dish or sweeping a floor became a repeat of what she'd seen the night before. It became harder to decide, as time went on, what was really happening and what was the dream. She would wake up hours before dawn, clutching nonexistent things in her hands, not sure if it *was* nighttime, or where she was.

Even when she was awake and knew exactly what was going on around her, simple things were starting to take on a surreal quality. One brisk morning she wandered out to the site of the building she'd burned down. Most of the trees had been cleared, and the Sector were building a new house now, bigger, and made of stone this time.

She watched, from what was left of the woods, as slaves and building materials appeared from nowhere and disappeared into thin air. She could see the metal disk set in the fire-blackened floor of the old wooden house, but the outworld technology made no sense to her and became another aspect of the nightmares.

In her dream that night, the noise on the steps turned into Raffail's boots, and the door opened with a gust of cold air. Costa pushed the blanket away in a panic, staggering to her feet.

"You're alone," the dream Raffail observed. He put his hand on her belly, and she backed away from him. "It doesn't matter," he said. "I already know." He reached under his cloak and pulled out a length of shiny chain. "I've been saving this one for you."

Costa flung her hands out to keep him away, scraping her knuckles on the stone hearth as she lay dreaming on the floor. In the vision, her hands clamped around his throat, and she woke up squeezing the life out of him.

Costa lay perfectly still in the silent, empty room, holding her breath, listening to the blood rush in her ears. There was no creaking step on the stairs, no sound of hooves in the street. She cracked the door cautiously and peered outside. The moons were beginning to set, each haloed by ice crystals, and snow clouds hung in the dark sky, but there was no motion except for the cold late-autumn wind in the trees. Costa shut the door, still unsure of how to judge the time between the prediction and the event, too confused to know how to accurately interpret the vision. All she was sure of was the feeling of immediacy. She looked around frantically for her bow, or a weapon of any kind, but Tomas had hidden everything. Even the kitchen knives.

Outside, a horse neighed in the cold, clear air, not yet so close, but not very far away, and the dream flowed back around her. Costa leaned against the wall, knowing that she didn't have the strength to strangle him, not alone, and that he would take her tonight if she let him. She made herself pick her blanket up off the floor, went into the bedroom, and crawled under the covers with Tomas.

He gave her a sleepy look of genuine amazement, and she put a hand over his mouth. "Raffail is coming," she whispered. "Be still."

Hoof beats stopped in front of their house, and the steps groaned. The bedroom curtain wavered in the chilly breeze as the front door opened softly. Tomas let his breath out. She shut her eyes, not wanting to see anything, waiting to be yanked out of bed and exposed.

Raffail pulled the curtain aside, watching for something to confirm his suspicions. Costa held perfectly still, her head nestled against Tomas' shoulder, and after a moment, the slaver moved across the creaking floorboards to the room where the babies were. Neither of the children made a sound.

When he finally left, Tomas slid his arm around her waist and didn't move it. "This is too much," he hissed. "He'll take us both, not just you." His hand fumbled with her clothes. She grabbed his wrist, but he'd finally made up his mind.

"Get off of me," she hissed back, jamming the heel of her hand into his chest.

He grunted, but it didn't stop him, and he forced her over on her back. "Give in, Costa," he whispered, holding her with his weight.

"There's nothing you can do to change things. You're no better than the rest of us."

Costa wrenched her hands free and wrapped them around his neck. "I'm doing what I have to do," she snarled. "Now get off."

He hadn't expected her to fight, and she felt his resolve disappear. She slid out from under him and threw her blanket over her shoulders, shivering.

Tomas leaned on one elbow, frightened and angry. "Don't expect me to help you if he comes here again."

"I never have," snapped Costa, and she walked out.

Outside there was no sign of anyone at all. Costa stood against the door, watching her breath rise in the cold air, trying not to shake. She didn't feel safe staying in the house tonight, but she had no idea where else to go. She thought she heard Tomas move inside, behind the closed door, and she hurried down the steps, toward the lake.

At the shoreline, she turned to see if anyone was following, but behind her, everything was quiet, stagnant, frozen. Costa let her shoulders slump and crouched down on the sand. She knew that tonight might be the last chance to make a decision on her own. She could go back to Tomas now, this minute, apologize and let him have his way, or go to the Sector and let them have theirs. Waiting any longer would make things harder. Perhaps the only control she had left over her life would be to voluntarily give everything up. She looked back at the lake. A thin film of ice on the surface told her how cold it was, and she wondered if she had the courage to simply walk into it and not come out. The thought made her shiver uncontrollably. Costa got to her feet, needing more time.

Walking to the far end of the lake, she crept out from under the bare, black branches, waiting for the first trace of sunrise. The eastern mountains looked thin and artificial now, like cutouts. Wind ruffled her hair warningly, and she turned to the water. The village hung in the mist on the other side, just another dream in the moonlight. Costa stumbled over the roots to the shore and crawled out on a long, flat stone. The lake wasn't a refuge for her anymore, more like a leash she could run to the end of and no further. She leaned over the edge of the stone—dizzy, disoriented—and started to put her hands in the water. But the image that stared back at her was wrong.

Costa pulled her hands away. The scum of ice made it hard to see clearly, but there were definitely two people watching her from the surface of the lake.

One was the strained, hungry face she'd seen in the fire. She tried hard to believe it was Ari, but the longer she looked, the more she understood it was her own image. The reflection of her other self touched the gleaming chain at its throat, and a second face came closer, slanting eyes under a shadowy cloud of dark hair. The face was almost familiar, very concerned, and . . . female?

A hand brushed underneath the surface of the water, and Costa felt something touch her arm. She jerked away, expecting Raffail or Jezr'el, or Tomas, but there was nothing behind her, not even a falling leaf. She looked back quickly at the water. The vision was gone, and now all she could see was herself, sad and exhausted.

Snow started falling not long after that, forcing Costa to return to the house. She would have gone regardless of the weather. In the vague reality her life had become, that particular hallucination began to seem like a rescue of some kind, and she clung to every detail of it. Her own nightmares and undependable prescience became less intense. She began to relax. Tomas never let on if he noticed any change in her. They were trapped together in the small house for the duration of the winter by the howling blizzards. He retreated into his normal, unaggressive self. She ignored him.

It had been about four months since Raffail had taken Ari when the next dream came. It left Costa breathless, and she woke up crouching in the middle of the room, clutching her own shoulders. She fumbled in the darkness for her cloak, pulled on her boots, and stepped quietly out into the snow.

Emielle was behind her house, lying half-naked in the shed. The bloody miscarriage steamed between her legs, and she moaned when Costa came in.

"It's me," whispered her cousin, "it's just me." She wrapped the girl carefully in the cloak. "Does Ephraim know?"

Emielle shook her head, tears rolling down her face. "I don't know what to say to you." She curled up in the darkness and put her head against Costa's knee, sobbing.

Costa stroked her hair, knowing that the Sector might come to collect them both within hours. "If you want," she said carefully, "I'll get the horses. We can still leave."

"How?" wept Emielle. "We'll get caught in the snow."

"No," said Costa. She glanced over her shoulder into the night. The moons were sharp as knives overhead. She knew there were at least two days of clear weather. "I had a dream."

When Emielle had the energy to stand, they went back inside and quietly collected her clothes, her bow, and a little food. Ephraim slept through their exit without missing a snore, and would be honestly unable to tell Raffail anything later on when he was interrogated about Emielle's disappearance.

By sunrise, the village was less than a speck in the frozen white distance. Costa scanned the rolling fields as they rode, but there was no sign of any other living thing, only a few skeletal trees.

The wind blew steadily from the north, the air so cold that the snow creaked as the horses moved across it. She pulled the blanket a little more closely around Emielle as her cousin slept against her in the saddle. In her dream, they'd had two days of uninterrupted riding, enough time to reach the foothills. Beyond that, things were unclear. The two of them were far from safe, with nothing more than a head start on the slavers. In Costa's mind, though, there was a kind of boundary ahead, something that she would be able to recognize. Past that, whatever it turned out to be, they would be out of danger. The Sector would be unable to touch them.

What worried her most was Emielle. The Sector had never encouraged the Jahari to master any form of medical knowledge. With a few exceptions, women who miscarried were collared. Costa had no way to know what condition her cousin was really in. Under the heavy clothes and blankets, she couldn't tell if the bleeding had stopped. Emielle hadn't woken up at all since they'd started.

By afternoon, the temperature had dropped considerably, and the mare began to lag under her double load. Costa slid off into the knee-deep snow, pulling her along by the reins. She knew there was a thicket of sheltering trees somewhere ahead where they could spend the night. She peered out at the horizon, searching for any thin line of shadow, but there was nothing, not yet anyway. She bent her head against the wind, grimly clinging to her own optimism, and began to break the trail for the horses.

She spotted the trees just before sunset, but by the time they got there it was almost completely dark. Emielle sagged in the saddle, barely conscious.

"Where are we?" she whispered.

"About halfway to the hills," said Costa. She held out her arms as her cousin moved painfully to dismount. "How are you feeling?"

"I'm bleeding a lot," said Emielle. Her voice was thin and exhausted. She let Costa walk her over to the trees and collapsed against one black trunk. "I'm freezing," she sighed.

Costa tucked the blankets around her tightly. "I'll get a fire going," she said, but her cousin didn't respond.

There were plenty of dead branches sticking out of the snow, and Costa snapped them off as fast as she could. The long walk and the cold had drained her. It was increasingly hard to fight down the panic she felt. If Emielle got too cold she would die, and that was not in the dream. Costa crouched over the pile of tinder and icy twigs, blocking the wind with her body, and struck the flints together with numb fingers. Sparks blew off in the darkness instead of into the wood. She pushed the tinder to one side and dug down into the snow, making a deeper shelter, then tried again. This time the fire caught. She blew on it gently, feeling the faint heat on her face. The flame hissed and fluttered as ice melted from the twigs. Costa dropped bits of dry tinder into it until it steadied. As she reached back for another handful of broken branches, she glanced up at Emielle. The fire glittered in her half-open eyes.

"Are you awake?" asked Costa.

Emielle nodded slowly. She watched as Costa built the fire up into a steaming blaze. "What if someone sees that?" she asked.

Costa sat back, rubbing her hands together. "I don't think there's anyone around here except us," she said, trying to sound encouraging. She groped in the food pack until she found a small pot and the packet of tea they'd brought along. She held it up. Emielle's eyes narrowed in a weak smile.

While she waited for the water to boil, Costa dragged out the biggest branches she could manage, arranging them against the trees to make a small lean-to. She covered the branches with one of the horse blankets and sealed the structure with snow. When she was done, there was just enough room for the two of them. With their combined body heat, it would be warm enough to survive the night.

Emielle managed to hold her own cup and had a sufficient appetite to reassure Costa somewhat, but as they curled together in the dark hut, she could feel the stiff crust of dried blood on her cousin's blankets.

Outside, the horses shifted patiently on their pickets as they tried to find the most sheltered place in the trees. The wind was steady, moaning in the branches overhead, almost articulate.

Costa held her eyes open in the blackness, letting her head rest against her cousin's shoulder, exhausted and too afraid to sleep. Emielle's breathing sounded shallow and painful. The dreams tonight would probably show just exactly how long her cousin had left to live and whether the Sector would find them before she bled to death. Even without the benefit of dreams, Costa could see that somewhere ahead, she would be forced to decide whether to save herself by avoiding the slavers, or save Emielle by seeking them out. The only thing that could help her cousin now was the Drug.

Suddenly the air around her was smotheringly warm. Costa pushed her heavy blankets back, sweating. Last night's vision had been precise, completely accurate, but she realized her mistake had been to assume that the dream was showing her a safe passage. Instead, she and Emielle were both trapped, with only another day of clear weather between them and the Sector.

Costa groaned to herself, cheated by her incomplete talent. Disastrous events she had no way of avoiding hung around her in the darkness, just waiting for her to close her eyes, and her own future twisted in on itself, like a long, long tunnel.

Emielle stirred next her. "Go to sleep," she mumbled, pulling her cousin's arm around her waist.

Costa rolled against her, cold again, too tired to stay awake any longer. She let her eyes shut, reluctantly opening herself to unwelcome visions.

That night it was no dream, but a stifling nightmare. She watched herself kick the skittish gelding forward, past gaping pits and huge piles of torn earth. A light snow was falling, and she was alone. There was no sign of Emielle. The horse clambered unwillingly up a steep bank of loose dirt, past splintered trees and broken fenceposts. Something was burning. The choking smell of ashes hung in the warm air, but there was no smoke. Costa's hovering soul floated behind her as she slid off the horse and crawled to the top of the slope. Far below, where the ground had been scraped down to bare rock, stalky winged things swarmed together, drifting on flimsy legs. At first they looked so much like ordinary garden insects, she couldn't understand why the gelding was frightened. He snorted and reared, almost pulling her down the hill. Then she realized how big they were, easily the size of two or three horses put together. And they stank, like rancid, burned grease.

She floated up slightly as her body got to its hands and knees for a better look. Animal bones and human skulls were scattered all along the sides of the pit, and just below her, two Sector in their white robes walked hurriedly past the enormous creatures. They didn't look up as Costa ducked away and flung herself into the saddle. The gelding plunged through the loose dirt in a panic. She woke up clutching the blankets, his mane, fighting for breath.

"You screamed half the night," Emielle informed her the next morning. She was even paler, and didn't have the strength to pretend she felt better than she looked. "What was it this time?"

Costa shook her head, stirring the coals. "I saw. . .creatures." She didn't feel like she'd slept at all, and the meager food wasn't helping. She sipped at the lukewarm tea. "We've got to find a cave," she said, trying not to sound as unsure as she felt. "This weather can't hold."

Emielle rubbed her belly, without the energy to respond.

The day dragged on as they rode slowly toward the hills. Emielle slept, and Costa held onto her, absorbed in worry.

There were absolutely no signs of reshie. Their migration would take them more to the south later in the season, but in past years when food ran low in the village, there had never been any problem with midwinter hunts in this area. She searched the empty whiteness without optimism. There were no tracks, no spoor, nothing.

Further ahead, the foothills were already obscured by a thin veil of falling snow. Costa watched the storm uneasily. It swirled in place over the hills, as if caught there, not drifting with what should have been a prevailing wind. Other things were wrong, too. On the ground, the snow was not as deep, and there were patches of ice, as though the surface had warmed up and then frozen again. Costa sniffed the wind suspiciously, but the air was crisp, uncontaminated.

As they got closer, the snow thinned to only a bare covering over scraped red dirt. Costa reined the gelding to a halt. There should have been herds of reshie here, winter grass and scrub trees. Instead, every-thing was ruined.

Emielle pulled the cloak away from her face and stared at the bare ground. "It's warm," she whispered. "What's going on?"

"I don't know." Costa glanced up at the shrouded hills. "No won-der they wanted to keep us away."

Emielle stiffened. "You think the Sector are here?"

Costa nodded. Even without the smell, things were starting to look unpleasantly familiar. She could see the flows of loose dirt running down the gentle slopes from this distance, and the tops of broken trees sticking out like helpless swimmers. It looked as if someone with an enor-mous shovel was trying to dig the hills right down to the ground and hadn't quite finished.

"What did you see?" demanded Emielle, twisting around in front of her. "What's going to happen to us?"

"I don't know," said Costa. "I know if I climb to the top of one of those hills and look down, I'll see creatures and Sector. That's all." She didn't want to tell her that there was no trace of her in the dream.

"So we can't get across?" Her cousin stared at the wrecked land-scape. "What if we just turn south and keep going?"

"We could try."

Emielle sagged against her. "You're not telling me everything. Is Raffail here? How long do we have?"

"I'm not sure," said Costa. "I honestly don't know."

She turned the horses south, paralleling the hills. Emielle was either too angry or too weak to ask any more questions, but she managed to stay awake as they passed deep, muddy gashes in the ground, and piles of dirt as big as houses.

The wind shifted, bringing a thickening flurry and the first traces of the stench from up above them.

Emielle covered her face, gagging. The gelding shied, skittering sideways, trying to turn and head for home, fighting with unusual de-termination. Costa shortened the reins, winding them around her fists, choking.

Behind her, the mare snorted in excitement, waiting to follow whenever the gelding made his break. Costa squeezed Emielle between her elbows and gripped the horse hard with her knees. If they were thrown now, they might as well lie in the mud and wait for Raffail to find them.

The wind changed, mercifully, and the horse gave up. Costa held him firmly as they splashed along, searching for any familiar landmarks from the night before. Higher on the hill, odd little posts were stuck in the ground. They were slender black things. She remembered them as fenceposts from the dream, but they were much too far apart for that.

"Look at those," she said to Emielle. "I can't figure out what they are."

Emielle's head lolled against her shoulder.

"Emielle?" Costa pulled the horse to a stop. Her cousin was limp, but not sleeping. Her face was white as dough. Her mouth hung open.

The wind changed direction, and the gelding took a sudden sideways step. Emielle's weight shifted too far to one side for Costa to hold her in the saddle. With one hand wrapped in the reins, she struggled to get her cousin on the ground. Snow drifted like ash, and the air seemed too dense to inhale.

She laid Emielle down as carefully as she could in the cold, red mud, and searched frantically for her pulse. All she could feel was a weak, thready heartbeat.

The gelding jerked her arm back. Costa got to her feet, dizzy with nausea. Nothing here looked familiar. She sensed that it wasn't the location but the events that were important now. She could ride up the hill, let the Sector see her, and try to escape before they found Emielle, or she could just leave: Emielle would die, and she would live like a hunted animal for the rest of her life.

She stared up at the ruined hill and boiling clouds, trying to remember anything from any dream that might guide her. All she knew for sure was that she could not lose Emielle the way she had lost her sister. Maybe, if she was cooperative, Raffail would let them stay together.

Costa untied the mare from the gelding's saddle and knotted her lead rope firmly around a half-buried branch. She swung up on her horse and kicked him hard, forcing him uphill past fallen boulders and the black posts. He labored through the slick mud and loose dirt, resisting her every step of the way. The smell got thicker and thicker as they climbed. Costa leaned forward in the saddle, sick to her stomach, almost ready to get off and lead, except she wasn't sure she could hold him. Just ahead, she could see the top of the hill, with steam rising from inside, like a huge cooking pot. She gave the gelding an encouraging nudge with her heels. He balked. She leaned over his neck, urging him up, but he was rooted, solidly.

Costa pushed herself out of the saddle, holding her breath, winding the reins around one hand, and crawled to the edge of the chasm. An immense channel ran the length of the hills for as far as she could see. Below, the fog drifted in grey, stinking clumps, hiding whatever was underneath. There was no movement or sound, only the smell.

She had to let her breath out and gagged, loosening the reins just a little. The gelding saw his chance and pulled hard, yanking her arm almost out of its socket. She fell backward, into the mud, and her hand came free of the reins. Her horse slid sideways down the hill, legs churning for balance. Hooves flashed, inches from Costa's face, as she wrenched herself out of the way, rolling in the dirt and mud and stones. He reached the bottom of the slope before she did and took off at a dead run, while she spat dirt out of her mouth, trying to call him back.

Costa staggered out of the mud, covered with it. Just below, the mare pranced around her picket, whinnying, and Emielle lay still. The scene was so unfamiliar, she found herself wondering if it might be a continuation of some dream she couldn't remember falling asleep for. She stumbled down the hill and knelt next to Emielle. When she looked back up, she was not surprised to see two riders charging toward her.

Raffail brought his horse to a quick stop while Jezr'el jumped off behind Costa, hauling her to her feet. His father dismounted and bent over Emielle.

"Is she dead?" whispered Costa.

"Not quite," he said, and glanced at Jezr'el. "Let go of her," he said. "I told you, we'll deal with her later." He reached inside his cloak and pressed the needle into Emielle's neck. Color streamed back into her face. She groaned, curling around her stomach. Raffail pulled the bloody blankets out from under her and threw them over Jezr'el horse. He glanced nervously up the hill. "Get her out of here."

Jezr'el didn't look like he wanted to, but he got back in the saddle and took the girl as his father handed her up to him. He gave Costa an unmistakable leer, wheeled the horse, and galloped back the way they'd come—south.

Costa watched him go, feeling Raffail's eyes boring into her back. She dropped to her knees, expecting the worst.

He walked around in front of her and pushed back the folds of the cloak from her face. "I was wrong about your sister," he said. "I see I should have listened to you."

Costa could not identify his tone. It wasn't gentle, but he didn't sound angry either. "Is she alright?" she asked hesitantly.

"She's doing remarkably well. At least she has the brains to keep herself out of trouble." Raffail walked around behind her again. "What happened to you?" he asked. "Why are you so dirty?"

"I fell, D'sha," said Costa in a voice too soft to hear. His indulgence unnerved her, and her damp clothes were beginning to chill her to the bone.

"You went up the hill," said Raffail. "What did you see?"

"Nothing, D'sha," said Costa. "There was too much fog."

"Why did you go up there?"

Costa shivered, afraid to tell the truth, afraid to lie. "I knew you'd come if I did," she said. "I couldn't leave Emielle."

"How responsible of you," said Raffail sarcastically. "I suppose you came all the way out here just to tell me how sick she was."

"I'm telling you the truth," whispered Costa. "I've never lied to you."

Raffail didn't say anything. Costa listened to the horses shift and the rustle of the wind. She got the impression he was waiting for something and wondered if it was Jezr'el. "What are you going to do with me?" she asked finally.

"That's a good question." He settled himself on a boulder, just to her right. "I don't know if there's any way for me to explain to you how much you've cost me."

Costa kept her eyes on the ground, wondering if this wasn't the crux of the matter, wondering why she wasn't already branded and chained.

"You're not pregnant, are you?"

"No D'sha."

"Have you been trying?" he asked doubtfully.

She shook her head.

Raffail let out an irritated sigh. "I want you to listen very carefully," he said. "I can arrange things so that you have twins, or even triplets, for the next ten, twelve years. That should just about make up for the children Ari and your mother should have had." He leaned forward with his elbows on his knees. "You could handle that, you know.

You've got the build, you're strong. And it would keep you out of collar."

Costa closed her eyes. "You'd take them all."

"That's right," said Raffail. "Your bloodline ends here. No more trouble for the sake of good looks."

She couldn't say anything. She didn't believe he was actually going to let her decide her own fate.

"Listen to me, Costa." Raffail put his hand under her chin and raised her head so their eyes met. "Don't suppose that being a slave is the easy way out. You're not the sort that does well in collar, believe me. Jaleela didn't do well at all."

"She's dead?"

"Close enough," said Raffail, "and it's such a waste." He took his hand away. "You have a choice," he said. "Just this once. You can get back on that horse, go home, and get in bed with your husband, or we can stay here and wait for Jezr'el. He's had his eye on you for a long time."

Costa stared at the ground, abandoned by her visions, trying not to think about what might be happening to Emielle right now. She opened her mouth and let the words come out on their own. "I'll stay," she whispered. As she said it she understood that these choices were just alternative traps, that her decision made no difference in the long run. She looked up, not sure if he'd heard, wanting to change her answer, but he was nodding.

"Good," said Raffail. He was holding a small pouch on a cord, and unfastened it to show her the pills. "Take these when you get home," he said. "We've wasted enough time." He looped the cord around her neck, tucking the packet inside her cloak. "Nine months," he said, and it was a command. "Twin girls." He stood up and helped her to her feet, walking her toward the mare. "Do you have enough food for the night?"

"Yes D'sha." The pouch was like a block of ice against her chest.

He must have felt her tremble as he helped her up onto the horse. "You're cold," he said with false concern. "I think you should come with me. I'll take you back by the short way."

"I'll be alright," said Costa quickly. She was afraid to spend even another minute with him, afraid he would change his mind, or she would. She held out her hand for the reins.

He frowned, sensing her indecision. "You won't get any more chances from me, Costa," he said. "Be sure you understand that."

"Yes D'sha." She let the mare dance back, and Raffail took a step toward her.

"Go straight home, girl," he said. "I'll be watching."

"Yes D'sha." She loosened the rein, and the mare leaped away, running from the stink and the mud. Costa wound her hands in the black mane, letting her choose her path, clinging with weak knees. Snow flew past her face. She pulled the cloak open, allowing the wind to blow through. The pouch swung against her chest, heavy as a rock.

By the time she caught her breath, the mare was already turning west, racing across the mud, heading for home. Costa looked back over her shoulder. Raffail was far behind her, completely out of sight. She shortened the reins, slowing the anxious horse, and finally stopped her.

Everything was quiet. Snow fell lightly, freezing in a thin film over the muck and broken trees. The mare snorted and pawed the ground, ready to run anywhere, as fast as she could go. Costa pulled the pouch from around her neck and opened it to look at the pills. She might avoid being raped by Jezr'el today, but he would only have her later, vicariously, through these unformed daughters. Maybe Ari had figured out a way to keep herself from loving her children. Costa knew she would never find that kind of strength inside herself, though. She already loved Ari. She already loved Emielle. Costa dropped the pouch into the mud, swung the mare to the north, and kicked her into a canter.

It wouldn't take Raffail long to discover he'd been tricked. Costa crouched over the horse's neck, trying to hold her back, wanting to save her strength, but the mare ran like a wild thing, dodging through the boulders, into deeper snow. Costa hung on as the decimated foothills fell behind them and the landscape became a little more normal, spotted with trees and winter grass. She leaned her weight to the right. The mare responded, heading for the thickly wooded hills, shelter from the impending weather.

The snow was finally too deep and the trees too dense for the mare to run headlong, and Costa managed to stop her. She listened in the stillness. Snow fell in clumps from the branches overhead, but that was the only noise. Costa had no doubt that she would be caught, and that her freedom might be limited to what was left of the day, but for the moment it was refreshing not to know when or where or how. She had no landmarks to avoid, so she rode according to her instincts, staying in the underbrush where her trail would be harder to follow, crossing and recrossing a creek, backtracking, circling, moving slowly toward the mountains.

It was snowing again by early evening, but there was still no sign of the slavers. Costa tied the exhausted mare at the bottom of a hill and climbed up to have a look around before dark. From the top, she had an indistinct view of the mountains as they edged the sky—black, bare rock, looming like a wall. Costa wrapped her face against the wind and started back down the hill. Halfway, she heard a noise and froze instantly, crouching in the underbrush. The wind shook the tree branches overhead, and bits of snow fell softly next to her. She listened intently, but there was no other sound. Costa crept down the hill, peering into the deepening shadows. She made her way to where she'd tied the mare and found the right tree. The horse was gone.

Suddenly the woods were full of eyes. She pressed herself against the tree, breathless, afraid to move. Now she could see another set of human tracks, and the imprints of the mare as she had been led away. The Sector had somehow circled around in front of her, cutting her off from the mountains. All the time she'd spent covering her trail had been wasted. They'd come from the other direction.

She was trapped and she knew it. Whichever way she ran, there would be someone waiting. She took a shaky breath. "D'Raffail?"

There was no answer, but she could feel his presence. Something rustled in the trees to her right. A horse snorted in the darkness just ahead. Finally, she understood that they were waiting for her to run, they wanted her to, and that the only thing she was to them was a kind of prey.

Costa moved away from the tree, panting, really afraid now. She took a hesitant step in one direction. Something moved right next to her. Panic poured into her body, and she fled back, the way she'd come.

The silence behind her broke as men shouted at their horses. She ran through the uneven snow, tripping on hidden rocks and broken tree limbs. The pounding behind her got closer. She switched direction, tearing along blindly. The hillsides were next to invisible in the dark, and she fell hard against sharp stones. She struggled to her feet, gasping for breath as the slavers closed in.

Jezr'el dismounted first and yanked her arms back. All she could do was gulp air, without the strength or courage to fight anymore as she felt the cuffs snap around her wrists.

Raffail walked up to her, calm, as tall as the trees. Jezr'el let go, and his father wound his fingers into the front of her shirt. Costa turned her head away as he raised her up on her toes and shook her hard, like an empty sack.

"No more chances, Costa." Raffail threw her to the ground and bent over with the needle. It stung against her neck. Suddenly, she felt warm, and her exhaustion vanished. She lay in the snow, amazed for a moment, then horrified. Jezr'el tore away her shirt, peeling it down to her waist. He snapped the chain around her neck with obvious impatience, pressing the metal brand against her shoulder. The flash of heat turned into pain, and she choked on the smell of her own flesh burning. Jezr'el pulled the brand away and glanced up at his father.

Raffail stood back, his arms crossed. "You can start now, if you like," he said, so Costa could understand. "Keep her for as long as you want but don't mark her."

Costa squeezed her eyes shut as Jezr'el pushed her into the snow. It was too late to fight, too late to run. The future was blackness, like the sky overhead.

4

t was taking much too long, and it was making Mira angrier and angrier. She checked the time again as the Cibban ambassador continued to read, aloud, the entire contract for mining rights. The Ulasz representative was listening with unbelievable patience, calm as could be, hooded in black, draped in it really, sitting cross-legged in her chair, nodding.

"We understand all this," said the Ulasz, finally interrupting. "What we don't understand is the part about the money." She turned to Mira. "Madame LoDire, perhaps you can explain again, a little more clearly, the language of this contract?"

"It's very straightforward," said Mira keeping her tone even, diplomatic, like she was supposed to. "It hasn't changed at all in the six months since I helped you negotiate the terms, or am I mistaken on that point, Mister Ambassador?"

The Cibban cleared his throat. "Intent," he said. "*Intent* is what we're discussing, not actual *content.*"

If it wasn't word for word what he'd said three hours ago, at the beginning of this session, it was pretty damn close. Mira rubbed the back of her neck. Her own deadlines were closing in fast, and she was starting to get the feeling that someone else was going to have to deal with this mess. That would be a nasty little mark on her record.

"Resolving this is simple," said the Cibban, more to the Ulasz than to Mira. "Pay us in cash, Emirate currency, and go on your way. Barter with somebody else. We just don't need what you have to offer."

"We don't use money," said the Ulasz. "We have furniture and we have vegetables from Maryl's World. That's what you said you wanted." She jabbed a finger at the contract. "That's what you and I and the Emirate agreed on." She looked back at Mira with a trace of real anger. "You're the authority here, you represent fair trade. Don't we have protection from this? You understand what's at stake."

Mira nodded wearily. The Ulasz were nomadic traders living a religious, moneyless life in ship-bound communities. They owned nothing, not even slaves, but to keep body and soul together, they had set up elaborate trading networks all over the known galaxy. If the Cibbans broke this contract, the Ulasz would lose virtually every trading partner they had in the quadrant, simply for the lack of this particular link in their chain. The trials and tribulations of the Ulasz were of no real concern to the Emirate. The real point of contention was the sanctity of the Emirate contract. No matter how uninspiring, that was what Mira was here to defend. She straightened in her chair, wishing there was some way to threaten this pompous Cibban. The battleship she was stationed on, the Merganthaler, was orbiting uselessly overhead, armed to the teeth, nothing but a prop, a holdover from earlier, more violent times.

"*My* objection," said Mira to the ambassador, as mildly as she could, "is that you've given these people absolutely no notice of these intentions of yours. I'm sure the Emirate would have no problem changing a few terms here and there, as long as everyone had time to adjust their schedules." She eyed the Ulasz representative, and the woman nodded quickly. It was as generous as Mira could be, officially, but she already knew what the Cibban would say. He wanted cash and he wanted it now. He had no interest in furniture and vegetables from Maryl's World.

The ambassador shook his head, and his jowls shook too. He had a folder in front of him and pulled out a sheaf of papers. "These are our mining agreements for the next two years," he said with obvious reverence. "The value of your barter goods simply can't match what our other customers offer."

"Why didn't you say that six months ago?" demanded the Ulasz, which is what Mira would have said, but more diplomatically.

The ambassador shrugged. "We always *try* to do things the Emirate way. Unfortunately, in this case, our goodwill isn't worth the financial strain."

The woman's face tightened. "We were told you were honorable people. Doesn't that reputation mean anything to you?"

Mira wondered where in the world she'd gotten *that* information. The Cibbans were well known for their parochial attitudes and greedy nature, but it did give her an opening. She turned to the ambassador and gave him a big smile. "How interesting," she said. "The Emirate was under the same impression when we agreed to extend our protection all the way out here." She raised her eyebrows at him. "How disappointed would you be if we reneged on that contract?"

The ambassador looked at her like she was kidding. "You can't do that."

"Can't I?" Mira sat back. He was right, but she was sick of this. "The military is being redirected, Mister Ambassador. Surely you've heard of the planned expansion into the Faraque?"

The Cibban pursed his lips and looked uncomfortable. Of course everybody had heard about that by now. Even the Sector slavers seemed to be taking the idea of losing their portion of the galaxy, their slave-breeding grounds, more seriously.

"The Emir has instructed the Diplomatic Corps to let our allies know that his protection is not to be taken for granted," Mira went on, enjoying the fact that she was the one to drop this official bombshell. "We can't waste our time on people who don't take our requirements, or our contracts, seriously." Actually, these days, the aging Emir's wealthy friends had graciously taken responsibility for what went on in his galaxy, and most people suspected that the military's expensive new incursion into Sector territory was probably not his idea at all.

The ambassador's jaw twitched a little. He glared at the Ulasz. "I suppose we could continue with the arrangement as it is for now," he said reluctantly. "But we can't afford it."

Mira was sure the Cibban economy would survive the blow. She stuck out her hand for him to shake. "Thank you so much for your cooperation, Mister Ambassador. The Emir himself thanks you." She gave him a wide, diplomatic smile, and held the door open for the Ulasz representative.

"You've been very helpful," said the other woman as they walked down the colonnaded breezeway toward the Ground Station. "Our contacts gave us the impression that the Emirate only looks after its own."

"The Emirate wants consistency," said Mira. "Everywhere, all the time." She gave the older woman a questioning glance. "I'm curious where you got your information about the Cibbans."

"We've engaged a new set of trading partners," said the Ulasz. "They're a lot like us, actually. They're nomadic. They also seem quite religious, although they keep slaves. Maybe you've heard of them. They call themselves Sector."

Mira stopped. "You're doing business with the Sector? All the way out here?"

The Ulasz frowned a little, but she nodded. "They've been helping us with our business deals for the last few months."

Mira took a deep breath, wondering how to tell this principled but uninformed woman what the Sector really were. "Have you ever been on their ships? Have you seen their cargo?"

"They say they're self-sufficient."

"The Sector are slavers," said Mira bluntly. "They don't just stick to the people on the government List, either. They breed people and sell them like animals. And when they don't make enough money doing that, they wait until nobody's looking and grab whoever's prettiest on planets like this." She groped in her pocket for her transmitter. The Ulasz were certainly not the first to be conned by the Sector, but Cibba was a long, long way from the slavers' traditional home in the Faraque, a thousand light years from here. It was *very* surprising to find them so deep in Emirate space.

"Mira?" said the voice on the transmitter. It was Vince Noi, the first officer. "Aren't you ready yet?"

"Almost. Have you been scanning the Ulasz group?"

"No," said Vince, "but I can."

"Start looking for Sector ships," said Mira. "They may be using jammers, but they're definitely there."

"This can't be," said the Ulasz. "They've dealt with us very fairly and they've never tried to take our children." She narrowed her eyes suspiciously. "And they warned us about the Emirate."

"I'm sure they have," said Mira. "What's your friend's name? Is it Ariet? or Rasha? Or is it Raffail?"

She hesitated. "Raffail."

"Call him," said Mira. "Get him down here, and I'll show you what he really is." The Sector were more than nervous about the new expansion, Mira thought. If they were this far from their breeding grounds in the Faraque, they must be scared enough to be running for high, safe ground. She listened as the Ulasz spoke softly into her own transmitter, in Emirate, the only common tongue among hundreds of dialects in the galaxy. At least there would be no secrets in this conversation.

"He'll meet us at the Ground Station," said the Ulasz.

That was a fitting enough place for this confrontation. The Ground Station, where the city's transport disk was located, was also the center of the slave markets. The slaves knelt in neat coffle rows on one side of the sunny courtyard, all dressed in the standard white shirt and pants, both boys and girls. Mira put her hands in her pockets and walked past them quickly, the Ulasz at her side. That, at least, was something she could admire about this woman. The Ulasz might be naive, but they seemed to object to the whole institution as much as she did.

Mira squinted in the bright light and caught a glimpse of Raffail and another Sector, probably Ariet, one of his dozens of nephews. Both men were swathed in white cloaks, their faces crossed by the unmistakable blue eye stripe. They seemed very absorbed in watching one of the coffles settle into place. The slaves were miserable and filthy, all chained collar to collar, and probably headed for the Cibban mines by the look of them. Mira came up behind Raffail and tapped him on the shoulder.

He turned, but didn't seem very surprised. "Madame LoDire," he said. "I wondered where you were when I saw the Merganthaler." He held out one hand. Mira kept hers in her pockets.

"I don't have much time," said Mira tightly. It was always difficult for her to keep her temper around him, and he was going to make this as hard as he could because Ariet needed to be shown how to deal with the Emir's diplomat. "I just want you to tell your 'partner' what you really do for a living."

"I have," said Raffail, in an easy, cajoling tone. "We're self-sufficient."

"Be more specific," said Mira.

The Ulasz was waiting expectantly. "She's told me your people are slavers," she said. "She's told me you've used us."

"Slavers?" said Raffail. "I think personnel transport would be more accurate." He smiled at Mira and crossed his arms.

Mira glanced over at the mine coffles, every slave kneeling, arms tied behind their backs. The boy closest to her was shirtless, staring at the ground, but she could see his brands clearly. "Boy," she said, and he looked up. Something had clawed him, across his face and neck. The white scars that made him worthless contorted his expression into a look of permanent fury. Or maybe he was furious. "When you were collared," said Mira, "who did it?"

The boy curled his lip. "Sector," he said, and because he had nothing to lose, he spat at Raffail.

The slaver acted like he hadn't even noticed. "You can see that Madame LoDire knows us very well," he said to the Ulasz. "I hope you've gotten what you wanted out of our partnership, though. I know we have."

The woman gave him an angry look. "Excuse me," she said to Mira, and turned abruptly away, through the doors of the Ground Station.

"You can leave anytime," said Mira to Raffail. "You might want to, in fact. We're having your ships searched by now."

Raffail shrugged and gestured to Ariet in the silent language Mira still couldn't translate. "If you're looking for unListed slaves," he said aloud, "you won't find any. Everybody on board is Listed and legal."

That was probably true. With the Merganthaler in orbit, he wouldn't have dared to make arbitrary raids and then risk having his cargo confiscated. Uncivilized as she considered him to be, Raffail was at least limited by the law to a specific lottery of names, a published List. Her own name had been on it, years ago.

"Aren't you a little far from home?" asked Mira. "What are you doing out here, besides lying, cheating, and stealing, as usual?"

"It's always so good to run into you, Mira," said Raffail, putting a restraining hand on Ariet's arm. "You always restore my faith in what the Emirate stands for." He reached into his cloak and pulled out a wad of folded papers. "As it happens, I have my own copy of the List right here, and the two of us are having a nice, legal look around on Cibba." He shook the papers open for effect, and they uncurled to show the columns and columns of names of the unlucky. "My biggest regret," said Raffail, "is that I didn't know where you were when your name was on here." He grinned at her. "I could have kept you for myself."

He'd done this to her before, but not in front of Ariet. The first time, she'd almost punched him right in the mouth. Now it seemed more like lines in an old play. "Get out," said Mira. "Before I have your damn barges dismantled."

Raffail bowed mockingly. "As you wish, Madame Emissary."

She didn't watch them leave. They would be back as soon as the Merganthaler was out of orbit, ready to find another unsuspecting ally like the Ulasz. Despite the fact that close to a third of the Faraque had been violently overrun by Emirate troops two hundred years ago, the Sector had managed to flourish, insinuating themselves into the vary fabric of what Mira considered to be more polite society. Now, faced with the promise of another invasion, Raffail was showing signs of real adaptability.

Mira made herself walk along the outside row of the Mine slaves, checking brands. Easily one out of every three had the Sector eye burned into their arms. She tried not to look at the slaves themselves since it was useless to be looking for Renee—still. Her transmitter chirped in her pocket, and she turned back to the Ground Station. She was already behind schedule.

Back on the Merganthaler, she was knee-deep in her belongings when Vince knocked on the door to her cabin.

Mira glanced up from what had once been carefully organized piles of clothes, files, and outworld souvenirs. "I suppose you're already packed."

"I've been living out of my luggage for a week," said Vince, sounding a little amazed. "Don't you ever throw anything out?" He waded through the junk until he was standing in a more or less empty spot and rubbed his thin scruff of beard, so dark it made his light skin look even paler. "Are you going to be ready in twelve hours?"

Mira straightened up, feeling her spine crack. "You don't think they'll wait for me?"

"Not this time," said Vince. "Not the Proviso." His slanting eyes nearly disappeared behind the grin. His new captaincy agreed with him, and for weeks he'd been unbearably enthusiastic about this transfer. She was not.

"If you're not on duty," said Mira wearily, "and if it isn't too much to ask, *Captain*, why don't you help?" She pointed at the stack of papers just to his right. "You can throw out anything more than two years old."

Vince settled himself on one of the trunks and began to sort through the things she should have filed months ago. Mira picked up another handful of clothes, folding them in silence. "When we get to Ankea," she said, "are you going to see Amrei?"

"I'm going to buy her this time," he said without looking up.

This was news. "Are you serious?" said Mira. "Can't you wait three months until we come back out of the Faraque? You can't take her into a war zone."

"It's not a war zone," said Vince calmly. "And it isn't going to *be* a war zone. This may be a temporary transfer for you, but I could be there for years. I might never see her again. Anyhow, I won't be the only one."

"Other people are taking their wives or their husbands. I can't think of anyone else who wants to take their whore."

"Be nice," said Vince. "She's my consort." He balled up a handful of paper and tossed it across the cabin into the overflowing trash can. "What's bothering you, Mira? When the Sector see the Proviso coming, they're not going to fight. They're going to fold their tents and run as fast as they can."

"That ship is a two hundred-year-old piece of junk."

"A refitted piece of junk," said Vince, "and it's a piece of junk with a reputation. The last time it went to the Faraque, it blew the Sector defenses to pieces."

"They didn't have any defenses. It wasn't even a contest."

Vince shrugged. "This time it won't be any different. They know it. We know it. All we have to do is make sure they don't ruin all those valuable planets the Emir's buddies want so badly." He grinned. "I'm glad that's your part of this job."

During the last invasion, the Sector had quickly come to the foregone conclusion that the key to their own survival was to give up the portion of the Faraque that bordered Emirate space. However, before they left their old territory, they had systematically destroyed whatever and whoever they couldn't take with them. In the years following the war, the Emirate had spent a tremendous amount of money—more than a hundred times the cost of the war itself—just to make the Frontier into a liveable place again. The current regime had decided that a real estate deal would be far cheaper than a war. The plan was to intimidate the Sector with the Proviso, then suggest a reasonable price for the rest of the Faraque. To the Emir and his friends at court, it was just another contract. For Mira, it was slightly more involved.

Vince watched as she shoved her stack of clothes into one of the trunks and slammed the lid down, leaning on it with all her strength. "This mission is practically a homecoming for you," he said. "I thought you'd be looking forward to it. You spent four years in the Faraque, right under Raffail's nose. It couldn't have been too bad."

"I spent four years sitting on a military outpost between slavers and man-eating aliens," said Mira. "It wasn't any fun, Vince." She snapped the lock shut and leaned her elbows on the trunk. She was exaggerating. The outpost had been completely shielded by jammers, invisible to the Sector. And that was when her aunt had given her Renee. There were times when she felt like those four years were the best she would ever have.

Vince wasn't really paying attention. He held up a handful of holographic snapshots. "This is the outpost? How can you complain about a place that looks like this?" He moved the picture back and forth, making the blue sea roll and the beach gleam in the sun.

Mira sat down next to him. The pictures had been taken almost ten years ago, just after her twenty-third birthday. "That's where we went for a vacation. It was my reward for getting into the University. And for staying out of collar."

Vince studied the holo. "I've never heard of anyone being on the List for four years. It's a long time to hide."

"I could have been in school," said Mira bitterly.

"This is Thea?" he pointed to her laughing aunt. "Is this your girl?"

Renee smiled back, even darker from the sun, her shirt half open, the chain collar shining around her neck. Mira just nodded.

"How long ago did she run away?"

"Five years," said Mira. "Almost six." She didn't talk about Renee much. Vince only knew about her because of one drunken, unguarded conversation they'd had, a long time ago. It wasn't proper to fall in love with your slave. They were too temporary, and it was unseemly to grieve for them when they died. Renee was certainly dead by now, runaway or not. Mira frowned at the pictures, surprised at how strong these emotions still were.

Vince flipped through the rest of the holos silently. Any other time he would probably have tried to talk her into coming down to the Pearl, on Ankea, where Amrei was, but at the moment the invitation would only make her angry, and he knew that. He peeled away a piece of paper stuck to the back of one of the pictures. "This is pretty old," he remarked, unfolding the map. Mira smoothed the yellowing paper. The date of the printout was her eighteenth birthday.

The largest part of the diagram was labeled *Emirate Territory*. On the far right side, two red lines swept along the natural curve of one galactic arm, *Faraque*, printed neatly between them. A line of faded blue dots bordered the farthest edge of the slavers' territory, where the military had established its observation outposts to keep a distant eye on the aliens, the Remini. The middle outpost, where Mira had spent those four long years, was circled.

"Did you ever actually see the Remini ships?" Vince asked.

"No," said Mira. "We could hear them, though. We taped all their transmissions."

"How long did it take you to decipher their language?"

"I didn't have anything to do with that," said Mira. She knew this was one of his favorite subjects. "Thea had it all worked out by the time I got there. She taught me what she knew."

Vince studied the map thoughtfully. "It's too bad you can't speak it."

"You'd need a lot of sandpaper to speak Remini," said Mira. "Anyway, we were under orders not to communicate. Not after what they've done." She shuffled the holos. "There's probably another map like this," she said. "I had one that showed which direction they think the Remini came from."

"I have one of those," said Vince. "*Galactic History, According to the Remini Path of Destruction.*" He pointed vaguely to the middle of the printout in Mira's lap, the Emirate section. "When I first joined up, we had a layover at a planet where they were excavating what was left of the culture the Remini wiped out. They were digging up buildings and machinery, but things were so old, they were all buried almost ten meters underground. Everything was covered with a layer of black smelly stuff, like ash, and there was nothing at all on top of that. Just dirt."

"You should have been an archaeologist."

"Maybe." He smiled. "What do you think? Are they going to turn around and gobble us up one day?"

"How should I know?" said Mira. "I only translate. I don't know what their plans are."

"Aren't you the expert?" asked Vince, teasing her. "Isn't that why you were assigned to this mission?"

"There are three other people who're probably twice as fluent as I am. But they have more seniority." She looked around the room helplessly. "Trent's going to call in less than six hours, Vince. How am I going to get all this stuff packed?"

Vince shrugged and tossed the holos into the nearest open trunk. "Do what I do," he said, "throw *everything* out."

When Trent did call, late as usual, Ankea was less than an hour away. Mira checked the room again. What she hadn't been able to fit into the trunks was stacked against the walls where Trent wouldn't be able to see it. She slipped into the chair in front of the monitor, ignoring the blinking red light that was her supervisor's incoming call. The monitor's screen was reflective, a dull silver, and Mira squinted into it, pushing back her disheveled hair. Her own dark face and slanting eyes squinted back from under a cloud of thick black curls. She wasn't even in uniform, she finally realized, and Trent would hate that.

There was no time to change now. Just finding a uniform could take forever at this point. She turned the screen on, and waited for the channel to clear. "Madame Ambassador," she said, as Trent's image solidified.

"Madame LoDire," replied Trent. She flashed a spotless smile at Mira and cocked her head to examine the rest of the room. "I see you're all packed."

"Yes, ma'am," said Mira, as brightly as she could. "I was just getting the last of my things out." The fact that Trent was easily twice her age had always intimidated Mira for some reason. She found it impossible to argue with this woman, not because of some misplaced patronizing respect, but because it seemed to her that Trent never, ever listened. Over the years, Mira had discovered that it was much easier to agree with everything Trent said than to try arguing with her. That approach seemed to work to some extent, except for now, this mission, when all Mira really wanted to do was say no.

Trent shuffled through her papers. "There are a couple of changes we need go over before you leave." She looked up. "You know there won't be any long-range communications once the Proviso crosses into the Faraque."

"Yes, ma'am," said Mira. That was, in fact, the whole point of this call. Neither the Emir nor the military wanted to risk the Remini picking up a stray signal.

"The itinerary is the same," said Trent, thumbing through her notes. "You have a brief layover on Ankea while you wait for the Proviso, three weeks of travel time to Traja, and another week to the border itself. There is one addition." She frowned at Mira. "Where's your copy? You should be writing this down."

Mira glanced helplessly over her shoulder. "It's packed," she said. "I can remember."

Trent looked doubtful. "You'll be stopping at the Point Seven Station, just this side of the border. I want you to contact Emissary Mahai while you're there. He's quite familiar with most of the Sector planets just inside the Faraque. He'll have some suggestions for your itinerary."

"Harlan?" said Mira, forgetting herself. "*He's* going to give me advice?" Harlan was one of those three other people, fluent in Remini, who had been allowed not to volunteer for this mission, even though his diplomatic territory adjoined Sector space.

Trent leaned back in her chair. "Is there a problem with that, Madame LoDire?"

"No, ma'am," said Mira quickly, and clamped her teeth together. In her opinion, Harlan Mahai's professional judgment wasn't worth what his parents had paid to get him his job.

Trent leaned forward, elbows on her desk, her face filling the screen. "Your job is very simple, Mira," she said. "By the time you and the Proviso get to the Faraque, the Sector should be ready to give you whatever you want. They haven't got the weapons or the guts to fight back. All you have to do is make them an offer." She narrowed her eyes meaningfully. "The Emir is counting on you, Mira. If you can talk the Sector into bowing out gracefully, then you've made history. I turned down a lot of requests so you could get this promotion."

"Thank you," said Mira. The last part was a lie, and she knew it. "Is there anything else I should know?"

"One thing." Trent hesitated, something Mira had never seen her do. "The Sector have a great deal of respect for people who make an effort to show the proper. . .decorum. I'm sure you understand how crucial it is to make a good impression."

Mira frowned. "I always make a good impression."

"Of course you do," said Trent. "What I mean is, it's helpful, in terms of image, to. . .blend in with the people you're trying to impress."

"I'm not following you."

"Then let me put it very simply," said Trent. "Before you set foot in the Faraque, get yourself a slave."

Mira felt her mouth drop open. "What?"

"I know how you feel about it," said her supervisor, "but your personal convictions aren't going to make a dent in something that's a thousand years old."

"Is that an order?" demanded Mira in disbelief.

Trent nodded. "If it helps, this wasn't my idea."

It didn't help at all. "I have to think about this."

"No you don't," said Trent. "I don't care if you get a boy or a girl. Just get one. Preferably School."

"What if I don't?"

Trent lifted one eyebrow. "Then don't bother coming out of the Faraque," she said. "It's that simple."

Mira wondered whether it was better to quit or be fired, or just give in. "Lend me your boy. At least he's got some experience."

"No," said Trent. "I've got two big conferences coming up and I need him. Mira," she said, trying to sound sympathetic, "it's not worth risking your career over this. It's just a temporary thing, anyway—whoever you buy, you don't have to keep."

"I can't afford School," said Mira angrily.

"I'll put a stipend in your account," said Trent. "I can get four thousand credits for you."

Mira stared at her hands, considering new avenues of employment. Six years was a lot of time to throw away. "Alright," she said finally. "But I'm doing this under protest."

"Submit a grievance," said Trent, with obvious relief. "I'll make sure it gets the proper consideration."

"Thanks," said Mira, trying not sound too sarcastic.

"You're overreacting," said Vince when she told him about the conversation. He raised his hands in mock horror. "And she's paying for you to get a School slave? What ever could be worse?"

"Never mind," Mira rested her chin in one hand and stared out the cafe window at the sluggish Ankean sunset.

Vince was killing time, waiting for the Pearl to open. She wasn't sure what she wanted to do tonight. They'd been informed at the Ground Station that the Proviso was going to be delayed by an extra two days, which gave them a total of three days in a city enthusiastically billing itself as the "Sex Capital of the Quadrant."

Vince put down his coffee. "You need to relax," he said, sounding serious, almost brotherly. "It's not the end of the world."

"Don't start," said Mira. "I'm not going with you tonight."

"That's not what I mean," said Vince. "I just think you're letting this business with Trent bother you too much."

"Why shouldn't it? First she drafts me into taking a transfer no one else will touch, and then she tells me I'll lose my job if I don't compromise the one thing I really believe in."

"But you've had a slave," said Vince gently.

"Renee was a gift," said Mira. "Thea gave her to me to keep me company on the outpost."

Vince moved his spoon around in the cup. "Correct me if I'm wrong, Mira, but you seem awfully jumpy about this mission, and it's not just because of Trent."

"I don't want to go," said Mira. "That's all it is. I have better things to do with my time."

"You don't want to deal with the Sector," said Vince. "I don't understand why you're afraid of them. You're not a pretty girl on the List anymore."

"I'm not afraid." She slumped down in the chair. "I saw Raffail on Cibba today. We had the usual conversation—he baits me and I give him a piece of my mind. The idea of having to treat him as a legitimate trading partner. . . ." She shook her head. "We've never dealt with the Sector on that level."

Vince shrugged. "So they're basically dishonest, undependable bastards. That's an accurate description of practically everyone you negotiate with. If they were nice, you wouldn't have to make them sign contracts."

"This is different," said Mira. "The other dishonest, undependable bastards don't get under my skin like he does."

"Ah," said Vince wisely. "The diplomat hates somebody."

Mira nodded without saying anything.

"So what are you worried about?" persisted Vince. "By the time we get finished in the Faraque, there won't be any Sector. Not in an organized sense, anyway."

"You think they'll give up? Just like that?"

"Why not? With this arrangement they get to make a huge financial killing. The Emirate expands without any blood spilled. You look great, I look great. Everyone comes out with a medal or two." He cocked his head. "What are you worried about?"

Mira sighed, staring out the window. "The last time we invaded, two hundred years ago, who really got the short end of the deal?"

"Their breeding populations," replied Vince. "Lots and lots of beautiful bodies, stacked up like cordwood. I've seen pictures."

"The Sector killed everyone they couldn't pack into their barges," said Mira. "Here we come again. If that happens this time, who's fault is it, really?"

"I thought the contracts were very specific," said Vince. "The Emir gets all mineral and organic rights. Rocks and flesh."

She shook her head. "We're talking about people who breed human beings like animals. You think the Sector are going to smile and roll over just because they've signed a piece of paper?"

Vince studied her, much more serious now. "You can't blame yourself for their bad habits, Mira. It's not going to be your fault if they decide to cut their losses by making off with the young and the fertile."

"And killing the rest."

"They won't," he said. "Why would they waste their time? I'm sure they'd be much happier to see the Emirate saddled with thousands of ignorant illiterates that they won't have to feed anymore."

Mira shrugged. "Maybe."

"They wouldn't waste the ammunition. You're overestimating them, Mira." Vince leaned forward and went on in a lower voice. "You could keep a lot of people out of collar by doing this. You know that."

"You don't have to talk me into it."

"But I have to live with you for the next three months," said Vince. "And you have to figure out a way to do your job without hating yourself." He stood up and stretched. "You're going to get mighty bored drinking coffee all alone tonight, Madame LoDire. Come with me to the whorehouses. You can window shop."

"No thanks."

"Then come and meet Amrei. You'll like her. She never does a thing she's told." He gave her a winning smile. "You don't even have to be tempted. I'll buy you dinner."

The Pearl was deep in the city's historic district. Mira followed Vince closely as he pushed his way through the narrow, crowded streets. Overhead, a few ruddy stars shone through the arching metal grillwork that spread lacily between the old buildings. Mira licked the sweat off her upper lip. Ankea was low on her list of favorite places. It was too hot here, and she didn't like the way it smelled. Still, not knowing where Vince was for the next three days was unappealing. Even if she didn't see much of him and his. . .consort, it was better than being alone.

"How do you know where you're going?" she asked, as Vince led her through an alley. Even off the main street, every window was complete with flickering candles, one for each vacant room.

"Instinct," said Vince. "The first time I came here I was completely plastered."

"What about the second time?"

A slave girl who might have been pretty with less make-up leered at Mira from an open doorway. "Buy me, D'sha!" she called after them.

"Frankly," said Vince, "I'm not sure if this really *is* the same place I went the first time. But I like it."

"I thought you went back because of Amrei," said Mira. "I thought it was love at first sight."

Vince gave her a dirty look. "Mind your manners," he said rather primly. "This is a respectable place."

He stopped in front of a rather large house with a pair of double doors set back under a slight overhang. Upstairs, through the open windows, Mira could hear some instrument being badly played, and someone laughing.

A lanky boy answered the door, dressed in nothing but a towel. "D'Noi," he said politely, "how nice to see you again."

Mira followed them in reluctantly. The hallway was cool, dry, compared to the eternal summer outside. They turned a corner, passed a set of stairs, and came into a small parlor, empty except for a couple of half-dressed slaves and a man sitting behind a desk. He glanced up as they walked in. "Mister Noi," he said, and he sounded surprised. "I didn't expect you so soon."

Vince smiled. "Is Amrei busy tonight?"

The man picked up a well-thumbed appointment book and flipped through the pages, almost at random. "She's not scheduled. I was going to give her the night off, to tell you the truth."

Vince reached into his pocket and pulled out the plastic card that would access his bank account. "I'm not just here for tonight. I've been transferred. I want to take her with me."

The man didn't answer. He put the book back on the desk and sat down heavily.

"Last time you said you'd take two thousand," Vince persisted. "I've got it now."

Mira could hardly believe her ears. A high price for someone with Amrei's history would be five or six hundred credits. What Vince was offering would buy School, easily. She had always known how much he liked Amrei. He'd been seeing her for the past six years. What she hadn't realized was that he really *was* in love.

"Go get her," said the man to the boy in the towel.

The man took Vince's voucher, turning it over in his fingers. "Two thousand." He gave a soft snort of a laugh. "I had no idea you were such a wealthy man."

Vince glanced back at Mira, and then looked past her.

"D'sha," said Amrei from the hallway. Her auburn hair was wet, pulled back from her angular face and green eyes. She wasn't very tall, but in the pictures Vince had of her, she always seemed to have a kind of bearing, which in a free woman might have been described as haughtiness. The pictures were all Mira had ever seen of her, and they didn't show how attractive she really was.

She walked past Mira and slipped under Vince's arm.

"He's here to buy you," said the man. "I didn't tell him. I think you should." He held out another card, not Vince's. Mira caught a glimpse of it. It was the girl's ID.

"Tell me what?" said Vince. He took the ID, examined it and then frowned in surprise.

Amrei pulled away a little. "I don't have a lot of time, D'sha," she said in a rather strained voice.

Vince was still staring at the card. "This is the end of your twentieth year?" he asked in disbelief, and Mira finally understood what was happening. "Why didn't you tell me?"

Amrei shrugged and tried to smile. "No one wants an old whore."

Mira took a deep breath and wondered how to leave. Amrei was going to Fail, that was obvious now. It might be a matter of days or weeks, or even hours, depending how close it was to the date she'd actually been collared.

Vince put his arms around the girl's shoulders. "You should have told me," he whispered. "I would've done this years ago."

Amrei didn't say anything. She closed her eyes and leaned her head against his chest.

"Amrei," said the man, "if you want to go with him, you can." He pushed the voucher back at Vince. "You've spent at least this much here already. You can take her, if she wants to go."

Amrei pulled back sharply. "I'll go," she said, as if there had never been any question about it. She took his hand and guided him past Mira, toward the street.

Mira looked back at the parlor long enough to see the man sink down into his chair, his head in his hands.

Outside in the smothering dark, Amrei had curled her fists into Vince's shirt and was speaking in a low, urgent tone. Mira closed the front door behind her, making sure it made some kind of noise.

Vince looked up. "Mira," he said. "I'm sorry about all this. I had no idea. . . ." He ran a hand through his hair, but kept the other over the girl's.

Amrei looked at Mira with sudden recognition. "You're Mira LoDire."

Mira nodded, surprised. She had not expected to be a topic of conversation for the two of them. "You don't need me," she said quickly. "I'll head back to the hotel."

She would have, too, except Amrei let all her breath out suddenly and sagged against Vince, her eyes rolled back in her head.

Vince caught her under the arms and sank down onto the pavement with her. "It's already started." He gave Mira a frantic look. "Don't leave," he said. "Not now."

Mira felt her insides turn into blocks of ice. She had seen slaves Fail, and it was always horrible, no matter how quick. It made her think of Renee, who must have died alone. She shuddered and made herself help him lift the girl up in his arms. "Where do you want to go?" asked Mira. "Back inside?"

"No!" groaned Amrei. She clutched Vince's hand and took a painful breath. "You know. Where we always go."

"This way," said Vince grimly. He set off into the dark, letting Mira trail behind.

She had no idea what he expected her to do except provide a little moral support. Beyond that, there really wasn't anything anyone *could* do. She hurried after them, through the maze of side streets, and wondered what Vince would do if Amrei's Failure took more than three days.

Somehow, in the midst of all the brothels, there was simply a hotel. Vince supported the girl as she stood, wavering in the street.

"They can't know this is happening," Amrei panted. "Don't tell them anything. Just get a room."

Vince nodded and pulled open the door. He seemed to have forgotten Mira for the moment, and she watched in amazement as Amrei straightened herself up and walked inside under her own steam, like nothing was wrong.

They handed Vince a key with a minimum of small talk, although everyone obviously recognized the two of them and wanted to know how Vince had been. The slaves behind the counter gave Mira half-hidden, sidelong looks, as if nothing could surprise them, certainly not anything as mundane as a trio in a single room. Vince put an arm around Amrei's shoulders, and Mira followed them to the end of the hallway.

The room was pleasant enough, airy and cool, but everything in it, from the curtains, drawn closed over dirty windows, to the faded bedspread, seemed worn, overused.

Amrei curled up on the bed and Vince crouched next to her. "We have to talk," she whispered. "I need to talk to you alone."

"Maybe I should leave," said Mira, still standing by the door.

Vince bit his lip. "Can you wait outside for a minute?" he asked. "I'll be right there."

Reluctantly, Mira stepped out into the hallway and waited. She leaned against the peeling blue wallpaper and studied the pattern of it on the opposite wall, serpentine, convoluted, and possibly floral. Nothing in the pattern supplied her with a metaphor that might make this easier for everyone. She put her head down and stared at her shoes, not thinking about Renee.

The door finally opened, and Vince came out slowly. "She wants to talk to you."

"Me?" said Mira. "She doesn't even know me."

"I've told her a lot about you," said Vince. "It's important." He put an unexpected hand on her shoulder and squeezed, hard, then walked back down the hall.

Amrei was propped up on pillows, so pale now that her skin seemed almost transparent.

Mira sat down gingerly on the edge of the bed. "He said you wanted to talk."

"You're the one who thinks slavery is wrong."

It seemed like an odd time to be discussing personal philosophies. "I don't like it," said Mira carefully, "if that's what you mean."

"Vince says you're a revolutionary," said the girl. "He says you won't buy a slave because you don't believe in the system."

That was really only one reason. Mira wasn't sure how to answer. "Maybe I should leave you two alone." She couldn't tell if Amrei was accusing her of something, or just stating a fact she had no business knowing.

"No," said Amrei, gripping her wrist, and holding her tightly. "You have to stay. You have to help him."

The door opened and Vince came in with two small buckets, each filled to the brim with ice.

Mira frowned. "Help him do what?"

Vince closed the door. "Help me free her."

It took a minute for Mira to convince herself she hadn't misunderstood what Vince had said. "Free her?" she repeated. "That's impossible." She pulled her arm away from Amrei. "What are you talking about?"

"It takes two people," said Amrei. "You have to stay." Her face was already flushing with fever as the Drug started its slow withdrawal from her body. It wouldn't be long before her temperature was high enough to kill her.

Vince pushed the door to the bathroom open with one foot, and Mira followed him in, watching as he dumped both buckets into the tub, and turned on the cold water.

"What do you think you're doing?" Mira hissed at him. "You're going to try to keep her alive through this? It doesn't work that way."

"She says she's done it before, with other slaves." He stared at the rush of water and the swirling ice. "She says she's done it twice."

Mira glanced back at Amrei, limp on the bed. "How can you believe that? You know that's not possible."

"It's what she wants me to do." He pulled off his uniform jacket, and pushed his sleeves back up to his elbows. "Are you going to stay?"

"And do what?" demanded Mira. "Torture her?"

Vince shook his head, but it was clear he was having the same thoughts. "If we can keep her temperature stable," he said, "she says she can get through it. You have to help," he said softly. "This could take days. I can't do it by myself."

"You seem very convinced," said Mira. There were lethal drugs made specifically for Failing slaves, drugs that were far more humane than this sounded. Try as she might, Mira couldn't come up with a single reason Amrei might have for wanting to be put through more pain than she was already in for.

The tub was almost full, and Vince turned the water off. "Mira," he said, urgently, but too softly for Amrei to hear. "It may not work, but you're the only person I can think of who would even consider helping. And if it doesn't—" he shook his head hard, "you're the only one I can talk to about her."

This was the most obvious reason not to fall in love with slaves, but he didn't need to hear that, especially from her. "What do you want me to do?"

In the other room, Amrei had kicked the sheets away. The tub had taken only minutes to fill, but she was already drenched with sweat, almost unconscious. Vince's hands shook as he helped Mira peel away the girl's plain white clothing. Together they carried her into the bathroom and laid her carefully in the tub.

The shock of cold water ran all the way through Mira, but the girl lay in it, unaffected, panting as Vince cradled her head, brushing her face with wet hands. Her body was so hot with fever that the ice melted wherever it touched her.

Mira sat back on her heels, resting her elbows on the edge of the tub. Vince's desperation was so obvious, it was painful to watch, but if it had been Renee, she knew she would have done whatever she could, for exactly the same reasons. Failure was such an undignified way of dying, almost anything else was acceptable. She wondered how many other people tried staving it off like this, and how many simply walked away, not wanting anything to do with it.

Amrei gasped and opened her eyes. The color had evaporated from her skin, suddenly, leaving her white as paste. Vince lifted her out of the water with an effort, and she hung in his arms as he carried her back to the bed, dripping and shivering.

"More ice," whispered the girl through chattering teeth. "I can feel the next one coming."

Vince got up without a word and hurried out.

Mira touched the girl's forehead. She was cool now, but her eyes seemed brighter than normal, delirious. "Take it easy," said Mira. "He'll be back in a second. You'll be alright."

"Will I?" said Amrei, trembling in the cocoon of blankets. "You didn't take long to convince."

"I'm not," said Mira, taken aback by her sarcasm.

"Neither am I, frankly," said the girl. She rolled onto her side and groaned. "This is already a lot harder than I thought it was going to be." She closed her eyes again, and sweat trickled off her temple, down her cheek.

The next six hours became an exhausting repetition of immersing the girl, warming her, and cooling her down again. By the third time, the blankets were soaked through, and Mira was the one who went to the front desk to get an armload of dry ones, avoiding the curious looks from the slaves, who were already wondering what was happening to all that ice.

Somewhere around dawn, the cycle slowed a little and Amrei dozed, her temperature more or less normal. Mira slumped into the only chair in the room.

"Is this why you need two people? So one can sleep?"

Vince nodded wearily. His clothes were soaked to the shoulders and to the knees. "I'll wake you up if something happens."

Mira let her muscles relax, watching him through half-open eyes as he wandered around the room, too anxious to sit still. "Vince," she said gently, "you could just let her go. She'll be unconscious. She'll never know."

"I can't."

"She can't survive this," said Mira. "We haven't done anything but put it off for a few hours. It'll be easier for her."

Vince stopped pacing. "There was a boy at the Pearl called André," he said. "Did I ever tell you about him?"

Mira shook her head. "Is this the success story?"

"You don't have to believe it," said Vince. "He Failed last year.

I checked the records and I know that's true. I saw him six months ago when you were negotiating the Trellian treaty. He was working as a skimmer pilot."

"Maybe he was Sector-bred," said Mira. "He might have come from a planet where they all look like that."

"But he was free," said Vince. "And he recognized me. He gave me a real strange look, like I was the one who was going to turn him in."

"He was out of collar?" asked Mira. "Dressed as a free man?"

"I know it was him," said Vince. "I was as close to him as I am to you right now."

"And she's responsible for that?" Mira asked, nodding at the sleeping girl.

Vince shrugged. "You don't have to believe it."

"It was somebody else," said Mira. "It had to be. If what you're saying is true, there'd be freed slaves all over the place."

Vince leaned against the window and pulled back the curtain. "I think there are," he said. "Hundreds."

It was that thorn of information that kept her awake. Her eyes were shut, and she pretended to sleep, but there was only one thing on her mind now: Renee had disappeared six years ago. Her Failure would have occurred shortly afterward. Mira had seen her again—three years ago—at the Ground Station on DeKastri.

Up until today she had managed to convince herself that the event had never really happened. She'd just finished a marathon three-day negotiating session, and was half napping, waiting for the ship. The familiar laugh woke her. She'd jerked awake, thinking she was still on Thea's outpost. Renee was standing across the room with another woman, but she wasn't dressed in the white uniform of slaves. Even in the wrong clothing, even at a distance, her rangy body, dark face and eyes were unmistakable. Mira remembered stumbling to her feet, staring. Renee—or her twin—saw her and stopped smiling. She purposefully hooked the other woman's arm and walked away. She turned once, but the look was fearless and the message clear: Don't follow.

There were no records of Renee's death. Mira had searched the files thoroughly for look-alikes, Identification number errors, anything she could think of. The fact was that after the girl had run away, she'd somehow vanished completely. The only thing Mira could think of was that she had not died from Failure, but someone had killed her and neglected to make a note of it. What she thought she had seen on DeKastri was not possible. It was a dream, or wishful thinking.

Mira opened her eyes. Vince had curled up next to Amrei and was sound asleep, one arm wrapped around her waist. Mira got up unsteadily and went into the bathroom to wash her face. Towels and blankets hung over everything, and the ice in the tub had melted into a thin layer of scum. In the mirror, she took a good look at the woman who had been searching long after searching was useless. If Amrei could in fact free herself, if Vince was right about the numbers, and if it had been Renee—Mira watched her reflection to see if the crumbling taking place inside herself was even slightly visible from the outside. Four years on the outpost. Five years of college that Renee had coached her through. Love that Mira would have sworn to, and could not let go of, even when she knew Renee was gone. None of these things could be seen. What if it had been Renee? Mira played it back in her mind again: the determined gesture as Renee took the other woman's arm, the assurance of her movements as she turned around, the look of warning as she walked out of Mira's life forever. Tears slid from her eyes, and the reflection blurred. Mira put her hands over her face, letting the loneliness of six long years flow out of her, hoping that there had been even a short time when she had been loved.

Vince was awake when Mira came out, and so was Amrei. She looked pale and ill, but she was sitting up.

"Are you alright?" asked Vince.

Mira nodded weakly, sitting on the bed. "What happens next?" she said to Amrei. "It can't be this easy."

"Usually convulsions. With Andre it was very bad." She held out one hand, and Mira could see the muscles shivering under her skin. "It's already happening," Amrei said. If she was afraid, no one would have been able to tell.

"How do you know what to do?" asked Mira. "Who teaches you?"

"Andre taught me when he needed help. I guess someone else showed him. I showed another girl when he Failed, but she's been sold, so no one at the Pearl knows what to do anymore." Amrei leaned her head against Vince's shoulder. "You always did have good timing."

Vince smiled. He looked very tired. "I thought you were the skeptic," he said to Mira. "What's the matter?"

"Renee," said Mira. "I saw her on DeKastri. I never told you."

There was enough time to get food but not to eat it. Mira made her way up the hall with an armload of things she wasn't sure she could stomach. She almost dropped half of it when she heard Amrei screaming.

Vince was hovering over the bed, holding Amrei as she thrashed uncontrollably. Mira dropped everything into the chair and grabbed Amrei's ankles. "How long?" she panted.

"Since you left," said Vince. "She hasn't stopped."

Amrei let out another shriek, and Vince glanced at the door.

"You can hear her all the way to the front desk," Mira informed him. "Are they going to come in here to see if you're killing her?"

"I don't think so," said Vince. "They know it's none of their business."

The convulsions went on long past what Mira would have considered the limits of her own endurance, and in Amrei's condition, they were absolutely debilitating. Even when she lost consciousness, her body writhed and jerked on its own. Mira kept a solid grip on the girl's legs. Her doubts had changed into a grim determination that Amrei *would* live, because that would mean that Renee was alive. Even though Mira might never see her again, it was better—much better—that her ultimate fate had been survival, not some arbitrary murder.

When the convulsions finally stopped, it was afternoon. Amrei had quit breathing.

Vince had already tried every method of resuscitation the military had taught him. Now he was crouched on the bed with his hands balled together in his lap, not looking at the pale corpse.

Mira was sitting on the edge of the windowsill, as far away as she could get without leaving the room. Outside, the sun was beating down, and everything had a kind of bronze cast to it. People moved slowly in the streets. The only shadows were from skimmer taxis floating like scavengers overhead. "We've still got a couple of days," she said. "How soon do you want to start drinking?"

He didn't answer, and she knew he was too close to tears to say much. "I'll be back," he said hoarsely, and walked out.

Mira made herself go over to the bed. Vince had put a clean sheet over Amrei's body, but not her face. She really had been a beauty, probably looking better and better with age. Mira started to pull the sheet up the rest of the way, worn too thin to know how to properly mourn for someone she'd met less than a day ago. Then Amrei opened her eyes.

Mira nearly jumped out of her skin and found herself backed up against the opposite wall. She had almost articulated the words *rigor mortis reactions* in her mind, when the girl closed her eyes again and took a deep, shuddering breath, like someone who'd been under water for a very long time.

"Vince!" shouted Mira, and bolted for the door, shrieking down the hallway until she heard him running back.

Mira slid out of the way as he charged back into the room, hunching over Amrei, whispering to her. Mira closed the door, bracing herself for another round.

Vince glanced up. "Find something sharp. Break a glass. Anything."

There were glasses in the bathroom. Mira broke one over the sink and picked out the biggest shard, watching warily as Vince held it up for the girl to see. Amrei kept her eyes open with effort, as he sliced quickly across her forearm. It was a little cut. Even at its lowest ebb, the Drug would have healed it instantly, but Amrei continued to bleed. The blood ran down her arm in tiny rivulets, and she let her head fall back in relief. Vince bent over and kissed her on the lips.

"Marry me," he whispered.

Amrei smiled at him with all the strength she had left.

Fortunately, the banging on the door of Mira's hotel room at four in the morning was not some secret goon squad sent to ferret out freed slaves and their law-breaking friends.

Mira had jerked awake from nightmares that included everything from police interrogations to Renee's accusing stare, but it was only a shore crew from the Proviso. The ship had finally arrived, early in a relative sense.

Getting Amrei on board was easier than she'd thought. Dressed in Mira's clothes, the young woman sagged and staggered on Vince's arm, looking more like she'd had too much of planetside pleasures than anything else. When Vince introduced her rather nervously as his fiancee, all he got was a few disinterested nods.

A doctor was what Amrei needed. Somehow the Failure had taken almost a quarter of her body weight, and now the skin around her cheeks was tight, hollow. She looked absolutely starved. Mira sat in Vince's small cabin, watching Amrei sleep, waiting for him to get back. The glint of the chain collar was just visible under a fold of her shirt. That could be cut off, the sooner the better, but the brands under her long sleeves were more permanent.

What Mira really wanted to know was whether she and Vince had actually done anything illegal. Dressing a slave as a free person, like Amrei was right now, was a punishable crime for everyone involved. But technically, Amrei was free. Wasn't she? The presence of the Drug in her body was what defined her as a slave to begin with. Now that it was gone, who would even guess what she had been? Mira closed her eyes, trying to imagine Amrei and Vince at some fancy function. It was remarkably easy; Amrei seemed to fit right in.

It was much, much later that night when Mira located her own quarters.

The Proviso was a prime example of engineering prowess, dating from an era when the military had come into rich favor with a more aggressive Emir. Despite the overall starkness of the rest of the ship, however, Mira's own quarters were surprisingly comfortable. Besides the rather microscopic kitchen set into one corner, there was a modestly sized main room, and beyond that, a bedroom. High ceilings swept gracefully toward a wall of view-windows, following the broad curve of the hull past banks and banks of heavy artillery and battle turrets. Beyond that, Ankea shrank rapidly in the distance, glowing in the haze of its own atmosphere, murky and uninviting.

Mira wandered into the bedroom, past the piles of her things, all neatly stacked, and back into the main living space. In the corner of the room there was a desk with a monitor already set up. The red light on the screen was blinking insistently and probably had been for some time. Mira eased herself down in the chair, already knowing who the call was from.

Trent shimmered into view, and she glanced past Mira's shoulder. "Well?" she asked, dispensing with any pretense of formality. "Where is she?"

Mira stared back blankly. "Where is who?" Then she remembered the slave she was supposed to buy. "Oh."

Trent narrowed her eyes into a piercing stare. "You had three days on Ankea. What were you doing down there, playing?"

"No, ma'am," said Mira. "I wasn't playing."

Trent glared, waiting for some excuse, but Mira was too tired to come up with anything convincing.

"Are you still in orbit?" Trent asked finally.

Mira glanced out the window. The planet was invisible now, just another light in a field of stars. "No, ma'am."

Trent gathered up the sheaf of papers in front of her and angrily tapped them together into an even stack. "Your personal beliefs are none of my business, but I just want you to know how close you are to being insubordinate." Her finger hovered over the button that would break the connection. "I hope we won't have to go through this again when you get to Traja."

"No, ma'am," said Mira. "You won't."

"I'll be waiting to hear from you."

"Yes, ma'am." Mira watched dully as the screen faded back to its reflective state, too exhausted to even feel guilty. She put her head down on the desk and went slowly, uncomfortably, to sleep.

Over the next few weeks, Amrei's condition improved considerably. Mira made it a point to see her at least every couple of days. If Vince was going to become permanently attached, it would not do to be left behind.

By the beginning of the third week, Mira found Amrei shoving empty crates out into the corridor.

"I can't stand it," she said, brushing off her hands. "Vince doesn't have time to unpack, and I'm having trouble even getting to the door." She glanced back inside the cabin. "I've got a pot of tea, if you don't mind the mess."

Mira stepped in, but it wasn't that bad. Most of Vince's things were stacked neatly or already stored away. "You can come to my place next," said Mira, meaning it as a joke. "My stuff is still in boxes."

Amrei gave her a terse, artificial smile.

"Sorry," muttered Mira. "I didn't mean—"

"It's alright." Amrei handed her a teacup, rather briskly. "I'm too sensitive. It's me, not you." She smiled. "You should see poor Vince. He's afraid to open his mouth around me anymore."

That sounded like a sure path to marital bliss. Mira sipped her tea in silence, trying to think of something to talk about.

"Vince says you're about to get a School slave."

"I was supposed to find one on Ankea," said Mira. "My supervisor was very upset when she found out I didn't do it."

"There aren't any School dealers on Ankea. Their reputation is too good for a place like that."

She wished she'd known. "What about Traja?"

Amrei nodded. "There's a huge market. You should be able to find whatever you want." She glanced at Mira. "Have you thought about what you want?"

Mira shrugged.

"Most people would be a little more excited," said Amrei. "Especially getting one for free."

"I can buy a lamp or a table," said Mira. "I don't think I can buy a person."

Amrei gave her an amused smile. "But you've had a slave."

Mira frowned. "Vince told you that?"

The smile became more sympathetic. "He talked about you all the time. For a while I thought you were lovers, but then he said you'd had a girl once." She cocked her head to one side. "She must have been very special if you've gone all this time without someone else."

It was a pointed question, and a rather nosy one. "Do you want to know if I was in love with my slave?" asked Mira bluntly.

"I won't make it public," said Amrei. "I was just wondering if that's the kind of revolutionary you are."

"It's not so unusual," said Mira, a little too defensively. "It's just not something you talk about. Anyway, I was a kid. I would have fallen in love with anything that moved." Mira scowled at the teacup. "It was a long time ago."

"Did you know how Vince felt about me?"

Mira shook her head. "He talked about you, but I never guessed how serious he was."

"I didn't know it myself for a long time." Amrei hesitated. "Would you like to hear about how we met?"

"Sure," said Mira, although it seemed fairly obvious.

"I knew who he was," said Amrei. "I mean, I recognized him when he came in, but he was just another sailor. You know."

Mira nodded, hoping this wasn't going to turn into some lurid story.

"There was another guy who came in once in a while, whose big thrill was to get rough. Really rough." She put her cup down. "One night, when he was done with me, Vince was downstairs, waiting. I walked in with this character, and I guess I must have looked pretty bad." She stopped. "Am I shocking you?"

"Not yet."

"Vince almost threw him through the wall. He never came back, either. I spent the rest of the night with Vince. It made me nervous in the beginning, to think that someone was watching out for me."

"You spent your whole time at the Pearl?" asked Mira. "The entire twenty years?"

"Only the last fifteen," said Amrei. "It could have been a lot worse. When the boss discovered I could out-haggle him at the slave markets, I got to do most of the buying. After a while he started feeling like he owed me something." She smiled. "He gave me a lot of rope. Probably too much."

"What about the first five years?" asked Mira.

"I swept floors in someone's house and fed their little brats." She grimaced. "I tried to be nice, but I guess I'm not docile enough. I don't think I've been docile in my whole life."

Mira didn't say anything. She'd never even asked Renee what she'd been before the slavers had come for her. It was supposed to be easier for everyone if the past was never mentioned. Now the rules of etiquette were balanced precariously on whatever Amrei chose to say next.

"Vince said you were Listed for four years," said Amrei, trading one uncomfortable subject for another. "You must have had a great place to hide."

"I was in the Faraque," said Mira. "Sector ships went past us every day and never stopped."

"Lucky for you. I was Listed twice."

"Did you hide?"

She shook her head. "I didn't even know about it. I was nineteen the first time, and no one bothered me. Then I got nabbed, just before my twenty-second birthday." She swirled the remains of her tea. "I was that close to having a normal life."

"When I was Listed," said Mira slowly, "my biggest fear was that I would end up in a place like the Pearl."

"It got easier when I found out there was a way to keep from dying in the end." Amrei hesitated, not looking up. "I don't believe I've thanked you yet."

Mira shrugged awkwardly. "You don't have to."

"But I'd like to do something for you." She paused. "I'd rather not unpack your boxes, though."

"Look," said Mira, "if you really want to help me, why don't you come down to Traja? The last thing I want to do is bargain for human flesh."

Amrei's eyes lit up like candles.

"If you don't mind," Mira added uncomfortably.

"Not at all." There was nothing she could do to hide her enthusiasm. "I'll make sure you get a really good deal, too."

"I just want someone nice."

"Don't worry about it, Mira." Amrei gave her a big, honest grin. "We'll find someone who's perfect."

5

n its heyday, when it served as the last stopover between Emirate space and the Faraque, Traja had been a haven for smugglers, illegal slavers, and a number of famous criminals. In the two hundred years since the Emirate had pushed the Sector back past their own border, Traja had become slightly more civilized. Safer. Overall, however, the planet's reputation had remained pretty much intact.

Amrei didn't seem at all worried though. Mira had to hurry to keep up with her as she pushed through the crowds around the Trajan Ground Station, out into the overcast afternoon and sprawling slave markets.

"Don't get lost," said Mira, finally close enough to grab her arm. "Vince would kill me if something happened to you."

Amrei gave her a huge grin. Dressed in Mira's old clothes, with her collar cut off, there was nothing in her walk or her face to give away what she was or what she had been. "How much do you have to spend?" she asked.

Mira hadn't actually checked. She was just as happy to let Amrei deal with this part of her job requirement. "Trent said she would give me four thousand." She squeezed the plastic voucher in her pocket. "Do you think that's enough?"

"More than enough. We might spend half." Amrei stopped and surveyed the stretch of covered pavilions. Beyond the market proper, Traja's capital city edged along the grey sky, interrupted, rather dramatically, by the sheer black walls of the arena.

Amrei pointed to a looming white tent at the other end of the main avenue. "That's the School tent. Come on."

"I don't even know why she wants me to get School," said Mira, hurrying along next to her. "All I ever hear about them is that they haven't got a brain left in their heads."

"Who needs a slave with a brain?" said Amrei without a trace of sarcasm. "It only makes them unhappy and undependable. Besides, with School you get the best sex training anywhere." She glanced at Mira. "They're very willing."

"How do you know all this?" asked Mira uneasily. School was sounding less and less like something she wanted.

"We had one at the Pearl for a while," said Amrei. "He was incredible in bed. Really amazing, in fact."

"What was he like?" asked Mira. "I mean as a person."

Amrei stopped and gave Mira a curious look. "He was a . . . blank, I guess is the best way of describing him. He just did what he was told. He never said much. They're all like that. It's the training."

"It's permanent?"

"Of course."

The School tent fluttered audibly, not more than a stone's throw away. "That's not what I want," said Mira. "I want someone I can have a conversation with."

"You want your girlfriend back," said Amrei in a low, unaccusing voice. "That's not going to happen, Mira. You can't be friends with them. They're property. They all know that."

"What about you?"

"I was different," said Amrei. "You would have been, too." She put her hand on Mira's arm. "Just buy a slave, Mira. Fall in love with a free woman. It's much easier."

"How am I supposed to free someone who's a robot?" Mira whispered. "That's the only reason I can do this with a clear conscience."

"You may not be able to," said Amrei. "Not everyone makes it through Failure. It has to be something you want very badly."

Mira pulled away, confused by her attitude. For herself, just seeing her name on the List had been enough to make her question the entire institution of slavery. For Amrei, even a lifetime in collar hadn't changed her mind. "Would you buy a slave?" she asked. "After everything you've been through?"

"I know what you want me to say," said Amrei, "but as soon this mission is over, we're getting a boy. I'm not going to wait on Vince hand and foot, certainly not after we're married."

"What are you going to do when he Fails?"

Amrei shrugged and took a step toward the School tent. "Are you coming?"

Mira followed her unwillingly, fighting down her dismay and unexpected resentment. She wondered if Vince knew or even cared that he would be owning a houseboy sometime in the near future. She tried to imagine Renee shopping in the markets of DeKastri, and it was surprisingly easy to visualize. There is no end to this, she thought to herself, walking past the lines of collared youngsters, if I'm the only one who thinks it's wrong.

It was just beginning to drizzle as they stepped into the huge drapery of the School tent. Inside, there were only a handful of people, including the sales staff. Apparently the high prices kept even the browsers away. From one end of the tent to the other, slaves knelt—docile, unchained—in precise rows: the boys on the right, the girls on the left, all arranged by the color of their hair.

An impeccably dressed salesman drifted over. "Is there something I can help you with?" he asked, trying not to cast a judgmental eye on Mira's Emirate uniform and Amrei's too-large clothing.

Amrei waited a second for Mira to speak up and then did it herself. "My friend is looking for a servant," she said. "For the Diplomatic corps."

"Ah," said the salesman to Mira, suddenly sensing money. "I didn't recognize your insignia right away. My apologies. What is your preference? Male or female?"

"Female," Mira muttered. She would make her peace with this later, she decided. Trent would be expecting her to call within a few hours, and if nothing else, she needed something to show just to stay employed.

"Any particular racial type?" asked the salesman a bit too pleasantly. "Blondes are very popular this year."

"Sure," said Mira.

There were at least twenty light-haired girls kneeling together in a tight line, with platinum blondes at one end, and pale redheads at the other. "Most of these girls are new graduates," said the salesman. He pulled back the nearest girl's shirt to expose her left shoulder and the series of brands there; her ID number, the School's mark, and the tiny hieroglyphic eye just between them that identified her as someone the Sector had taken.

"I won't buy Sector," said Mira shortly.

The salesman blinked in confusion. "Our highest quality comes from them," he said. "This group is all Sector, from the Faraque. They're bred for their obedience."

"I know," said Mira. "I won't buy Sector."

Amrei had wandered down the line, examining brands as she went. She looked up from a girl midway through the row. "This one's not." She pulled the girl to her feet and pushed the shirt off her shoulder for Mira to see.

She was very pretty, and had probably been collared on the day she'd turned eighteen. Her hair was bright gold and fell to her shoulders. She kept her eyes glued to the ground, standing passively for inspection.

"What's your name?" asked Amrei.

"Whatever you wish, D'sha."

Amrei nodded in approval. "How many years in collar?"

"Just one," said the salesman. "But she's had the full ten months of instruction, including the Sixty-Nine Nights."

Amrei shrugged as if it were the most unimportant thing in the world, and Mira could see that the bargaining had begun. "My friend doesn't need a bedwarmer," she said. "She needs someone who can serve a hundred hungry dignitaries and not drop anything."

There was a long table set up at one end of the tent loaded with food and a dozen different kinds of wine. The salesman nodded to the girl and pointed at the table. "Show her."

Mira watched as she moved gracefully across the floor and poured two glasses, exactly two-thirds full. As she knelt at Mira's feet and held them out for her to choose, Mira met her eyes, just for a second. They were strikingly sapphire, like jewels, and empty. There was no intelligence behind them, not a single cognizant thought. Somehow she had succeeded in learning what she had been taught by the slavers, and had been able, essentially, to turn herself off.

Mira took both glasses and handed one to Amrei, feeling completely trapped.

"That's not much of a demonstration," said Amrei.

"If you'd like, you can see how she performed on her tests," said the salesman. "We record everything from the first day they're here. Of course," he added, "when it comes to the Sixty-Nine Nights, we realize our customers need a little more than just visuals."

At the moment Mira couldn't imagine anything more distasteful than taking this creature into some back room and putting her through her paces for the next hour or so. She opened her mouth to decline, but Amrei stopped her.

"Do you want to?" she asked. "Or would you like me to try her out?"

"No," said Mira. It was an empty offer anyway, considering that Amrei was still clearly branded under her long sleeves.

"I have a few others," said the salesman, misinterpreting Mira's response. "But if you don't want Sector, you're limiting yourself. You should at least see what you're missing." He snapped his fingers, and the girl began to open her shirt.

"That's alright," said Mira quickly, embarrassed. "I guess she's fine." Aside from her looks, this slave was no different from any of the others in the tent, Sector or not. She was School, and that was the only thing that really mattered. "I'll take her," said Mira.

"How much?" asked Amrei.

"Four thousand."

Mira was reaching into her pocket for the voucher, but Amrei curled her lip at the man like he was out of his mind. "You've already told us she's not top quality," she said. "What makes you think we'll pay that kind of money for her?"

The salesman glanced at Mira. She could tell he'd spent his time sizing her up as the buyer, not Amrei. "You have a point," he said. "I suppose I could take a little less."

"Two thousand," said Amrei.

"Thirty-five hundred," said the salesman, finally giving her his full attention. "Any less is an insult to the School. And to the girl."

Amrei snorted. "I'm certainly not worried about her feelings. Twenty-five hundred, and that's more than generous."

Mira watched the girl as they haggled. She was as unresponsive as a chair at an auction, even as Amrei began pointing out the things she considered flaws, from the size of her ears to the shape of her face. Nothing anyone said could affect her. She would only take orders, she would never be more than politely friendly, and the concept of being free one day would never enter her mind.

The salesman gave in, and Amrei compromised around three thousand. Mira handed him the voucher, and gave Amrei a convincing smile as she glowed with her own victory.

The salesman turned back from his monitor where he was scanning Mira's account. "Are you sure this is the voucher you want to use?"

It was the only one Mira had. "What's wrong?"

He moved to one side and pointed at the screen. "You only have nine hundred in this account."

"What?" Mira peered at the numbers, but there was no sign of Trent's stipend. Only her most recent balance was listed. "It has to be in there." She paged back and forth through the file, but there was nothing.

"I thought you had money," said Amrei in a low voice. "Didn't you check?"

Mira shook her head angrily and took the voucher out of the machine. "I'm sorry," she said to the salesman. "I guess I've wasted your time."

"Not at all," said the salesman crisply. He gave Amrei a final, withering glance, and turned to put the girl back in the coffle.

Mira caught up to Amrei just outside. The afternoon had turned wetter and darker, and she was standing just out of the rain in the shelter of the tent. Water dripped at her feet. She looked cold.

"Sorry," said Mira. "Sometimes Trent is more trouble than she's worth."

"You should have checked," said Amrei. She didn't sound angry, but Mira suspected that she was. "What do you want to do?"

"I don't know." Across the plaza, dealers were closing down early, and the crowds had thinned to no more than a few dozen people hurrying to get out of the rain.

"Let's go back to the ship," said Amrei. "We can try again tomorrow. Maybe you can get the money straightened out by then."

"You can go," said Mira. "I just want to get this taken care of."

"He's not going to let you have her for nine hundred. Not even *I* can get him down that low."

Mira sighed. "Trent didn't say that I had to get School. She just said that's what she preferred." She pointed down the street to another tent. "They're still open."

Amrei looked doubtful. "What kind of deal do you think you're going to get if there's no competition?"

"It's better than nothing," said Mira. "Anyhow, I get reimbursed. Do you want to come?"

Amrei took her arm, friendly, forgiving. "Only to save you from yourself."

Unlike the School tent, the second place was drab and wet. The slaves huddled together, most of them sleeping. One boy jerked awake as Mira and Amrei came in. "Buy me, D'sha," he mumbled, holding out his chained wrists. Mira stepped past him and wished she had gone back to the ship.

The dealer moved out of the shadows in the back. "You're just in time," he said. "I was about to close down for the night." He took a long look at Amrei, obviously judging her age. "What can I help you ladies find?"

"A nice girl," said Amrei, looking him right in the eye. "Someone with a little class."

He scratched his head, surveying his lot. There weren't really that many, and most of the slaves were boys. "How much were you planning on spending?" he asked innocently.

"That depends," said Amrei. "Let's see what you've got." She pointed to a dark-haired girl in the back who was watching them intently. "Are you set on a blonde?" she asked Mira.

"No," said Mira. "I guess not."

The dealer made his way over to the girl and unfastened her from the coffle. She wasn't cuffed at all, Mira noticed, just a thin chain from her collar, like a leash.

Amrei pulled the shirt off of the girl's shoulder. She kept her eyes down, but she seemed tense, not oblivious, like the School slaves. "How many years?" asked Amrei.

"Six, D'sha," said the girl. "I was a house servant on Ankea for the last five."

"Why did they get rid of you?" asked Mira. She was attractive in a rough kind of way, light-skinned, with a strong, stocky body, and her hair cut short.

The girl shrugged. "They needed money." She paused and quickly added, "D'sha."

Amrei was rubbing her chin thoughtfully. Mira couldn't tell if she approved or not. "What are you worth?" she asked, to keep her talking.

"Oh, five or six," said the girl. She smiled at Mira, attempting to look guileless. "It depends what you want me to do."

She forgot to add the *D'sha,* and Mira couldn't decide whether that appealed to her or not. She seemed very bold, very confident, as if she were in possession of some secret knowledge which made her life easier.

"Mind your manners," said Amrei.

The girl ducked her head. "D'sha," she said, as Amrei came closer and pulled her left ear forward.

"I thought so," she said to Mira. "She's wired." She turned the girl's head so Mira could see the number printed on her scalp. "Did she run away from you?" she asked the dealer. "Or did you pick her up from somewhere?"

"I was about to mention that," said the man lamely. He held up a palm-sized box, the Governor, which could be set to deliver a paralyzing shock if the slave went past a certain boundary. It was considered a humane alternative to beating runaways and sending them to the Mines. "She's got plenty of good points. Just a little mistake once. Right?"

The girl nodded emphatically, but Amrei pushed her away in disgust. "Let's get out of here."

They wandered out into the gathering darkness, past the empty, wet pavilions, heading for the Ground Station. Amrei was clearly worn out, and Mira was discouraged.

"Do you think she was really that bad?" asked Mira. "There isn't anywhere to run on the Proviso."

"I wouldn't trust her," said Amrei. "She was too smooth. I've seen her type before, and they never work out. They outsmart themselves and end up in the Mines."

The Ground Station loomed in front of them, dark and gleaming in the rain. Amrei stepped through the door. "Aren't you coming?"

Mira shook her head. "I want to walk for a while. I'll be up later."

"In this weather?" Amrei frowned. "Is something wrong?"

Mira shrugged, because she couldn't begin to articulate how wrong it all was. "No," she said. "I just need some time."

"Don't go back for that last one," said Amrei. "She's no good at all."

"I know," said Mira. "I won't." She let the door close and walked off into the night, feeling Amrei's eyes on her long after she knew she was too far away to be seen.

It wasn't that she expected to find an open dealer and then the perfect girl. It wasn't that the weather had cleared; it hadn't. Rain fell steadily, but not uncomfortably on Mira's face and shoulders, muddying the grime she felt accumulating on her soul. The girl at the School tent was simply a human robot. The other one would have cajoled Mira, lied to her, until an opportunity presented itself. Then she would have disappeared without a trace or afterthought. Mira shoved her hands in her pockets and put her head down, closer to tears than she had been in a long time. She needed more than this. She needed what Vince had finally found.

She wasn't even sure where she was when it began to really pour. Water trickled down her neck and into her shoes. She headed for the nearest shelter, a dark, dark tent. She thought it was empty until she pulled the front flap aside and stepped in.

There were no more than a dozen slaves, most chained hand and foot, the girls shirtless, the boys completely stripped. They looked at Mira from the corners of their eyes, silent, as motionless as they could be. Mira froze, and recognition stuck in her throat. This was the Mine tent. There was no question about it. As her eyes adjusted to the dim lights, she could see the marks on the slaves that made them worthless. One was missing a hand, another had his mouth taped shut, his back a labyrinth of scars. One muscular girl was eyeless, an arena brand looping across one shoulderblade.

There was a movement from the back of the tent, and a big woman in a dirty coat came out. She cocked her head at Mira, looking for the slave she was no doubt here to drop off. "Help you?" she asked suspiciously.

Mira pushed back her dripping hair. "I'm a little lost. How far is the Ground Station?"

The woman moved closer. "Walking?" She jerked a thumb to the right. "It's about twenty minutes." She listened to the rain on the canvas for a moment. "You can wait until it lets up, if you like." Her tone was friendly, but the slaves at her feet bent away from her, almost imperceptibly, like flowers in the wind, and Mira had no doubts about the sort of person she was. "It's late to be shopping," she remarked.

Mira nodded warily.

"Didn't you find what you were looking for?"

It was an innocent enough question. "Not really," said Mira, and immediately wished she hadn't said anything at all.

"You look like the sympathetic type," said the woman. "Maybe you can find something here."

With what she had in her account, Mira knew she could buy every slave in the tent and still have money left over. "I don't think you have what I want."

"I think I might," said the woman. She crossed her arms. "It's so hard to buy loyalty these days, don't you agree?"

Mira didn't say anything. The dread silence all around her was thick as paste. The slaves shifted in their chains, listening to the conversation. Suddenly, Mira was a way out: it was only a question of who would get her.

The woman reached down and pulled a skinny boy to his feet. She held him under the jaw as though he were a fish and shook him roughly. "Here's one," she said. "Very dependable. Just stupid. Go on," she said to him, "tell her what you did."

"D'sha," he gasped, "I tried to run."

She let him drop. "He'll never do it again," she said to Mira. "Now he's as faithful as a dog."

"I don't think so," said Mira. The sound of the rain was even louder overhead, or she would have left right then.

"As for the girls. . . ." The woman rubbed her chin, looking around. "I've got a couple of nice ones."

"Please," said Mira nervously. "I just wanted to get out of the rain. You don't have to sell me anyone."

"No?" said the woman. "What about her?" She hauled the blinded girl up. Her arms were cuffed behind her back, a sure sign of a violent past. "She'd be grateful for a new pair of eyes. Wouldn't you?"

"Buy me, D'sha," whispered the girl.

Mira turned away, unable to bear it, and pushed open the tent.

Curtains of water sluiced off the roof, blocking her way.

"Wait," said the woman. She put a big hand on Mira's shoulder and pulled her back. "I do have one you should see."

"I'm not interested," said Mira tightly.

"You should be," said the woman. "She's School."

"No chance," said Mira. It had to be a lie. A School slave wasn't capable of ending up in the Mine line.

The woman smiled slowly. "It never hurts to look."

Mira bit her lip and looked at the coffle. "Which one?"

"She's in back," said the woman. "She's mine—for now."

Against her better judgment, Mira followed her under a drape of canvas to a dingy back room furnished with only a table, two chairs, and a battered monitor. Mira found herself wishing that Amrei had come along, just for moral support. Even without her, Mira knew she could spot a fake School brand. The ID card took care of that, but there were a lot of ways to get cheated in this game.

A girl was kneeling in the shadows in the corner. She didn't look up as they entered, but Mira could see her body tighten.

"Get up," snapped the woman, and the girl obeyed instantly, eyes on the ground. The woman turned to Mira. "See for yourself."

Mira gingerly pulled the shirt off the girl's shoulder. The cloth was stiff with dirt, and the girl wasn't much cleaner. Her hair was tied back in a clumsy, tangled braid. Possibly blonde, Mira couldn't tell. The brands were clean, untampered with—her ID, the Sector eye, and the School mark—but Mira wasn't convinced. "Why are you here?" she asked.

"Show her," said the woman.

The girl slipped out of the shirt, never looking up. Haphazard marks from a beating wrapped around her back and waist. They were not the signs of a considered punishment, more like something done in a fury.

"What did you do?" asked Mira.

"I ran, D'sha."

"They had to hunt her down with horses and dogs," said the woman. "They told me it took almost a week." She pulled the shirt back up. "Get us something to drink."

The girl answered inaudibly and darted away to the back of the tent. She was wearing ankle cuffs, Mira finally noticed, and the chains jingled softly against her bare feet.

"Well?" The woman sat down at the table and leaned toward Mira. "What do you think?"

"Let me see her card," said Mira.

The woman peeled back her coat, fishing in her pockets. She held up the card in her fingers and twirled it around. "Let's have a look at your money."

Mira pulled out her voucher. "How much do you want for her?"

"I don't know," said the woman. The girl came back with two cups and a steaming pot of tea. "Maybe a thousand."

Mira waited as she poured. Her hands shook, and her body was braced, as if she expected to be hit for the smallest mistake. As she turned away from her mistress to kneel on the floor, Mira saw her face. Under the dirt, what she caught a glimpse of was a tightly controlled panic, not the trained unconsciousness that the School should have equipped her with.

Mira sat down and checked the dates on the ID card. The girl had been in collar less than two years. "How long have you had her?"

"Sixty-five nights," said the woman smugly. "But she's been with us for about four months. She's made the rounds, if you know what I mean."

Mira only nodded and started to put the ID into the monitor's slot, but the woman stuck her hand in front of it. "Not so fast. First I have to know if this is going to be worth my while."

Mira put the card down wondering what she wasn't supposed to know. "I'll give you five hundred," she said flatly.

"Don't be ridiculous," said the woman. "She's School." She was about to go on when a gust of cold air blew through the tent as someone came in from the front.

"Excuse me," said the woman. "I'll be right back." She picked up the ID and glanced at the girl. "Keep your mouth shut."

The girl nodded silently, eyes fixed on the ground.

Mira waited until she was well out of earshot and leaned over. "Why won't she let me see your record?" she whispered, but the girl wouldn't answer.

In the front of the tent, Mira could hear someone objecting to how much they were being offered for a slave they no longer wanted. It didn't sound like a discussion that would last very long. "Look up here," she said to the girl, who tilted her head up a little, but wouldn't meet Mira's eyes. "Is she going to put you back in the coffle if I don't take you?"

The girl hesitated and finally nodded, just barely.

Mira chewed her lip, undecided. Once the girl was in chains with the rest of the rejected slaves, no buyer would take a second look at her. It meant that her next stop would be the Mines, and there was no way out after that. "I still don't understand," said Mira. "Why won't she show me your record? Did you kill somebody?"

The girl glanced up with an odd expression, as though it was an idea that had occurred to her. "No D'sha," she said, and lowered her eyes again. "At the School . . . ." She hesitated. She knew she was taking a big risk. "I couldn't pass half my tests. I'm not much good, I guess."

"Oh," said Mira. This admission made the School brand a nominal mark on the girl's arm, as close to a fake as it could be and still remain genuine. The fact that she'd come through the training at all was probably the result of some internal decision at the School that kept them from throwing her out and losing whatever money they could make on her.

Mira leaned back in her chair as the woman ducked back into the room. The girl didn't appear to have moved, but the woman looked at Mira suspiciously. "Let's be serious. You know five hundred's too low."

Mira shrugged. "I don't have a thousand."

The woman put her hands into her pockets, still standing. "What did she say to you?"

"Nothing," said Mira uneasily. "I just don't have it." She didn't relish the idea of losing her entire paycheck in this deal, but she started to get the feeling it was going to happen. "I'll give you seven."

The woman turned to the girl, who cringed visibly. "What did you say to her?"

"Nothing, D'sha," she whispered, gasping as she was yanked to her feet.

The woman held her by the front of her shirt. "She may not be great School," she said to Mira, "but she's worth what I'm asking. Of course," she snarled, turning to the slave, "I might have to give you a deal on damaged goods." She drew back her arm and hit her hard, not a slap, but a solid punch. The girl dropped to the floor covering her face, trying not to make any noise.

The woman reached down to do it again, but Mira grabbed her

arm and pressed the voucher into her hand. "Stop it," she said. "Here's nine hundred. Just give me the ID."

The woman straightened up, a knowledgeable and unpleasant grin on her face. "A thousand."

"I don't have it," said Mira. "If you break her neck you won't get anything for her."

She looked down at Mira's voucher and stuck it in her pocket. "It's always so nice to do business with humanitarians," she said sarcastically. She dropped the ID into Mira's palm, and Mira understood that she would have beaten the girl no matter what, until Mira had either walked out or paid enough to make her stop.

Mira helped the trembling girl to her feet, supporting her as she tangled in her chains. "Don't take those off," the woman shouted as they stepped into the downpour. "Don't give her any ideas!"

They got as far as a street lamp before Mira had to turn up her collar against the pelting storm. The girl fell to her knees on the streaming pavement, already soaked to the skin. She looked worse in the rain, her hair sticking to her face, her clothes plastered to her thin body.

Mira leaned over to unlock the chains. They were free-keyed and slipped off her ankles when Mira touched them. "Don't even think about running," she said. "You'll end up right back here." She hadn't meant to sound so harsh and held out a hand to help the girl to her feet. "What's your name?" she asked, forgetting that School slaves didn't have names.

"Costa, D'sha," said the girl, then quickly covered her mouth. "Whatever you wish, D'sha," she corrected herself, and bowed her head, waiting for a slap.

Mira wanted to tell her that she couldn't care less, but didn't know how to say it. Instead she pulled the girl up off the ground and spread half of her coat over her shoulders. "Come on," she said, and started walking toward the Ground Station.

6

Back on the ship, it was well after midnight and the corridors were deserted. That was fine with Mira. The fewer people who saw her leading this dripping, dirty child to her quarters, the better. She'd almost made it, when Vince came around the corner.

He saw Mira first. "There you are," he said. "Amrei told me you'd—" He saw the girl, who dropped to her knees. "This is your bargain?"

"Don't say anything," said Mira. "And please don't mention this to Amrei yet. I have the feeling she won't approve."

Vince put out a hand, but the girl flinched away from him. "Is it just men?" he asked, "or is it everybody?"

"I think it's everybody."

He shook his head. "This could be a big mistake."

"Maybe," said Mira. "Maybe you would have done the same thing."

Her quarters were quiet and dark, lit from the outside by Traja's hazy crescent. Mira touched the walls for light, feeling the girl's eyes on her. "You might as well know where you are. This is the battleship Proviso. I'm Mira LoDire. I'm a diplomat for the Emirate."

"D'LoDire," whispered the girl, standing frozen against one wall.

Mira came a little closer, watching as Costa tensed with every step.

She stopped. "No one here is going to hurt you."

"Yes D'sha."

She didn't sound a bit convinced, and Mira wondered if it was worth trying to explain how different things would be from now on. "I want you to wash," she said firmly. "I'll show you where everything is."

Mira turned the water on in the tub and let it run while she dug through one of her trunks for Renee's old clothes. Costa knelt silently behind her in the bathroom, clearly expecting something awful to happen, bracing herself for it. Mira shook out the soft white clothing and draped it over one arm. There was no way she could think of to make this any easier. If nothing else, the girl would need help washing her hair, which fell to her waist in dirty, complex tangles, and besides, Mira thought, I'm no rapist. The sooner she finds that out, the better.

She came back into the bathroom, careful to move slowly, but Costa crouched into herself and turned her face away. "This is nineteen," she whispered. "I don't remember nineteen."

Mira eased down on the edge of the tub and turned off the water. Maybe she's crazy, she thought. That might explain a lot. "What's nineteen?" she asked.

"I don't remember how to do it. I can remember forty and seventeen." She clutched the front of her shirt and pulled it open with a nervous jerk.

She was talking about the Sixty-Nine Nights, Mira realized suddenly. "What does number nineteen have to do with a bathtub?" she asked, and smiled in case the girl looked up.

She didn't. She stared at the floor as if she were racking her brains for the answer. "I can't remember," she whispered at last. "D'sha."

Mira dipped a hand into the hot water and swirled it around thinking of Amrei, covered in ice. "Let's just get you washed up," she said softly. "We can save the sex for later. Alright?"

The girl took a sharp breath and pulled off her clothes quickly, before she had time to decide not to, and stood naked and shivering in front of Mira, her head down, her hands clenched at her sides. Mira reached over to help her into the tub, but she shied away, stepping into the water, sliding to her knees.

"Relax," said Mira. "I've never hit anyone in my life." She picked up a bar of soap and pushed the girl's braid out of the way. Dirty puckered lines ran across her back, random and deep. Mira lathered up her hands and began to scrub. "I've never heard of School running away," she said. "What happened?"

"I ran, D'sha," said the girl, exactly the same way she'd said it in the Mine tent.

"I know," said Mira. "I want you to tell me why." She slid her hands over her shoulderblades and down her spine. Every muscle was steeled, tight as a spring.

"It's on my card, D'sha."

"Okay," said Mira, "what does it say on your card?"

"I wasn't any good," said the girl softly, anxious. "I ran away one night. They had to chase me down with horses and dogs."

"But School doesn't run," said Mira. "School slaves only do what they're told. Isn't that right?"

"Yes D'sha."

"So what happened?"

There was a long, long silence. Mira waited, washing the last traces of filth away from the thin shoulders. The water had turned grey, but as she leaned over to set the system to recycle she saw the tears streaming down the girl's face.

"What happened?" insisted Mira. "Did he tell you to run?"

Costa nodded and covered her face. "They chased me like I was an animal," she whispered.

Mira slid down to the floor so that the two of them were at eye level, and gently pried her hands away. "Nothing like that is going to happen here."

Costa just shook with fresh sobs. "Don't hurt me," she begged and put her head on the edge of the tub. "Please don't hurt me."

"Take it easy," said Mira, not knowing what else to say. She stroked the girl's back, the mats in her hair, making soothing noises, saying anything she could think of that might sound reassuring. In the end, though, Costa seemed too worn out to keep crying or even react as Mira rinsed the soap away. Underneath the grimy suds, there was a rich remarkable gold in her hair, dark with water. Mira slid a hand under the girl's chin, tilting her head up. Grey eyes looked back, deep as the sea, resigned and afraid—but nothing like the vacant jewels in the School tent.

Mira touched the wet hair again, smoothing it back from Costa's forehead. "I don't think you'll have to cut any of this."

The girl swallowed hard and turned her face away. "Thank you,

D'sha," she whispered, and carefully stepped out of the tub.

Mira ate her dinner slowly, trying not to watch as her slave knelt on the floor, wolfing down everything on her plate.

By Mira's calculations, it was somewhere around four in the morning where Trent was. There would be no chance of getting through to her supervisor if she called right now.

As she stared at the monitor screen, waiting for the channels to clear, she could see Costa's reflection eyeing her. In a perfect mirror, she might have been able to tell what her expression was, but the silvering made things look blurry and indistinct, like the surface of water. Mira resisted the urge to turn around. It would take a long time for real trust, not just dinner and a bath and a few friendly words.

She left a message with the recording of Trent's secretary, turning the screen slightly so Trent wouldn't be able to see the girl. Mira cut the connection, then checked if she was still being watched, but Costa was kneeling, eyes down, and the plate was spotless.

"You can sleep out here," said Mira. "If you don't like the windows open, just tell them to close."

The girl nodded wearily. "Do you want me tonight, D'sha?"

"I want you to get some sleep," said Mira. "That's all." She hesitated. The door to the corridor was locked, keyed to her own handprint, but she didn't relish the idea of this stranger roaming around the cabin at will all night. Locking the bedroom door seemed too paranoid. Her coat was hanging on the back of her chair, and Mira reached into the pocket for the ankle cuffs. "I'm not doing this to scare you," she said. "I just want you to stay put tonight."

"Yes D'sha." She stretched out on the floor, and Mira snapped the chain around her leg, then the sofa's. If she really tried, she could get away, but she looked too exhausted for that kind of effort.

"Pleasant dreams," said Mira, and left her alone.

In her own bed, Mira turned over restlessly and stared out the windows at the nebulous clouds that trailed across Traja's surface. Fifteen years ago, this had been her last stop on her way into the Faraque. It had taken two months to travel from her home on Newhall to Thea's shielded listening post, and she'd been terrified the entire time. Forged identity papers, and the temporary things she'd done to change her eyes, hair, and skin, had all suddenly seemed like very weak and amateurish ways of fooling anyone, especially seasoned slavers, who, in her mind, were lurking behind every door. It had been her father's idea to send her to her aunt. She'd agreed completely at the outset, but as she got closer and closer to the Faraque, all she'd wanted was go back home and take her chances. The fact that the Sector would never dream of setting foot on an Emirate outpost hadn't seemed at all comforting, or even realistic, at the time. She'd been safe there, however, and in retrospect, it was her imagination that had made the eight-week passage so frightening.

Thea had bought Renee on Traja.

Mira sat up, too tense to sleep. Suddenly she wanted to know everything about the girl sleeping in the other room, not just her misfortunes, but what sort of person she was—or had been. Mira got up and went quietly to the door. Social convention might prohibit her from asking this slave about her life before she'd been collared, but it could not prevent her from wondering.

She pushed the door open a crack, with less than a breath of noise, but the girl wasn't asleep. Costa was leaning against the windows, at the end of the chain, silhouetted against the radiant planet. There was no way she could have heard the door, but she clearly heard something. She stiffened, not turning, and sank back down to the floor out of sight behind the sofa, tense and unmistakably awake.

Trent called even before Mira's alarm went off.

Mira fumbled in the dark for her robe and staggered out of the bedroom, her head still thick with the dream of some emergency that explained the incessant beeping of the monitor. The sight of Costa kneeling by the sofa, still chained, took her by surprise until she remembered why Trent was calling at this hour. She peered at herself in the screen, puffy and tangled, and turned the monitor on reluctantly.

"Good morning," said Trent, frowning. "What time is it where you are?"

Mira checked. It wasn't as early as she'd thought. "I had kind of a late night," she croaked, and cleared her throat.

"I see," said Trent. "So where is she? How come you're answering your own calls?"

Mira glanced over at the girl, still crouching by the windows, and despite everything, still not very clean. "Just a second."

"This is my supervisor," whispered Mira as she snapped open the cuffs. "Don't say anything."

The girl nodded and followed her, head down, across the room.

Trent's face wrinkled into instant displeasure, almost anger. "I told you to get School."

"I did," said Mira, ready to tell the whole story, but Trent interrupted her.

"Let me see her arm."

Costa turned her face away as Mira pulled the loose shirt down. The School mark showed clearly, and so did the whip marks over her shoulder.

"For God's sake, Mira! You got her from the Mines?"

"There was no stipend in my account," said Mira coolly. "I spent everything I had. She was the best I could find."

"*Naturally* the money's not in your account!" snapped Trent. "Didn't you check with the ship's paymaster?"

"No, ma'am," said Mira. "I didn't know I was supposed to."

"Now you know." Trent stared hard at the girl. "Are you still in orbit?"

"Yes."

"Take her back," said Trent. "Do it this morning. I don't care if you miss breakfast. Just do it."

"Yes, ma'am," said Mira, trying to sound like she was really going to. Behind her, Costa let out a tiny, agonized sound.

"One other thing," said Trent, her mouth thin and tight. "The Corps does not sleep in, even on extended missions. Do I make myself clear?"

"Very clear," said Mira.

"Then get busy," said Trent. She reached out and broke the connection with a sharp, angry stab.

Mira rubbed her eyes and leaned back in the chair. "Stop worrying," she said to Costa. "You're not going anywhere."

The girl was standing helplessly in the center of the room, her panic a tangible thing. "But you said . . . ." Her voice shook and she covered her mouth.

"I have to live with myself," said Mira. "I know what'll happen if you go back." There was a vehemence building inside of her that she couldn't pinpoint the source of. It had a lot to do with Trent's clear lack of sympathy, and also the fact that Mira knew she had done exactly what was right, what anyone should have done. Anything so morally correct could only have good consequences. She hoped.

Somebody knocked impatiently at the door.

The girl hurried to answer it before Mira could stop her. As she had expected, it was Amrei, with Vince right behind her.

"I'm not dressed yet," said Mira, without much hope that they would go away.

"We don't mind." Amrei stood to one side as Vince entered sheepishly with an armful of breakfast trays. He gave Mira an apologetic look and set them on the table.

"This is so thoughtful of you, Captain," said Mira sarcastically.

Amrei gave Costa a critical once-over as the girl fell to her knees by the door. "I knew I should have stayed with you. How much did this set you back?"

"She's fine," said Mira. "Leave her alone and let's eat. Since you're here."

"But she's *filthy*," said Amrei. "I'd almost say she was—" She pulled the shirt off Costa's shoulder and saw what was there. "School in the Mines." She snorted. "And I thought I'd seen everything."

Mira sat down at the table across from Vince. "Tell her to stop," she said, low enough so only he could hear. "I already know all this, and I just went through it with Trent."

"Have some breakfast, Amrei," said Vince. "It's getting cold." He pulled the chair out for her, but she didn't sit.

"I hope you didn't pay too much," she said to Mira. "That brand's a fake."

"No it isn't." Mira reached into her coat pocket and pulled out the ID card.

Amrei snatched it out of her fingers and examined it doubtfully. "It looks real." She settled herself at Mira's desk, in front of the monitor, and slid the card in, peering at the screen. "She's a runner," said Amrei. "She's no different from that last girl we saw yesterday, except she's not wired."

Mira scowled at Vince.

"Maybe she has a point," he muttered over his food. "It doesn't hurt to listen."

Amrei ran her finger along the screen, reading as she went. "Here's her School rating. On a scale of one to twenty, she got a two on food prep, a two on table service, a three on personal service, a two on appearance. And those are the high scores." She paused. "Wait, there's one more. A ten in bed." She gave Costa a skeptical look. "A ten? That sounds pretty artificial to me."

"Isn't that good?" asked Mira blandly.

"If she remembers any of it," said Amrei.

"What do you mean?" asked Mira. "How can you forget sex lessons?"

Amrei was still waiting for the girl to respond, one way or the other. "We could watch your tests," she said.

Costa looked up, flushed with embarrassment. "D'sha," she said, "it's an artificial score."

"What are you talking about?" demanded Mira.

"Enhancers," said Amrei. "She must have been drugged to her eyeballs."

Mira turned to Vince. "What the hell's an Enhancer?"

"It's a type of aphrodisiac for slaves," said Vince. "They do whatever they're told, but they don't remember a thing the next day." He pushed his plate away. "She doesn't sound very reliable to me, Mira. Especially if she's a runner."

Mira decided it wasn't worth trying to tell them Costa's version of what had happened. She wasn't entirely convinced of it herself. "There's nowhere to run up here," she said. "Anyway, so what if she didn't do so well in School? Renee wasn't School and I survived that."

"This is different," said Amrei. "School training is thorough, or it should be. If she went through all that and still disobeyed, then something's seriously wrong with her. She might be dangerous, Mira. She might try to kill somebody one day."

Mira rolled her eyes, but Amrei shrugged. "You don't have to listen to me. I can tell you right now, though, she's completely useless. I'll bet she can't even make a decent cup of coffee." Amrei pointed at Mira's tiny kitchenette. "Go ahead, girl," she said. "Prove yourself to this nice lady."

"I don't want coffee," said Mira, but Costa had already hurried off into the corner of the cabin.

Amrei sat down at the table. "How much longer are we going to be in orbit?" she asked Vince.

"Another hour."

"I'm not taking her back," said Mira shortly, keeping her voice low. "And frankly, Amrei, I think you should have a little more compassion."

"I think you should be realistic," said Vince. "What exactly did Trent tell you to do?"

"She told me to take her back."

Vince frowned. "You're disobeying a direct order?"

"She'll be killed," said Mira. "I can't do that to her, or to anybody."

"You don't even know her," said Vince incredulously.

"I didn't know *her*," said Mira, nodding at Amrei. "Have you ever been to one of the Mine tents, Vince? It's very compelling."

Vince looked away, not answering as Costa leaned over Mira's shoulder with a pot of fresh coffee, and stepped back while she took a sip. It was strong enough to make her teeth ache. "It's fine," she said to Amrei.

"You're serving from the wrong side," said Amrei to the girl. "You clear from the left."

"Yes D'sha," whispered Costa. She moved over to Vince's right and poured, filling the saucer, but only half of the cup.

Amrei pursed her lips. "I hope she does a good job with laundry. You'll probably end up with most of your meals in your lap."

"It won't make a very good impression when you negotiate," said Vince quietly. "Especially in the Faraque. The Sector take this sort of thing very seriously."

Costa was poised over Amrei's cup, cautious, tense. She flinched at the mention of the Sector.

"Raffail's opinion means *so* much to me," said Mira as sarcastically as she could.

Costa's arm jerked, and the coffee pot sailed through the air, bouncing off the edge of the table, splattering Amrei with hot, black liquid.

Amrei shrieked and jumped out of the chair. "*Look* at this!" she shouted, clutching at her soaked clothes. She turned on Costa as the girl backed away, and her hand flew back, fingers arched like claws.

Without thinking, Mira caught her wrist and pulled her around roughly. "Don't you dare," she hissed. "Not with *mine!*" Her own tone shocked her, and she let go.

Amrei stared at her, rubbing her wrist. "She's no good," she said in a low, hoarse voice. "Anyone can see that. You'll save yourself a lot of trouble by getting rid of her now. It only gets harder if you wait."

"It's my decision," said Mira.

"It's her decision," repeated Vince. He took Amrei's arm. "Let's go," he said gently, and guided her out the door without a backward glance.

Mira took a couple of deep breaths. She and Vince had had enough conflicts in the past six years for her to know that it would take more than this to make a permanent rift between them, but with Amrei involved, it might take a lot longer before he would talk to her again.

"Take me back," said the girl from where she was crouching on the floor.

"Back?" Mira stared at her in amazement. "After all that? Are you kidding?"

"I'm not what you need." She edged away, trembling as Mira took a step toward her. "You need real School, D'sha," she insisted. "I spill things. I do things wrong. I'm not good enough for you."

She was positively babbling. Mira stopped where she was. "It was just an accident," she said. "Amrei could rattle anyone."

"Take me back, D'sha," whimpered the girl. "You're a friend of Raffail's."

It was an accusation, as though Mira's every cautious motion were just part of a charade. "I am not," said Mira. "Where did you get that idea?"

Costa eyed her. Wary. Suspicious. "You know him."

"I'm a diplomat," said Mira. "I come into contact with a lot of slime. How do you know him?"

The girl hesitated. "He took me."

"I see." Mira sat down again, carefully avoiding the pools of spilled coffee. "Raffail's not one of my favorite people, but I have to deal with him once in a while. If you're really that scared of him, I suppose I could take you back to the Mine line. But only if it's what you really want."

Costa shook her head slowly, just as frightened by her own suggestion. "D'LoDire," she said, "if I had to serve him, and . . . I did something wrong, would you send me back to Traja?"

"No," said Mira, flatly, so there would be no doubt.

The girl took a nervous breath. "He might not even remember me by now," she said, softly, without much confidence. "I can do whatever you want, D'sha."

Mira nodded, encouraged by even this microscopic step forward. "Good," she said, "because you belong to me now, not him."

Mira sat at the monitor, watching Costa as she emptied the trunks in the bedroom. Everything from the Merganthaler was still packed, even after three weeks on the Proviso.

With enough time and distance, Mira theorized, the girl would eventually become more of a normal, less anxious human being. Right now, though, her shoulders were hunched against Mira's eyes, and she never looked up from what she was doing. What Mira had hoped would be a low-stress task, Costa had apparently interpreted as a test of her own obedience and efficiency. It was painful to watch her agonize over which drawer Mira's underwear should go in, and more painful to watch her try to decide to ask for instructions.

Costa reached into the bottom of the trunk and pulled out the stack of holos of the beach vacation with Renee that Mira had tied together and thrown in three weeks earlier. She hadn't actually tied them. They were really just wrapped loosely with a little bit of string, and as the girl straightened, they flew out of her hands. Costa crouched behind a pile of uniform jackets and began to gather up the pictures as fast as she could. She never checked to see if Mira was watching, but even from a distance, Mira could feel the tension surrounding her, tightening like a fist.

"Let me help." Mira picked her way across the room and bent down for the remaining stray holos. Renee's image grinned at her, waist-deep in the calm sea. It was a knowledgeable, superior smile.

"Thank you, D'sha," whispered the girl, as Mira handed her the snapshots, like it was some great act of generosity.

"There's no need for you to rush through this stuff," said Mira. "I've been to a lot of interesting places. If you have questions about anything, you should ask."

"Yes D'sha." She glanced at the holos, very briefly, without any discernible interest. "Where should I put these, D'sha?"

"It doesn't matter," said Mira. "As long as you know where they are."

Maybe the only School training that *had* worked was the part that had killed her curiosity. Mira retreated to the monitor and cleared the screen. She could feel the hard plastic edge of the girl's ID card in her pocket, and she pulled it out reluctantly. She hated to think of Amrei as a good judge of character, but the facts were very straightforward. Costa was a product of the School, and if she had been bred in the Faraque by Raffail and his kin, as Mira was beginning to suspect, she should have been the picture of obedience. Even if she had been ordered to run away, eluding some maniac with horses and dogs should not have been something she was capable of.

Mira pressed the card into the monitor's slot and turned the screen so there was no chance the girl could see it.

A date flickered into view, almost two years earlier, and a holo materialized underneath it—Costa, with her arms locked behind her. She kept her eyes on the ground while someone outside the frame ordered her, in Emirate, to look at the camera. Her clothes were fresh, but her expression was exhausted, deeply afraid, and she stared at the camera as if she had no idea what it was. A hand reached out and turned her to one side, pulling the sleeve off her shoulder to reveal new brands: her number and the Sector eye, but no School mark, not yet. A voice barked a command in some foreign language. She dropped to her knees, head down.

The language was unfamiliar, probably an obscure Faraque dialect, but recognizing Raffail's voice was easy. Mira paged forward grimly.

Another holo of Costa appeared, this time just underneath the School's elaborate, looping logo. Her face had been daubed with makeup, and her hair was pulled back into a stylish braid. Mira checked the date. Her entry into the School was easily three months after Raffail had gotten his hands on her, and the effects of spending that much time under the Sectors' tight control was obvious. The girl's face was expressionless, blank as the slaves Mira had seen on Traja in the School tent.

The holo shrank in size to make room for the list of training tests that the School had recorded on the card. There were dozens, including everything from table service to the Sixty-Nine Nights. Costa's ratings were listed next to each one, and most really were abysmally low. At that moment in the other room, Mira heard the girl catch her breath. She looked up in time to see Costa grab for something small and fragile, catching it just before it hit the floor. Mira rubbed her forehead and accessed the table service tests.

The screen wavered for a second, then dissolved into a shot of a luxurious dining room. Well-dressed men and women sat around the table, waiting, as a tense blonde slave poured drinks. There was nothing graceful about her movements. Her face was a study in anxiety as she served everything from the wrong side. One of the diners, apparently a trainer, tried to correct her, one last time, speaking slowly and loudly in Emirate. He pointed to his glass and plate as he spoke, and she, obviously not understanding a word he said, poured the wine out in rapid glugs until the glass overflowed.

Mira checked the date of the test without enthusiasm. Halfway through a ten-month program, and the girl was still quite obviously far from fluent. To an unsympathetic eye, such as Amrei's, her mistakes looked idiotic, maybe even purposefully antagonistic. Mira studied the girls tense shoulders in the next room, looking carefully for some obvious sign of guile, willfulness, or even plain deceit. If it was there, it was incredibly well hidden.

The last tests on the list, which seemed to be chronological, were from the Sixty-Nine Nights. Mira skipped past them, totally uninterested in seeing exactly what Enhancers could do, and paged forward until she found the man that the girl had run away from.

His name was Regis, and he'd paid less than two thousand for her. There wasn't much information on him except for his location—a long, long way from Traja. His commentary was short and to the point. The girl was uncooperative and had resisted him, especially when it came to sex, and she had run away. There were two pictures of Costa. In the first one, just after he'd bought her, she was hardly recognizable under the lipstick and rouge. In the second shot, her face was hidden behind the tangle of her hair as she knelt in the dirt, bloody and disheveled, identifiable only by the brand on her arm. He'd kept her for barely six months.

The Mine entry was next. There was no picture, just a date of purchase from about four months ago.

Mira tapped the key that would allow her to record new data and then stopped. The information on a slave's ID was necessarily a matter of public record. By law, anyone who bought another human being was required to record the transaction so that runaways could be traced and stolen property recovered.

Mira frowned as the image of Trent's angry face came back very clearly, almost as though it were actually on the screen right now. Anyone who knew Costa's ID number could search a general registry to find out where she was. If Trent were feeling meddlesome—and that was not unheard of—Mira had no doubt that whatever moral victory she had achieved by saving Costa from the Mines would be rapidly eclipsed by instant unemployment. She put her hands in her lap, breaking the law as she sat there, and wondered exactly what it was that made these actions so compelling.

It still felt odd to be closing the bedroom door after all these years of living alone. Mira sat on the bed, listlessly pulling a brush through her hair, watching the indistinct shadow of her reflection as it moved in the mirror across the room. She hadn't chained Costa tonight. It really didn't seem necessary.

Earlier, she'd led the girl through the maze of corridors to the mess hall, past the conservatory and the observation levels, in hopes that the change of scenery might provoke a question or two. Costa had followed her silently, invisible and correct, two steps behind, apparently oblivious to everything but Mira's desires.

At dinner, the girl had waited on her with painstaking perfection. Her tension transferred itself by degrees to the pit of Mira's stomach, making it virtually impossible to eat, much less attempt a conversation. By the end of the meal, Mira decided it was best to interpret the entire day as an exercise in overwhelming gratitude. She went to bed very early to avoid any more of it.

Mira undressed slowly and crawled under the covers. With Amrei becoming more of a thorn between her and Vince, and this uncommunicative stranger in her own quarters, it was starting to look like a long, long mission. It was rather ironic, she thought unhappily, that after the trouble she'd gone through to avoid getting a slave emptied of all personality, she'd ended up with one who was intent upon doing the job herself. Mira shut her eyes, trying not to think about it.

There was a very timid knock on the door.

"Yes?"

Costa pushed the door open and stood in the sliver of light. "Please, D'sha. Do you want me tonight?"

Mira sat up uneasily, not sure for a moment what she meant. "Oh. No. I mean. . .haven't you had enough of that?"

The girl stepped into the room and it must have taken all her courage. "I just want to do something right for you today, D'sha."

"You're doing fine," said Mira nervously.

Costa stopped. "You don't like girls."

"Yes I do."

Costa moved further into the room until she was standing in front of the view-windows. Outside, the effects of light speed had changed the stars into a vast field of frozen fireworks, and her silhouette hugged itself. "It's the marks," she said. "I'm ugly to you."

"You're not," said Mira.

Costa came closer, making herself do it, and knelt on the floor next to the bed. "I just want you to be glad you bought me," she said. "I don't think you are. They told us the first night was the most important, and I didn't. . . I didn't do anything."

"As I recall," said Mira, "you were chained to the sofa."

"I can make it up to you," said the girl desperately, as though it were her fault.

There was no easy way out of this, Mira realized. Telling her to leave would just make her feel like a failure. Letting her stay wouldn't really solve anything, either.

"Look," said Mira, "you can stay in here tonight, but you're going to have to do something for me first."

Costa bowed her head. "Yes D'sha," she said, as though it was what she'd been expecting all along.

"You're going to have to talk to me," said Mira. "Proper or not, we're going to have a conversation."

The girl looked up uneasily. "D'sha?"

"Conversation," repeated Mira. "And then if you're still in the mood. . . ." She shrugged, "We'll see if *I* am."

Costa blinked in unguarded confusion. "What do you want to talk about?"

Good question. Mira pulled the sheets around herself, feeling very self-consciously undressed, and patted the mattress. "Come up here."

The girl perched on the very edge of the bed, hands knotted together in her lap. Her shirt was already partly open, and her pale skin gleamed under the folds of white fabric.

Mira reached for the hairbrush, feeling Costa watch her, all nerves, as if this were the moment of truth that would reveal bedroom horrors even the School hadn't prepared her for.

"Turn around," said Mira, and she made a vague gesture at the girl's long hair, still tangled. Costa had been raking at it with her fingers for most of the day, but without much visible progress. She hesitated, and Mira held the brush out with a shrug. "You're welcome to do it yourself."

Costa turned, shoulders hunched, and Mira tugged at the first of the knots, as gently as she could.

Except for the husk of the brush, it was suddenly very quiet. "Why didn't they let you wash?" Mira asked after a moment.

"It was my punishment, D'sha."

"For what?"

"For being School, D'sha."

It made as much sense as anything else. Mira worked her way through the snarls, waiting for the girl to relax, even by a fraction. She didn't, and after a while, the silence was too thick, too expectant.

"Your Emirate is really flawless," said Mira, trying to sound unconcerned. "You must be good at languages." She felt the girl tense under her fingers, gathering the courage for something other than a yes or no answer.

"They had to teach me with machines, D'sha," she said softly. Mira nodded. Machine-assisted language learning was hardly uncommon. "How long did it take?"

"Two months? Three? I'm not sure, D'sha."

Even the switch to Emirate from some obscure Faraque dialect should only have taken a couple of weeks. After all, it was done while you slept. Mira had learned most of her Remini linguistics from machines on the outpost, and it was usually very effective.

Mira pulled through another knot. "That seems like an awfully long time. Maybe they were trying to teach you something else while you were sleeping?"

The girl actually trembled. "I couldn't sleep," she whispered. "I haven't slept—" She stopped herself, hands clenched in her lap.

Mira frowned. Maybe something really *was* wrong here. She smoothed the thick curls. "What's the matter?"

Costa took a deep, controlling breath. "Nothing, D'sha."

Her face was still turned away, but Mira could see her reflection in the mirror across the room. The strange, surreal light from the stars rippled across her face, wavy patterns that caught in her hair, turning it silver instead of gold. The mirror glimmered, almost like a pool of water, and Costa's vague image shivered there, like something below the surface, close enough to see, but just out of reach. Mira found herself staring, not at the success of Sector eugenics, but at what had come out of the Faraque in spite of it.

Costa turned around cautiously to face her, and Mira looked away from the mirror and into the girl's eyes. The anxiety was still there, but what was even more obvious was the extent of her exhaustion. Mira touched her forehead without thinking, but there was no flinch this time. "When was the last time you had any sleep?"

Costa blinked and bit her lip, like she was counting. "It's been a long time, D'sha," she said finally. "Not since I was collared."

"You haven't slept in two years?" Mira frowned. "That's not possible."

"It's true, D'sha. At the School. . . ." She hesitated. "I couldn't learn anything. I have terrible dreams."

It was certainly understandable that after spending three months with Raffail and his minions, one might very well be too terrified to close one's eyes for more than a few hours. Add the School regimen on top of that, and insomnia was practically a guarantee. "Did you sleep at all last night?" asked Mira, knowing perfectly well that she hadn't. Costa shook her head. Mira patted her hand lightly, dismissively. "I think we should save the sex until you've had some rest, don't you?"

She meant it as a joke, but the girl glanced up in sudden alarm, and her hand pressed against Mira's knee, through the sheets. "I'm not tired, D'sha."

The actual physical contact ran through Mira's body like an electrical shock. She caught Costa's hand before it went any farther. Cool, slender fingers met hers, and a moist palm. There was no resistance, no tension. And no discernible interest.

Mira held the hand as long as she dared. "Maybe you're the one who doesn't like girls."

"That doesn't matter."

"Yes it does," said Mira, and let go.

Costa sat in silence, utterly trapped by her conditioning.

"Do you even know what you like?" asked Mira after a moment. "Or did they tell you to forget your preferences?"

The girl nodded slowly, not looking up.

Mira leaned against the headboard, wishing that putting her arms around this pathetic child was the proper thing to do. "Well?" she said. "What do you prefer? Boys or girls?"

"I don't know, D'sha."

"What do you mean you don't know? You can't remember because of the Enhancers?"

Costa stared at her hands. "I never. . .we couldn't. . . ." She licked her lips nervously. "I never really knew, D'sha."

No doubt in the Faraque, the Sector collar their virgins, Mira thought in disgust. They probably made more money that way. "Look," she said wearily, "we're not going to have any sex tonight. Is that clear?"

Costa didn't answer, but her shoulders tensed. "I'm sorry—"

"Don't be," said Mira. "I think I'm the one who's too tired." She pulled the sheets up over her shoulders and curled up against the pillows. "Get some sleep, Costa," she said. "Consider that an order," she added.

Mira shut her eyes and felt the girl move off the edge of the bed. The sound of her bare feet on the thin carpet moved toward the doorway, then stopped.

Mira looked up through slit eyelids to see Costa standing in the middle of the room, staring at the mirror. From where she was, Mira could barely make out her own image, ambiguously dark against the sheets. Costa touched her face, oblivious to the fact that she was being watched, and spread her hair over her shoulders with a sort of bewildered hesitation. She studied the reflection for another moment, and then went slowly into the main room.

Mira kept her eyes open as long as she could, waiting for the girl to lie down, but she didn't. She just stood there, in front of the open view-windows, a vague shadow against distorted stars. Even after Mira fell asleep, her dreams were thick with that emanating wakefulness.

7

She was still tired when she woke up. Mira huddled under the covers a little longer, staring at the silent explosion of colors in the blackness outside her window. This morning it bothered her that the actual trappings of morning, such as a sunrise, were missing from the ship, and the best she could look forward to was an extension of last night. Mira closed her eyes again. It irritated her to think that Amrei might just be right, that there really was no possibility for friendship: Costa would simply have to learn to be a slave, while Mira learned to be the master.

The smell of coffee floated in from the next room, but she resisted and took a shower first. She soaped herself resignedly in the tiny stall, while the weak stream of water splashed on her shoulders. The mission was hard enough without the extra issue of worrying about the mental welfare of someone she barely knew, someone who, quite simply, was born for the position she was now in.

Mira toweled her hair with a vengeance, watching herself in the mirror as it billowed out into an uncontrollable black cloud. She draped the towel around her neck, scowling at her reflection. "I don't have to care," she said, but it was too obvious a lie.

Costa was kneeling by the window staring absently into space, quite literally, thought Mira. She closed the door again, a little more loudly this time, and the girl jumped to her feet.

She looked as worn out as Mira felt. "Good morning, D'sha," she mumbled politely, and hurried to pour a cup of coffee.

"Good morning," repeated Mira, even though it didn't look all that promising. She took the cup and bent over the monitor, keying in the codes for last night's dispatches.

There was a note from Harlan Mahai at the Point Seven Station, but nothing else. Mira read it as it printed out. It was Harlan's usual style, flippant and verbose, full of obscure references to current politics, and, as usual, very little of it seemed to pertain to what she had to do. Mira was ready to throw it away when she saw the last few lines:

> . . . *have also compiled a complete decipher-*
> *ence, if you will, of the confounded hand-*
> *language the Sector use. Maybe you have some-*
> *thing to trade? Where you're going, you'll prob-*
> *ably need it.*
>
> *Yours/Mahai*

The idea of being indebted to Harlan for something was enough to kill her appetite. She balled the letter up and sat down at the table anyway.

Costa stood quietly behind her, just to the right, still holding onto the pot of coffee. Mira set her cup down. The girl immediately refilled it.

"Have you eaten yet?" asked Mira.

"Yes D'sha."

"Come over here where I can see you."

The girl obeyed, head bowed. The only thing that seemed to be keeping her from falling to her knees was the fact that she had to keep an eye on the table.

"I don't suppose you got any sleep," said Mira.

"No D'sha."

No wonder she dropped things and couldn't concentrate. Mira ate in silence, trying to remember what she knew about the Drug and its side effects. She'd heard of people who'd lost their vision or even their hearing upon being collared, and she'd met slaves who couldn't sweat—a variety of peculiar things. But she'd never heard of a slave with insomnia, certainly not two years' worth.

She pushed her plate aside wearily. "I'm going to put you to work today," she said. "Come on."

She sat the girl down in front of the monitor and reached over her shoulder to bring up the first portion of Trent's briefing on the Faraque. The file was huge, ambitious even for Trent. It contained every map, every scrap of history, and the opinions of a good many people Mira had absolutely no respect for. If nothing else, when Costa was through reading this, the two of them would have slightly more to talk about, maybe even things to disagree on.

Mira leaned on the back of the chair as Trent's image glowed on the screen. "Remember her?"

The girl nodded, but didn't seem terribly certain. "Ambassador Trent?"

"Very good." Mira keyed forward and brought up the next page, the printed information. "Have you used this kind of system before?"

"No D'sha."

"It's easy," said Mira. She pointed to the only two buttons that Costa needed to touch. "This one pages forward, this one moves back. Just read everything in the first section. . .that's the overview for the mission. We'll discuss it when you're done."

"Yes D'sha."

Her voice was small and tight. Something seemed to be wrong, but whatever it was, it wasn't obvious.

"If you have questions," said Mira, "ask." She picked up a handful of papers lying on the desk and started to walk away.

Costa was staring alternately at the screen and the keyboard, her hands wound tightly in her lap.

"What's the matter?"

The girl took a deep breath. "I can't read this," she said in a tiny voice. "Can you make it talk?"

"Talk?" repeated Mira. "What do you mean you can't read it?"

"I was never taught, D'sha," she said helplessly.

Mira leaned over the chair again and stared at the screen herself to make sure there wasn't some kind of glitch scrambling the letters. There wasn't. Everything was perfectly legible. If one could read. She rubbed her head, not knowing what to say. It was incredible to her that the School would risk its reputation by letting an illiterate slip past.

"I can learn this, D'sha," said Costa urgently. "Just make it talk."

There was a setting for the visually impaired. Mira changed the machine's bias and turned away as the thing began to speak in its flat monotone, neither male nor female. She sat back down at the table and poured another cup of coffee while the girl concentrated on the screen, staring at the writing as though she could decipher it if she watched and listened at the same time.

Mira looked away in despair. There were machine programs to teach reading the same way the School had taught Costa to speak the common language, but they were expensive. In this part of space, Mira doubted if they were even available. She stared at her own paperwork, trying to focus through the endless monotone, but it was too distracting. The droning stopped at the end of its page, and Mira waited for the next one. She could hear Costa tentatively tapping the keys, but other than that, the monitor was silent. The girl had probably closed the file by accident and was now most likely lost in the system, erasing things. Mira got up quickly to see what she could do about it.

A hard-eyed young man stared out of the screen at her, the blue Sector strip crossing his face. The Sector file was still incomplete, and Mira wasn't sure who he was. Harlan had promised to send background information on all the Faraque regulars, but she was still waiting. It had been over six weeks.

Mira touched the key that would exit the file. "This is for later," she said. "I don't even know these guys yet."

"I do."

The key was sticking and Mira tapped it again. "I'm sure you do," she said, "but I need to know family relationships. Who's in charge, things like that."

"He's Raffail's son," whispered Costa. "His name is Jezr'el. He's Raffail's right hand."

Mira hesitated. She'd never been under the impression that Raffail liked women enough to produce a child. "How do you know?"

"I was his."

Mira frowned at the man, insensitive and harsh under the blue paint. The name was certainly familiar. He was mentioned in a number of reports from the Faraque. "What else do you know about him?"

"He's different from his father," said the girl softly, as though the image itself might hear. "He's. . .unpredictable."

She was afraid of him, that much was very clear. "Who else do you know?"

"His uncles. Raffail's brothers."

Mira paged the file forward to the next unfamiliar face, an older man, Raffail's age. "Do you know him?"

She did and she named him. She knew his sons, and the names of his wives, although she'd never seen them. She knew how many slaves he owned, and the name of his ship. Mira let her move through the file, just listening. There were gaps in her knowledge, and things she obviously wasn't sure of, but Mira suspected that this was not the kind of information she would ever get from Harlan. It was far more detailed, more personal, much more useful.

"How do you know all this?" asked Mira. "Were you told or did you just overhear?"

"I overheard most of it, D'sha," she said. "A lot of it was in Emirate, but they spoke my language too. There were too many slaves who didn't understand anything else. No one cared if we were listening."

"Why did you listen?" asked Mira. "What difference did it make to you?"

"I was looking for someone. I thought I could find her if I could find the right person to ask."

"Did you find her?"

Costa shook her head. It was almost a shudder. "They got rid of me."

"You know a lot more than I do," said Mira. "You probably know more than the people at Point Seven. I'll bet you've seen more of the Faraque than anyone else around here."

Costa looked up questioningly. "The what, D'sha?"

"The Faraque," repeated Mira, and she smiled before the girl remembered to avert her eyes. "I'll show you."

She found Trent's stash of maps and put the first one on the screen. "You recognize this?"

"Galaxy," said the girl.

Even without an accent, it was easy to tell that neither the picture nor the concept was terribly familiar. Mira brought up the next map, the one that showed border delineations. She pointed at the dot that was Traja. In the scale of things, the Frontier between Traja and the red line that edged the Faraque was no more than a finger's width. "This is where I bought you. See the red line?"

She nodded.

"That's where the Emirate ends and the Faraque begins. Everything past that line belongs to Raffail and his family."

"The Faraque," repeated Costa. "That's where they keep their slaves."

Smarter than she acted. "Right," said Mira. "But technically, they're not slaves. We refer to them as breeding populations." Mira moved her finger along the blue line that included Traja. "That's the old border for the Faraque. Two hundred years ago the Emirate drove the Sector back across a third of their territory."

"They didn't fight?" Costa's vague reflection was just visible, frowning in the dark sections of the map.

"They tried," said Mira. "Then they gave up and ran for their lives. This ship was part of the attack."

"What about their slaves?" The girl traced the swath between the blue and red borders, ignoring Mira's semantic distinction.

"The Sector took a lot of them further into the Faraque," said Mira. "But they didn't have time to be very picky. If they were in a hurry, they just. . .well, eliminated everyone who was too much trouble."

"There was no one left when the Emirate came?"

"Actually," said Mira, "there were quite a few survivors. They're citizens now. They don't have to worry about their children being made into slaves."

Silence. Mira wondered if she was making any impression at all. "Want to see where we're going?" she asked.

"Please, D'sha."

Mira tapped the very center of the Faraque itself. "We're not invading this time," she said. "Not in the traditional way. We're going to see if we can buy our way into Sector territory."

Costa didn't say anything, but her hands gripped each other more tightly and her knuckles whitened.

Should have waited to tell her that. She might have asked an intelligent question or two. Mira gave herself a mental kick and went on anyway. "Nobody has the money to waste on another war," she said. "The Emirate is expanding, though, and the Emir's friends have convinced him that it's actually cheaper to pay the Sector for the planets we want than it is to launch the fleet. Of course the military has a few doubts about that, but they're not as worried about the Sector as they are about what's out *here.*" She tapped the edge of the map where the Faraque ended and, for all practical purposes, the Remini had control. "The only aliens we've ever come in contact with are out here someplace."

"Aliens?" Costa hadn't taken her eyes off the map. The idea of being taken right back into the heart of Sector space probably scared her to death.

"Commonly called the Remini. No one's ever actually seen one . . . it doesn't seem like a good idea to get too close to them, but they seem to be headed away from us. If we don't bother them, they may not even notice we're here."

"What do you need me for?" asked the girl nervously.

Mira patted her on the shoulder. "All you've got to do is pour the drinks and serve sandwiches. It looks very low-class when I do those things myself."

"Yes D'sha."

"So, what's your opinion?" asked Mira.

"Opinion?"

"Sure," said Mira. "There are thousands of people on the planets we plan to buy. They come with the asking price. What do you think we should do with them?"

"D'sha," said Costa hesitantly, "they're slaves."

"Not until they're collared." She shut her mouth and waited. There was still an intelligence under all that abuse, and it was time to find out what she really thought.

"D'sha," Costa said after a long moment, "they'll be moved to other worlds?"

"Not according to the contract," said Mira. "We get the planets and all resources, mineral and organic."

The girl bit her lip. "Make them slaves then."

"We've got plenty of slaves. Too many if you ask me."

"You'd free them?" Costa blinked at the map. "They'd be citizens?"

"Assimilation can be a difficult thing," said Mira, trying to sound offhand and unconcerned. "Do you think they could do it?"

"I don't know."

Maybe she really didn't, but Mira doubted it. "Give it some thought," she said. "We can talk more about this later."

Mira reached over Costa's shoulder and tapped the key that would bring her back to Trent's tedious introduction, but the screen flickered momentarily, and then switched itself off somehow, fading to dull silver.

Mira hit the reset as fast as she could, picturing all her files disappearing into electronic oblivion. Nothing happened. The only thing on the screen was her own reflection, a mass of black hair and the glint of eyes in her own dark face, floating next to Costa's uncertain expression. Mira puttered frantically, awkwardly with the keyboard as Costa sat there, staring at the reflective surface, one hand at her throat. The girl reached for the screen, oblivious to what Mira was doing and put her fingers against it. For a second Mira thought she saw something flickering in the glass, something more than two indistinct images. She brushed Costa's hand away, and peered intently at the monitor, at her own face. The girl's image stared back in obvious amazement, like it was the first time they'd ever seen each other.

Mira straightened, panicked now. "Get up," she said. "Let me see if I can fix this thing."

Costa stumbled out of her way as the files reappeared, neatly menued and intact. Mira glanced at the girl, relieved, but Costa was still staring at her with an unidentifiable expression on her face. It was tempting to call it recognition.

Mira frowned. "Is something wrong?"

Costa shook her head wordlessly.

Mira brought Trent's file back onto the monitor feeling oddly self-conscious. "Keep working on these," she said. "I'll be in the other room if you need help." Mira scooped her papers up and retreated into the bedroom.

It took a long time for her to get her mind back on what she was supposed to be doing.

Mira sat on the bed in the center of her paperwork, staring out the window, trying to decide what, if anything, had just happened. On the one hand, it was easy enough to dismiss the girl's off-centeredness as a result of physical stress and mental trauma, but she was starting to think there was more to it.

The reflection was the problem. It was difficult for Mira to pin down exactly what made the girl's reaction to the blank screen so disturbing. There had been something very odd about that single moment. Just thinking about it was making her skin prickle, like it was much colder in her bedroom than it should be. Mira rubbed her arms and frowned at the paperwork, trying to make herself concentrate. If there was something fundamentally wrong with Costa, it would surface again. The next time, she would be ready, waiting to put a name to it.

An hour later Mira looked up to see the girl standing in the doorway. "Are you stuck?"

Costa nodded and took a cautious step inside. She was holding a small piece of paper in one hand, palming it. Mira couldn't tell what it was. "I got to the schedule. After that I didn't understand what she was talking about."

Mira raised an eyebrow. "You're not the only one."

Costa sat on the bed, one knee drawn up under her, but surprisingly close. "I know Ankea and Traja, D'sha," she said. "But I don't know Point Seven."

"That's the Emirate military base on the edge of the Faraque," said Mira. "We'll be there tomorrow. It's the last stop before we cross the border."

"And Harlan Mahai is there? The other diplomat?"

At least she really did seem to be trying. Mira smiled. "We use the term loosely with Harlan," she said dryly.

Costa looked at her—actually did look at her—with a questioning frown. "What do you mean?"

"Let me put it this way," said Mira. "Harlan is the best source of pertinent gossip in the entire quadrant, but as far as his job goes, he's got a boy who does all his work for him. If he didn't have Jeremy, he'd be way over his head out here."

"You don't like him?"

Mira shrugged. "I'm just jealous. His parents are bigwigs in the government, and they had him transferred out here when it looked like an easy posting. Now, when there's something to do in the Faraque, Trent won't make him go."

"Maybe she knows his slave does everything."

It was possible. And Trent wasn't one to risk treading on political toes by making a fuss about something like that. "Maybe," said Mira. "I prefer to think of it as favoritism." She smiled. "You'll like Jeremy, though. He's one of the smartest people I've ever met." In fact, he was the only reason she had to look forward to arriving at Point Seven. Mira pointed at the paper in Costa's hand. "What's this?"

It was one of the old holograms of Mira and Renee on the beach.

Costa laid it on the bed. "Can I ask you something, D'sha?"

"Sure." In the picture, Renee caught her from behind, her dark face partly obscured by Mira's wild hair. Mira ran her thumb along the edge of the holo. "This was a long time ago," she said.

"You don't look any different."

Actually, it was hard to tell. The sun had been too strong for the camera, and all that was really visible of her younger self were her eyes. Eyes and hair and brown skin. "You can hardly see me."

"It was dark," said the girl.

"What?" Mira looked up from the blindingly blue sky of a world almost a parsec away.

Costa bit her lip. "Was she your slave?"

Mira nodded, still wondering what she'd said.

"Was she School?"

"No." Mira smiled, trying to picture Renee being even a tiny bit submissive. "I don't think she was what you'd call School material."

"When I saw the picture the first time," said Costa, "I thought she was your sister. I didn't see the collar."

Was the relationship so obvious, Mira wondered, that this stranger could see the depth of it from a snapshot? "She was a good friend," said Mira quietly.

"What happened to her?"

"She's dead by now."

"She Failed?"

Mira sighed and put the picture down. "She ran away from me one day. I never hurt her," she said quickly. "She just got tired of me. I don't know where she ended up. I looked for months, but after a while it seemed pretty useless."

Costa didn't say anything, and Mira couldn't tell if she even believed the story. "She might have gotten caught," she said at last. "They would have put her in the Mine line."

"I looked," said Mira. "I spent so much time trying to find her I nearly got fired."

"Is that why you were in the Mine tent on Traja? You were looking for her?"

Mira shook her head. "This was six years ago. I was just trying to get out of the rain that night."

"You weren't trying to find someone?"

"No," said Mira, confused. "I was lost."

Costa picked up the holo. "Is this where you lived?" she asked, tracing the edge of the beach. "By a lake?"

"It's an ocean," said Mira. "We were just visiting."

"Could you see yourself in it?"

Mira shook her head, confused. "You ask the strangest questions."

Costa looked up at her. "Why did you buy me, D'sha?"

"You were School." Mira shrugged, not understanding what she wanted to know. "You were in trouble. Aren't those the right reasons?"

Costa nodded slowly and rubbed her eyes. She leaned forward, and to Mira's amazement, wrapped her arms around her neck. "You saved me," she whispered. "How do I thank you for that?"

Mira held her tightly. "You don't have to." Unexpected emotions were crowding inside her chest. She closed her eyes and stroked the girl's back, running her hands across the flat, distinct scars. Mira pressed her face against the soft curls, waiting for her to relax, wanting her to be able to sleep—like this, warm and finally secure.

It was late in the afternoon when Mira woke up. Her arm was sound asleep, and so was Costa. Mira untangled herself carefully. The girl was curled up against the pillows, peaceful. Very young-looking, Mira decided, and painfully vulnerable. She gathered up her papers and tucked the covers around Costa's bare feet. Better that she would wake up by herself than in strange company. Mira kissed her lightly on the forehead and left her alone.

Sometime around midnight, Mira's eyes started closing by themselves. Costa hadn't moved except to turn over, and now she was squarely in the middle of the bed. Mira's resolute intentions about letting her sleep alone, for as long as she needed to, were starting to waver as it got later and later. She took her shoes off at the bedroom door and came in silently. She'd almost decided that the couch was a more honorable option, but it was too narrow and hard. Mira pulled her clothes off except for her shirt and crawled under the blankets, carefully arranging herself away from Costa's arms and legs. The position she ended up in was awkward enough to make her think twice about the couch, but it was too much work to get up again. Mira lay back, listening to the girl's slow breathing.

Half an hour later, she was still wide awake.

Mira turned over carefully. From outside, the lacework of light silvered in Costa's hair, shimmering over her face as her eyelids fluttered in dreams.

How old had she been when Raffail had taken her away from her home? Eighteen? Nineteen? Had she fought? Had she tried to run? Would anyone on her homeworld have dared to help her? Or had she been completely alone when the slavers came?

Mira let out her breath. This kind of curiosity was pointless, frustrating. Whatever questions she had, she would never be able to ask them. The best she could hope for was that one day, Costa might tell her a few of the details of her time with the Sector—but after they had kidnapped her, not before.

Costa sighed and opened her eyes.

Mira moved away, abruptly embarrassed, feeling a little too voyeuristic. Costa blinked at her. "You're awake."

"I couldn't get to sleep," said Mira.

"Oh." She pressed the heels of her hands against her eyes. "I had a dream about you." She looked at Mira with sleepy conviction. "It was you." If anything, she sounded relieved. "What do you dream about?"

"Me?" Mira shrugged. "I can never remember."

Costa frowned, like it wasn't the answer she'd expected. "Why didn't you buy someone else when your girl ran away?"

"I didn't want to."

"You've spent six years by yourself?"

"Well," said Mira, "I haven't been alone. I have Vince. I have friends." It was odd to be having a conversation in the middle of the night, but, Mira thought, better now than never. And it was terribly refreshing not to be called D'sha in every other sentence.

"I wouldn't have run away," said Costa.

Mira smiled. "Amrei thinks you'll be gone the minute we set foot on solid ground."

"Do you think so?"

"No."

"Six years is a long time." The girl rolled over a little closer, and Mira edged back.

Costa blinked up at her. "What's the matter?"

"You don't have to sleep in here if you don't want to," said Mira nervously.

"Do you want me to leave?"

Mira hesitated, completely unsure of the right answer.

The girl took her hand, very gently, by her fingertips. "You think I'm still afraid."

"Aren't you?" breathed Mira.

She shook her head. "I know who you are now."

Who am I? Mira wanted to ask, but the kiss stopped any words. It was a sleepy, soft, compelling kiss, and Mira tried hard to push away the undeniable craving inside of her that felt more like starvation. Costa moved even closer. Mira lay back on the bed stiffly, expecting the School's skillful indifference in the girl's touch, working up the strength to tell her to stop.

Costa leaned over and kissed her again, lightly. Her hand slid inside Mira's shirt and Mira shivered, her convictions crumbling as delicate fingers explored the curve of her breast.

Warm lips brushed her neck, down around the collar of her shirt. Costa started to open the fastenings. Mira caught her wrists, but it was already too late to stop.

"Which night is this?" she asked breathlessly.

Costa gave her a puzzled look. "It isn't any of them. I can't remember enough." She pulled one hand away and touched Mira's face. "What's wrong?"

"I don't want you to do this because you think you *have* to," Mira whispered desperately.

The girl pulled her other hand loose. "But I want to," she said. "I had a dream about you."

Mira closed her eyes as warm hands touched her and the soft mouth traveled along her body leaving a trail as hot as fire. The last traces of her resistance drifted away like smoke. She stroked the girl's hair, her shoulders, twisting closer as Costa pressed against her hips.

To Mira's relief, there was nothing especially practiced about the way the girl touched her. Instead of being professionally seduced, Mira began to feel more like she was being explored, even savored. The girl moved lower, searching and probing until she found the very center of Mira's desire. Mira felt the touch of her tongue and the rest of her self-control vanished. She squeezed her eyes shut against the irresistible wave of sensation, holding her breath until the she couldn't anymore. Six years of loneliness and denial ended too quickly, shaking her, wrenching her.

Costa moved up the bed, and Mira rolled against her, panting, pulling her close, kissing her wet mouth. She nuzzled the girl's throat, her ear lobes and shoulders, kissing and caressing until she finally noticed the unmistakable tension in Costa's body. Mira pulled away abruptly, afraid she'd already gone too far.

"I'll stop," Mira whispered, "if it's what you want."

Costa shook her head nervously and lay back on the pillows, flushed even in the darkness.

Mira slowed down, watching her face, searching more carefully for the boundaries that had no doubt been formed by two years of abuse. She ran her hand over the girl's shirt, tracing the edge of one small, practical breast. Costa took a sharp breath and caught her fingers.

"It's alright," said Mira. "I'll stop."

"No. . . ." She guided Mira's hand inside. "Don't."

Mira pushed the rest of the girl's clothing away, cautious, gentle. Except for the scars, there was not a single flaw on her, not physically. Mira moved one hand past her waist, her navel, lingering over the soft curves of her belly and hips. Generations of breeding had gone into this graceful figure, small-boned, delicate but not fragile. There was an unexplainable sturdiness to her that had nothing to do with her size or her build. It was an invisible thing, a deep kind of strength the Sector and the School had missed entirely, and that she had done her best to hide, even from herself.

Mira moved her hand slowly to the tangle of crisp hair and the promising wetness there. She waited for the flash of passion she remembered from her years with Renee, but what she felt instead was a steady patience, a compelling desire to share the intimate pleasures this girl knew so much about and, at the same time, so little.

She slid her fingers into the warm, distinct terrain, exploring tentatively over familiar hills and valleys. Costa's breath came out as a short rush of air against her ear, and Mira found the crease of her sensitivity, moist, deeply hidden. She ran her fingers over the whorl of flesh, smoothing away all traces of the Sector and the School, until she was sure the girl was focused entirely on her and what she was doing.

Costa shivered against her, one lip caught between her teeth. Mira dawdled over her until she groaned.

"I could stop," whispered Mira. "If you like."

The girl took a couple of panting breaths, inarticulate words catching in her throat. Mira caught the rhythm of her breathing and copied it with her fingers, pinching softly, pressing harder, alternating until the tension in the girl's hips broke and she jerked hard, too surprised to even make a sound. Her body arched, rigid, and she fell back on the bed, damp and breathless.

Mira smoothed the curls away from her forehead. "Did I scare you?" she said, only partly joking.

Costa shook her head and let out a sigh. "That's what you pay for?"

"My dear," said Mira. "You're the first time I've *ever* paid for that."

Costa made a soft noise, like a laugh, and Mira eased herself back, letting the girl lay on her chest, a dense, comfortable weight over her heart. Costa's breathing slowed. Mira put a protective arm over the girl's shoulders, drinking in the scent of her, beautiful, fragrant, and, as she drifted off to sleep herself, more familiar than Renee had ever been.

8

n its previous incarnation as a nameless, lifeless moon, the Point Seven Station had been a rather uninviting place. Now that the military had covered it with atmosphere domes, open-air housing, and a number of choice weapons systems, it had lost the advantage of its anonymity, and seemed more like a target than a place to live.

The skimmer that Harlan had so graciously sent to pick up Mira from the Ground Station let her and Costa off in front of what Mira could only describe as a comfortable little bungalow. The front yard was neatly mowed, and layers of flowering vines shaded the trellised brick walkways.

The sight of it all was enough to make Mira intensely jealous. She knocked on the door loudly.

The boy who answered wasn't Jeremy. It was a slave Mira didn't recognize, strikingly Oriental, and unmistakably Sector-bred, with straight black hair that fell to his shoulders. As he knelt on the doorstep, Mira realized with a sinking feeling that Jeremy was gone and that Harlan had managed to get himself a School slave.

"I'm Mira LoDire," she said. "Is this Emissary Mahai's house?"

"Yes D'LoDire. He's expecting you."

They followed him around to the back of the house, past lush and ostentatious landscaping. Harlan was sitting next to the pool in a lawn chair, a towel around his shoulders, sunning himself on the patio.

"Mira!" he said, "what a pleasure. And you're on time, too." He looked past her at Costa, and an amazed grin slid over his face as the girl dropped to her knees. He started to laugh. "I can't believe my eyes. Mira LoDire bought a slave."

"And you got rid of yours," replied Mira. She sat down without being invited and nodded at the boy. "Who's this?"

"I haven't decided what to call him," said Harlan. "I keep thinking of names like Ashley, or Drew. Nothing seems quite right." He held out his hand, and the boy knelt next him like a good dog, while Harlan caressed his cheek.

"What did you do with Jeremy?"

Harlan shrugged. "I sold him. I'd rather have School, wouldn't you?" He glanced pointedly at Costa. "Well?"

"*Well*, what?" said Mira. "Why didn't you tell me? I would've taken him off your hands."

"This is new," said Harlan, grinning even more. "First, she actually buys a slave, now she wants a *boy*. What's wrong, Mira? Mid-life crisis?"

"Not at all," said Mira icily. "I just wondered how you were going to get your reports done without him."

"You never change," said Harlan. He chucked Drew or Ashley under the chin. "Get her a drink. Heavy on the alcohol so she can loosen up."

"Don't bother," said Mira. "I'm here on business, Harlan, and I don't have all day. Didn't you tell me you'd made some major breakthrough with the Sector?"

"Oh, that." He reached into his pocket and pulled out a plastic information card. "It's all right here. The entire Sign vocabulary, with oodles of examples taken from real-life negotiating sessions." He raised an eyebrow. "Pretty impressive for a guy with limited language skills, don't you think?"

"I never said that." Mira held out her hand, but she knew he wouldn't just give it to her. "I'm extremely impressed."

"You should be. But there is a price for this information."

"I know," said Mira. "You've never heard of professional courtesy."

"All I want is gossip." Harlan leaned forward with his elbows on his knees. "What did Trent tell you about what's really going on in the

Faraque?"

Mira frowned. "What?"

Harlan gave her a vaguely surprised look. "Surely you've heard the rumors."

"What rumors?"

"About the Sector," said Harlan. "About the new weapons they have. Trent *must* have told you *something,* Mira. Don't play dumb with me."

"What new weapons?" asked Mira suspiciously. It wasn't beyond Harlan to fabricate some piece of drama just to make her nervous. "What are you talking about?"

Harlan looked at her with genuine exasperation. "When you were on Traja, didn't anyone mention the number of refugees and runaways coming from the Frontier? Haven't *you* heard the rumors?"

Mira shook her head doubtfully.

Harlan settled back in his chair with an air of complete superiority. "In the Frontier they're saying that the Sector have some kind of secret weapon and are massing for an attack on the Proviso."

"In their dreams," said Mira.

"Maybe," said Harlan, "but I understand there may be a problem with one of the far outposts as well. You know, the ones that monitor the Remini."

"What kind of problem?"

"Loss of signal."

Mira relaxed. "That happens all the time. When I was out there, we stopped transmitting for a month while we waited for the repair crews."

"This time it seemed rather sudden."

"Sudden like what?" she asked skeptically. "A Remini attack?"

Harlan sipped his drink and didn't answer.

Mira started to grin. "Are you saying that someone thinks the Sector have figured out a way to control the Remini, and that's their secret weapon?"

"I say nothing," replied Harlan. "I only hear."

"That's ridiculous," said Mira flatly. "If the Remini were turning around, every ship in the fleet would be on alert. This whole mission would have been canceled. We'd be at war."

"Exactly," said Harlan, still sipping. "No new territory for the Emir and his friends. Just piles of dead bodies and scorched earth."

Mira frowned at him. "You're not sure of any of this. You're just trying to scare me."

Harlan shrugged. "All I can say is I'm glad I'm not the one who got picked to go out into the wilderness."

"It was a promotion," said Mira. "And it was free."

"You get what you pay for." He smiled at her and squinted past her shoulder at Costa. "Now about this quiet little creature over here. How much did she set you back?"

What she really wanted was more information, but Harlan was never one to be pushed. She leaned back in the chair. "Enough."

"Let's have a look at you," said Harlan to Costa.

The girl stood, turned slowly, always keeping her eyes down, and sank back to the ground. "Good lord," said Harlan. "She's School." He stared at Mira. "On your salary?"

"I saved up," said Mira with a straight face. "I've always wanted one. How'd you get yours?"

"Birthday present," murmured Harlan. "I don't suppose you'd be interested in trading for a couple of hours?"

"Now Harlan, you're forgetting yourself." She held out her hand, and he gave her the information card. "I appreciate this," she said. "But about the business with the Sector—"

He held up a finger to stop her, and then pointed at the girl. "Information is expensive, Mira."

She hesitated. "Just tell me how much you really *know*, Harlan. It's my neck out there, not yours."

He smiled. "If Trent didn't mention it, it's hardly my place to say anything more."

Mira pocketed the information card in disgust. "Aren't you going to wish me luck?"

Harlan caught one of her hands in both of his. "Good luck," he said, and grinned. "Better you than me, darling."

Mira pulled off her jacket and threw it on the sofa. No matter how much she disliked him, it would be a fabulous irony for someone as nonessential as Harlan to decipher the Sector's secret language. She sat in front of the monitor and slid the card in.

Costa leaned over the back of the chair. "What is this?"

"It's a long story," said Mira, "but basically, whenever the Sector are involved in negotiations, they talk to each other in some kind of sign language. Nobody's been able to figure it out so far." The screen flickered, then focused on two of the Sector that Costa had identified in Mira's files. There was no sound, only subtitles, and they sped along the bottom of the screen as the two men spoke with their hands.

"This may be Harlan's contribution to the ages," said Mira. She ran the file back to the beginning. "I'll read it. You watch."

Costa gave her a strange look, but didn't say anything.

"Okay," said Mira, concentrating on the tiny, fast-moving print. "This one says, *There's no time to waste. We must move now, or we'll lose money.* And the other one says, *No, no. It's better to leave. He is too clever.*" She stopped, frowning at the screen. "This doesn't sound right."

"It's not," said Costa. "They're not saying that at all."

"What?" Mira twisted around in the chair to look at her. "How do you know? They taught you Sign?"

"No," said the girl. "But I know it."

Mira glanced back at the screen in the awkward silence. What she wanted to ask, she could not know, any more than the girl could volunteer the information. "What are they saying?"

"They're deciding how to cheat him," said Costa. "The last part, where you said, *He is too clever,* is almost right. But he's really saying, *He is a complete idiot.*"

Mira started to laugh. "What else?"

"They know he's recording them. Most of it's just nonsense so he'll think they're talking."

"Wonderful," said Mira. "I'll bet they do the same thing to me. Can you teach me this?"

Costa shrugged nervously. "I guess I can. It's complicated though. We always tried to—" She stopped. "Yes D'sha."

Mira smiled at her. One day there would be a time to talk, she could feel that. "Show me what your name looks like."

"It's just this." She held out one palm and brushed it two or three times with the other hand. "It's the edge of the waters."

"Like a beach," said Mira. "That's what your name means?"

Costa nodded. "What about you?"

"Mira doesn't mean anything. It's just a name."

The girl looked around the room thoughtfully. "It sounds like *mirror.*" She held an open palm up to her face. "Like this."

Mira tried it, and watched her suppress a big grin. "What else does this mean?"

"Nothing really." She blushed. "Sometimes it means *beautiful.*"

"You're not supposed to make fun of me," said Mira with mock severity.

"I'm not," said Costa. "I mean, yes D'sha."

The Proviso crossed into the Faraque uneventfully, sometime around midnight. Mira lay on her back, watching the undulations of the distorted stars, one arm under her head. Costa was curled against her, close, and sound asleep—one small victory.

Everything seemed so much easier now. Despite Harlan's vague half-warnings, Mira could feel an interest, even an enthusiasm inside of her that had been missing for a long time. No matter what kind of intricate machinations were going on around the Emir at court, she realized that what she and Vince had discussed in the Ankean cafe over three weeks ago had been absolutely correct. With this mission, she could single-handedly break the Sector's hold on millions of people, beginning once and for all to close the door on the slavers' way of life. She didn't care if anyone knew she was responsible. Fame like that would get her in trouble. If Costa was the only one aware of what she really wanted in the Faraque, that was enough. Mira sighed into the girl's hair, feeling protective and strong. She closed her eyes, savoring Costa's warmth, her permanence.

The whole bed jerked. Mira snapped awake, her hands out to fend off whoever was doing the shaking. She caught Costa's arm as it flailed near her face. "Wake *up!*" She pushed off the covers and grabbed the girl's shoulders. "Hey!"

Costa wrenched away and flung herself out of the bed like it was on fire. She banged into the opposite wall, hard, and slid to the floor on her hands and knees.

". . . Jezr'el . . ."

Mira untangled herself from the sheets and crouched next to her. "It's just a dream." She tried to put her arms around Costa's shoulders, but the girl was rigid with fright.

She looked past Mira with feverish eyes. "What's the name of the planet?"

"What?"

"The one on Harlan's schedule. The one we're going down to today." She didn't even sound like she'd been sleeping.

"It's called Veral," said Mira.

"Jezr'el is there." Costa took a deep, shaky breath and then another. "He's waiting to kill you."

She said it with such dread and certainty that for a second Mira was almost convinced. "It was just a nightmare. But you don't have to come along if you're afraid."

Costa pulled away. "You can't go. I know he's there."

She was utterly convinced, that much was clear. How naive, Mira told herself, to think that the effects of two years of abuse could be erased in less than a week. "It's alright," she said, keeping her voice soft, soothing. "Come back to bed. We'll talk about it in the morning."

The girl stood unsteadily and leaned against the wall. "I'll just keep you awake, D'sha. I can't sleep. . . ."

Mira watched as Costa stumbled into the darkness of the next room. She didn't want to admit that Amrei might have been right about Costa's mental state, but she was starting to suspect that what kept the girl from sleeping was inside her own head. It had nothing to do with the Drug or its side effects.

Mira got back into bed slowly, wide awake now, and chilled. She curled up in the warm spot where the girl had been and wondered what to do next.

"Did you sleep at all?" Mira asked as Costa refilled her cup the next morning.

"No D'sha."

Back to square one, thought Mira. She hadn't been able to make eye contact even once this morning, and her attempts at conversation were beginning to feel like a waste of breath.

Mira sipped at the coffee. It was still too strong, but she was getting used to that. "I want you to stay on the ship today. I can handle this by myself."

Costa looked at her sharply. "You're going?"

"It happens to be my job."

Costa set the pot down on the table, and Mira could see her hands trembling. "Why aren't you afraid of them?"

"I am," said Mira. "But I would never let them see that."

"What would you do if you knew they wanted to hurt you?"

"They wouldn't dare," said Mira. "This battleship is here to protect *me*. The Sector know that. And they know how upset the Emir would be if something happened to his representative. They can't risk that kind of reprisal."

Costa studied the table. "I'll come with you."

"That's very brave of you," said Mira gently, "but what if Jezr'el really is there?"

Costa shook her head. "Maybe he won't be." She put one light hand on Mira's arm. "I can do whatever you need me to do."

Mira looked up in surprise. "You're sure?" she asked. "It's business this time, not just Vince and Amrei."

"I'm sure," said Costa, a little too quickly. "I really am."

There was no actual Ground Station on Veral, just the metal disk set into a stone platform with a blue, blue sky overhead. Trees clustered around small thatched houses, and Mira could see the locals staring at her from every door and window.

She stepped off the disk onto the cobbled pavement and held out her hand to the tall, dark-skinned man who came forward to greet her.

"I am Alshar," said the man in halting Emirate. He gripped her hand awkwardly and shook it.

Mira introduced herself, smiling broadly, taking a quick look around as she and Costa stepped off the disk. There were no Sector in sight, but that didn't mean anything. "It's a great pleasure to be here," she said. "The Emir is very glad to have your cooperation."

The man nodded and smiled, a little too tense, Mira thought, and she wasn't sure he'd understood a word she'd said. "Keep your eyes open," she murmured to Costa.

Alshar pointed to a thatched building that was slightly larger than the rest. "This way," he said. "Please, please D'sha."

D'sha? Mira frowned as he led them across the small plaza. There was no trace of a collar and brand on him. He wasn't young enough anyway. She hadn't thought about it before, but now it occurred to her that one of the reasons that slaves from the Faraque were so obedient was that they were treated as slaves from the day they were born. She glanced back at Costa again and wondered what had gone wrong.

In fact, Jezr'el *was* there, waiting inside. He looked older than the picture in Mira's files, leaner, almost voracious. He curled thin lips around his teeth, but it wasn't a friendly smile. "I've heard a great deal about you Madame LoDire," he said. "My father speaks of you often."

I'll bet he does, thought Mira. She gave him a firm handshake. "The Emir extends his respects to your family," she said. "Your cooperation is appreciated."

Jezr'el nodded and looked past Mira. "My father never mentioned that you had a slave."

"She's new," said Mira quickly, not wanting him to investigate. "Why don't we sit down and get started?"

Costa was kneeling behind her, head down, her hair loose and obscuring her face. Jezr'el leaned over, examining her. "School," he said. "You got one of ours." There was no recognition in his voice, just professional interest. He turned away, and Costa shuddered, brushing at her face where he'd touched her.

Mira sat down across from Jezr'el and Alshar. She smiled politely. "Excuse me, Jezr'el, but does your friend speak any Emirate at all?"

"No," said Jezr'el, "but I'll be glad to translate."

"Forgive my cynicism," said Mira, "but how will I know if I'm getting his opinion or yours? He does belong to you, doesn't he?"

"You misjudge me, Madame LoDire," said Jezr'el. "My father and all of the Sector understand what's at stake here today. We're perfectly willing to listen to what you have to say rather than risk our independence. No one wants an invasion like the last one." He leaned back. "I can assure you that whatever you say will be exactly what Alshar hears."

Mira glanced at Costa, who had placed herself just behind Jezr'el where Mira could see her. Mira caught her eye for half a second. She was listening too, and didn't seem at all convinced.

Mira looked back at Alshar, who knew just enough Emirate to say *D'sha*, and decided to see how far Jezr'el was willing to go with this charade.

"Excellent," she said. "You can start by telling him that this planet falls into a category which is often extremely rich in rare metals. I have a survey team waiting to do an appraisal of Veral's actual worth, but I'll need someone's permission before they start digging."

Jezr'el cocked his head at her. "What kind of metals?"

"I'm no expert," said Mira. "All I can say is that mining rights on Veral could easily be worth ten times the value of its population." Jezr'el's little speech about the sacrifices the Sector were prepared to make had the hollow sound of rotten lies to her. Put the possibility of even bigger profits in front of him, and Jezr'el's true intentions would probably surface.

"Well?" said Mira. "Aren't you going to translate for me?"

His flash of dislike for her was too strong for him to hide completely, but he turned to Alshar and began speaking in a quick, clipped language. Mira shot another glance at Costa and ran a finger over one eyebrow. *Understand?* she asked in Sign, but the girl shook her head.

Alshar answered more slowly, no more than a sentence or two, and gave Jezr'el a questioning look.

"Your survey team is welcome," said Jezr'el. "But Alshar wisely requests a show of good faith from the Emir."

Jezr'el wants hard cash, thought Mira. "Yes?" she said. "That's very encouraging. What does he have in mind?"

"A percentage of estimated value."

"Fine," said Mira. "You'll have the results in less than a week. I'm sure we can manage some kind of credit arrangement."

"No credit," said Jezr'el. "Cash. And since you seem so sure about the worth of these. . .metals, he wants the money before your geologists set foot on his planet."

"Ah," said Mira. "Alshar is a very savvy gentleman. I see he's learned the Sector technique for driving a hard bargain."

Jezr'el flushed a little behind his blue stripe. He turned back to Alshar and said something else, probably instructions, thought Mira, as Alshar began to nod his head energetically, watching his master for the signal to stop. "Alshar desires a recess," said Jezr'el. "He needs time to think about your offer."

"By all means," said Mira. "Tell him to take all the time he needs." Raffail would never have let himself get flustered, thought Mira. It surprised her that he wasn't here. Jezr'el obviously didn't have the experience to play this game the way his father could. In fact, it was not like the Sector to send a boy to do a man's job, especially in a situation like this. Maybe Jezr'el had some hidden talent she hadn't seen yet, but she doubted it.

"It's customary on Veral for guests to accept refreshments," said Jezr'el. He signaled to Alshar, who shot out of his chair and retrieved a tray with two ceramic cups and a pitcher. He started to pour, but Jezr'el stopped him and pointed at Costa. "You," he said, "you'll serve."

"They make an excellent wine here," said Jezr'el, watching the girl as she laid a cloth correctly over her arm, concentrating on every move she made. "It's very well known inside the Faraque."

"How nice," said Mira. "But I think you're missing a cup."

"So we are." He turned back to Alshar and snapped a harsh command. "Go on," he ordered Costa as she hesitated with the tray.

She set the first cup down in front of him, properly, from the right, and put the second at Alshar's empty seat as he returned with the third, and handed it to her. *Now* she was trembling. Mira watched the girl inch around the table, holding the cup as though it was about to bite her. Instead of just setting it down, Costa dropped to her knees, below the edge of the table, where Jezr'el couldn't see her. She looked up anxiously and held the cup out. Mira reached for it, and the girl let go.

The crash of pottery was like an explosion, incredibly loud in an oddly expectant silence. Mira pushed her chair away, amazed at the girl's audacity. Costa had done it on purpose. It was no mistake, no clumsy error. She turned to Jezr'el to apologize, but the young man was on his feet, red with fury.

"It was an accident," said Mira. She moved away from her chair as Costa crouched on the floor, wiping up the mess. "My fault. Surely you have an extra glass?"

Jezr'el unclenched his fists and jerked a thumb at Alshar. "Of course," he said, and made an abysmal attempt to smile. "Have a seat please, Madame LoDire."

There was a small sound from Costa, still on the floor, and Mira looked down. The girl was holding up the cloth she'd used to wipe up the wine. The purple stains were slowly changing color, and Mira could see black blotches forming, thinning the cloth, dissolving into huge holes. Mira made sure the expression on her face didn't change. Unpredictable, Costa had said. And poison was certainly not something she'd expected. She glanced at Jezr'el.

"On the other hand," she said, "I hope you'll be kind enough to tell Alshar that he can contact me on the Proviso." She stood up abruptly and started for the door, with Costa at her heels.

Jezr'el didn't answer, but his eyes were like sharp points between Mira's shoulders as they hurried across the deserted plaza and onto the transport disk. The open windows and doors were shut now, as if Jezr'el's anger had been carried through town on the warm breezes. She glanced back at the low thatched building as she pulled her transmitter out of her pocket. The young slaver was standing in the doorway, swathed in his white robes, livid even at this distance.

"Proviso," said Vince's voice.

"I've got some trouble," said Mira. "Get us out of here, Vince."

She pulled Costa off the ship's disk and grabbed her shoulders. "How did you know?" she demanded. "How did you *know?*"

"Last night," whispered Costa, pale as paper. "I told you last night."

Mira let go and shook her head, shaking away the fear that this child was crazy. "No," she said. "You're going to have to come up with something better than that. What was different? The color? The smell?"

"Nothing," whispered the girl. "It was the same."

The door opened and Vince ran in, breathless. "What's wrong?"

"I just got finished talking to Raffail's son down there," said Mira, fuming. "A real nice kid. He just tried to poison me."

Vince gave her a concerned look. "You're alright?"

Mira glanced at Costa. "I'm fine," she said. "Give me five minutes. I'll give you a full report."

One of the things Mira had the ability to do very well was repeat conversations exactly as she had heard them. Vince was smiling behind his hand as she went through the part where Jezr'el was pretending to speak for Alshar, but this time it didn't amuse Mira at all. She was watching Costa, who was going to have to speak her piece. "No dreams," Mira had hissed to her in the corridor. "Tell him *anything* but that." She'd gotten a perfunctory *Yes D'sha*, but the closer Mira got to that part of the story, the more nervous she felt.

"She dropped it?" asked Vince, very seriously.

"Right on the floor," said Mira.

"You should have brought a sample." He looked over at the girl. "What made you think it was poisoned?"

"It had a different color, D'sha," said Costa. "It had a strange smell."

Mira let out a sigh of relief, and Vince raised his eyebrows. "What's going on down there?"

"I don't know," she said. "I can't believe Jezr'el is a loose cannon."

"You think Raffail is behind this?"

"I think the Sector are ready to start shooting to protect their interests here," said Mira. "Naturally they're nervous about an Emirate battleship inside their territory, but I never thought they'd pull this kind of stunt."

"It doesn't make any sense, though," said Vince. "Killing you wouldn't have scared us away. If anything, we could have gotten two or three more ships in here."

"But it would take time." Mira leaned her elbows on the table, suddenly feeling very worn out.

Vince studied Costa and then looked back at her. "Attempted murder of an Emirate official isn't something we can pass off as a misunderstanding."

"You wouldn't be able to prove anything," said Mira. She shook her head. "Veral isn't a place they'd even feel a reprisal. Let's wait. I'll be more careful next time."

Mira sat in her quarters, staring at the lunch she had no appetite for. The whole episode this morning had scared her more than she wanted to admit, and the next stop on Harlan's schedule was less than a day away. She pushed the tray toward Costa. "Do you want any of this?"

"No D'sha." Costa started to clear the table, but Mira pointed to the other chair.

"Sit down."

The girl obeyed, hands in her lap.

"You have to talk to me," said Mira. "You have to tell me what really happened down there."

"I've told you the truth, D'sha." She hesitated. "I can imagine how it sounds to you."

"It sounds absolutely crazy to me," said Mira bluntly.

Costa stared down at her hands. "I did warn you, though."

It was true, and there really was no arguing that point.

"Look," said Mira. "If I ask you about these dreams, it's not because I really believe all this. It's because I'm curious, understand?"

"Yes D'sha."

"Well?"

"It was exactly the same as what happened today," said Costa. "Except I didn't drop the cup in the dream."

"I drank that stuff?" Mira rubbed her eyes, still not convinced. She remembered what had happened last night, vividly, but could not bring herself to believe it was anything more than a *very* odd coincidence. "So why does he want to kill me?"

"I don't know." Costa was watching her carefully, judging her reaction. "What you said in the meeting was probably right. Jezr'el does whatever Raffail wants him to."

Mira sighed. "Do all your dreams come true?" She smiled, but Costa was nodding.

"You don't have to believe it," said the girl, "but I knew what he wanted to do to you. I couldn't let that happen."

Mira looked down, embarrassed. "You saved my life."

"You saved mine."

Mira couldn't meet her eyes. She wasn't sure if she was going to cry, or if this surge of emotion in her chest was something more complicated. "I've got to lie down," she muttered. "I'm not feeling very well."

Ain-Selai was the next planet on Harlan's itinerary. Mira stared at the vague information about the planet as it swam on the screen in front of her. It was almost midnight now, but she was still too wound up to sleep, her stomach working itself into tighter and tighter knots.

She hadn't told Costa anything about tomorrow's schedule or the impending planetfall. She was worried enough for both of them, and another round of nightmares was not something she wanted. The idea of ordering the girl to stay on the ship for the duration of the mission had occurred to Mira, but going alone to Ain-Selai, or anywhere else in the Faraque, seemed less than intelligent. The Sector would certainly have some kind of follow-up planned. Taking along armed guards had occurred to her, but she knew that would only make negotiations harder and the Sector more jumpy. Her best bet was still Costa. Mira turned off the monitor and crawled into bed, exhausted. She curled up against the girl's sleepy warmth and fell asleep almost immediately.

When she woke up, Mira was under the impression that it was already morning, but then that didn't seem right. Costa had moved to the other side of the bed, and there had been a sound, but whatever dream the girl was having, it seemed to Mira to have started some time ago and that she had been shouting.

"Emielle," moaned the girl, very clearly, and then something more in a language Mira didn't recognize.

"It's alright," Mira whispered. "Everything's okay." She put her arms around the girl and waited for her to relax. Instead, Costa twisted against her, clinging close, fists knotted in the sheets.

"It's the blood," she whispered in Emirate. "They love it."

Tiny hairs on the back of Mira's neck raised themselves up, one by one. She shook off the unexplainable chill. This was not her nightmare. "Wake up," she said. "You're dreaming."

"Emielle," repeated Costa. She wrapped her arms around Mira and squeezed her hard enough for it to be painful.

Mira tried to pull away, awake now and worried. "Costa!"

"Don't!" cried the girl, and her eyes opened.

"Wake up," said Mira slowly, clearly. "You're having another nightmare."

Costa stared at her, breathing hard. "You didn't tell me."

"About what?" Mira put a hand against her face. She was damp with sweat.

"Ain-Selai."

Who had told her? "I didn't want you to worry," said Mira, hiding her unqualified surprise. "I wanted you to sleep."

"You can't go. You have to listen to me this time. You can't *go.*"

Mira moved away from her, just slightly. This intensity was new, a little unnerving. "I have to. We've been through this before. I'm flattered that you worry about me, but you have to stop talking like that."

"What about yesterday?"

"Coincidence," said Mira. "I'm sorry, but I've never met anyone who could tell the future. Now go to sleep." She turned over with her back to the girl, hoping that she would be quiet and do what she was told.

There was just a moment of thick silence. "Raffail is there," said Costa. "So is Jezr'el, and two of Raffail's brothers."

"Raffail is a million kilometers from here," said Mira. "I saw him a month ago in Emirate space. If he is on Ain-Selai he'd have to be moving pretty fast."

"They'll hold you hostage."

Mira sighed. "Am I too hard to kill?"

"You have to believe me," said the girl, and this time she sounded scared. "The creatures are there too."

Maybe it was better for her not to sleep, Mira thought. Obviously she couldn't distinguish her dreams from reality, but as craziness went, it seemed more delusional than dangerous. She turned over, just wanting to go back to sleep. "If I listen, will you shut up?"

"Yes D'sha."

Mira closed her eyes. "Go ahead."

There was more about the creatures, something about the name, a cousin? Mira wasn't sure as she drifted off . . . a room full of candles, which seemed to concern the girl a great deal, and then there was a snowstorm which turned into part of Mira's own dream as she fell asleep again.

What she had hoped would be a decent breakfast turned out to be worse than usual. Mira sawed at the artificial ham with a dull knife, and finally ended up pulling it apart with her fingers.

Ain-Selai was an hour away, less, and absolutely nothing felt right. The long-range scans of the planet showed at least three Sector ships and a full complement of barges. The numbers alone didn't bother Mira. A dozen Sector ships wouldn't stand a chance against the Proviso, but three-to-one odds on the surface didn't appeal to her at all. Neither did the thought of dealing with Jezr'el again. She pushed the tray aside and glanced at Costa.

Costa was distracted this morning, off in some other world. Whatever Mira had said to her in the last hour, she'd had to repeat. "Is that all you're going to have?" asked Mira in a loud voice, pointing to the untouched cup of coffee.

The girl blinked at her. "I'm not very hungry."

"You need to pull yourself together," said Mira. "Things may get messy down there. You've got to be awake for this."

Costa stared at her coffee and didn't say anything.

Mira felt a prick of anger at this unslavelike attitude and the girl's air of supposed knowledge. A couple of unpleasant comments surfaced in her mind, but there was a knock on the door before they turned into actual words. "You can get that," she snapped instead.

It was Vince. "You look beat," he said as he walked in.

"Thanks," said Mira. "That's just what I needed to hear."

"When are you leaving?"

"As soon as she takes that back to the mess hall." She shot Costa a meaningful look and the girl picked up the tray.

"I want you to bring a couple of security guards with you," said Vince. "It's too dangerous for business as usual."

"I'll call if I need help," said Mira. "If the Sector see guns, they tend to jump to conclusions."

"Don't you think it might be worth the risk?" asked Vince. "You can't underestimate them."

"You sound like a grandmother," said Mira.

"What if they have weapons this time?"

"They always carry weapons," she said. "Raffail never shows up to a meeting without some kind of peacemaker." Mira grinned at the joke and how weak it was. She patted the pocket where her transmitter was. "I'll check in every fifteen minutes."

It didn't really seem to satisfy him, but he turned to the door. "Good luck down there."

"Thanks." She watched him go and looked back at Costa, still standing there with the tray. "Come on," Mira said, more tired than angry. "Let's get this over with."

About halfway to the mess hall, she slowed down a little to walk beside the girl. "Stop worrying."

"I'm not," said Costa, sounding very tense. "I'm fine."

Mira reached over to put a reassuring arm across her shoulders and happened to look down at the tray. The uneaten meat lay in a pool of sticky egg yolk with the fork and spoon, just the way she'd left them. Mira had put the knife there too. She remembered doing it. Now it wasn't anywhere in sight. She let her hand fall down to Costa's waist and felt the brush of something hard stuck into the band of her pants. "Hold it."

The girl stopped, eyes down, as Mira pulled the knife out of her clothes.

"Exactly *what* were you planning to do with *this?*"

"I'm just trying to help, D'sha."

"Go back to my quarters," said Mira angrily. "You're not going *anywhere!*"

"You can't go by yourself." Costa looked at her in genuine horror and dropped to her knees. "I'm sorry, D'sha. It was a stupid mistake."

"That has to be the understatement of the century," snapped Mira. "Weren't you listening when I was talking to Vince? Can you imagine what the Sector would do if I went down there with an armed *slave?*"

Costa put the tray down and laid her head at Mira's feet, wrists crossed, like someone who had actually learned something in the School. "Forgive me, D'sha," she whispered. "Just don't leave me here."

Mira was infinitely glad that Vince was not around to see her with this lunatic girl lying on the floor next to her half-eaten breakfast. "Get up."

"Please let me come."

"Absolutely not," said Mira. "What were you going to do, anyhow? Stick Jezr'el a couple of times?"

Costa looked up desperately. "I won't do anything wrong, D'sha. If you don't take me, at least take the guards."

The truth was, Mira had no choice. Going alone was too frightening: she would miss something and she would die. "You'd better watch your step down there," Mira said, sounding as threatening as she could. "If you pull anything like this again—" she shook the knife for emphasis, "I'll get rid of you. I swear I will."

By the time they reached the ship's transport disk, Mira had calmed herself down somewhat. She stepped onto the disk and pushed her hair back, clearing herself of emotional excesses that would only cripple her on the surface. She took a deep breath and glanced back at Costa. The girl was the proper two steps behind, but on the wrong side, and she seemed more tense than ever. Mira shook off her anxieties and nodded to the technician.

"Let's go."

9

The first thing she saw was Raffail. Mira opened her mouth in surprise, but someone grabbed her from behind, clamping a hand over most of her face. She twisted against whoever it was and saw Jezr'el, his lips drawn back over his teeth, awful, like some animal. She heard Costa shriek, caught a glimpse of her as she dodged away from two other men. Jezr'el's hand tightened around her jaw, squeezing hard. Mira plunged her hand into her pocket for the transmitter, but Jezr'el caught her wrist, wrenching it behind her back, up against her shoulderblades, forcing her to her knees.

"That's enough!" snapped Raffail. Jezr'el let go of everything but her arms, and Mira staggered to her feet.

"Get your hands off me!" shouted Mira. She yanked against Jezr'el's iron grip.

"Take her transmitter." Raffail looked past Mira to the back of the room. "Bring that one over here."

The two other slavers dragged Costa across the floor. Mira recognized them and struggled for their names. They were both Raffail's brothers.

He gave the girl a nudge with the toe of his boot. "Get up."

"What the hell do you think you're doing?" Mira demanded.

"Don't you know?" He jerked Costa to her feet. "I'm sure she's already told you everything."

Mira had seen Raffail in a number of different moods, but she had never seen him really angry. Right now he was barely controlling himself. "Let her go," said Mira. "Let us go. You're in deep trouble, Raffail. You can't hold an Emirate official—" She stopped before the word *hostage*, and the echo of last night's conversation. Was this the nightmare? Mira swallowed hard, more frightened now. If Costa had an inkling of what was going on here, it was too late to ask, too late to listen.

"It's so good to see you again, Costa," Raffail snarled at her. "You must be very pleased with yourself. You're still alive, and you managed to bring the biggest ship in the Emirate fleet to kill me. You must be *very* pleased." He wound one fist into her shirt and pulled the other one back. "What did you tell her, Costa? I want to hear your exact words."

"Nothing," gasped the girl. "I didn't!"

"What are you talking about?" demanded Mira. She took a step forward to stop him, but Jezr'el grabbed the back of her neck. Mira froze as Raffail hit the girl as hard as he could.

"Stop it!" Mira shouted, as Costa collapsed on the floor.

"When she talks I'll stop." Raffail hauled her up, shaking her until her eyes opened. "Tell me," he said. "Why did you bring this woman here? What could she possibly want in the Faraque?"

"The Emir," said the girl thickly, desperate. She cringed as Raffail pulled his fist back again. "It's not what you think, D'sha, it's just a mistake!"

"Go on," said Raffail. "Tell me all about it."

"Those things," she panted. "I never knew what they were called. I never said anything because I didn't *know*."

Raffail hesitated and then lowered his arm. "You're lying."

"I'm not, D'sha. It's the truth."

He almost let go. "Tell me what you saw."

"Nothing, D'sha."

"But you did," he snapped, furious again. "You must have, because you know exactly what I'm talking about." He pointed at Mira and started to shout. "She's here, and you're trying to make me believe this is a coincidence?"

"It was a dream, D'sha! I never really saw them!"

"I'll get it out of her," said Jezr'el impatiently.

"No," said his father. "She's stubborn, but she's not stupid enough to lie." He nodded at one of his brothers. "Get your girl. We'll solve this problem right now."

In the instant of silence as the other man left the room, Mira pulled away from Jezr'el. "Tell me what's going on," she said. "Before you kill her you have to tell me what you're trying to get her to say, because she hasn't told *me* anything." She wondered how long she could keep him talking, and how many of her fifteen minutes passed. She would be rescued. She just hoped Costa would be in one piece when it happened.

Raffail frowned. "You're not keeping very good records, Mira. The registry says she's still in the Mine line." He shook his head mockingly. "I should have guessed that's where you'd do your shopping."

For the first time, Mira was genuinely afraid of him. She glanced at Costa, kneeling now, motionless, but watching everything. "What are you trying to do?" she asked. "You must know they'll come after me when I don't check in."

"Then I suppose you have nothing to worry about." He crossed his arms. "Tell me, Mira, how does the Emir expect this invasion to succeed if he only sends one ship? How many more are behind the Proviso?"

"This isn't an invasion," said Mira in amazement. "The Emir thinks he can buy the Faraque for cash. I was sent to find out what your price is. That's all."

Raffail shook his head. "I thought you'd be a better liar."

The door opened, and his brother came back in, followed by a slave girl with short blonde hair. There was something familiar about her, but Mira couldn't quite put her finger on it until the girl looked up. She was enough like Costa to be an identical twin.

"Emielle," whispered Costa.

Mira remembered *that*. There was no room for doubt anymore, and she tried hard to recall what Costa had said while she was ignoring her, trying to sleep.

Raffail pulled Costa to her feet. "The truth this time."

"But I've told you everything, D'sha."

"Have you?" He nodded to Jezr'el, who stepped behind Emielle and pulled a knife out of his cloak. "What did you see the day you were collared?" asked Raffail as his son laid the knife against the other girl's throat. "I have her version. Now I want yours."

Costa took a shaky breath. "We camped in the snow the night before. I had a dream."

"That's not what I'm asking about," hissed Raffail. "Tell me what I want to know."

"There were creatures in the mountains," whispered the girl. I saw human bones and animal bones. I saw you walking next to them, and they left you alone."

None of this made any sense to Mira, but she could see how jumpy Jezr'el was. Once he had an excuse to start cutting, she doubted if he would stop with Emielle. "What's she talking about?" she demanded loudly.

Raffail ignored her. "How many ships are coming behind the Proviso, Costa?"

"There aren't any," said the girl. "I never said anything. It was only a dream."

Raffail shook her hard. "Why do you keep saying that?"

"She talks like that all the time," said Mira. "She's out of her mind."

Raffail scowled at her. "What do you mean?"

Mira shrugged, trying to stay cool and convincing. "She can't tell what's real and what's in her head. I think somebody beat the sense right out of her."

Raffail made a motion to his son, and Jezr'el lowered the knife. He pushed the shirt off Costa's shoulders and examined the marks on her back. "If she's crazy, why do you keep her?"

Mira couldn't tell if he believed her or not. "She was the only School I could afford."

Raffail snorted and let go. "She hasn't told you anything?"

Mira shook her head. "Give me back my transmitter," she said. "Let us out of here, and I'll forget the whole thing."

"It's not that simple." Raffail studied her for a moment. "Aren't you the expert on the Remini?"

Mira shrugged nervously. "More or less."

"Have you ever seen one?"

"Of course not," said Mira. "Nobody has."

"Your little slave did," said Raffail. He nodded at Costa and Emielle. "These two decided to run away from home a couple of years ago. We found them right outside the Remini base on their planet."

"A base?" said Mira doubtfully. "Which planet might this be?"

"I'm sure you've never heard of it," said Raffail. "We call it Jahar."

"There must not be much of Jahar left," Mira said carefully. "Why are you settling breeding populations beyond the Faraque anyhow? The Remini destroy anything they can find."

"Jahar is on our side of the Remini border."

Mira stared at him, searching for any sign of a bluff in his face. "They've turned around?" she whispered. "They're here?"

"Closer than you think," said Raffail.

"My god," said Mira. "Why didn't you say something? We would have sent the entire fleet!"

"I'm sure the Emirate would have rushed right in to save us," said Raffail acidly. "But it's not an attack. We've been in communication with them for almost three years. We invited them." He watched her struggle for a reply and smiled. "I never thought I'd be the one to break the news to you, Mira. It really is a pleasure."

"You thought Costa told me that?" asked Mira. "That's what this is all about?" She looked desperately at the girl. "Why didn't you say something?"

Raffail grinned. "Because someone beat the sense out of her."

But she *had* said something, last night. "You've managed to make some kind of deal with those things?" asked Mira. "They seem awfully destructive to be good trading partners."

"They aren't especially intelligent," he admitted. "In fact, most of their technology seems to be stolen from the cultures they've destroyed. They're just scavengers. All they really want is a constant food supply, and as long as we give them that, they're very cooperative."

"And what do you get in return?"

"Ah," said Raffail. "We've found that their weapons fit very nicely into a standard slave barge."

Mira took a sharp breath. "You're attacking the Proviso."

"Even as we speak." He held out his hand, and Jezr'el gave him Mira's transmitter. "I certainly understand if you're skeptical," he said, pressing the small box into her palm.

She took it numbly, knowing that he would never offer her this escape if the Proviso was still capable of taking her aboard. She keyed in the emergency sequence and waited for a reply. All she could hear was the hiss of the open channel. "It's been destroyed?" she asked. "Or have you just chased them away?"

"Destroyed," said Raffail. "We don't want the Emir to find out about all this until we're ready."

Mira rubbed her head and wished she could sit down.

"Obviously you won't be leaving."

"Obviously." Mira found she was too afraid to say anything more.

"There is something I want you to see." Raffail pointed to a set of sturdy double doors in the opposite wall. "Just stay where you are, Mira," he added.

Everyone in the room took a step back. Jezr'el reached down for Costa, but she caught Emielle's arm and pulled her away, retreating into the furthest corner. Mira watched nervously as the doors creaked open. Something moved inside, hissing in the darkness.

The creature itself was so tall it had to crouch on its insect legs to get out. It had wings too, filmy, useless-looking things that reached even higher, brushing the ceiling. Mira moved away from it, her heart pounding. Back on the outpost, she'd come up with her own vision of what the Remini *should* look like. It was nothing at all like this mantis-thing swaying in front of her. Raffail had said they were scavengers, but right now she wasn't sure she believed him. The Remini eased toward her, lowering the front of its body to her level, tasting the air around her with long, wet cilia streaming from its mouth, and that was when she got her first breath of it. Mira backed away until she was against the far wall, choking on the unholy stink. "Raffail!" she gasped. "Call it off!"

She heard Jezr'el's harsh laugh. "Talk to it," Raffail suggested blandly. "Give it a message of goodwill from the Emir."

The thing took a quick step toward her, hissing, rasping its wings. The sounds were barely familiar, and without special equipment, there was no way for her to talk back. Mira pressed herself against the wall, gagging as the creature came closer. The room swam around her as she felt her legs give way. The Remini exhaled in frustration, crouching to investigate. Mira slid to the floor, squeezing her eyes shut against its size and its smell. As she lost consciousness, the only word she could make out was *Alive.*

She opened her eyes in a cold, dark room. Someone was leaning over her, silhouetted against the light of an open door. Jezr'el.

"It's about time you woke up." He eased down next to her on what seemed to be a narrow cot, uncomfortably close.

Mira managed to sit up, pulling away. "What do you want?" She could hardly remember what had happened. Her head hurt and her clothes stank. "Where's Raffail?"

"He's gone to see what's left of your ship. I'm in charge while he's not here."

His tone was soft, incredibly threatening. Mira took a deep breath. She had expected the alien to kill her, not this obnoxious boy. "Get out of here," she snapped.

"If you like," said Jezr'el. "But if you cooperate, I could make things easier for you. Maybe keep you alive."

Until he's done with me, thought Mira. "Get out," she said, as nastily as she could.

To her relief, he shrugged and got to his feet. She could barely see it as he reached into the folds of his cloak and pulled something out, something thin and metallic—a knife.

Her mouth went dry. All she could think of were the things she'd said to Costa when she'd discovered the pathetically dull mess hall knife in her clothes. Was she already dead? Chained somewhere? With Raffail? I could fight him, Mira thought weakly. If I fight, maybe it won't take long. She braced herself, but Jezr'el dropped the knife on the cot.

"You have about six hours until my father and the Remini get back," he said. "Naturally we'd rather not murder an Emirate official in cold blood."

"I see," said Mira weakly. "It's better for you if I do it myself."

"Faster," said Jezr'el. "For everyone."

Mira watched wordlessly as he stepped out of the tiny cell into the light of the corridor.

"D'sha," said Costa's voice from just outside. "Let me say good-bye to her, please."

"Quiet."

At least she was still alive. "Costa!" Mira swung one leg over the side of the cot as Jezr'el slammed the door shut.

Mira held her breath, listening. The conversation was no longer in Emirate, but the content was clear. Costa spoke in a sultry, servile voice, the way the School had taught her, the way she sounded when she was most afraid.

The door swung open again. "Hurry up," snapped Jezr'el.

Costa slipped in, a dark rush of breath and sweaty palms. She wrapped an arm around Mira's neck and hugged her very hard.

Mira clung to her as Jezr'el eyed them. "Costa," she whispered, too softly for him to hear. "Costa, I believe everything you told me."

"I know." she pulled herself loose with a jerk as Jezr'el moved back into the room. "Good-bye, D'sha," she whispered.

"Yes, good-bye," said Jezr'el, mimicking her. He grabbed the back of Costa's shirt and shoved her out into the hallway. "Good night, Madame LoDire," he said, and this time, he locked her in.

The darkness was total, disorienting. Mira felt her way to the door and ran her hands over the flaking inner surface—corroded metal—searching for a knob, or a latch, but there was nothing. There had to be a way out. This was an old, old cell. It smelled dank and unused, and there was probably enough rust around the lock for her to dig through and dismantle it from the inside. She groped along the edge of the cot to the place where she thought Jezr'el had dropped the knife, but it wasn't there. She felt along the length of the bed, twice, and got down on her knees to search the filthy floor, desperately hunting for what she knew was gone. With nowhere left to look, she crawled back onto the cot, panting. She wasn't even sure when Costa had taken the knife. She had known exactly where it was, exactly what to say to Jezr'el to get him to let her into the cell, like reading from a script. Mira shivered hard in the darkness, colder now and chilled with sweat. There was something about this other girl, Emielle, that she needed to remember. *Were* they twins? No, cousins. And if she were in Costa's position, forced to choose between escaping with a blood relation or a woman she'd know for barely two weeks. . . . Mira closed her eyes, listening hard for any small sound, praying that she had not been abandoned.

She had no idea how long it had been before she heard the whisper of noise in the hallway. Mira struggled off the cot.

"Costa?" she hissed. "Costa!"

There was a soft click as someone turned a key in the lock. The door opened, and Emielle moved back into the light of the hallway. She ran a finger quickly over her eyebrow. *Understand?* she asked in Sign.

Little, Mira signed back. She brushed one hand over the palm of the other. *Costa?*

The girl jerked a thumb over her shoulder nervously, as if she was in a tremendous hurry.

"Is she alive?" Mira whispered.

"No E-mi-rate." Emielle took a step away from her, pointing down the corridor, and Mira followed.

It was even colder in the hallway than it had been in the cell. Mira could see her breath and patches of ice on the floor as Emielle rushed her along through the deserted dungeon.

The girl made her stop at the foot of a stone stairway, holding a finger to her lips. She pointed up the stairs. *Costa,* she Signed. Mira nodded and then frowned at the wide, draping gestures.

"Remini," whispered Emielle, making her hands like the mantis arms. She walked her fingers across one palm.

Remini moving around free? Mira nodded again. "Sector?" she whispered.

Emielle held up four fingers.

The floor above was warmer, dark and empty except for a faint tang in the air, like something had been burned recently. The sound of boots on stone echoed down the hallway, and Emielle grabbed Mira's wrist, painfully tight, crouching in the shadows by the wall.

Mira held her breath as the slaver passed within a few meters of them without pausing, but Emielle's grip didn't loosen. Mira tried to pull away, then stopped. Even in the dim light, she could see the determined scars that ran from the inside of the girl's elbow to the palm of her hand, a naive suicide attempt. The Drug would have healed her before she could have bled to death. Hadn't she known that? Mira looked up and met the girl's grey eyes. There was no innocence left in her, no hope. Emielle let go and turned away, creeping through the shadows of the corridor.

Mira followed her through the labyrinth of the slavers' fortress until Emielle finally stopped in front of a tall wooden door. She gestured frantically, and Mira understood why she'd been brought here. The door was free-keyed. Emielle was locked out. Costa was trapped inside with Jezr'el, or whatever was left of him.

It suddenly occurred to her that this was a trap, that Costa was dead and she would be next. "Costa?" she whispered.

"Mira!" The girl's voice was light and frightened. "Can't you open it?"

Mira touched the latch and felt it give. She pushed against the door, but something inside was blocking it. Emielle pressed behind her before she could tell what it was, crowding her through the narrow opening.

She wasn't prepared for all the blood. Jezr'el was slumped against the door, his eyes still open. He had been cut from the belly, all the way up, completely gutted. Mira leaned against the wall, her stomach knotting. Costa stood in the corner, still shaking, spattered with gore, the knife clenched hard in one hand.

"Are you hurt?" Mira managed to ask. The girl jerked her head. *No.* He probably hadn't had time.

Emielle squeezed past her and hurried Costa into a small alcove that seemed to be a bathroom. Mira stepped gingerly over Jezr'el's body, listening to their voices, soft behind the sound of running water. It was their own language, and she couldn't understand a word of it.

Costa turned to her, shrugging into a clean shirt as her cousin wiped the rest of the blood from her face and her hair. "Do you know what a Governor looks like?"

Mira looked at her blankly. "It's just a little box."

"There's one here somewhere. We have to find it."

"We have to get out of here," said Mira. "There's a Remini wandering around out there somewhere. If it smells Jezr'el—"

"Go if you want to," said the girl sharply. She turned back to her cousin and said something else.

Emielle pointed at a trunk at the foot of the bed and glanced at Mira. She touched her left ear and tapped the side of her head.

She was wired, Mira realized suddenly. There was no way for her to leave without setting off every alarm in the building unless they could find her control unit. Costa was already deep in the trunk, rooting through Jezr'el's belongings.

"I thought you dreamed this," said Mira. "Don't you already know where it is?"

"I couldn't find it in the dream." She pulled out one last piece of clothing and threw it furiously at the body. "Where did you *put* it?"

Emielle had opened a cabinet on the other side of the room and was pulling the drawers out of it, pawing through trinkets and cash, unidentifiable objects. Mira bent down next to her, sifting through the junk. Was this also the dream, she wondered, and would the Remini lead the Sector in to find the three of them like this? How fixed were the events that Costa could foresee?

Emielle stood up suddenly and jabbed a finger at the door,

whispering emphatically. Costa ignored her, searching Jezr'el's pockets.
The room was completely ransacked now, even the bed was stripped.
Costa took her hands away from the corpse, wiped them on the sheets.
"It's not here," said Mira nervously. "We've got to go, Costa. That
thing'll be here any minute."

Emielle stepped past her and edged the door open. The burnt
smell in the air outside had thickened considerably, wafting into the room
like smoke. Emielle grabbed Costa's hand and pulled her through. Mira
followed. The hallway was still empty, but the unmistakable sound of
rasping wings was too close. Emielle led them back the way she and Mira
had come, around a corner, and stopped to look back.

Behind them, the shadowy form of the Remini filled the corridor,
pressing against the low ceiling. It moved slowly from door to door until it got to Jezr'el's room. Mira could see it trying to manipulate the lock
with its spindly forelegs. "What if it can't get in?" she whispered to Costa.

"It will," said the girl. "Watch."

The Remini bobbed in the hallway, creaking with frustration and
hunger. It leaned against the door, not even very hard, and the heavy
wood gave way, splintering in the darkness like bones.

Emielle let out a shaky breath and said something.

"It's the blood," translated Costa. "They love it."

They made their way silently through the empty corridors, the
two girls gripping each other's hands, Mira trailing behind. A lot of things
made sense now. It was obvious that Emielle was the one who Costa had
been searching for during her time with the Sector. With Jezr'el as her
master, it was no wonder she couldn't sleep.

Raffail clearly had no knowledge of Costa's ability. Mira wasn't
sure if that was surprising or not. Surely the Sector knew every detail
of their gene pools. Freaks and mutations weren't supposed to exist in
the Faraque. But perhaps the Sector were getting overconfident these
days, and careless. Mira hurried along behind the two girls, wondering
how deep their similarities ran.

The corridor made a sharp turn ahead, and Mira felt a draft in
the air, distinctly cold, as though there was an opening to the outside
somewhere further ahead.

Emielle tapped Mira on the shoulder, pointing to a small narrow
door in the wall, like a closet. Mira pulled it open and peered inside.
It was a weapons locker, nearly empty now except for a half dozen belts

with some kind of bulky, antique-looking ammunition. Emielle stepped past her and slung the belts over her shoulders. Mira watched uneasily. She needed to have a closer look, but she was pretty sure Emielle was carrying enough thermal grenades to destroy a ship the size of the Merganthaler.

Emielle hurried ahead. Mira caught Costa's arm.

"What happens next?" she whispered. "Do you know?"

"We have to get out," said Costa. "Raffail comes back at dawn."

Mira glanced down the hall. "What about your cousin? Does she get out with us?"

"She has to," said Costa shortly. "It doesn't matter what I saw. I've been wrong before." She broke into a run and raced down the corridor, leaving Mira behind.

Mira followed, her heart pounding. Emielle's options were very, very limited. Realistically, the only way for her to escape the Governor's control field would be by transport disk. Walking, running, even riding in a skimmer would be next to impossible. Mira had seen slaves cross past the edge of their wire—or attempt to. Even if Emielle did make it somehow, the three of them were no match for the Sector, who would be sure to follow.

She rounded a corner to see Emielle crouching on the floor, emptying the grenade belts, her cousin watching anxiously. There was a door just behind them, and a line of coveralls and cloaks hanging on the wall. Outside there was a continuous whining moan, either wind or machinery, and it was much, much colder.

Mira stopped. "For god's sake, Costa, tell her to be careful with those things."

Costa looked up, worried. "She won't tell me what they are."

Mira bent to examine the fist-sized cylinders. Emielle glanced at her without expression, without stopping. "These are thermal grenades," said Mira. "Tell her she can't use them without a launcher. We'll all be killed if she tries throwing them."

"This isn't right," said Costa. "There's a fire. It starts with candles. The last thing I saw was a room full of candles." She started speaking in her own language, translating.

The other girl took the last of the grenades out of its pocket and held it gently, listening, but Mira was pretty sure she already knew exactly what she had in her hand, and what its capabilities were. She said something very softly and twisted the ring that would arm the grenade. A tiny yellow ready-light went on as she set it down on the floor. Now it would go off on impact. It really did look like a candle.

Costa stared at it in horror, then at the rest of the unlit cylinders. Emielle picked up another grenade and calmly armed it.

She had no intention of even trying to leave, Mira realized. She would stay here until the Sector returned, and blow them all sky-high. She had missed her chance with Jezr'el, but she would kill his father.

Mira shivered. The Sector had a lot of nerve making these people into slaves. She touched Costa's arm. "We've got to get out of here."

"No!" she caught Emielle's hands before she could pick up another bomb and spoke in a low, urgent voice. Emielle shook her head and answered impassively. The only thing Mira could understand was Raffail's name, and Jezr'el's.

Mira moved away, not wanting to watch them argue when the outcome was already too clear. She put her hands against the door to try the lock, then jerked them away with a gasp. The metal was cold enough to freeze bare flesh.

Emielle was pointing at her as Mira rubbed her hands together, trembling. Was it that cold outside? Colder? Maybe Costa was wrong after all, and there was no way out for any of them.

Costa got to her feet, on the verge of tears, and stumbled to the cloaks. She struggled into one and pulled a set of coveralls off its hook. "Put this on," she said to Mira. "Hurry."

Mira slid into it, feet first. The material was thick, heavy, with gloves sewn onto the ends of the sleeves. It stank of ashes, like the Remini. "Is she coming?"

Costa shook her head. "She can't," she said hoarsely. "She won't." She took down a second cloak and threw it over Mira's shoulders, fastening it at the throat. "Cover your face. Cover as much as you can."

Mira pulled at the fabric with clumsy hands, trying to copy what Costa was doing. Emielle reached up to help, draping a heavy swath of scarf over her mouth and nose. She secured it somehow, and turned back to her cousin, her face set.

Costa gave Mira a pleading look, nothing but a pair of desperate grey eyes over the scarf. "Tell her to come. You're free. She'll do what you say."

Mira swallowed and looked at Emielle. "It's suicide," she said, knowing Emielle couldn't understand a word. "If she comes they'll be able to track us." She glanced back at Costa. "You've had your revenge. Doesn't she get hers?"

Costa didn't answer. She squeezed her eyes shut as Emielle pushed the thick folds of cloth away from her face and kissed her. Costa threw her arms around the other girl's neck, but Emielle pulled away, hauling on the door until it opened. Outside it was pitch black. Wind howled around the side of the building, and snow blew in like a solid wall of needles.

Mira took a step back in amazement. She'd been in a lot of places and seen her share of weather, but this was different, impassable. She shook Costa off as the girl reached for her. "Are you crazy?" Mira shouted over the wind. "We'll never get through this!"

The girl just nodded, her eyes flooded with tears. She pulled hard, and Mira had to follow as they stepped through the door and into the gale. Behind them, Emielle stood shivering in the arch of light, her clothes beating against her body. She raised one hand, but Mira wasn't even sure Costa saw it as they fought their way through the knee-deep snow. Then the door closed, and they were alone together in the freezing blackness.

"Where are we going?" shouted Mira.

Costa bent against the wind and led her off to the left.

There was a small building just ahead, barely visible. The wind gusted hard, blowing Mira onto her knees in the snow. She fell against something hard. Metallic? Mira ran her hands over whatever it was, squat and familiar.

"There's a skimmer here!" She could hardly see Costa. "Help me get it open!" She fumbled with the cowling release through thick gloves but couldn't make it budge.

Costa appeared next to her. "It's frozen shut. Don't waste time with it. They can't fly in this kind of weather anyhow."

"Have you ever tried?" snapped Mira, but she was probably right. "We're not going to last ten minutes out here." She struggled with the catch. It was completely solid.

Costa tugged on her arm, and Mira stopped trying to resist. Even through the coverall and cloak, the wind was sharp, draining. If Costa's dream had shown her a way to walk out of this place and still be alive by morning, it would be nothing short of a miracle.

A dim rectangle of light floated ahead in the driving blizzard. Mira stumbled toward the open door, tripping against a hidden stair and collapsing inside.

At least it seemed warmer. She untangled herself from the cloak and looked around, trying to catch her breath. Huge, shaggy black animals loomed over her not ten meters away. It took a minute for her to realize they were horses. Their coats were so thick she could hardly see their eyes.

Costa shut the door, muting the sound of the howling wind. Mira sat up in her bulky clothes as the girl knelt next to her, breathing hard. "Are you alright?"

Mira shivered. Her face was so cold it felt like it was made out of wood. "I think so. What now?"

"We're going to ride out."

"In what?" asked Mira, and then she realized that wasn't really the question. "What do you mean *ride?*"

Costa didn't answer. She went over to the line of horses and chose two, the two biggest.

Mira watched her with a terrible feeling in her stomach. "You've got to be kidding."

"We can be out of the valley by daylight. We'll see the explosion from the hills."

Costa sounded tired and strained. She kept her back turned while she saddled and bridled the animals, easily, as though this was something she'd done all her life.

"Did you see all this?" Mira asked. "How do you know we won't freeze to death?"

Costa pulled a girth up tight enough for the horse to grunt. "Maybe we will," she said. "Maybe we should stay."

The lack of sarcasm in her voice was abruptly more frightening than riding through the storm on horseback. Mira struggled to her feet and got within an arm's length of the smaller of the two animals. Costa adjusted the stirrup and held out a hand, still avoiding Mira's eyes. Mira took a breath, wanting very much to tell her how genuinely sorry she was about Emielle, but couldn't think of anything that wouldn't sound insincere and patronizing. "I haven't ridden a horse since I was twelve," she said instead.

"I know," said the girl. "Just stay close to me."

The creature lurched as she clambered into the saddle. Mira hung on as Costa led both horses to a tall door on the other side of the building. The door creaked on its rollers, opening like a curtain onto the black and the blizzard. Mira shrank deeper into her clothes. The wind was straight on, right into her face.

Costa swung up onto the other horse. "We'll be alright. I know what I'm doing."

"How?" asked Mira, unable to keep her voice from shaking.

"It's much worse where we come from." Costa pulled the cloak up around her face, and urged her horse out into the storm.

It was hard to imagine anything worse. Mira crouched in the saddle, trying not to get blown off, while the horse slogged reluctantly behind its stablemate. Snow flew into her eyes, and the wind blew right through everything she had on. In a few minutes, she lost sight of the other horse. When she squinted, she could see what she thought was Costa's cloak flapping in the gale, but then she wasn't sure. The wind changed direction suddenly, or maybe she had. Mira peered into the snow below her, looking for the tracks the other horse must have left, but all she could see was a confusion of prints, rapidly filling with snow. Her horse gave an outraged snort and pulled his head to one side. Mira let him do what he wanted, assuming he knew where Costa was and would follow. The wind struck her hard from behind as the horse broke into a shambling trot. Mira realized he was heading back for the barn. She hauled on the reins in a panic, trying to turn him back into the wind. He did finally stop, even turning for her, but he wouldn't budge beyond that. Mira pounded his sides until her legs hurt, shaking with a blind panic she'd never felt in her life. The storm closed in around her, and she pulled the cloak away from her face to shout for help. She opened her mouth and felt the heat of her body escape, blown off like a thin layer of dust.

She'd never been lost. She'd never been terrified like this, and she'd never imagined that wind could make a scream sound so insignificant. Mira huddled against the horse's neck, positive that this was the spot where she would die, either by freezing or Emielle's grand suicide. Her friends were already dead. She doubted that anyone else would ever know that she had been off the ship during the Remini attack, that she was, at least for the time being, the Proviso's last survivor. Except for Costa.

The horse shifted under her, and Mira was almost grateful, thinking that this animal was about to take some initiative and would get her out of the penetrating cold.

"Mira," said the wind in Costa's voice.

The reins pulled out of her hands, and Mira looked up. Costa slipped the reins under her own leg and fastened the scarf back over Mira's nose and mouth, tight against the wind. Suddenly it was much easier to breathe.

"Don't leave me," Mira whispered, but she could hardly hear herself say it. Costa turned away, not responding.

It seemed like years before the horses began to labor against the gently rising ground, and an eternity before it occurred to Mira that she had absolutely no idea where they were going. They would be safely out of range of the explosion by dawn, but then what? This planet was controlled entirely by the Sector, and even if they could stay out of sight for a few days, it was only a matter of time before they were discovered. The idea of being pursued by Raffail's vengeful relatives occupied Mira for quite some time. She almost didn't notice the change in the darkness as the storm began to weaken, but when she looked up, it was distinctly lighter and not as cold.

Snow still blew around them, but the sky was a sort of transparent grey now, with a trace of sunrise in it. They were at the top of a small hill. Costa had stopped her horse and was peering into the haze behind them.

"What's the matter?" Mira tried to ask, but her voice rasped over the words.

Costa slid her leg out of the loop of reins and handed them back. "We have to hurry now," she said. "I don't think we're far enough." She waited until Mira had a firm grip, then kicked her horse into a gallop.

Mira hung on as her horse bounded through drifts that reached his chest. She lost the reins and wound her hands into the long mane.

The blast caught her by surprise. Soundless light flashed behind them, and a gust of hot wind nearly lifted Mira right out of the saddle. Her horse leaped out from under her, sliding sideways in the snow, and Mira fell for what seemed like a very long time. She hit her head on something. When she opened her eyes, she found herself studying the little clouds that were floating overhead. Mira moved her arms and legs. She managed to roll over on her side and saw Costa running toward her. The horses were nowhere in sight.

The girl sank down in the snow, breathless. "Are you alright?"

Mira touched the back of her head. The glove came away bloody. "I guess not."

Costa explored the wound with gentle hands that Mira could hardly feel. "It's just a cut. Can you get up?"

Mira held onto her, struggling to stand, trembling with exhaustion or cold—she couldn't tell anymore. Costa supported her, leading her down the side of the hill to where she'd tied her own horse, helped her mount, and got on behind her.

"Where are we going?" asked Mira thickly.

"There's a cabin further ahead. Emielle told me they came out here to hunt."

"Hunt?" Mira leaned back against her, too tired to be really curious, or even that concerned.

Costa poked her in the ribs. "Don't go to sleep."

"I'm warm," Mira lied. "I'm tired."

"You're frozen," said Costa. She kicked the horse into a jarring trot. "You can rest in a little while. Not now."

Mira hung on with all the energy she had left, concentrating on keeping her eyes open. The early sun glared off the snow. Suddenly she noticed that there was already a trail in front of them, freshly broken. "Somebody's ahead of us!" she said in alarm.

"It's your horse," said Costa gently. "He's heading for the nearest stable."

Under other circumstances, it might have been a relaxing, refreshing change from the pressure of her job. The sun climbed slowly. The air got warmer. The open, white fields gave way to a scattering of trees and rougher, higher ground. Costa slowed the horse, letting him pick his way through hidden rocks, and finally got off to lead him through the tangle of bare trees. Ahead, just visible in the cleft between two hills, was a small cabin and a shed. Mira's horse was waiting patiently at the gate.

Costa stopped, peering anxiously ahead. "There's no smoke," she said. "They would have taken the horse in by now."

"You think somebody's in there?" asked Mira.

"I don't know."

"I thought you dreamed all this."

"Only up to the explosion."

"Oh." Mira squinted at the cabin, and that made her head ache. "It looks pretty deserted to me. Anyhow, if I was going to attack an Emirate battleship, I'd take all my troops."

As they got closer, it was pretty obvious that they were alone. The cabin door hung open. Inside, snow had drifted on the floor.

Mira slid off the horse shakily. The cabin wasn't much: tiny, actually, with a table, a couple of chairs, and a cold, ashy fireplace with a pile of furs in front of it.

Mira tottered over to the furs and collapsed. It wasn't very warm in here, but at least there was no wind. She watched for a moment as Costa crouched in front of the fireplace. Then she let her eyes close. Her hands stung, and she couldn't feel her feet at all. It all seemed very useless, suddenly, to get this far and still be in danger of dying from the cold. Maybe the Sector knew how to construct a fire, but she did not. Her survival skills, she was discovering, were not what they needed to be. She found herself on the edge of sleep, entering some awful dream with the Remini in it, complete with the smell of smoke. Mira opened her eyes in alarm. Costa was arranging pieces of wood in the fireplace, carefully encouraging a tiny flame.

"How?" Mira croaked. She pushed herself up on one elbow. "How'd you do that?"

"I'll show you sometime." She set a larger chunk into the fire, and Mira watched in amazement as the flame caught and quickly turned into a respectable blaze. Costa looked at her expectantly. "It's much warmer over here."

Mira gathered her strength and crawled over to the hearth, as close as she could without catching fire herself. Costa unfastened the coverall. "Let me see your hands."

Mira held them out. They were ruddy and stiff, painful when Costa rubbed them. "Stop," she said. "I just want to sleep."

"I know. Let's see your feet."

Her thin uniform boots were soaked with melting ice. Costa pulled them off, and her socks. Mira clenched her teeth, expecting it to hurt, but everything was numb.

Costa slapped the soles of her feet, massaged her toes. "I can't tell if you're blue or purple," she said. "You're so dark."

Mira groaned as her flesh thawed. The flow of blood was agonizing, like a limb that had been asleep for hours. Costa didn't stop until she'd revived every nerve, and by that time, Mira would have been just as happy to cut off both feet. She pulled an armful of the furs around herself, exhausted, watching as Costa set a pot of snow into the coals. "What are you doing?"

"Making tea. You should have some. Then you can sleep." She sounded very matter of fact about it, but there was something else in her tone.

"Is it really this primitive on Jahar?" asked Mira.

The girl stared at the fire. "I thought we weren't supposed to talk about that."

"We don't have to," said Mira. "I was just curious."

Costa rubbed her eyes. "Jahar," she said, "is like Veral. But we have more snow. Like this."

"Do you miss it?"

Costa shook her head a little too emphatically, pushing another piece of wood into the fire. She sat back on the hearth, her hands over her face, and didn't say anything for a while.

Mira waited, watching the snow in the pot melt into a smaller and smaller island until it disappeared altogether and began to steam. "I'm sorry about Emielle," she said finally.

"Did you see how she cut herself?" whispered Costa.

"Yes. "

"I didn't even say good-bye." She took a breath and tears began to roll down her cheeks. Mira put a tired, clumsy arm around her shoulders and held her while she shook, choking on her anger and grief. "At least she killed him," wept Costa. "You were right. It's what she wanted."

Mira stroked the girl's hair, smoothing it back from her burning ears. If Raffail had been in the building, there was certainly nothing left of him now. No doubt the Sector would investigate the explosion, but hopefully there would be no search for saboteurs. The blast had taken place close enough to the weapons locker for any evidence to point to an accident, and there would be no trace of Jezr'el's murder. Nothing to make anyone suspect that the diplomat and her troublesome slave were still alive.

Mira wrapped the girl a little more tightly in her arms. As long as they were together, and Costa's disturbing visions were accurate, maybe they could survive here until a search party came looking for the remains of the Proviso. She squeezed her eyes shut against her own tears for Vince, and even Amrei.

10

It was dark again when she woke up. Outside, the storm had strengthened and was beating against the wooden door in furious, uneven gusts. Mira pushed away the swaddle of furs and sat up. The only light in the room came from the fireplace, and Costa was sitting cross-legged on the hearth, staring into the flames.

She looked up when Mira moved. "How are you feeling?"

"Better." She rubbed her eyes. "Is there anything to eat around here?"

Costa nodded and gingerly took the pot out of the fire. There was a large ceramic mug on the hearth, and she dipped it into the dark mixture.

"What is it?"

"It's supposed to be soup."

It was thin, but there were substantial, meaty-tasting things in it, and Mira drank it as quickly as she could without hurting herself. Her coverall was spread out to dry along with the cloaks, and the snow had been completely swept out of the cabin. There was also a new stack of wood by the fireplace. "You've been busy," she said. "Didn't you sleep?"

"I will tonight."

Mira blew on the hot liquid, considering her next question. "Will you know what happens tomorrow?"

"Yes."

"How far ahead can you see?"

"A day usually. Sometimes a little more."

"A week?" Mira wasn't sure why she was hedging. It certainly wasn't because of any lingering skepticism on *her* part. "More?"

"I saw you two years ago."

Mira frowned. "But that would have been—"

"It was before I was collared," said Costa quietly. "I wasn't even asleep. I looked into the lake and saw you in the water. It was night. . .you were so dark. I could hardly see you."

"Maybe it was just a reflection," said Mira. "If it was that dark, it could have been anyone."

The girl shook her head. "It was you. For a long time I thought you'd be like me. I thought you'd be searching for me because your dreams told you to."

Which finally explained the peculiar conversation that night on the Proviso. "I found you by accident."

"I know." She pushed the end of a stick into the coals, stirring them. "But if I hadn't seen you, I would have run away sooner. I'd have ended up in the Mine line one way or another. You wouldn't have found me, though. You would have been too late."

"Someone else would have gotten you out," said Mira. "That woman was just waiting for the right amount of money."

"She told me whoever bought me would kill me," Costa said. "When you came in, I thought that was what you wanted."

Mira shifted uncomfortably. "You talk like this is some kind of destiny. I just did what anyone should have done."

"But you helped me," said the girl. "You're the only person who's ever helped me. Just knowing you were out there somewhere got me through a lot of things."

Mira hesitated. "But you didn't recognize me."

"No," said Costa. "After the Enhancers, I could hardly remember my own name."

Mira looked down at what was left in her cup. Firelight flickered off the oily surface of the soup. She could barely see the shape of her own face in the liquid, a glint where her eyes were, and a cloud of dark hair. Was that all that Costa had seen? Was that what she'd clung to for two years? Mira put the cup down. She didn't believe in fate, but whether it was pure chance or providence, Costa had found the person who would free her.

"When did you know it was me?"

"When you were showing me the maps and the monitor shut off. You were looking over my shoulder and I saw the same reflection. Then I knew I was safe."

And then she'd finally gone to sleep. "You've got a lot of faith in these dreams," said Mira. "Didn't you say you'd been wrong before?"

"I make the wrong decisions. When Emielle and I ran away, it was the wrong thing to do. I thought we had time to get to the mountains and hide. She was too sick. All we found were the Remini. And Raffail." She rubbed her forehead. "Sometimes I think if I could change one thing, everything would turn out differently. But I never know what to do until it's too late."

"Like staying on the ship," said Mira. "If I had listened to you, none of this would have happened."

"I couldn't think of a way to make you listen," said Costa. "I could have killed one of them right away if I'd had a knife when we first went down."

Mira shook her head. "The Remini would have come out the second it smelled blood. Anyway, that knife wasn't sharp enough for butter." The furs were hot from the fire, and Mira tucked them around Costa's bare feet. "What did you see last night?"

Costa touched her face where she'd been hit. "I saw Raffail. I knew the Remini was there. And Emielle." She leaned against Mira's arm. "I knew Jezr'el would give you a knife."

"Did you know you would kill him?"

"Yes."

Mira wondered if the girl had any qualms at all about what she'd done, and doubted it. "What about the grenades? What did they look like in the dream?"

"Candles. I was sure that's what they were."

"But I told you what they were. Didn't you see that?"

Costa thought about it. "If I did, I don't remember. Things are very distorted. It's hard to know what's really happening."

"You have a general idea of events? Not any details?"

She nodded. "It feels strange to talk about this. I never told anyone except Emielle."

"When I remembered who she was, I was afraid you'd left without me."

Costa slipped her hand into Mira's, and the press of it was warm and sure. "I wouldn't have done that. Even if we could have gotten out by ourselves, I would never have left you there."

Mira held on, carefully savoring this feeling of being genuinely needed. "Did she have dreams too?"

"No."

Mira stared at the fire, trying to decide how much more she had the right to know. "Did anyone else in your family?"

"My mother might have," said Costa. "They say I'm a lot like her. I never knew her though."

"She's dead?"

"She's a slave. She was collared when I was four years old."

"A slave?" Mira frowned. "I thought they only took people who couldn't have children."

"She was trouble," said the girl bitterly. "So was I. So was my sister."

"You're all . . . ." Mira wasn't even sure how to ask. "How big was your family?"

"Just the three of us. Raffail took my mother and then my sister. He gave me her husband and her babies." She pulled her hand away and got up to put another log on the fire.

It was easy to see why these were such forbidden subjects. "We don't have to talk about this," said Mira.

"I want to." Costa sat next to her again, closer. "I had a choice once," she said. "Raffail told me to decide whether I wanted to be a slave or have twenty children." She shuddered. "When I thought about what Jezr'el would do to the girls—"

"So you ran away? That's why he made you a slave?"

"That was part of it." She hesitated. "I tried to kill Raffail once. I tried to burn his house down."

"*What?*"

"He blamed my sister. When I tried to tell him the truth, he didn't believe it." She squeezed her eyes shut. "I don't know what happened to her. It's been two years since I've seen her."

"Do you think she's alive?"

"I don't know. I asked about her once. Raffail said she was alright, but I don't know now."

"We can find out," said Mira urgently, because Costa was about to start bawling. "We'll find her," said Mira. "We'll just scan the registry until you see her." And then what? Mira had a sudden and uncomfortable vision of herself with two or three lovely slave girls. "As soon as we get out of here, we'll start looking."

When she realized she was by herself, Mira opened her eyes. The fire was no more than a pile of smoking coals. The pot and mug from last night were gone. She sat up stiffly, sore in every joint and hungry. Quite hungry. Morning light sifted through the chinks in the door, and outside she heard a heavy, distinct *thunk*, like something being hit.

Mira scrambled to her feet, tangling in the furs. The Sector were here? It had been stupid to stay in one place for so long. She crept to the door and peered through the cracks expecting to see Raffail in a fury. But outside there was only fresh, undisturbed snow. Mira opened the door carefully.

Costa was standing barefoot by the shed, oblivious and alone. She was holding a long, slender piece of wood—or plastic? There was a string involved somehow, and another short stick. She pulled the string back and the stick flew out of her hands. Mira watched it hit a tree more than twenty meters away. Then she heard the *thunk*.

"What are you doing?" asked Mira.

The girl looked up in surprise. "Shooting."

"I thought someone was beating you up out here."

Costa smiled and shook her head. The cold had turned her cheeks pink, and her hair was so completely gold in this light it hardly looked real.

"What's that?" asked Mira, nodding to the strung stick.

"It's a bow." She handed it to Mira. "Haven't you ever seen one?"

It was made of smooth, smooth wood, shaped like two frowning brows, no longer than her arm. Mira ran her fingers along the taut string. "What's it for?"

"It's a weapon." Costa took it back and held up one of the shorter sticks. "This is the arrow. You just set it in . . ." She adjusted the arrow on the string, and pulled the contraption back. Mira didn't even see her let go. The arrow brushed through the air and hit the tree. "I found it in the shed."

"Why do we need a weapon?" asked Mira. "What happens today?"

"Well. . . ." She stopped, like she was trying not to laugh. "We have to do some hunting."

"Hunting?" echoed Mira. "I thought there was food here."

"Not any more."

Mira squinted nervously at the trackless snow. "We're going to kill something?"

"Just reshie," said the girl. "It won't be hard."

"We're raiding somebody's farm?"

Costa laughed. "They're wild. The Sector never let us herd them. It's the same on all their planets, I think." She pointed at a pair of big felt shoes sitting by the door. "I found some boots for you. We can leave when you're ready."

At least the horse seemed more cooperative, or maybe he was tired too. Mira adjusted the coverall carefully. Every time she moved, her muscles ached. By the time she'd muffled herself up in the cloak and scarf, she was in real pain. The horse lagged, and Mira let him nose the snow for nonexistent grass. Ahead, Costa whistled cheerfully, some unrecognizable tune that carried clearly in the bright, cold air. The sky was cloudless overhead, a sharp, almost cutting blue, and it fit precisely over the little hills like a glass bowl. It was a gorgeous day—even with the Sector and the Remini lining up for an attack along the Emirate border—Mira had to admit that.

The cabin was far behind them now, not even visible in the distance. Mira had kept an eye on it for a while, turning around, an intermittent black dot on the horizon which rose and fell as the horses labored through the low hills, past invisible obstacles under shoulder-high drifts. Any unlikely rescue would probably check the cabin first for survivors from the Proviso, but so would the Sector. Mira urged the horse forward as it dawdled. Realistically, there was nowhere that she and Costa could expect to hide on Ain-Selai. The only solution was to keep moving and hope they weren't noticed, at least until the war was resolved, one way or another.

Costa pulled her horse to a halt and glanced back, her hair blowing in bright strands around her face, perfectly at home in this freezing, unforgiving place.

"Where are your reshie?" asked Mira.

Costa waved vaguely at the distance. "Over there. We'll see a line of trees and a frozen lake. They're just past that."

Mira let her horse move forward so they were riding side by side. "That's all you saw? Just hunting reshie?"

The girl hesitated. "There was something else. It wasn't very clear though."

"What was it?"

Costa squinted into the distance. "I think there's a city. I think it's some kind of port."

Mira felt her heart jump. She pushed away outlandish hopes. "It must be a Sector port. We're too far into the Faraque for smugglers."

"It might just be a village," said Costa. "It's two days away. I won't be sure until tonight."

"Anything else I should know?"

Costa gave her a sideways look, trying not to grin. "I get to teach you how to hunt."

Was it going to be that entertaining? "What happens?" she asked. "Do I fall off?"

Costa laughed, and Mira shortened the reins a little, trying not to look as nervous as she was starting to feel. "When does this happen?"

"While we're hunting. You don't have to help if you don't want to. I can do it by myself."

Mira pointed at the bow slung over the girl's back. "Don't you just shoot?"

"You have to get close enough. It takes two riders." Costa held her hands up, palm facing palm. "You have to pen them with the horses, so they run between."

"And then you kill it?" Mira frowned. "That doesn't sound very hard."

"It's not," said Costa. "But reshie are fast, and they hear *everything.*"

Mira tried to imagine sneaking up on anything on horseback. "I can stay on," she said with as much confidence as she could muster. She wondered if Costa knew anything about setting broken bones. "What do we have to do?"

It didn't sound difficult or complicated. The only thing that seemed risky, and potentially embarrassing, was the speed involved. Mira glanced down at the horse's knees, deep in the fresh snow. A really *fast* charge at some unsuspecting and much smaller animal didn't seem very probable.

At the crest of the next hill, Costa pulled her horse to a stop and pointed across the shallow valley. "Those are the trees."

An inauspicious clump of tall shrubbery straggled across the top of the next hill—and the one further on.

"Are you sure?" asked Mira.

She nodded. "Here's the lake."

Mira looked down at the featureless snow below them. There was a faint outline, a vague frozen oval she would never have noticed otherwise.

"You have to be quiet," said the girl. "This is why we have Sign." She gestured deliberately with her hands. *Stay to the left. Stay close. Leave room for the—*

Reshie, Mira guessed. A quick brush of thumb against all four fingers. She nodded silently and felt her nerves tingle.

Costa led the way around the edge of the valley, staying away from the frozen lakebed, letting the horses pick the easiest path. Without conversation, even the muffle of hooves in snow seemed loud. Mira glanced at the girl, riding without reins, restringing the bow, unconcerned. Perhaps it was only the sound of human voices that would make the animals run.

The trees were thicker than they looked from a distance. Mira ducked under branches, flat on the horse's neck. Costa motioned her to come alongside and pointed, through the tangle of limbs to a collection of black shapes in the valley.

Costa tapped her on the shoulder, pointed and held up four fingers. *The fourth one from the right,* she Signed and pointed again to the smallest of the group. *Stay left,* she repeated with her hands, and edged her horse away. *This much space.*

Mira nodded and gathered up the reins. Her heart thumped nervously, but she found it hard to be afraid. At least not yet.

Costa set an arrow against the bowstring and crouched low, moving carefully out of the trees. Mira paralleled her until they were at the very edge of the woods.

"Now!" hissed the girl and kicked the horse hard.

Mira's horse gave a huge bound and flew after her, plunging straight down the hill. Ahead, the reshie raised their heads as a single creature and promptly scattered.

Mira had enough time to gasp for breath before she lost the reins. Each stride made her land farther and farther back in the saddle, and all she could do was try to hang on. When she had the chance to look up, she saw Costa plowing through the snow, hair streaming behind her, completely in control and somehow quite far ahead. The slope ended abruptly, and Mira's horse stumbled. Through some miracle, Mira found herself correctly placed on his back, scrabbling for the reins. She saw Costa glance back, grinning. The girl veered to the right. Mira's horse followed.

Ahead, two reshie fled together, black tails flagging as they tore along through the snow. Costa caught up with them, and they changed direction almost instantaneously, charging off to the left while the horse churned snow.

"The smaller one!" shouted Costa. "Stay next to me!"

Mira hauled on the reins. The horse wheeled under her, breaking into a gallop as his stablemate flew past. In a second, Mira found herself within an arm's length of Costa, the horses running side by side.

"Good!" Costa leaned away from her, widening the distance between them, and brought up the bow. The reshie were heading for the far side of the valley and the rest of the herd, which was already halfway up the hill.

They were no match for the speed of the horses, Mira realized, as they gained on the frightened animals. One was clearly younger, a fawn or a calf, and it was already losing ground. It tried to dodge to the right as the horses closed in on it, following its mother, but Costa was in the way. It swung to the left, almost tangling with Mira's horse, and then ran in a straight, terrified line between them, its ears flat against its skull, the thick winter coat rippling over straining muscles.

Costa leaned over it, bowstring back, an easy, graceful motion. Her expression was calm, intent, waiting for some particular moment. Mira never even saw her let the arrow go. The reshie jerked and dropped in its tracks. Costa slid her horse to a stop in the suddenly bloodied snow. Mira kept going.

The fall wasn't even frightening. She slipped off as her horse charged up the hill, unstoppable. Mira lay in the pillow of drifts, catching her breath, dizzy with the cold air. Blue sky stretched overhead, flawless and deep. It had not occurred to her to ask when, exactly, or how she would fall. The single way to have avoided it would have been to stay back in the trees and not participated. Had there been a choice?

Below her, Costa knelt in the scatter of red, methodically working the dead calf with Jezr'el's knife. The other horse stood patiently next to her, a black point at the center of new tracks. Whatever else Raffail had required her to learn, Mira thought, he had also given her the skills for her revenge. Maybe Jezr'el's death was no different than this one, a question of survival. But Mira had to admit, she felt much sorrier for the calf.

She got up slowly, brushing herself off, and made her way back down the hill.

Costa looked up from what she was doing and smiled. "Now you're an expert rider," she said. "You've fallen off twice."

"I think I lost the horse." Mira crouched in the snow, trying not to watch. Costa had emptied the carcass and was in the process of skinning it. Mira shuddered. "Maybe I should try to find him."

"He'll come back." Costa grimaced, peeling back the hide, working the knife between the skin and raw, red muscle, up to her elbows in gore. "We could eat now," she said. "Are you hungry?"

"No," said Mira, trying not to gag. "Not at all."

By late afternoon, she was ravenous. The rolling hills had become steeper, almost mountainous, and thick with trees. Mira rode doggedly behind Costa, cold again. They'd found her horse at the top of the hill, but the climb had been exhausting. The sky was beginning to cloud over, and the thought of spending the night in a blizzard began to preoccupy her to the point of extreme anxiety.

"Do you think its going to snow?" she asked finally.

Costa glanced back. "Probably. But not until later. Are you cold?" Mira nodded helplessly. "Is there another cabin out here?"

"No," said the girl. "We'll build a shelter. We should stop now anyway." They were riding along the edge of a frozen gully, and Costa guided her horse down its slope. The small valley was heavily wooded, windless, and broken branches stuck up through the snow like arms and legs and fingers.

Mira slid off the horse, shivering. What she wanted to do most was lie down and sleep. The snow was starting to look very soft and inviting.

Costa took the reins, studying her face. "You're freezing. And you must be starved. Why didn't you tell me?"

"I can't eat that thing," said Mira earnestly. "It was alive." She sank to her knees, too sore and too tired to stand, but the girl pulled her back up.

"At least help me build a fire," she said. "All you have to do is pick up some of the wood around here. Make a stack about this high." She held her hand at about knee level.

It didn't sound too hard. Mira wandered aimlessly around the small clearing, breaking off what she could, piling the sticks and twigs while Costa leaned bigger branches together and covered them with saddle blankets. It didn't look at all weatherproof to Mira. "Is this enough?" she asked, pointing to the stack.

"It's good for kindling," said Costa. "See if you can find five or six big pieces. How are you feeling?"

Mira realized she was sweating. "Better."

The girl smiled and turned back to the shelter.

By the time Mira had collected the rest of the wood, the lean-to was covered with a thick layer of snow, packed down and hard as ice. Costa was crouched next to the pile of kindling, hovering over a tiny flame, carefully nursing it with twigs.

Mira sat down next to her. "You'll have to show me how to do that one of these days."

Costa gave her a handful of kindling. "Just feed them in, one at a time."

Mira did, watching as they caught fire and shriveled into twisting coals. It was darker now, and the snow flickered redly with the flames. Four tiny moons, like asteroids, edged through thickening clouds, and trees creaked softly in the wind.

Costa laid a few of the larger branches on the coals and began sharpening a stick. Mira watched as she pierced an unrecognizable part of the dismembered reshie and set it over the flames.

"You don't have to eat it," said Costa. "I know it's a lot different than what you're used to."

Juices from the meat dripped into the fire, smoking and hissing. The aroma was suddenly overwhelming, and Mira swallowed back her hunger.

"You know," she said, and had to swallow again, "the food on the ship is all artificial. I think its generated from algae or something."

Costa looked at her with a disgusted expression. "That explains a lot. Your technology is very interesting, but your food is awful." She turned the spit a little.

"How long does this take?"

"Not long." Costa skewered a bigger piece. "You have to be patient," she chided. "You wouldn't want to eat it raw."

Mira grinned weakly. She'd just been considering it.

Despite its size, there wasn't much left of the calf by the time they were done. Mira rubbed a handful of snow between greasy fingers and wiped her mouth. She was finally warm, well-fed. Even the impending weather didn't seem worth worrying about.

The shelter was less than a hut, low and dark and cramped for two people. Mira pressed herself against one side, twigs digging into her back, as Costa sealed the entrance. The darkness was abruptly total. Costa's hand touched hers, and she felt the girl curl against her. Mira lay back on the thick furs and blankets with Costa's head nestled on her shoulder, inhaling the scent of smoke in her hair.

Outside, the wind moaned a little more loudly. One of the horses whinnied from its picket in the trees.

"Are you sure they'll be alright?" asked Mira.

"Yes."

Mira lay in the dark with her eyes open, tired but briefly energized by the food. She felt Costa shift, and a hand moved across her shoulders, brushing her face. "Aren't you sleepy?"

Costa yawned. "I will be." She sighed and didn't say anything for a moment. "Can I ask you something? About your other slave?"

"Renee? What do you want to know?"

"What was she like?"

Mira thought about that. Her perceptions of Renee had changed considerably in the last month. "She was very intelligent."

"Why did she run away from you?"

There must have been dozens of reasons. "She was in her eighteenth year. Maybe she just wanted some freedom for a little while."

"Was she. . ." Costa started, and stopped herself. "Did you. . . I mean, were you. . .did she like girls?" she asked finally.

Mira smiled in the darkness. "She was my first. Is that what you want to know?"

She felt the girl nod. "She was much older than you."

It was an odd statement. She'd never really thought about it before. "In actual years. . . ." Mira added the numbers with difficulty. "I guess she was about thirty-eight when she left me. I think she was collared when she was twenty."

"In the holo, you looked like friends," said Costa. "When I first saw it, I thought she loved you very much."

Mira shook her head. "I don't think she did. Not toward the end anyhow." Something had caught in her throat, making her voice sound more emotional than it should have been.

"Maybe she loved you in a different way. Like you were a daughter, or a sister."

The image of Renee, arm-in-arm with another woman, walking determinedly out of Mira's life, reappeared as vividly as ever. "I don't think so," she said, too hoarsely.

Costa was silent for a while. "You were in love with her."

Mira nodded slowly in the darkness. "I was too young to know better. I even told her." She stopped, clenching her teeth. It was too long ago to still feel this way.

The girl moved a little closer. Her lips brushed Mira's, lightly. "I love you," Costa whispered.

Mira pulled her close, as tightly as she could. The words were there, and the emotion was genuine. She put her mouth against the girl's ear. "I can free you," she heard herself say.

"What?" Costa untangled herself from Mira's arms and sat back, not touching her anymore.

Mira pushed herself up on one elbow, wide awake now, wishing she hadn't said anything. She was afraid to repeat it. Out here in the middle of nowhere, it was hard enough for *her* to believe. The only thing that made it a solid fact was the memory of Amrei. "You don't have to die," she whispered. "There's a way to get past the Failure. I've seen it done. I've helped. I can help *you*."

"No you can't," said the girl flatly. "I saw everything in the Mine line. Nobody survived, no matter how long they took."

"It's not how long you can last," said Mira urgently. "There's a method. It's all body temperature. It *works*."

"Every time?" She didn't bother to hide her skepticism. "Who have you freed?"

Even if Amrei was dead, she had a right to her secrets. Mira hesitated. "You've never met her."

Costa didn't say anything. She didn't have to. Her disbelief was a density in the air itself.

"Renee is free," Mira blurted. "That's why she left. She found someone who could do it. I saw her three years ago. She was alive. She was free."

"You must have imagined it."

Mira shook her head emphatically, uselessly in the dark. "It was her."

"The Drug must have been bad to begin with," said Costa. "Diluted, or too strong maybe. It's not possible."

"It is," insisted Mira. "I wouldn't lie to you about something like this."

Costa hesitated, considering that. "Why are you telling me this now?" she asked finally. "I have another eighteen years. What if I belong to someone else when I Fail?"

"You won't," said Mira. "I can promise you that."

"It's a lot to promise," said Costa softly.

"I mean it."

Costa was silent. "When I was collared, I knew what would happen to me. Sometimes I wished for it. What you're telling me now. . . ." She laughed a little in the dark hut. "Who will I be when I'm free? Costa LoDire?"

"Maybe," whispered Mira. "It'll be your choice." She reached over and found her damp palm. "Just stay with me that long."

Costa put her arms around Mira's neck, fingers wound in her hair. "How many of these slaves do you know about?"

"Only two for sure," said Mira. "But the one I helped knew three or four others. I think there must be a lot more." She laid back on the furs with Costa curled against her.

"Would you be able to tell if you saw a freed slave?" Costa asked after a while.

"I don't think so."

"What if I was free and called someone D'sha?"

Mira smiled. "You haven't even called *me* that for the last two days."

11

t was the slap of cold air that woke Mira up, not the shouting.

Costa was outside the shelter, on her hands and knees in the snow. Mira pushed away the furs and crawled out into the frozen, pinkish dawn.

"What was it?" Mira knelt, cradling her, rocking her slowly until she stopped gasping. "Tell me."

"There's a city. It's a half day from here."

In itself, that was very encouraging. But this was another nightmare, not something pleasant like a reshie hunt. "What's in the city? Sector?"

Costa shook her head. "Smugglers. Murderers. We can't go."

Mira smoothed her hair. "What happens if we do?"

"There's a man with a ship. He'll offer you passage. Then he'll kill you and keep me." She shivered hard. "We can't go."

"We have to," said Mira. "Is he the only one with a ship?"

"I don't think so."

"Why would we beg him for a ride?" asked Mira. "I've got money."

"No you don't." Costa rubbed her eyes. "Your card was on the Proviso."

Of course it was, but Mira pulled the coverall open anyway and searched every pocket. The card had been on her desk. She knew exactly where. It was atoms now, with everything else. She pulled the heavy clothing back around her, trying not to let her teeth chatter. "What if I turn him down?" she asked. "If I know he's going to kill me, why would we go along?"

"You're in a hurry to get out. You think you can handle him." Costa got to her feet slowly, leaning against a tree trunk for support. "We can't leave," she said. "Not yet anyway. It's too dangerous."

And how long before it was safe? By now every smuggler in the Faraque would have heard about the Proviso's destruction, and possibly even the presence of the Remini. It wouldn't be long before the port in Costa's dream was nothing but a ghost town. Then, no matter how safe it was, they would be stuck here for good.

"We have to go," said Mira. She stood up and brushed off the snow. "There's bound to be someone else with a ship."

"No," said Costa. "I won't take you there."

She said it with such finality and determination that Mira could only stare. "Yes you will."

The girl shook her head. "You know I'm right. It's the only way to stop those things from happening."

Mira turned away. Ordering Costa to shut up and saddle the horses was not an option. She tried to picture herself spending the next several months—even years—chasing reshie and waiting for a rescue that might never come. It didn't sit well in her stomach. "I suppose I could try to find this place myself."

"You'd freeze first."

That was true. Mira rubbed her head, trying to shake off the cold and the sleep. "Didn't you say something about making one change in the things you dream about?"

"I don't remember."

No matter how calm she sounded right now, it was easy to see just how afraid Costa really was. As long as they stayed here in these frigid woods, she was in control. Beyond that, the best she could expect was to be at the mercy of the events she could foresee. "You were talking about when you and Emielle were captured," said Mira gently. "You said you tried to find the one thing you could change to make the outcome different."

"There was nothing I could do," said Costa. "They took us because we ran away. We ran away because Emielle miscarried. They would have taken her anyway."

The miscarriage was not something Mira had known about. Was that how the Sector chose which girls to collar? Clearly it wasn't the best example to use. "What about when Jezr'el tried to poison me?" she asked. "How did that dream end?"

Costa didn't answer. "It's not the same," she said finally. "There's only one way to leave. You make the decision to go with him, and there's nothing I can do. I can't let you go alone."

"Because you think you can save me from him?"

"Yes."

Mira touched her arm. "You're already trying to change the one thing," she said. "You're dreams aren't fate, Costa. They're only options. They're warnings, or different paths to follow. Things go wrong when you don't have enough information."

Costa shook her head and sat down heavily against the tree. "This is already different."

"How?" She suspected it was only a matter of time until she could talk the girl into going against her better judgment. It might not be the best idea, but there didn't seem to be a lot of choices. "How did the dream go?"

Costa sighed. "We argued. You went off by yourself. I followed you. The city is straight east of here. All you'd have to do is ride for a couple of hours and you'd see it."

"This conversation didn't happen?"

"No."

"Tell me about this man," said Mira. "How do we find him?"

"There's a Ground Station. You try to talk your way onto a ship. They want money, and you don't have any. They offer to buy me, but you turn them down. The man follows us out and asks you where you want to go."

"What do I say?"

"Anywhere over the border."

Mira nodded. She could picture it all. "What then?"

"He's very friendly. He offers you a job for passage."

Too solicitous, Mira thought. Too openly generous for this part of space. "And I agree because there's no other way out?"

Costa nodded. "Once we're on board, he's not so nice." She

hugged herself and shivered.

"But there are other ships, aren't there?" asked Mira. "Isn't that what you said?"

"I'm not sure. He might be the last one. I'm not sure."

Nothing was worth getting killed for. "Look," said Mira, "if he's the last ship out, no matter how safe it seems, we won't go. We'll stay here and you can teach me all about living in the woods. If we can find someone else, we'll go with them. You've still got the knife?"

Costa nodded unhappily.

"We'll be careful." She'd expected this prior warning to make her feel safer. Instead it made her more uneasy, like waiting for the murder in a play. "Tell me what he looks like."

"He's taller than you, older. His hair is long, mostly grey."

"He's white-skinned?"

"Yes."

"Alright." Mira held out her hand. "Let's get started."

Neither of them said much as they rode. The sun had risen right into another bank of clouds. It was much windier, much colder, dark with the threat of heavy snow.

Mira wrapped her face a little more tightly and continued to cut away at the Emirate insignia sewn to her uniform. Every time her horse slipped, Jezr'el's knife would make another gash in the cloth. Finally the foolish winged lettering came loose, and she threw it behind her.

She had no idea how far Raffail's arm extended on Ain-Selai, but it was a fair guess that news of a woman in an Emirate uniform with her slave would not take long to get back to whichever Sector had survived the explosion. Better to look anything but official.

Costa was no problem. Her clothes were dirty from the camp fire, bloodstained from the reshie, and her hair was tangled from wind and sleep. There was no danger of anyone mistaking her for School. As for herself . . . . Mira fidgeted with the scarf around her mouth and nose. If everyone on Ain-Selai were as light as the man they had to avoid, she would stand out like a black pebble on a white beach.

There wasn't much she could do about it. She jogged her horse forward until she was next to Costa and gave her back the knife. "How close are we?"

"We should be able to see something from the top of this hill."

She frowned at Mira's bundled head. "Are you that cold?"

Mira shrugged. It was too hard to explain. "When we get there," she said, "be careful how you talk and how you behave. If anyone suspects you're School, I'll turn around and you'll be gone. We'll never see each other again."

"I don't think anyone here knows what School is."

"Smugglers always know."

From the top of the hill, the city sprawled in the distance, much bigger than Mira had imagined. The road that wound toward it through the valley below was absolutely jammed with people. There were hundreds of them, all heading for the city like a swarm of insects, packed with all their worldly belongings.

"They're running from something," Costa frowned. "The Remini? Sector?"

Mira felt her stomach contract. "Something must have happened. Either the Remini are loose, or there's a search on for us." She pulled the horse's head up as he snuffed for grass. "Let's get out of here."

The way down was easy, a rolling descent. They picked up speed, passing from a canter into a gallop. People in the road heard them coming and began to point. Most obviously mistook them for Sector, with their white clothes and black horses, and fell to their knees in the icy mud.

Mira couldn't help but stare. They were pathetic, miserable, even scrawny. Costa glanced back with an expression of obvious contempt. They were slaves—even without a collar and brand. This exodus might be the only act of resistance in generations.

Still, it was hard not feel some sympathy as they passed family after family, muffled and hooded in ragged black, with everything they owned on rickety wooden sledges. If they expected to leave the planet, Mira couldn't imagine how they would pay. Even if they could afford it, there would never be enough ships.

Her horse slowed abruptly, and Mira looked up. The crowd of refugees was thicker just ahead. They would have to go around.

Costa reached back and caught her horse by the bridle. "They'll try to keep us here," she hissed. "Don't go near them."

"Why?"

Before she could answer, a rough-looking man pushed out of the milling fray, dragging a boy behind him. He shook his hood back and looked straight up at Mira, babbling in his own language. He pushed the boy to his knees in the slush and uncovered his head. The boy was no more than sixteen, raven-haired, with skin like porcelain, and blue, blue eyes. "D'sha, D'sha," was all Mira could really understand of what the man was saying, but *Buy my son* was what he meant. Mira turned away, not sure if she should be impressed or disgusted. Would this man resort to anything to save his child? Or was the boy's safety incidental to his own passage out? She didn't look back as Costa led her away from the refugees, across a field of deep, clean snow.

"Is it like this on Jahar?" Mira asked finally.

"You mean do people sell their children?" Costa spat into the snow. "They would if they had the chance." She kicked her horse angrily, and Mira followed at a floundering canter until they got back on the road.

The Ground Station was the most modern-looking building in the city, and it was a decrepit antique. To call this place a city was stretching things. What Mira had thought were outlying residential areas turned out to be huge, disorganized encampments of refugees. The middle of town was no better. Every alleyway was packed, and only the flow of still more people kept the streets from filling up with children, tents, and sledges.

Mercifully, at least for outworlders, the apron in front of the Ground Station had been blocked off with concrete barriers except for one opening. People were packed all around it, but no one was going in. Costa edged through the crowd and slid off to lead the horses through the narrow space.

Mira dismounted stiffly, rubbing her knees. Beyond the windowless blockhouse that was the Station, she could see the slave market. Apparently the local population wasn't allowed to circulate there either, and the pavilions seemed completely deserted. It was starting to look like they were already too late.

She turned to Costa, swallowing back her panic. "Don't go anywhere. I'll be right inside. Don't talk to anyone."

Inside the Station itself, it was much warmer. Mira pushed the scarf away from her face and looked around.

It was a different sort of Ground Station. There wasn't the usual airy openness designed to hold huge numbers of people and their luggage. This one had an admittance office, with a waiting area. The man at the front desk guarded another set of double doors, wedged open with someone's dufflebag. She could see the metal disk at the far end of the next room, gleaming like a prize.

"Good morning," said Mira.

The man eyed her doubtfully. He looked like he hadn't slept for days. "Where the hell did you come from?"

There were two more men sitting at the back of the waiting area where it was too dim for her to see them clearly. They'd been talking when she came in. Now they were watching her. "I need passage out," she said.

He grunted. "Don't we all." He waved at the battered monitor sitting behind him on another chair. The screen was blank except for a handful of number sequences. Ship registrations. Ships still in orbit. Mira leaned forward eagerly, trying to read them, but he switched the screen off. "Two of those have left already." He narrowed his eyes, and she wasn't sure he was telling the truth. "I can guarantee you passage on the other one. Costs money though."

"How much?"

"A thousand. Emirate credits only. Plus a finder's fee."

"I can work my passage," said Mira. Was she wasting time? She glanced back at the other two men, able to see a little better now. One was stocky, short. The other had hair down to his waist. She turned back to the man at the desk. "Anybody need crew?"

"Not that I know of." He looked past her. "How about it, gentlemen? Need crew?"

There was no audible response. Mira wondered why they were even here, what they were waiting for. "Thanks a lot," she said. As she pushed the door open, the taller man stood up and stretched. She stepped back outside.

Costa hadn't budged. "Well?"

Mira just nodded. Behind her, the door opened again. Steam puffed out from the warm room. Or rose off of him.

He shut the door and leaned against it, very casually. No rush. "You must like cutting things close," he said. "Everyone else left yesterday."

"Looks like it," said Mira.

He was exactly the way Costa had described him: about fifty, greying hair, balding a little in front. Light skin, slightly freckled. He had an easy smile that would have fooled her completely if she hadn't been warned.

"Where you headed?" he asked.

"Over the border," Mira repeated, and felt Costa tense across a meter and a half of space.

He nodded and surveyed the girl, up and down. "I might have a job for you," he said. "My next stop is Traja. Interested?"

Mira took a breath. There were other ships still here. There had to be. "No," she said. "I don't think so." She turned away, feeling the mistake in the pit of her stomach. The Sector were already searching for them. Staying on Ain-Selai would be like hiding in a fish bowl. He was the last ship out. She could feel it. She got back on the horse and didn't say anything.

He frowned, confused and suspicious. "You'll never get out of here," he said. "Look, I'll pay you for the girl. Five hundred, Emirate. You can watch the scenery if you want."

Mira shook her head and followed Costa away from him, into the deserted slave market.

Costa glanced back as the station door slammed. "You did the right thing," she whispered.

"God, we're in trouble," said Mira. Her heart was pounding and her teeth were clenched so hard, they hurt. Turning around and begging for the ride she'd just turned down did occur to her, but Costa jerked on her sleeve.

"Look over there!"

There were still two tents at the very far end of the market. One sagged heavily and was in the process of collapsing in a billowing heap.

"They're packing up," said Mira. "Come on!" She booted the horse into a clattering run, bolting through the empty stalls with Costa right behind her.

She realized as they got closer that these were the Mine tents. It was only natural, but she hadn't thought of it. They were always the last ones out.

She pulled the horse to a sliding halt, scattering the dirty slaves as they tangled in the long chains holding them together. One tent had already been folded into a filthy wad, and they were getting ready to start on the second. A free man with a greasy beard scowled at her. "What do you want?" he shouted. "We're closed."

"Passage!" Mira shouted back. "I can pay!" Somehow, she thought.

He raised his eyebrows. "How much?"

"Five hundred," said Mira hopefully. Even this was better than nothing.

The man held out his hand. "Show me."

She hesitated, and he turned away in disgust, shrieking at the slaves to move faster.

There was nowhere to go but the next tent. Mira slid off the horse and handed the reins to Costa. She looked just as scared.

"We may not be able to do this," Mira whispered. We may not get out of this alive, she said to herself, just to get used to the idea.

Best not to look too afraid of being left here. Mira straightened herself up and started walking across the icy little space. She could hear Costa leading the horses, but she didn't look back. People were moving inside the second tent as the slaves were lined up to be put to work. There was something else, too. One boy stood outside with his back to her, hands on his hips, frustrated and impatient, even from behind. He wasn't part of the Mine coffle. He was waiting for someone to come out. It was his hair that looked familiar, a reddish shock that never stayed combed. Mira walked faster. It couldn't possibly be him. He felt her eyes and turned around, frowning.

"Jeremy," she gasped, and he stared at her in astonishment.

"Mira LoDire?" He shut his mouth and opened it again. "D'Lo-Dire? What are you doing out here?"

"Trying to get out." She was terribly glad to see him, but the first thing she needed to know was if he could help. "I'm in trouble, Jeremy, and I'm broke."

"You were on the Proviso," he said, suddenly comprehending. "Wait." He ran to the opening of the tent and grabbed someone by the arm, a young man with a thin, razor-sharp face. "D'Tiago," said Jeremy, giving Mira a meaningful glance. "This is Mira LoDire. I know her. She's worked with jammers before. Her ship left without her, earlier today."

Tiago looked at her very carefully. "Why?"

"Pay dispute," said Mira quickly. It had been ten years since she'd touched a jammer. She hoped Jeremy knew that.

Tiago looked past her, at Costa. "You could have bought passage," he said. "She's worth plenty. Sector bred, I'd say."

"She's not for sale," said Mira. She moved a little so she was blocking his view of the girl. "Or for rent." There was something strange about him that she couldn't pin down. Part of it was the way he looked at Costa—not greedily, like most men—but with real concern.

Behind them, the second tent deflated around itself. Jeremy looked over his shoulder nervously. "We don't have time for this," he said. "She's alright. I know her."

She couldn't understand his hesitation, either. If they needed a jammer operator so badly, what was he waiting for? Finally Tiago nodded and held out his hand. "I'm Esau Tiago," he said. "My ship is the Tantilla. Welcome aboard."

"Thanks," she said, with immense relief. "Thanks a lot."

The ship was almost as old as the Proviso, but seemed to have been through considerably more action. The corridors looked like they'd been split apart and welded back together by someone in a real hurry. The metal was blackened beyond the welding, as if there had been a fire, and the soot made the place even gloomier.

She glanced back at Costa padding silently behind the three of them. She'd left the bow behind, on the planet, but the knife was still hidden under her clothes. Mira disliked the fact that she felt better knowing the girl was armed and as dangerous as she cared to be. It bothered her that Jeremy was involved in what was clearly a smuggling operation, that he was with this Tiago character. It didn't look like Tiago hit him, at least. She hoped he didn't.

"This is where you'll be spending most of your time." Tiago touched a button and an old-style pressure door slid to one side. "Have you used military jammers before?"

It was a trick question since the honest answer was yes. Mira edged past him into the room, crowded with equipment: three monitors for the jammer and a wall full of related electronics. Mira sat down in one of the three chairs and ran her hands over the control board. The jammer was practically the same one she'd used on Thea's outpost. Mira wondered where he'd gotten it. "I've only used commercial models," she lied. "This one doesn't look too different."

Tiago sat down next to her. "Let's see what you can do."

Mira switched on each of the monitors and unwrapped her scarf.

It was warm in here, and she suspected he was going to try to make her sweat. She opened the coverall, but not enough to show what she was wearing. Even without insignia, she felt vulnerable. Jeremy would not have lied for her if the Emirate was at all welcome on the Tantilla.

The whole point of a jammer was to hide things. Big things. The military used them to hide planets, moons, spy ships. Smugglers like Tiago used them just to hide. It was almost a fantasy machine for some people, not just a "cloak." Jammers provided an electronic field that could be shaped into anything—a battleship disguised as a pleasure cruiser, a smuggler as something much more legitimate. It was a handy although far from foolproof tool for crossing in and out of the Faraque without being questioned.

The first monitor showed a schematic of the Tantilla, gridded off with green lines. Mira adjusted the power, and the grid began filling in until the ship was entirely obscured. They would appear as an unfocused image to anyone scanning, difficult to locate, but obviously a ship in the process of disguising itself.

"Alright," said Mira, "what do you want to look like?"

"An ore freighter," said Tiago. "Alpha class."

He could hardly have picked anything bigger. Mira turned to the second monitor and brought up a menu of preprogrammed images. The Alpha freighter was at the very beginning of the file. She engaged it, boosting the jammer's power to maximum.

The image of the freighter on the second screen solidified, then began to flutter wildly. Mira checked the output indicators. Two of the six weren't even working. Back on the first screen there were gaps showing large parts of the schematic, even though most of the green grid was completely filled in. "There's something wrong," she said. "You haven't got the power to maintain an image that size. Not for long, anyway."

He nodded in what seemed like approval. "Try common transport. That's what we usually look like."

Mira lowered the signal strength and engaged the smaller image. The grid reassembled to completely cover the schematic, but the projection on the second monitor was still wavering as if it was under water. She made a few adjustments and it steadied, at least for the moment. "This really needs to be fixed."

"I know," he said. "But there's no time for that now. Just hold it together until we get where we're going."

Mira nodded as casually as she could. "Where's that?"

"The border," said Tiago unhelpfully. He reached in front of her and tapped the keyboard for the third monitor. "Here's something you can watch in your spare time."

The screen fuzzed briefly and resolved into an unfamiliar ship. Mira looked more closely. Sector barges were moored to the bottom of it, like remora on a shark. It was a Remini ship, she realized with a jolt. It was immense. "When did you see that?"

He gave her a suspicious look. "You know what it is?"

"I've never seen one before," she said, quite truthfully, "but it's got to be Remini."

"It passed us two days ago." He watched the ship move across the screen. "We saw that and started running. We wouldn't have stopped, either, except we lost the slave who used to operate this thing." He gestured at the jammer.

"What happened to him?" asked Mira.

"She Failed." Tiago got to his feet. "Jeremy'll show you where you can get cleaned up. We'll be eating in a couple of hours. You can meet the rest of the crew then. Any questions?"

Mira shook her head and watched as he squeezed past Jeremy, disappearing into the corridor.

She sighed and leaned back in the chair, absolutely spent. "Thanks," she said to the boy. "You saved our necks."

"Come on," he said. "We can't talk here."

It was someone else's cabin or had been. She couldn't tell if a man or a woman had lived here. Mira stood in the tiny bathroom using a toothbrush that was not her own, gratefully scrubbing away two, three days of fur. She spat into the sink, ran the water until it was hot, and washed her face again. Costa sat on the lid of the commode, combing out the last tangles. Jeremy had brought them clean clothes and was on his way back with more coffee. All that plus a shower had made the Tantilla seem a much less threatening place.

"Are we still in trouble?" asked Costa quietly.

"Depends." Mira kicked her dirty uniform under the pile of coveralls and cloaks. "We're not over the border yet. Tiago doesn't trust me." She shrugged. "Could be worse, right?"

Costa put the comb down. "Do you think he's bad person?"

"Why do you ask?"

"He gave me the strangest look back by the Mine tents. Like he was worried about me."

"I saw that. Maybe he thinks I beat you."

Costa grinned and leaned her head against Mira's hip. Mira ruffled the girl's hair and went to answer Jeremy's knock.

"I saw Harlan about a week ago," she said, sitting on the bed, carefully holding the hot cup. "When did he get rid of you?"

"It's been two months." He grimaced. "I'm glad it happened."

The bed was quite low, just a couple of mattresses stacked together. It was nice, not so awkward as sitting up high on a chair, having a conversation with people who were kneeling on the floor. Mira took another cautious sip. "Are you alright here?"

He gave her an odd smile. "I'm fine, D'sha."

"You're sure?" she said. "You could leave with us when we cross the border."

"I'm fine," he said again. He put his cup down and said in a low voice, "You know what happened to the Proviso?"

Mira nodded, not looking at him. "The Sector are using Remini weapons and hiding them in barges. They blew that ship to pieces."

"You were in an escape pod?"

"I was on the surface thinking it was a standard negotiating session. They're not even afraid of taking hostages now."

He shook his head grimly. "There's no sign of anything happening on the Emirate side of the border."

"We were under orders to keep radio silence. The attack was so fast, they could never have sent a distress call. No one out there has any idea what's going on. The Sector could cruise by Point Seven and start shooting whenever they feel like it."

Jeremy fidgeted with the cup. "We're not going near the Emirate bases," he said. "Esau doesn't want any trouble. You can understand that?" He looked up apologetically.

Mira shrugged. It wasn't his fault. She would think of some way to contact the people who needed to know. Right now, it was enough to be alive and warm.

"So," said Jeremy, with curiosity he couldn't hide, "they took you hostage?" He glanced pointedly at Costa. "Both of you?"

"It was very dramatic," said Mira wryly. "I saw my first Remini.

They stink," she said at his incredulous expression. "They're not very smart, and the only reason they have any love for the Sector is because they get fed regularly."

"What do they eat?"

"Anything," said Mira. "People. Reshie. I think they'd probably eat each other if they were hungry enough."

"How did you get away?"

She'd known he would ask, anyone would want to know. "There was an explosion," she said, and made it into an accident. She left out Emielle and the part about Jezr'el's murder. No one would ever know about that if she could help it. Slaves who killed free people were not dealt with gently, even if there were mitigating circumstances. She left out the part about the reshie, too. By the time she was done, most of the events of the last three days had been substantially edited into a rather difficult camping trip.

"I never knew you could ride a horse," said Jeremy, but he did sound impressed. "Now you can play polo with Harlan." He turned to Costa. "You're very quiet about all this. What's your name?"

She answered in a shy, proper voice, while Mira kicked herself for her own bad manners.

Jeremy studied the girl's face. "I suppose you've already heard about Mira's reputation for self-righteousness when it comes to owning people." He smiled. "I think you were expensive, too."

"Overpriced," replied Costa, and didn't say anything else.

The tension at dinner seemed to start when Costa reached automatically for the platter in the middle of the table and began serving. Up until that moment, Mira had been fairly sure it was just her, and all that coffee on an empty stomach.

Tiago took the plate away from Costa. "We do things a little differently here," he said. "Sit down." He held a chair, and she obeyed, looking at Mira uncomfortably.

Mira made sure she didn't react. Tiago was watching her as well. She turned to Jeremy instead. "Pass that, would you please?" She pointed at the bread. Tiago could bait her later. Anyway, it had become normal for Costa to sit at the table, although never with other people around. She concentrated on the bread, trying not to gulp it down.

"Let me introduce you to everyone," said the older man sitting across from her. "I'm Cyril Frei, ship's doctor."

He had a trace of Asian ancestry in his eyes and high cheekbones, like she did, but he reminded her of Vince for a painful second. "Nice to meet you," she mumbled.

Frei gestured to the sandy-haired young woman on his left. "Korei Alba, the pilot, and everything else." She smiled, bobbing her head, nervously, Mira thought. She had a long, ragged looking scar over one eye. "You know Esau and Jeremy." He gestured at the empty chair between her and Costa. "Jesse sits here, but she's not feeling very well right now."

"This is Costa," said Mira, nodding at the girl, who was hunched indecisively over her plate. "I'm Mira LoDire."

Esau glanced at her. "What ship did you say you were on?"

She hadn't. "It's the Jahar. Have you heard of it?"

Naturally not, but it was a name Costa could remember without any trouble in case somebody asked.

"What were you carrying?" asked the pilot.

"Nothing important," said Mira. "How about you?"

Esau stiffened, then relaxed enough to smile. "Right now we're not loaded," he said. "We're just running like hell."

She knew she was going to sound too concerned, but she asked anyway. "Did you see what happened to the Emirate ship?"

"Well," said Frei, "we didn't actually see it happen." He glanced at Esau, and some silent communication passed between them. "We saw the pieces though."

Mira swallowed hard. She hadn't realized how much she'd been hoping that the ship had somehow escaped.

"It's too bad," said Frei. "They didn't expect it. The Sector always play dirty like that."

"They deserved it," said Esau indifferently. "Let the Remini have the Emirate. We'll pick up whatever's left."

Jeremy shifted uncomfortably, and suddenly Mira wasn't sure who he might agree with.

"There won't be anything left," said Mira. "And what makes you think the Sector can control them?"

"They've made their own bed," said Korei. "I hope those things eat them in their sleep."

Mira frowned, surprised at the amount of venom in her voice. Here was someone else who would cut out Jezr'el's heart without a second thought.

Korei had already piled her plate with enough food for two people. She stood up. "I'll see how Jesse's doing," she said to Frei, and walked out quickly without waiting for him to answer.

Frei waited until she'd shut the door. "You'll have to excuse her," he said to Mira. "She can't even listen to talk about the Sector. It makes her furious."

"I can understand that."

Esau leaned back in his chair. "So what's your prediction? What happens when the Sector and the Remini cross the border?"

"The worst things you can imagine," said Mira. "If the military doesn't organize itself fast enough, the Sector could be clear out to Traja in a matter of weeks. Maybe farther."

Esau nodded, almost smiling.

"You like the idea," said Mira softly.

Frei put his hand on Esau's shoulder. "What my inarticulate friend is trying to say is that he would give his right arm to see the Emir on his hands and knees before Raffail himself. Isn't that right, Esau?"

"But there are millions of innocent people—" She had a lot more to say, but someone kicked her under the table. She turned to Costa in angry surprise, but the girl held her hands down where only Mira could see them, thumbs hooked together, the right fist dragging the left along in a couple of quick jerks. Fish on a line, Mira thought. She was right. Shut up. "Maybe you have a point," she said, and looked back at her food.

She managed to say very little for the rest of the meal and tried not to listen as the two men bantered casually about the future of an entire civilization. Jeremy hadn't said a word so far. She caught his eye once, searching for some opinion, but couldn't tell what he was thinking. She knew how he felt about Harlan, but she couldn't believe the boy was as vengeful as his new master seemed to be.

The jammer was equipped with proximity detectors sensitive enough to pick up the presence of even small asteroids at ten thousand kilometers. Mira set the alarms to go off at a deafening level if anything came within a quarter light year of the Tantilla and went to bed early to stay out of Esau's way.

"I don't understand him," she said later, as Costa cuddled against her in the darkness. "I don't think any of them have the slightest idea what the Remini are capable of."

"Does Jeremy know?"

Mira nodded. "I'm sure he does."

"Do you think they listen to what he has to say?"

It was a good question, one that Mira had to think about. All this effort at appearing fair and equitable. How deep did it actually go? "Maybe they don't trust him either."

Costa didn't answer. Mira moved one hand lightly across her shoulders. "Do me a favor," she whispered.

"Mmmm."

"Dream something really nice, like Esau has a change of heart and makes an anonymous call to Harlan."

There was no response. Mira put an arm behind her head, staring up at the black ceiling and fell asleep wondering exactly where they were.

No nightmares was her first thought when she woke up. She reached across the narrow bed. It was empty, but she could hear the water running in the bathroom.

"You're up early," she said when the girl came out. "How did you sleep?"

Costa sat next to her, drying her hair. "I had a dream about my sister."

Oh, the sister. "Good dream?"

"I couldn't tell. There were a lot of horses. It seemed like a warm place." She shook her head. "I don't know what it means."

"There's a monitor we can use in the jammer room," said Mira. "We'll see if we can find her."

The third screen was generally used for keeping track of other space traffic, but they seemed so completely alone, Mira wasn't worried about using it for something else. Besides, the proximity detectors were still on. She cleared the screen and tapped in the codes for the general slave registry. Without an ID number, however, this kind of search could take all day.

"What does your sister look like?"

Costa was hovering behind her. "She's like me, but taller. She's two years older."

"Same eyes? Same hair?"

She nodded quickly.

What a place Jahar must be. "She was collared before you?"

"Yes."

"How long before?"

Costa thought about it. "Four months? Maybe five."

"Alright," said Mira doubtfully. She keyed in the information and got up. "The computer is searching for girls who look like you who were collared two years ago. All you have to do is watch the screen and push this when you recognize someone." She pointed to the right button.

The first face was already on the monitor, a sad-eyed blonde in a torn shirt. Costa glanced back at Mira anxiously. "You're not going to help?"

Mira shook her head and crouched down to unscrew the guts of the jammer. "I'm going to fix this piece of junk."

Before long, she found herself totally absorbed in the task. There wasn't that much she could do without turning the jammer off, but she eventually discovered the source of the problem and understood why no one had dealt with it before.

The jammer took all its power from the engines. Since it was big enough to hide a medium-sized moon, it could easily use all the energy the ship itself could provide. That would make for a perfect image in an Emirate scanner, but no juice left for the Tantilla to escape.

Someone had already cut the jammer's intake by a third, which explained the two indicators she'd thought were broken, but now there was an imbalance in the mechanism—the false image they projected probably wasn't very convincing. Mira made all the adjustments she could, but what the machine really needed was an overhaul. There was something else, too. It seemed to her that for all that the jammer drained the engines, it worked the other way around as well. If the Tantilla were running at top speed, there was no way that the obscuring field could cover the entire ship. Anyone chasing them would be able to tell exactly who they were.

Mira sighed and wiped her hands. If the Emirate border patrols were looking for them, a weakness like that would be an advantage for her. With the Remini and the Sector, it was just another worry.

"Here she is," said Costa abruptly. "I found her."

Besides the obvious family resemblance, the look of frightened determination was very familiar.

Costa had her finger pressed so tightly against the *Stop* key that her knuckles were white from the pressure. Tears were rolling freely down her cheeks. "Tell me where she is. Tell me if she's alright."

Mira keyed into the file. "She's at one of the arenas, training horses. Her price is pretty high, so I don't think she's been hurt." Or marked at least. "She's on a planet called Newhall. My parents live on Newhall." It was a long, long way off.

"How much is she?" wept the girl.

Mira squinted at the tiny print. "They bought her right from the Sector. Looks like seven hundred."

She wasn't sure if it was the amount or the relief, but Costa shook with sobs and couldn't say anything.

They ended up sitting together on the floor. Mira made comforting noises, trying to decide what she could realistically promise to do. "I don't want to get your hopes up," she said finally. "But I could send my next paycheck home and get my father to see if they would sell her. They might not."

"Would he do that?"

"He's a very tender-hearted guy."

Costa wiped her eyes. "I saw a lot of people I knew."

Other relatives? Mira hesitated. "We might be able to find your mother."

The girl leaned against her. "I don't know what she looks like. I was too young when they took her away. I'm not even sure she's alive anymore." She sniffed hard. "Ari might be able to recognize her."

The door hissed and slid open. Korei stepped in, frowning. "Everything alright?"

Mira nodded, but she could feel the young woman's suspicion from across the room. "We're just talking. How's your friend?"

"She'll live," said Korei, as though that was something that might have been in doubt. She came a little closer, but she seemed very hesitant, almost shy. "We're heading for some pretty thick asteroid fields. Would you mind if I turned the proximity detectors off?"

"It's your ship," Mira smiled, but Korei turned away quickly, her cheeks flushing.

Costa pulled her arm away from Mira's neck with a questioning frown, and Mira got to her feet. "Can you tell me where we are? I'd like to know how much longer I need to worry about the bad guys."

"It's another twelve hours to the border, or at least to where Esau wants to cross."

So they were paralleling the border, getting as far from Point Seven as possible. "Can you show me?"

Korei slid into the chair by the third monitor. Ari's tired face stared back at her. She glanced quickly, curiously, at Costa. "Can I clear this?"

Mira waited for the girl to answer.

"Go ahead," said Costa.

Korei's hands moved across the keyboard, and the navigational displays from the bridge appeared, one after another. Mira wondered how long she'd been doing this job. There was no trace of indecision as she flipped through the technical read-outs, stopping at the one that simply showed the ship in relation to standard landmarks.

"This is the border." Korei traced the red line to the right of the green dot that indicated the Tantilla. "Here's the asteroid field we're headed for. Saragasso, we call it."

A perfect place to hide, thought Mira, staring at the enormous collection of white specks. The ship would drift over the border like one more rock, and when they were far enough away, Esau could set a course for anywhere. "But where are we exactly?"

"You mean between the Points?" She expanded the map to include the two Emirate bases, numbers Seven and Eight. Days and days away, Mira realized. The asteroids were almost midway between them, probably a vague place on the scanners to begin with.

"Thanks," said Mira. "That's what I needed to know." She sat down heavily in the next chair.

Korei cleared her throat. "We'll be working pretty closely from now on," she said. "Is that how it was on your last ship?"

Mira nodded. Pilots and jammers were an almost symbiotic relationship, depending on each other for speed and cover. That's why she's really here, thought Mira, to find out about me. Nothing to do with the proximity detectors. She shook off her anxieties with an effort. Any new ally on this ship would be a help. "Esau told me about your last operator. Was she yours?"

"She was Frei's." Korei hunched her shoulders. "It was so sudden. No one expected her to Fail."

"She must have been pretty good," said Mira. "You'd have to be to work this thing."

Korei just nodded. She gestured vaguely at the second screen. "You've adjusted it. It looks better, not so foggy."

"Thanks." Shy was the wrong word for her, Mira decided. Maybe it was just nerves. "You seem like you've had a lot of experience. How long have you been here?"

"A couple of years." She stood up abruptly. "Could I ask you a favor?"

"Sure?"

"Jeremy's busy, and I need help with some things. Can I borrow her?" She pointed at Costa.

"I guess so."

Korei beckoned to the girl and walked out without another word. Mira watched the door close, frowning to herself. She'd missed something, and she had no idea what it was.

12

osta came back later, tight-lipped with fury. She sat down next to Mira. *Bad people!* she Signed emphatically.

"What?" Mira blinked in surprise. "What's wrong?"

The girl pointed to the intercom speaker. She put a finger to her lips, and began Signing slowly, so Mira could understand. *Korei—*, she brushed her forehead to indicate the scar. *I helped her carry things. She asked questions about you.*

Questions? Mira repeated with her hands.

Where you come from, do I like you. Her eyes narrowed with anger. *Do you hit me.*

You said?

I said you saved me from the Mine line. I showed her. . . she gestured at her back. *Not the brands.* One hand clapped over her left shoulder, and then a gesture Mira didn't understand.

"Esau!" she hissed, and motioned again, an open hand with the thumb brushing her cheek. The sharpness of his face, Mira guessed.

He saw the marks? she asked.

Costa nodded. *You did it, he says. Doesn't believe me.* Costa glanced at the intercom again. *He's angry, angry, angry,* she motioned with quick chops.

Mira pointed to herself and raised her eyebrows. *At me?*

Costa opened her arms to embrace the air. *Everything. Everybody.*

Why?

The girl shrugged. *Told me to—*

Something. *What?*

Two fingers tapped hard into the opposite palm. *Stay,* Costa mouthed it silently. "Told me to *stay.* You go. I stay."

I sell you? Or would someone throw her overboard?

Costa shrugged and scowled at the controls.

"Did you see Jeremy?" Mira asked in a low voice.

Costa shook her head.

"I'm going to find him." She stood up and turned the alarms back on. "I'll be back."

Careful, said the girl, in Sign.

She found him on the bridge. "I have to talk to you." Mira nodded at the intercom panel. "Privately."

Jeremy hit a couple of switches. A few of the green lights turned red. "What's the matter?"

She sat down in the chair next to him. The bridge wasn't much bigger than the jammer's large closet, and even more tightly packed with equipment. There was barely enough room for the two of them, much less some hidden listener. "There's something you need to know about Costa," she said in a low voice. "I found her in the Mine line on Traja."

Jeremy looked surprised. "I wouldn't have guessed that."

"Your boss saw her marks," said Mira. "Now he's convinced I did the dirty work, and he's talking about keeping her here. It doesn't sound friendly, Jeremy."

The boy let his breath hiss out through his teeth. "Esau gets very paranoid about certain things. If he thinks you're beating her, he'll jump to a lot of conclusions."

"But I didn't do it," said Mira urgently. "And even if I did, it's certainly none of his business."

"It's his ship," said Jeremy, "so, it's his business."

"But I didn't do it! Can't you tell him that? I thought he listened to you."

"Not always." He shifted uncomfortably in the chair. "He's been asking how I know you."

"What did you tell him?"

"I said you were one of Harlan's connections. Nothing specific." He hesitated. "I'm not trying to scare you, but bringing you on board may not have been the right thing."

"I'm already scared," said Mira. "What are you saying?"

"As long as Esau needs you on the jammer, you should be safe," Jeremy said softly. "I'll do everything I can, but once we're over the border, I'm not sure what he'll decide to do."

"I'm not interested in getting killed," said Mira. "Is that what we're talking about?"

Jeremy licked his lips. "It depends what he thinks you've done and what he thinks you know about him."

"I don't know anything about him. I don't even care."

"I know. I'll talk to him again."

It struck Mira suddenly that this must be the way Costa's dreams went. Things kept happening and there was no apparent way to stop them. "What about Costa?"

"She's safe here. Safer than most places, probably."

Did that make her feel better? She wasn't sure.

"Stay out of Esau's way," said Jeremy. "That's the best advice I can give you, D'sha." He reached over and squeezed her hand hard, unexpectedly. "I'll see about keeping him distracted."

Jeremy brought them dinner in their cabin that night, joking about room service, but Mira felt far from reassured. She'd repeated the conversation on the bridge for Costa as well as she could in Sign, and in whispers when they were alone in the cabin.

Now she sipped the cold dregs of her coffee in the pitch darkness, trying to stay awake. The warm weight of Costa's head lay in her lap as Mira sat braced against the wall, keeping a wary eye on the door that didn't lock. Less than two hours to the border, she'd figured, depending on their speed. The knife was a hard lump under her right leg, and she shifted a little. Even under these circumstances, she found it difficult to picture herself stabbing someone.

Costa jerked in her sleep, muttering something unintelligible. She'd been dreaming off and on for the last few hours, but it was impossible to tell how normal or how prescient any of it was. Mira rested a hand on the girl's cheek and felt her relax slightly.

Maybe these really were fateful dreams, she thought. After all, the events they'd tried to avoid by turning down the offered ride on Ain-Selai were manifesting right now on this ship. Was there a use for this sort of predestiny, Mira wondered, or would her own death be violent, pointless, and much too soon.

"Stay away!" snapped Costa, and every muscle went rigid. Mira took a breath and resolved not to wake her up until she was sure it was over.

"Mira." Costa moaned, and twisted away. "Remini!" she cried and started screaming.

It was blind, inarticulate screaming, and it froze Mira from the inside out. She hit the lights and reached for the girl, crouched at the end of the bed, face to the wall.

"Wake up!" she whispered, and held on until the noise stopped and Costa lay weakly against her. "It's okay," said Mira, trembling herself. "What was it?"

"Remini," repeated the girl. "They're hiding in the asteroids."

Holy gods. "Have they seen us?"

"Not yet. They won't . . . I'm not sure." She pulled away. "You'd better hurry."

Mira fled down the corridor and didn't remember the knife until she got to the jammer room. Too late now. She checked the monitors and the alarms. There was no sign of any problem, not yet anyway. She tapped the intercom speaker. "Korei? Are you there?"

"Yes." She didn't even sound sleepy.

"We may have a problem. Are you scanning the asteroids?"

"No," she said. "There's too much interference to get a clear reading. What's wrong?"

"I think we've got company," said Mira, her voice shaking. "There may be Remini out here."

There was a pause. "You're dreaming," said Korei. "Go back to bed."

"Run a scan," said Mira. "Just run a scan."

"I've already got visuals on."

"Do it!" Someone was shouting in the corridor. Jeremy's voice?

Mira glanced over at the third screen. Printed information from the scanners flickered over it, green letters on black. Heavy footsteps pounded down the hallway, too heavy for Costa.

"Esau, don't!" shouted Jeremy.

Esau filled the doorway, breathing hard, holding a wad of bulky fabric in one hand.

Mira got out of the chair, slowly. She'd never seen anyone so angry and so afraid at the same time.

He threw the cloth onto the floor. Her uniform, dug out from the pile under the sink. "You're a cop," Esau snarled at her. "You're an Emirate cop."

"I'm not," she breathed.

"She's *not*." Jeremy grabbed his arm, but Esau shook him off and moved into the room.

"I'm not what you think," whispered Mira. "I'm the diplomat from the Emirate ship." She backed away from him until her elbows knocked against the wall behind her. "Whatever you people are doing, I don't give a damn. Just let us leave, put us down anywhere."

Esau shook his head, too close now. "What you did to that girl—"

He pulled his fist back, Mira managed to move just enough for him to hit her right across the face. The wall slammed against the back of her head, and she fell instantly, nothing but black and red, black and red in front of her eyes and a peal of bells in her ears. I've never been hit before, she thought, and looked up.

Someone's dirty foot caught Esau in the stomach, two quick kicks. He staggered, and Costa stepped back. The knife hung above Mira's head, gripped in the girl's hand, blade down. Esau was furious or surprised, it was hard to tell. He pulled his fist back again and hesitated. Costa already knew that. She cracked the hilt of the knife against his jaw and kneed him hard in the belly. Esau doubled over. She punched him in the back of the neck, knocking him to the floor. Someone was shouting for Frei. Mira wanted to cheer, but there was too much sticky warmth in her mouth. Esau rolled on his back, groaning, and Costa dropped onto his chest, the point of the blade pressed lightly against his throat.

"Don't move," she said breathlessly. "I'll kill you."

Mira found she could just get to her knees, and braced herself against the wall. There was blood everywhere. It seemed to be dripping off her chin. When she looked up again, Frei was standing in the door.

"Stay away," snapped the girl.

"I will," said Frei, "don't worry about that." He said something to Jeremy, and Mira could hear his running footsteps. Everything hurt now. She put a hand against her face, but that only made it worse.

"You're friend is bleeding quite a bit," said Frei. "Let me help her. You don't have to move."

Costa glanced over at her, anxious now. "Mira?"

Mira made the mistake of nodding her head.

He'd gotten a medical kit and a wet cloth from somewhere, Jeremy, she guessed. The boy was back, hanging just inside the door, keeping his distance, watching Esau.

Frei eased down next to her and tilted her head back gently. "You'll be fine," he said. "A black eye and a headache, I think." He took something out of the kit and pressed it against the bridge of her nose. It stung, but the blood slowed down and her head stopped spinning.

Frei wiped her face carefully and started on her hands. "What's going on, Esau?" he asked, very quietly.

"She's with the Emirate." He started to move, but Costa pricked him and his hand dropped back onto the floor. "I found her uniform. I thought she was a cop."

"I'm not," repeated Mira, her words thick as soup.

Frei sat back on his heels. "You're the one who knows her, Jeremy. Let's have it."

"She's the diplomat from the Emirate ship. She was trapped on Ain-Selai. She's a friend."

"A diplomat like D'Mahai?"

"Nothing like Harlan."

"I see," said Frei. "What about this girl?"

"She's from the Line, on Traja."

"Is that a fact?" Frei frowned skeptically at Costa. "But there was blood on your shirt when you came aboard. If this woman hurts you, you should tell me. I'm sure I could pay her price."

"I killed an animal," said Costa, and she sounded really angry now. "You're going to let us both go." She laid the edge of the blade just below Esau's ear. "I don't mind doing it," she said fiercely.

"I can see that," said Frei.

"Call her off, Mira," whispered Jeremy.

Now that was something else that seemed out of place, Mira thought. Why would Jeremy be so concerned about someone he'd been with for only two months? And although he'd never been the kind of slave Mira would have described as submissive, it was still strange to hear him refer to his master by his first name, never as *D'sha.*

She leaned back against the wall, trying to think. As far as diplomacy went, this was as classic an impasse as one could hope for—a chance to collect her wits. It was only a question of time until someone spotted the Remini. Or maybe it would be the other way around. She wished she had the energy to ask. She turned to Costa, just to see if the girl looked like she was counting minutes. The movement hurt her head, and Mira blinked hard. When she could focus again, she found herself staring at Esau's arm.

His hand was close enough for her to touch if she'd wanted to. His sleeve was pushed up halfway to his elbow, and now it was easy to see the circling of deep scars on his wrists. Mira closed her eyes. She'd seen marks like that in every Mine line, and the fresh wounds from struggling against cuffs and manacles. No wonder he was afraid of the police. No wonder everything seemed so askew here. For a second, she understood him completely.

"Hey," said Korei's voice on the speaker. "How did you know about—"

The howl of the proximity alarms drowned out whatever she was about to say.

Costa moved off of Esau's chest, easily, just following the script. He pushed himself to his feet as fast as he could before she could change her mind.

"It's the asteroids," shouted Esau. He switched off the alarms.

"Its the Remini," said Mira in the sudden silence.

"Esau, get up here!" Now Korei sounded scared, and her voice boomed on every speaker up and down the corridor. "There must be a dozen ships!"

Only a dozen? thought Mira.

Jeremy shot a single questioning glance at her and at Costa, then hurried after Esau.

Frei kept his distance as the girl helped Mira into a chair and sat down next to her, but he didn't seem to be leaving.

"Don't you have a battle station?" Mira asked wearily.

He shrugged. "I'm just the doctor. I'm not much good with these gadgets."

She didn't know if he was sticking around because none of them trusted her, or because he thought she might keel over. Either way, having him there made her even more nervous. Mira leaned over carefully and brought up Korei's navigational chart on the third monitor.

The Tantilla's green fleck drifted precariously among the white shapes of asteroids and the indistinct, shifting blue dots that indicated the Remini.

Mira turned to Costa. *What now?* she asked with her hands. *Don't know. Woke up.*

"I'm cutting everything," said Korei from the bridge, and the lights went out abruptly. "You've got access."

"Access?" repeated Mira.

"She means you can tap directly into the engines," said Frei. He pointed to the glowing readouts. Now there was enough power available to hide two or three ships. "What's the plan, Korei?"

"We'll hang here until everyone else is gone. Do something quick. They're making random scans."

The most sensible thing was to project the image of another nondescript asteroid. The Saragasso's natural interference would make it more than convincing. Mira started to check the jammer's menu of preprogrammed images, but Frei stopped her.

"That's standard stuff," he said. "If you want to make a rock, you have to build it yourself."

She'd never done that. She'd repaired the outpost's image any number of times, but the actual fractile construction had taken months, and Thea had done it all.

"Are you alright?" asked Frei. He sounded very worried now. He sat next to her, his face edged with the greenish light of the control board. "Can you do this?"

Mira nodded weakly. She keyed in a couple of random geometric shapes and overlaid them, one on top of the other. Her hands shook as she tried to modify them into three dimensions. It wasn't right. She struggled with the image, but it still looked like a piece of folded paper, nothing like stone.

"That's no good," said Korei, apparently watching on her own screen. "Can't you do any better than that?"

"I need more time," said Mira. She glanced at the navigational chart. They were already in the midst of the alien fleet. There was no more time.

Korei hesitated. "Frei, are you still there?"

"Yes."

"She needs help," said Korei. "It's just luck they haven't seen us yet."

"Alright," said Frei softly. He reached for the intercom and changed the setting. "Are you awake?"

"Yes," said a different voice. Tired-sounding.

"We need you up here. Can you manage by yourself?"

"Yes."

"Hurry," said Frei. He leaned back stiffly. "I think you should go back to your cabin," he said to Mira. "Both of you."

Excused on account of uselessness, thought Mira, but her head hurt too much to think of a good argument.

The intercom crackled. "There's a transmission," said Jeremy. "Can you translate this?"

Familiar alien rasping, much too loud, mixed with static from the Saragasso. Mira adjusted the volume and bent over the speaker. It was the tail end of some conversation, finishing with a string of numbers.

Coordinates? She keyed them in and watched the third screen. A point began flashing among the asteroids, just over the red line of the border.

"What the hell was that?" Frei was on his feet now, nervous.

"Remini," said Mira. "That's what they sound like." She turned the volume up and down, but now the channel was clear.

"You can understand them?"

"It's my specialty."

"So what are they saying?" he asked skeptically.

"They're trying to locate something. . . ." Possibly some other unlucky smuggler, she thought, or maybe they'd already caught a glimpse of the Tantilla.

He didn't seem to be listening. Mira glanced up and then past him at the girlish silhouette in the doorway. Jesse wasn't expecting anyone but Frei, and when she realized Mira was in the room, she gave a little gasp, one hand flying to her throat. Not before Mira saw the glint of metal there. She turned back to the monitor. Of course. This was the slave who'd Failed. Mira wondered why she hadn't figured that out sooner. She looked over at Costa, trying to decide if she'd seen the collar too, but the girl was a silent shadow. There was no way to tell.

"It's okay," said Frei. There was a soft rustling as he helped her into the chair.

"Korei, I'm here," said the girl. Her voice was much stronger, more resonant than it had sounded on the intercom. "Give me a minute." She tapped the keys quickly, and Mira heard Korei sigh with relief.

"Perfect," she said. "Nice to have you back, love."

And somehow, that was no surprise either. Mira glanced at the second screen and blinked at the picture-perfect asteroid she'd constructed, literally in seconds. "How'd you do that so fast?" she asked in amazement.

Jesse gave her an uncertain, distrustful look. "It's easy," she said. "It's just a copy of one of those." She pointed to the mass of white specks on the third screen. "I make a couple of changes and project it. That's all."

Did it take twenty years in collar to out-think the Emirate engineers who'd worked long and hard to come up with convincing exteriors for listening posts on the Remini border? Mira nodded appreciatively. "I've never seen anyone do that. It really is perfect."

"Thanks." She'd buttoned the pajama top all the way up so the chain around her neck was no longer visible. In the light from the control board, Mira could see how striking she was. Her hair fell to her shoulders in thick black curls, and her eyes slanted over high cheekbones. She had the same starved appearance that Amrei'd had for weeks after her Failure, but that was the only thing that kept her from looking almost exactly like Frei.

Mira tried hard to swallow back the recognition and couldn't quite do it. She was his sister? His daughter? He'd bought his own child and freed her?

"Are you *listening?*" demanded Jeremy over the intercom. There was more static, but this time it was a human voice. It took Mira a second to figure out who it was.

"You may not understand this," said Harlan in a thin, wavering voice, "but what you're doing is an act of war." He waited for the mechanical rasp of the translator to finish.

"Of course they understand," Jeremy muttered. "That's why they brought those battleships, you idiot."

"What's he doing out here?" Mira whispered, listening for the Remini reply at the same time. "Where's his ship?"

"Take a look," said Korei, and switched Mira's monitor.

The Proviso hung just across the border, barely visible as it shielded itself with asteroids the size of mountains. The hull was a blackened, battered mess. Entire sections of the ship seemed to be missing altogether. Then everything blurred. She wiped the tears off her bruised face.

"That's yours?" asked Frei, and Mira nodded. "You can stop worrying then," he said gently. "The Emirate obviously knows what's going on. We'll drop you off somewhere in a couple of weeks. You can tell them you were lost behind enemy lines. You might even get a medal."

She couldn't tell if he was being sarcastic. She squinted at her ship again. It seemed to be alone and practically weaponless.

"I'm still waiting," said Harlan.

"I've told you already," said another voice, equally familiar. "They really have no interest in conversation."

"Raffail!" hissed Costa. "How—"

Mira held her hand up, and the girl stopped herself. There was something else in the transmission from the Remini ship, one alien voice reading off coordinates, another one counting.

"What are they saying?" asked Frei uneasily.

"Hang on—"

She glanced back at the navigational chart. The Tantilla was no more than a thousand kilometers from the border, drifting closer and closer to the red line and the flashing point on the grid she'd marked earlier. Now she understood that the aliens had already spotted the Proviso. They were just waiting for it to drift to an area where they could have a better shot. The counting was something she'd heard a number of times from the safety of the outpost. It was the charging sequence for the weapons that could dispose of entire planets, and if anyone on the Proviso could hear it, they would be running for their lives.

"What are they saying?" Frei demanded.

"New coordinates," said Mira. "They're verifying a target."

"What target?" asked Korei sharply. "Who're they aiming at?"

Mira's hands hovered over the control board. The charging sequence was only halfway complete, but the aliens had the Proviso dead in their sights now. With the Remini weapons at less than full power, the Proviso might be able to survive the first volley. Certainly no more than that.

Mira held her breath and keyed in new coordinates, false ones, directly over the Tantilla. She put her hands in her lap and closed her eyes, waiting. This was as close to suicide, or murder, as she ever wanted to be.

Korei saw the fictitious information flash on her screen and started shouting. "They've seen us!"

"They're about to start firing," said Mira numbly. The Remini would spot the Tantilla as soon as it started moving, but she had no idea whether the aliens would shoot at anything so small.

The engines wailed, resonating through the walls. Jesse's jammer went dark as she cut its power completely, giving Korei access to every bit of speed the ship could muster.

On the monitor, Mira watched the Tantilla's tiny green dot jerk and angle directly for the red borderline. The alien voice on the intercom stopped for a moment, then calmly read out a new set of numbers. Mira didn't even have time to translate.

They were less than five hundred kilometers from the border when they were hit. Not that it would have been any safer on the other side. Mira lay in the dark, not moving from where she'd been thrown, praying that the atmosphere seals would hold. Costa's sweaty hand caught hers, and Mira moved closer. Frei was still conscious. She could hear him breathing, panting really.

"Damn you," he said to her. "They didn't see us until she cut the jammer."

"Well. . ." said Mira, and gave up. "Right."

He didn't say anything. Mira couldn't hear Jesse at all. "Is she alright?"

"She's alive, if that's what you mean." He was angry, and sad, and when the lights came on, he would probably break her neck. If he could get past Costa.

"She's your daughter?" asked Mira, because she really wanted to know.

"None of your damn business." His voice shook. "Esau's right. All you Emirate people are exactly the same."

"We're not," said Mira. "Some of us are just like you."

Somebody on the bridge knocked against the intercom. "Hey down there," said Jeremy breathlessly.

"We're okay," shouted Frei. "Esau! You were right about her!"

Jeremy tapped the speaker again. "This is broken too," he said to someone else. "Can you check—" More static.

Frei swore to himself in the dark, and Jesse groaned.

"Mayday, Mayday, Mayday," said Jeremy. The intership channel made his voice sound tinny and distant. "Proviso—well, we can't *stay* here, Esau. Mayday, Proviso, request a tow."

"Proviso responding," said somebody else, far away.

Only a few of the lights were coming back on. Mira crawled out from under a pile of debris. Her monitor flickered weakly, showing the rearward view as they trailed behind the Proviso.

She grabbed Costa and struggled to her feet. "Look!"

The girl wiped dust out of her eyes, squinting at the screen. Behind them, the immense boulders that had hung around the Proviso were slowly dissolving as the jammers were turned down. Mira counted seven, ten, over a dozen Emirate battleships as they came into focus and opened fire, one by one, on the Remini fleet.

"Did you see that? Did you see it?" shouted Jeremy to nobody in particular.

They haven't won yet, thought Mira, and she was still up to her neck in trouble. She bent down to help Frei out from the tangle of chairs and cables. Jesse looked pale but unhurt. Frei pushed Mira's hands away and glared at her. "Get off this ship," he snapped. "Go back to your friends."

"Not yet." Esau stood in the doorway with his arms crossed.

Mira took an uneasy step back. He was furious, dirty, and he'd been out-maneuvered. Costa reached for the knife, but Mira stopped her. "Don't. It'll make things worse."

"How could it be worse?" demanded Esau. "You've destroyed my ship, you've risked our lives. It wasn't necessary. They had things under control before we got there."

"I didn't know that," said Mira. Unfortunately, most of what he was saying was true. "I'm sorry about your ship. I'll get a repair crew for you. They'll fix you up any way you want."

He looked at her like she was out of her mind. "I don't want your help, lady diplomat, or whatever you are."

Jeremy came up behind him. "Somebody on the Proviso wants to talk to you, Mira. Somebody named Noi? Vince Noi?"

She was incredibly, indescribably glad that he was in one piece.

She reached for the intercom, but Jeremy jerked a thumb over his shoulder. "That's broken. You'll have to take it on the bridge."

She followed him through the door, past Esau and Frei and Jesse, and they all watched her go like she was the plague.

Esau tapped Costa's shoulder as she tried to squeeze by. "Stay here for a minute," he said in a much kinder tone.

Mira just nodded at her. She already knew what he was going to say. He would have figured out some way to pull the girl aside before she could get off his ship, and it might as well be now. Hopefully it wouldn't make any difference at all.

The bridge was a complete shambles. Korei was holding an empty fire extinguisher, and the air stank of chemical foam. She gave Mira a furious look, pushing past her to the corridor.

Mira leaned wearily over the intercom. "It's me," she said. "How's everything?"

"We're very banged up," said Vince. "We lost a lot of people. I thought we lost you." He couldn't hide the relief in his voice. "Are you alright? You took a bad hit."

"Everyone here hates me," said Mira, and she tried to smile. "I told them you could send a repair crew over since they made such a big sacrifice for the Emir, but they don't seem very enthusiastic. Do you have some spare parts you could donate?"

He started to laugh. "I'll see what I can do."

"One more thing, Vince." She glanced at Jeremy. "This ship has no name or registration as far as you're concerned. If you can keep it out of your log, that'd be even better."

"No problem." He said it without hesitation.

"I'll be there as soon as I can."

Jeremy leaned against the console as she closed the channel. "You do know what's going on here."

She nodded. "I didn't know you were. . . involved in this sort of thing."

"When did you figure it out?"

"I saw Esau's arms." She rubbed her own wrists to show him where. "I know someone else," she said. "I helped."

He looked at her thoughtfully. "Does Costa know that?"

Mira nodded and glanced back at the door. "Esau's talking to her right now. He's trying to make her stay here." And hate me like he does, she thought. It was enough to make her head ache.

Jeremy took her arm. "Let's find out how he's doing."

Costa was kneeling at Esau's feet, and it was easy to see how uncomfortable that made him. He was speaking in a low, intense voice, but he stopped when he saw Mira.

Costa looked over her shoulder and raised one doubtful eyebrow. "Oh, D'LoDire," she said in a soft, School voice. "Tell me what to do, D'sha. These people are making me such promises."

Jeremy nearly choked, trying not to laugh.

"D'sha, this man says he can free me."

Esau glanced up suspiciously. "I'd like to see you do better."

"That's a pretty generous offer, Costa," said Mira. "It's your decision. You can stay if you like."

Costa gazed up at Esau, a little too dramatically, Mira thought. "Do it now, D'Tiago," she said. "Free me now!"

Esau hesitated. "I can't. . .yet. I mean. . .how many years have you been in collar?"

"Two, D'sha," said Costa. She crossed her wrists and put her head on his feet. "Free me now, D'sha!"

"I can't." He looked at Jeremy. "She doesn't believe it? Or she already knows?"

"I think she knows," said Jeremy. He grinned at Esau.

Costa sat back on her heels. "I suppose I could stay here and wait," she said. "You wouldn't treat me as a slave?"

"Of course not," said Esau.

"I could do the things that are important to me?"

He frowned. "What do you mean?"

"I need seven hundred credits to get my sister out of the arena on Newhall," said Costa. "Do you have that much?"

"The ship has to be repaired. Maybe in a couple of months. . ."

"I can't wait," said Costa. "What if someone's hurting her?"

Esau glanced at Mira. "You knew about this? You have that kind of money?"

Mira nodded.

Esau didn't say anything. Costa got to her feet, hands on her hips, bristling. "I hope I never see you again." She seemed like she had a lot more to say, but she turned to Mira instead. "Can we go now?"

It was tempting to gloat, but Mira didn't have the energy for it. She walked slowly behind Jeremy, who had his arm hooked through Costa's.

"Are you really School?" he was asking, and the girl nodded.

Jeremy gave Mira a sly grin. "I'm sorry about your eye," he said. "Esau would never apologize for it, but he should."

Mira shrugged. Her eye was so swollen she couldn't see out of it. The door for the ship's disk swung crookedly in front of her and she pushed it open. "Why don't you come with us?" she said. "I could use some help. I'll keep you out of Harlan's way."

Jeremy shook his head. "Esau needs me anyway, but he really needs me now."

"You've known him a long time," said Mira cautiously.

"Since I was sixteen. Before this." He tugged at his collar and gave her a curious look. "You really want to know?"

"If you want to talk about it."

He smiled at the floor. "Well . . . they took him a year before they took me. We ended up at the same auction one day. Harlan got me, and Esau went to one of the arenas. That's how he met Frei."

"How does Frei fit in?" asked Mira. "He's not freed, is he?"

"No. He was the doctor that traveled with one of the arena teams. You know, fixing them up after tournaments. You should hear him talk about it. He makes it sound like war time."

"Esau fought?" Mira never went to the arenas, but even she knew that Esau was far too light to hold his own in the ring.

"No," said Jeremy. "He was part of the stable."

Costa frowned. "Horses?"

He almost smiled. "The other kind. You know. Anybody's boy."

"Oh." Another casualty, Mira thought, like Amrei.

"He got sick of it and wouldn't do what he was told. They beat him up and sent him to the Mine line. Frei went looking for him. It's not the first time he's done that."

"How did you get involved?"

"Esau remembered Harlan and tracked me down at Point Seven." Jeremy shrugged. "It's not that I have to stay here, Mira. I want to. I'm the only one he can still love."

Mira nodded, not sure what to say.

The boy sighed. "Next time you see Harlan, would you do me

a favor?"

"Sure."

"He's so disorganized," said Jeremy. "And that boy he has now is completely brainless." He grinned. "But would you tell him that the reason he can't find his dress uniforms is because I buried them in the backyard before I left?"

13

S orry about the mess," said Vince.

What was left of her cabin on the Proviso was a shambles.

In the main room, the sofa was lying on its back where the repair crews had thrown it, bent into a peculiar new shape from being sucked against the bedroom door by the sudden escape of air. The door itself had been welded shut and was sealed with a yellow sticker that read, *Pressure Lock: Do Not Attempt To Open.*

Mira sat down on the deformed sofa. Costa was standing by the view-windows, intermittently lit from behind by the blue flares of airless welders as repair crews went back to work on the hull. Mira glanced back at Vince. "How many people did you lose?"

"Almost half the crew, and a lot, a whole lot of civilians." He sat down too, like it was suddenly too hard to stay on his feet.

"What about Amrei?"

"She's fine. She got knocked around like everybody else." He tapped his left eyebrow. "How'd you get the black eye, Madame Diplomat?"

"It's a long story." She touched the bruise lightly. All she really wanted to do was lay down and sleep. "Can we talk in the morning, Vince?"

"It is morning." He hesitated and glanced at Costa. "See if you can find us a pot of coffee," he said, more of a hint than a command. "And take your time." He waited for her to shut the door, then turned to Mira. "You *do* know she's carrying a knife under her clothes."

Mira nodded wearily. Outside, floodlights glared as exterior tugs hovered over ruptured metal, remounting the damaged battle turrets. When the lights turned away, she could see the faint trails of distorted stars. "We're moving?" she asked. "Where are we going? To Point Seven?"

"We're heading back into the Faraque."

She twisted around to face him. "They're sending you back while you're under repair? Don't you still have civilians on board?"

"Only Amrei," said Vince. "And she leaves on the next shuttle for Traja."

The idea of going back into Sector territory to face a live and vengeful Raffail was enough to make every bit of her exhaustion vanish. Mira straightened up on the sofa, suddenly aware that Vince was watching her very carefully.

"We've had a lot of contact with Raffail lately," said Vince. "He absolutely refused to believe me when I told him you'd been killed in the explosion on Ain-Selai. He kept insisting that you were hiding somewhere." Vince leaned over his elbows. "What happened, Mira?"

"Jezr'el was there," Mira said slowly. "He stayed behind after Raffail left. He was dead before the explosion, though." She hesitated. "If Raffail knows I'm alive, he probably thinks I'm responsible for that."

"Are you?"

"Not exactly," said Mira. "I mean, yes. I guess I am."

Vince gave her long, doubtful look. "Costa killed him."

Mira nodded reluctantly.

"He attacked you?"

It was more or less the truth. She nodded again. "Someone must have gotten away and told Raffail what was going on. I know they were searching for us, but I didn't think he'd be able to figure out what really happened. We didn't leave a lot of evidence."

Vince nodded slowly. "So now he wants your neck, is that it? To hell with invading Emirate space—all he wants is Mira LoDire?"

"And Costa." She glanced nervously out the window. "I could take her on the shuttle, Vince. We could keep an eye on Amrei and you could tell Raffail I'm still missing in action. He never has to know where we are."

Vince shook his head. "You can't go. We have to have a translator on board, and if someone wants a cease-fire, you're the official negotiator."

"Let Harlan do it."

"Harlan's already gone." He gave her a look of genuine sympathy. "You've got my permission to go," he said. "But you'll have to convince Trent to send Harlan back. Even if she's feeling generous and lets you off the hook, what are you going to do when you get to Traja?"

Mira frowned. "Get passage home."

"You haven't heard the news," said Vince. "On Traja, they think the Remini are winning. If you had six thousand credits, you might be able to get yourself a corner in a cargo hold, but you'd be risking your life just to get to a transport disk. People are so desperate to get away, they've had riots around the Ground Stations for the past week."

She hadn't heard. Still, there was the entire Frontier and most of the Faraque between Traja and Raffail. "What if I resign?" she said softly. "If I'm a civilian, you have to send me out."

He shrugged. "You could quit. You could walk out of here right now, but I want to make sure you know what the consequences are going to be."

Mira scowled at the floor. She already knew.

"If you desert a battle duty, there's an inquiry, right?"

"Call it a court martial," she said. "That's what it is."

"Whatever. They're going to want to know your reasons for leaving. What are you going to say?"

"The same thing I'm telling you," she said. "I'm scared to death of Raffail."

"Anyone with common sense would be," said Vince. "But he's not interested in murdering just anybody. It's because of what your girl did to his son." He shook his head. "It'll come out. If you try to lie, it'll be even worse, for both of you. She'll be wired, Mira, and that's just the beginning."

It was all true.

"You don't have to leave the ship," said Vince. "I'll give you the entire security squad if you absolutely have to go somewhere, but I can tell you right now, Raffail's probably going to get caught in the cross-fire at some point. You may not have anything to worry about."

"Thanks," said Mira.

The door opened in the sudden silence, and Mira looked up to see Costa, grimly holding onto the pot of unwanted coffee as Amrei pushed past her.

"Mira!" Amrei dropped onto the couch and threw her arms around her neck. "You're alive!" She pulled away when she saw the black eye. "I hope you hit him back, whoever he was."

"I almost destroyed his ship," said Mira.

Amrei laughed, but Vince's face tightened. "You're supposed to be waiting for the shuttle."

"I couldn't leave without seeing Mira." She smiled hugely, but it seemed very forced.

"Now you've seen her." Vince got to his feet. "I'll walk you down to the docking bay."

Amrei narrowed her eyes. "I told you, I'm not leaving."

"You are," he said. "It's not open for discussion. We've had too many civilian casualties already."

All the false humor went out of Amrei's expression, and she looked like she might start shouting. "I won't go," she said in a voice that was supposed to sound dangerous, but only came out as a quaver.

"I'll have you carried off," said Vince, "if I have to."

Amrei was afraid, Mira realized. If Vince didn't come back, she would be stranded, without money or people she could turn to. Mira started to say something, but Amrei shook a finger at Costa.

"What about her?" she demanded. "*She's* going back in, and she's certainly not military personnel."

"She's property," said Vince coolly. "Are you?"

The muscles in Amrei's face quivered "No D'sha." She heard herself say it and put a hand over her mouth. She shot a look at Costa, who'd heard it too.

Costa's jaw dropped open in amazement, and for a frozen second the two of them stared at each other. "You!" the girl hissed.

Mira and Vince both grabbed her as she lunged forward.

Amrei scrambled away, one hand at her throat. "How did she know?" she gasped at Mira. "You told her!"

"I didn't say anything," grunted Mira. "You just did. I only told her what was possible."

Costa stopped struggling and began to shout. "You wanted to send me back to the Mine line! Do you know what they did to me? Do you *know?* What kind of person *are* you?"

Amrei straightened herself, haughty as ever. "I'm free, for one thing." Her hand twitched, but Costa curled her lip.

"I'll knock you down, *D'sha!*"

"That's enough," snapped Mira. "Now you know all about her. That's more than enough." She loosened her grip cautiously, but the girl didn't pull away.

"Come on." Vince touched Amrei's arm. "It's time to go."

Costa watched them leave and turned angrily to Mira. "What's wrong with her?"

"Calm down," said Mira. "So she's a heartless bitch. You're not the only one who thinks so."

Costa pushed her hair back. "She's the same as Esau." She shivered. "Maybe its what's left of the Drug. Maybe it makes you mean and crazy."

"It's the kind of people they were to begin with," said Mira. "You won't turn out that way."

"She's not even marked," said Costa.

"Not where you can see," said Mira.

Mira's letter to her parents, with her last paycheck and the copy of Ari's ID, went out with Vince's military dispatches just before midnight.

Hours later, she was still awake, sitting cross-legged on the floor of her quarters, too tense even to lie down. Beside her, Costa slept soundly on a borrowed mattress.

Less than eight hours from their own border, the aliens were officially retreating, breaking ranks and fleeing across Sector space. Orders from the Emirate admiralty were to pursue at all costs, crossing the alien border if necessary. It was clear the military wanted to study the technology that had given the Remini the upper hand for so many thousands of years, and they wouldn't mind having a live alien either—but winning was a priority. If there was something left over for the researchers, that would be fine.

For the Proviso, the sole object of pursuit was a single Remini craft, small, but quite fast. The life-sign readings from the ship were distinctly human, and even without an answer to Vince's repeated hails, Mira was sure she knew who was on it.

The ship was far ahead, well out of weapons' range, but close enough for it to seem to Mira that the Proviso was following Raffail's lead, rather than running him to ground. The suspicion that he somehow knew that she and Costa were on board had formed a tight knot inside her belly, big as a fist.

Costa turned over in her sleep, one hand clutching convulsively on the pillow. Mira watched, but there was nothing more. No matter what the girl dreamed tonight, Mira didn't need a fortuneteller to know that by morning, her range of options would be narrower still, limited by unavoidable decisions that would position her opposite Raffail in a time and place of his choosing. The only thing that would keep her in one piece would be an opening in events he did not expect, which, at the moment, she could not imagine.

Mira slid between the sheets without undressing and laid her head against Costa's arm. The girl rolled against her, warm and embracing, and Mira pressed close, exhausted, struggling in the low ebb of alternatives.

"Wake up." Costa shook her again. "Wake *up!*"

Mira pushed herself up on one elbow trying to see what time it was.

"You have to listen," said the girl urgently. "Are you listening?"

Mira rubbed her eyes hard. "You had a dream?"

"Raffail is on the small ship," said the girl, hurriedly, like the details would escape her at any moment. "He's going to call and say he wants to surrender."

"He does?" He *does?*

"It's a lie," said Costa. "He wants to meet with you and when you go, he'll kill you."

Alternatives, thought Mira thickly. One thing to change. "I'll take the security squad," she said. "He won't get near me."

The girl shook her head. "They won't be with you when you get to the planet. He knows we're here. He's got something that only transports the people he wants and keeps out the rest."

"That's impossible," said Mira. "If we're all on the disk together, we all arrive together."

"Not this time."

It was easy enough to believe there was some Remini device Raffail had figured out how to use. Mira sat up, stiff from the hard bed and not enough sleep. "Is he alone?"

Costa nodded quickly, nervously. "Take me with you," she whispered. "I'll kill him."

"No." Mira pushed herself off the mattress and made her way to the bathroom, running water in the sink until it was ice cold, then scrubbing her face with it.

Costa hovered in the doorway. "I'll never see you again," she said in a small, frightened voice. "Please don't go."

"I'll be armed," said Mira. "He won't be expecting that."

"He will," said Costa. "You can't fight him. You can't go."

Mira dried her face, watching herself in the mirror. Costa's fear was so palpable Mira could feel it, like static.

"Tell me the dream," said Mira. "Tell me everything."

It was graphic. Not just the gory details at the end when Raffail finally finished her off, but even the incidental parts, like how many men Vince would assign to the security squad, which pocket she would put her side-arm in, and even what the scenery would be like on the planet's surface.

"Take me with you," persisted the girl.

Mira shook her head again, staring at the knife that lay on the floor between them. "He'll kill us both." She picked the weapon up by the tip. "If he knows I have a gun and he takes it away, why don't I just stick him with this?"

"It's harder than that," said Costa. "You've never killed anything. You don't know how."

From what Costa had already told her, Raffail's call would come when they were only hours from the Remini line. At the moment, the Proviso was closing in fast on the alien border.

"Take me with you," said Costa.

Mira closed her eyes. "He'll try to kill you, Costa. You won't be able to help me."

"You don't know that."

"Neither do you," said Mira. "What happens if you *do* come along? Which one of us does he take apart first? Who gets to watch?"

The intercom buzzed. Mira jumped.

"Mira?" Vince's voice from the bridge. "We're in contact with the Remini ship. Guess who's on it?"

She didn't have to. She eased down in front of the monitor and

Vince's tired face, feeling the prickle of sweat on the back of her neck.

"Raffail wants to talk terms with you," said Vince. "He says he wants to surrender."

"No terms," Mira said quickly. "You can tell him that."

Vince hesitated. "I understand how you feel, but he's got an undamaged ship and he sounds like he's open to making some kind of arrangement. Otherwise we'll spend the next six months chasing him. It's not worth it."

"He's been asking for me? Specifically?"

"He always does."

Mira glanced up at Costa, standing behind the monitor with her fists clenched. "Alright," she said. "Put him through. You'll be listening?"

"Wouldn't miss it," said Vince.

Mira rested one finger on the key that would open up the communications channel. "Don't say anything," she said to Costa. "I don't want him to know you're here."

She nodded, and Mira pressed the key.

Raffail flickered into view, smiling. "How nice to see you looking so well, Madame LoDire."

His false friendliness only made her heart beat faster. "Let's hear your terms, Raffail."

"I understand you want this ship."

Personally, she did not. "Not necessarily."

His smile vanished. "Maybe we have nothing to say to each other, Madame LoDire. You win and I lose. Very simple."

"Then prepare to be boarded," said Mira shortly.

"I wouldn't try that," he said. "There's a destruct sequence in progress here. It doesn't take much to trigger it. I wouldn't want you to lose any more friends."

He wasn't cornered, not by any stretch of the imagination. He was fast enough to outrun the Proviso. He could escape just as easily as stay where he was. Mira touched the key that would distort her image on Raffail's screen and mute her voice. "Where are we?" she asked Vince.

"Three hours from the Remini line. He's in orbit around a planet we can't find on our charts."

Costa motioned very deliberately with her hands. *My world. Jahar.*

So that was why she knew so much about the planet's surface. And why had he come here of all places? Mira took her finger off the distort key. "What do you want, Raffail?"

"A conversation with you, for one thing."

"I've got plenty of time," she said. "Go ahead."

"Not this way," he said. "That's my only condition. I just want to talk, face to face. Then you can have me, and the ship."

Costa shook her head emphatically, gesturing, *No, no, no!*

"Forget it," said Mira. "We'll talk when you're over here."

He shrugged. "It won't look very good if you're the one responsible for making me destroy this little trophy."

Vince cut in, blurring her screen before she could tell him what an obvious, overconfident liar he was.

"We can't lose the ship," said Vince. "He's right. You'd be disciplined up one side and down the other."

"I don't care," said Mira, eyeing Raffail's indistinct image. "I'm not getting on board with him."

"Then go down to the surface," said Vince. "The scans say there's practically nothing down there, just some agriculture. You can have the entire security squad. He'll never touch you."

NO! Signed Costa.

There was no choice. There was really no choice. To refuse now meant too many questions later from people who had no interest in anything but the truth. And the truth was that Costa had killed a man. Mira took a breath against the tide of unstoppable consequences. "Alright," she said. "Let me talk to him."

The channel reopened with a click.

"I'll give you five minutes, Raffail," she said, keeping her voice terse, uncompromising. "I'll meet you on the surface of the planet, though. Not on your ship."

He nodded easily, and she realized he'd already anticipated this. Maybe even planned on it.

"No tricks," she said. "I'm bringing the biggest security squad you've ever seen."

"Bring the whole crew if you like," said Raffail. "Bring that girl of yours too."

"She's dead," said Mira.

"Is that so?" He raised one doubtful eyebrow under the stripe of blue paint. "She was clearly alive at the port on Ain-Selai. My sympathies, Madame LoDire." He moved his hand, and the screen went blank.

"You can't do this," hissed Costa. "I won't *let* you." She took a step to block the door. Someone knocked rapidly, but she didn't move to answer it.

"Madame LoDire?" said a man's voice on the other side. "We're ready when you are."

"Take me with you," whispered Costa.

Mira shook her head hard, not at all ready for suicide, but even less inclined to watch Raffail tear Costa to pieces. "If I don't come back, Vince'll take care of you. He'll send you to Newhall, to my parents. To your sister."

"With the rest of your things?" said the girl bitterly. "You really think I'll be safe there?"

"What do you mean?"

"Raffail *knows* I'm here, and he knows what I did to Jezr'el. When he's finished with you, where do you think he'll go next?"

Mira hesitated. "He'll never get off the planet."

"You're wrong, Mira," whispered the girl. "You can't fight him alone, and neither can I."

The guard knocked again, and Costa opened the door. Outside, the security contingent was filing down the corridor, two by two, every man armed to the teeth. The sergeant gave Mira a stiff salute and waited for her to follow. Mira glanced at the girl, still rumpled with sleep, one fist clenched around the knife.

For a moment Mira had a very clear vision of what Raffail had in mind for her, and the thin silver blade was like a bridge between events—what was unchangeable, but also what might remain fluid. Her heart pounded just inside her throat, and she knew there was only one thing that could possibly be changed in this tightening spiral. She swallowed very hard.

"I think," she said, "you'd better come along."

Bright noonday sun blinded her. Mira shut her eyes. She caught the scent of flowers in the warm air, then the smell of stagnant water. Her head lolled over to the left, away from the intense light. She opened her eyes again.

Rickety-looking wooden houses covered the lower slope of a long hill. She could see people crowding in the doorways and windows, staring at something. Mira spotted a young girl with long blonde hair. For a moment she was sure it was Costa. She looked harder and saw another girl, almost the same age, nearly identical. Mira squinted at the others. Every last one of them was either a male or female version of Costa, different ages, different heights, but the same face and the same hair, and they were all looking, she realized, at her. Or something behind her.

A shadow fell across her face. Mira made a tremendous effort to see what it was, what everyone was watching, but she could barely move her head. Somebody's hand caught her chin and made her look up at the sky again, but this time Raffail was blocking the light.

Mira lay on her back in the warm sand, staring up at him, absolutely unable to move as he searched her pockets and took her side-arm.

"Not very diplomatic to bring a weapon, Mira."

Instead of the normal snap from one reality to another, the way disk-transport usually felt, there had been an unfamiliar dizziness, and now, virtual paralysis. Raffail let go and her head rolled the other way, more or less downhill. Costa was lying behind him at the edge of a low, dirty-looking pond, not moving. And the security squad? Mira didn't need to look very hard to know that they were still on the Proviso with Vince, wondering what had gone wrong.

"Let us go," mumbled Mira through numb lips. "I can get you safe passage out of here."

Raffail crouched beside her and pressed his thumb against her throat. "Safe passage to where? A prisoner of war camp? Or a courtroom where they'll try me as an enemy of your precious state?"

"You'll be stuck here," she whispered and winced as he pressed harder. "They'll find you. It won't do any good to kill me."

"My son is dead," he said softly, with just a hint of the rage he felt. "You gave her the knife, and she murdered him. And you don't think it'll do me any good to kill you?"

Behind him, Costa opened her eyes. "Wait," breathed Mira, "Just wait. We need to talk."

He shook his head slowly, clearly furious. "It's too late for talk." He reached into his cloak and brought out a pair of cuffs. She felt the warm metal clamp around one wrist and tried to resist as he pushed her onto her side. Her arms moved weakly, and the second cuff ratchetted shut behind her. Raffail rolled her onto her back again, so that both hands were pinned beneath her body. Out of the corner of one eye, Mira saw Costa sit up, reaching under her shirt where the knife was. Whatever the Remini transport device had done to them, Costa seemed to be recovering faster than she was. So far, Raffail wasn't aware of that. As long as his back was to the girl, she would have time to make the move that Mira couldn't manage.

"You can't think you're going to get away with this," Mira said, in as much of a normal tone as she could. "You'll never get off this planet. You'll spend the rest of your life hiding."

"Will I?" He pulled his fist back, letting it hang over her face. She took a breath to say something, anything. Across the strip of beach, Costa struggled to her feet, the knife glinting in one hand. In moments, she could be behind Raffail with the knife against his throat. Mira blinked at the slaver's fist and knew there simply wasn't that much time. She gathered every tiny bit of strength she had and rolled away, bringing her knees under her.

She heard Raffail's amused snort, then the scuff of bare feet on sand. When she looked back up, Costa was between her and Raffail, visibly trembling, the knife gripped in both fists.

"Get away!" Her voice was high and absolutely terrified. "Let us go!" Costa jabbed the knife at empty air as Raffail stood, slowly and unconcernedly.

"Put the knife down, Costa."

Costa froze, and for a minute Mira was afraid the girl was going to do exactly what she was told. If Raffail had considered her dangerous at all, Mira realized, he would have cuffed her too. Mira got one foot under her and then the other, pushing herself up unsteadily, hoping Costa could hold him off for a few more minutes, at least until they both had the strength to run. She could feel the cuffs very distinctly now. The one on her left wrist was painfully tight, but the other seemed loose enough to pull her hand through if she had enough time.

Raffail gave Costa a menacing smile. "Welcome home." He nodded at the houses and the silent audience. "I told your family you were coming. Nice of you not to disappoint them by pretending to be dead." He held out one hand, impatient. "Give me the knife."

Costa took a quick look over her shoulder at the village, then at Mira. "Let her go," she whispered breathlessly. "I did it, not her."

"Give me the *knife.*"

He made a grab for it. She dodged away, slashing the air. Raffail jerked his hand back and blinked in surprise, as though he couldn't quite believe she would have cut him. Costa grabbed Mira's arm in a painfully tight grip, and Mira stumbled against her as they backed away together along the water's edge.

Raffail eyed the knife and started after them—following, not chasing. "Keep going, Costa," he said. "You're only making it worse for yourself. And for your dear friend."

"Let her go," hissed Costa desperately. "You can have me."

Raffail shook his head. "What does it take to teach you?" He took another step, the girl swung wildly, and Mira ducked away. She heard him roar in absolute disbelief and looked up to see him crouched on the beach, bleeding on his white robes, drawing the length of the blade out of his right hand.

Costa stood where she was, clutching Mira's arm, completely frozen, too amazed and too frightened to breathe.

Raffail looked up from his wound. "Come here," he snarled at the girl. He held out his bloodied hand, as if the very sight of it might cure her disobedient nature.

Costa took a terrified gulp of air, not moving. Behind Raffail, the local population was just as still, riveted on this tiny portion of beach.

Raffail got to his feet, seething, holding the knife awkwardly in his left hand. Mira elbowed Costa as hard as she could. "Run!"

Costa grabbed Mira's arm, practically dragging her along the narrow strip of sand. Mira staggered next to her, moving as fast as she could, even clumsier with her hands behind her back. She yanked her wrist against the looser cuff, compressing her hand inside the loop of metal so tightly that her bones hurt, but there wasn't enough room. Or time. She could hear the scrape of Raffail's feet in the sand behind them, and his painful breathing. Costa twisted to see how close Raffail was and how murderously angry. She let out a frightened yelp as Mira lost her footing, pitching face down in the sand. She rolled over fast, shaking off the girl's hands as Raffail closed in. "Don't stop!" she shrieked. "*Run!*"

Raffail grunted, slicing empty air as the girl jerked away. He didn't even bother to chase her as she fled to the very edge of the lake and stopped. Instead, he crouched over Mira, panting. "Tell her to come back."

"Tell her yourself," snapped Mira.

She thought he would hit her, and she squeezed her eyes shut, flinching away from the blow, but instead, the blade pricked her lightly, just under her jaw.

"D'sha!" cried the girl, "Don't!"

"Come back," said Raffail through his teeth. He moved the blade, and a drop of warmth trickled across Mira's neck.

"Get out of here!" shouted Mira, but the girl didn't move. She just stood in the water with her fists over her mouth, like she was making herself watch whatever came next.

Raffail twisted the knife, staring into Mira's face, feeding on her panic, and Mira gasped, trying to stare back defiantly into his blue-striped eyes. She couldn't. Costa's dream had been right this time, she thought frantically, except that they would both die. And even if Raffail had lost the larger war, he would win this pointless battle.

The slaver glanced back at Costa, then at the village. "Stay and watch," he said to the girl. He moved the knife to Mira's belly, pinning her with a knee on her chest. "I'll kill her the way you killed Jezr'el."

There was a moment of thick silence. Mira heard Costa take a short, frightened breath. "You don't have any idea how I killed him," she whispered.

He raised the knife. "Don't I?"

"That's not what I mean, D'sha. You don't know how he died."

Raffail's face tightened. He glared across the beach.

"He bled like a reshie," said Costa, her voice shaking. She started to back off, deeper into the water, up to her knees. "He tried to get away, but I wouldn't let him!" She shot a look up at the village, hesitated, and then repeated herself in Sign. "I had him on his knees before he died, begging for his life!" she shouted. "What a coward you had for a son!"

Raffail got to his feet without a word, stepping over Mira as the girl fled into waist-deep water. Mira wrestled with the cuffs. The heel of her hand slid out, but the joint of her thumb jammed tight.

Costa stopped and turned to face Raffail as he slogged toward her, deliberate and furious. He stopped, an arm's length away, holding the knife just above the surface of the water. He said something Mira couldn't hear and lunged. Costa wrapped both hands around his neck, and he sank the blade into her side.

Mira yanked against the cuff as they thrashed together in the shallow water. She jerked hard against the sharp metal, not caring how much it hurt, and her hand came free.

Every time the knife went deep, Costa let out a breathless gasp. It was a gruesome contest: who could do the most damage first. Mira waded towards them as fast as she could, the loose cuff dangling from her wrist like an oversized bangle. If anyone knew how to push the Drug past its capacity to heal, it was Raffail, and there was nothing random in the way the slaver drove the knife into Costa's body.

Raffail's breath was coming in short coughs, and he didn't seem to hear Mira as she moved up behind him, splashing and panting. The length of chain between the cuffs was only a handspan. She'd never even imagined what it would be like to strangle another human being.

He jammed the blade between Costa's ribs, as deep as he could and the girl slid against him. Mira looped the chain around his neck from behind, pulling it tight.

Raffail's good hand flew out, and the knife fell into the water with a quiet splash. He let out a high, wheezing, suffering sound, twisting and fighting. Mira hung on as Costa clung to him, her eyes squeezed shut. Her thumbs were caught under the chain Mira realized suddenly, and resisted the urge to let go.

It took a long time for him to finally fall. His hood slipped off, and his long, silvery blond hair blew against Mira's face. Costa pressed him under the surface as he struggled, his breath coming up as trailing bubbles. Mira felt his body relax, felt him go limp in the cloudy water.

Costa pulled her hands free of the chain, shaking hard. Her shirt was soaked pink, darker red on the one side. She swayed unsteadily. Mira caught her under the arms and half-carried, half-dragged her back to the shore.

Long, deep gashes cut across Costa's right side. Mira peeled the bloody shirt back as the girl lay panting in the sand. She glanced up at the village, but as far as she could tell, no one had moved. They were just staring. Mira couldn't even tell if anything they'd seen had shocked them.

"Don't you have family up there?" she asked. "Why won't they help?"

"Reshie," gasped the girl. "That's all they are. They don't even know they're free."

Mira squeezed her hands. They were as cold as Amrei's ice water bath. "Didn't you see any of this last night?" she asked, trying to keep her voice calm.

She shook her head weakly. "Not last night. A long time ago. I had my hands around his neck, but it was only a dream. You weren't there. I couldn't do it alone." She took a couple of painful, ragged breaths. "Am I Failing?"

Mira shook her head hard, but she had no real idea. It was impossible to tell if the wounds were starting to heal, and she was afraid to touch them to find out. "You'll be fine," she whispered.

The distant whine of approaching skimmers sent the locals abruptly back inside their houses. Mira jumped to her feet, waving madly at the distant specks, shouting at the top of her lungs. One swooped in close, hovering over the beach as Vince scrambled out.

He saw the cuff dangling off Mira's wrist. "Are you hurt?"

Mira shook her head quickly. "Costa—"

Vince bent over the girl, carefully examining the wounds as the rest of the security squad touched down.

"I'm Failing," whispered Costa.

"You're not," Vince said. "Stop trying to rush things. You'll get your chance." He glanced around the beach. "Where's Raffail?"

Mira nodded at the lake. There wasn't even a ripple to show where the body was. "I can give you an official report," she said in a low voice. "But none of it's going to be true."

"As long as it makes sense, I don't care." He took her arm, guiding her out of the way as the medics descended, clustering around Costa.

For some reason she'd let Trent talk her into taking a leave of absence instead of quitting outright. At least it was a long leave, open-ended in fact, and there were some distinct advantages to still being a government employee. The trip to Newhall was free, for one thing.

A little more spartan than a commercial cruiser, Mira thought, but Trent had pulled some considerable strings to get them a private cabin on this transport ship. For as long as it took to get home, they would at least be comfortable.

Costa was almost asleep, naked against her, dozing with a hand still caught between Mira's thighs. Before leaving Point Seven, Mira had called home to let her parents know when they would be arriving. Ari's face had materialized on the screen, another version of Costa, just a little older. While Mira had stared stupidly at the almost clonelike resemblance, Costa elbowed in front of her, hands against the screen, laughing and crying, prattling on in Jahari. Mira still wasn't sure how the girl was going to contain herself for the next three weeks.

Mira shifted a little, propped up on the pillows. Starlight glinted off the tiny sliver medals she'd pinned on Costa's shirt, hanging on the closet door. The awards ceremony on Traja had been lengthy and acutely embarrassing. At least there had been enough food and alcohol to make it worthwhile. The medals were hers, not Costa's. There was one for bravery under fire and one for being wounded. Mira held up her right wrist, examining it again. Marked like a Mine slave—just like Esau—but the cuts were healing and there would be no scars. It was just as well.

Trent had given her the medals, practically bursting with pride, as though Mira's fictionalized deeds were something she'd suggested herself. As soon as she could get away, Mira had found her way to the courtyard where the slaves were, collected Costa, and hidden in the vast formal gardens behind the Trajan governor's mansion, waiting for Vince to show up.

She'd fumbled with the pins on her uniform, almost pricking herself, and fastened them to Costa's shirt.

"I like this one," said the girl, squinting down at the one for being wounded. It was filigreed and fancier. Mira had to agree: It was the more attractive of the two.

Giving them away was almost as embarrassing as getting them. "Shouldn't you get something for all that work?" she'd asked.

"I do," said Costa. "I get you. For a long time."

Vince had walked in on their clandestine necking with a large bottle and three glasses filched from the bar inside. He sat down and waited for Costa to stop giggling. Mira pushed her hair back, blushing in the darkness.

"I can't find her," he announced, and started pouring. "There's no message, no nothing."

Either Amrei had never boarded the transport she'd been booked on, or she had gotten off before the ship reached the military base near Ankea. Vince had been combing passenger lists for the past two days and still hadn't been able to find her.

It was hard for Mira to believe she'd really left him. More than anything else it made her think of Renee. "What are you going to do?"

"Nothing." He was rumpled and dirty. It was just as well he'd missed *his* award. "If she wants her own life, I can understand that. I just wish she'd said something. It's not like I would have forced her to stay."

It was difficult for Mira to push away the feeling that she was abandoning him as well.

Costa moved sleepily, one hand brushing Mira's face. "You're still awake?" She turned over, her body fitting smoothly under Mira's arm, a warm, comfortable arrangement that could last all night. Mira pulled the girl even closer, and Costa's hand slipped into hers. There was this surety between them, beyond gratitude or favors or violent, angry dreams. She closed her eyes, feeling the vague vibrations of the ship as it moved into light speed, casting forward into distorted, twisting stars.

Other titles from Firebrand Books include:

Artemis In Echo Park, Poetry by Eloise Klein Healy/$8.95

Beneath My Heart, Poetry by Janice Gould/$8.95

The Big Mama Stories by Shay Youngblood/$8.95

A Burst Of Light, Essays by Audre Lorde/$7.95

Cecile, Stories by Ruthann Robson/$8.95

Crime Against Nature, Poetry by Minnie Bruce Pratt/$8.95

Diamonds Are A Dyke's Best Friend by Yvonne Zipter/$9.95

Dykes To Watch Out For, Cartoons by Alison Bechdel/$6.95

Dykes To Watch Out For: The Sequel, Cartoons by Alison Bechdel/$8.95

Exile In The Promised Land, A Memoir by Marcia Freedman/$8.95

Eye Of A Hurricane, Stories by Ruthann Robson/$8.95

The Fires Of Bride, A Novel by Ellen Galford/$8.95

Food & Spirits, Stories by Beth Brant (*Degonwadonti*)/$8.95

Free Ride, A Novel by Marilyn Gayle/$9.95

A Gathering Of Spirit, A Collection by North American Indian Women edited by Beth Brant (*Degonwadonti*)/$10.95

Getting Home Alive by Aurora Levins Morales and Rosario Morales/$8.95

The Gilda Stories, A Novel by Jewelle Gomez/$9.95

Good Enough To Eat, A Novel by Lesléa Newman/$8.95

Humid Pitch, Narrative Poetry by Cheryl Clarke/$8.95

Jewish Women's Call For Peace edited by Rita Falbel, Irena Klepfisz, and Donna Nevel/$4.95

Jonestown & Other Madness, Poetry by Pat Parker/$7.95

Just Say Yes, A Novel by Judith McDaniel/$8.95

The Land Of Look Behind, Prose and Poetry by Michelle Cliff/$8.95

Legal Tender, A Mystery by Marion Foster/$9.95

Lesbian (Out)law, Survival Under The Rule Of Law by Ruthann Robson /$9.95

A Letter To Harvey Milk, Short Stories by Lesléa Newman/$8.95

Letting In The Night, A Novel by Joan Lindau/$8.95

Living As A Lesbian, Poetry by Cheryl Clarke/$7.95

Making It, A Woman's Guide to Sex in the Age of AIDS by Cindy Patton and Janis Kelly/$4.95

Metamorphosis, Reflections On Recovery by Judith McDaniel/$7.95

Mohawk Trail by Beth Brant (*Degonwadonti*)/$7.95

Moll Cutpurse, A Novel by Ellen Galford/$7.95

The Monarchs Are Flying, A Novel by Marion Foster/$8.95

(continued)

More Dykes To Watch Out For, Cartoons by Alison Bechdel/$7.95

Movement In Black, Poetry by Pat Parker/$8.95

My Mama's Dead Squirrel, Lesbian Essays on Southern Culture by Mab Segrest/$9.95

New, Improved! Dykes To Watch Out For, Cartoons by Alison Bechdel /$7.95

The Other Sappho, A Novel by Ellen Frye/$8.95

Out In The World, International Lesbian Organizing by Shelley Anderson /$4.95

Politics Of The Heart, A Lesbian Parenting Anthology edited by Sandra Pollack and Jeanne Vaughn/$11.95

Presenting. . . Sister NoBlues by Hattie Gossett/$8.95

Rebellion, Essays 1980-1991 by Minnie Bruce Pratt/$10.95

A Restricted Country by Joan Nestle/$8.95

Sacred Space by Geraldine Hatch Hanon/$9.95

Sanctuary, A Journey by Judith McDaniel/$7.95

Sans Souci, And Other Stories by Dionne Brand/$8.95

Scuttlebutt, A Novel by Jana Williams/$8.95

Shoulders, A Novel by Georgia Cotrell/$8.95

Simple Songs, Stories by Vickie Sears/$8.95

The Sun Is Not Merciful, Short Stories by Anna Lee Walters/$7.95

Tender Warriors, A Novel by Rachel Guido deVries/$8.95

This Is About Incest by Margaret Randall/$8.95

The Threshing Floor, Short Stories by Barbara Burford/$7.95

Trash, Stories by Dorothy Allison/$8.95

The Women Who Hate Me, Poetry by Dorothy Allison/$8.95

Words To The Wise, A Writer's Guide to Feminist and Lesbian Periodicals & Publishers by Andrea Fleck Clardy/$4.95

The Worry Girl, Stories From A Childhood by Andrea Freud Loewenstein /$8.95

Yours In Struggle, Three Feminist Perspectives on Anti-Semitism and Racism by Elly Bulkin, Minnie Bruce Pratt, and Barbara Smith/$8.95

You can buy Firebrand titles at your bookstore, or order them directly from the publisher (141 The Commons, Ithaca, New York 14850, 607-272-0000).

Please include $2.00 shipping for the first book and $.50 for each additional book.

A free catalog is available on request.